THE RETREAT

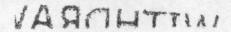

FORGE BOOKS BY SHERRI SMITH

Follow Me Down
The Retreat

THE
RETREAT

SHERRI SMITH

FORGE

A TOM DOHERTY ASSOCIATES BOOK
NEW YORK

THE RETREAT

Copyright © 2019 by Sherri Smith

A Forge Book
Published by Tom Doherty Associates
120 Broadway
New York, NY 10271

www.tor-forge.com

Forge® is a registered trademark of Macmillan Publishing Group, LLC.

The Library of Congress Cataloging-in-Publication Data is available upon request.

ISBN 978-0-7653-8673-1 (hardcover)
ISBN 978-0-7653-8675-5 (ebook)

Our books may be purchased in bulk for promotional, educational, or business use. Please contact your local bookseller or the Macmillan Corporate and Premium Sales Department at 1-800-221-7945, extension 5442, or by email at MacmillanSpecialMarkets@macmillan.com.

First Edition: August 2019

Printed in the United States of America

0 9 8 7 6 5 4 3 2 1

*For my bold and brilliant daughter, Rowan—
don't do any of the things the characters in
this book do and you'll probably be okay.
Love, Mom*

This place had made a killer out of her.

How about that for a testimonial! The retreat really did deliver on its promise of a complete transformation. She'd arrived a failure and was leaving a total success.

Everything she'd hoped to accomplish here had been checked off. Her core was stronger than ever, her joints looser, and she'd achieved a level of mindfulness that made her certain she could manifest any reality she wanted, simply by thinking about it really hard.

Most important, her head was finally quiet and that sad stinging in her chest was gone. The disguise she'd been hiding behind had been shed, and her true nature was now out in the open. She was awake, balanced. The sky should be ablaze with fireworks because she fucking loved herself.

A wheeze, a gurgle, then a sudden gulp of air and kicking feet.

She rolled her eyes and pressed harder on the tree branch, hoping she'd hear the conclusive snap of a windpipe and she'd finally get to move on. "Just die already," she said in a tired voice, then at last, it was quiet. No more movement. She waited a beat to be sure she'd really finished the job this time. Even took a moment to appreciate the inky beauty of moonlit blood as it oozed and pooled on the rocks. The peaceful silence after death. Finally, she was living in the moment.

She climbed out of the ravine, and as she started back toward the retreat she blissfully sang: *"One, two, three, four bodies are left on the forest floor. Oh wait, make that five. Five, six, seven, eight, I feel pretty great. One, two, three, four, I am a perfect warrior."*

She always knew she could do it. All she had to do was believe in herself.

When people fail, it's their own fault. It comes down to laziness and a lack of self-discipline. You have to be willing to suffer to achieve your goals. You need to accept a certain level of agony if you want to become your best self. It's as simple as that.

There were no witnesses either. Or at least, no credible ones. No cameras or nearby neighbors to report when the screaming started. Just the black sky.

What would she say? About the trail of bodies in the woods? Anything. She could say anything at all.

She was the last girl standing.

Three days earlier . . .

FRIDAY

KATIE

Katie jerked awake, eyes popped open at the foreign trill of an alarm set at full volume. She bolted upright, startled and confused, as if a gun had just gone off in her bedroom. First thing she did was assess where she was, which was the waking habit of not *only* a drinker but also a clinically diagnosed sleepwalker, *thank you very much*. Her Sphynx cat mewed his displeasure at being disturbed, needing her body heat like a kitty-vampire.

Katie sank back down into the bed.

She was not an early riser.

Her mornings, and sometimes afternoons, were usually spent sulking in bed, thinking about what other people were doing, daydreaming she also had someplace important to be, then happy she didn't because she was prone to hangovers. She said it just like that—*I am prone to hangovers*—like they were allergies and she was helpless to fend them off.

When she did finally get up, the remainder of her day was just as aimless.

That there was the lifestyle of the previously rich and famous.

Katie lived off her trust fund—a fast-deflating cushion of money she'd earned playing the loveable kid detective Shelby Spade. A monthly allowance was doled out to her by an accountant named Mr. Walt Maloney. He'd been managing her money since she was seven years old when she was already flush with commercial earnings. He was a paunchy, smiley man with spiced meat breath—she'd called him Baloney-Maloney as a child—who'd say things like, "And to think, all this money and you haven't even hit the double digits yet," in a way that wasn't entirely nice.

Now he called her every few months about her extra withdrawals, to ask her if she knew what a drain was. "Go into your bathroom, fill your bathtub, then pull the plug. That little hole at the bottom of the bathtub, y'know where all the water goes? That's a drain. I know it looks like a lot of money, but not at this rate. You need to start making deposits, topping it up in some way. This money could be a nest egg that lasts you the rest of your life if you manage it well. You tried college and a few other things—is there anything else you want to do? What comes next for Katie Manning?"

What to do next? Now that was the question, wasn't it?

Katie had been working since she was four years old. By the age of seven all the way through to a geriatric fifteen, she was Shelby Spade, Kid Detective and already the official family meal ticket for her brother, heavily Botoxed stage mom, and disappearing father. Her mother, of course, pushed her to keep acting, giving her the usual speech that she was a natural performer right out of the womb, which was really just Lucy's way to justify selling off Katie's childhood. But Katie knew her red hair, cutesy chipmunk cheeks, and freckled nose did not translate well into adulthood going by the roles she was offered—mostly soft porn or murder victims because people like to watch self-piteous, spoiled ex–child stars get either fucked or murdered—and then of course there was the scar.

But before delving into an existential crisis—she had all weekend to do that—she should probably get up first and pack.

She'd meant to do it the night before, but somehow she just *hadn't*.

Katie did a floppy roll out of bed, wandered over to her closet, pulled out her suitcase, and started tossing in Lycra pants, matching tank tops, and pullovers, tags still on, purchased solely for this trip.

Just one suitcase—she wasn't going to pull a Lacey Evans, who brought nine suitcases to summer camp in season 1, episode 11. This pathetic mental reference to Shelby Spade's mean-girl enemy refreshed Katie's self-loathing.

She was twenty-seven now, the age when celebrities (and yes, she used *celebrity* loosely) died from their bad habits. Their tender, bloated, black-hole bodies, where nothing was ever enough, simply gave out. And here she'd cynically muse about how the long-dead Shelby Spade franchise would get a bump in revenue, maybe even a reboot with some other, cuter girl to replace her.

Just last week, she saw her face in one of those "Stars you loved as a kid—where are they now?" clickbait sideshows. It read:

Just admit it—if you were born in the '90s, you probably owned a Shelby Spade lunch box or doll or duvet set or gut-wrenching perfume. For seven seasons Katie Manning played the adorable—and, let's face it, annoying as hell—Shelby Spade, Kid Detective. Her signature line, "I'LL SOOOOOLVE IT," had us all glued to our TV sets to follow squeaky-clean Shelby's slapstick sleuthing to solve banal crimes from stolen P&J sandwiches to missing library books. This was the orderly world of Shelby where all wrongs were righted and evildoers spent a month in the "hole," also known as detention. It was a balm to the budding adolescent's growing confusions about the world at large.

Katie skipped over the part about *the Incident* that derailed her life.

Katie then went on to attend the Tisch School of the Arts at NYU but dropped out after her first year. She spent her free time club-hopping and making it onto TMZ.

Just when it seemed Manning had finally drifted into obscurity (aside from her overactive Instagram account), she resurfaced again last year when an award-winning director cast her to play a Hooters waitress and girlfriend to a suspected killer in what would have been a career comeback (though it probably wouldn't be much of a stretch for Miss

Manning if anyone remembers how well she filled out her trench coat in that last season of *Spade*).

But then, she recently doled out a highly offensive tweet that resulted in her being fired. The part was recast, and Manning was forced into hiding or at least online banishment (bye-bye, Instagram shots of Manning's hairless cat).

Shelby Spade would not be impressed and would probably sentence Katie Manning to the longest after-school detention EVER!

What the clickbait missed was that Katie was depressed. Profoundly depressed. The most interesting thing about her was over a decade old. Obviously, she wanted a better answer to the *Whatever happened to* question than being a walking ex–child star cliché. *What to do next?* It had plagued her since the series ended. Oh, sure, she'd come up with dozens of things she'd like to do in theory: open a cupcake shop or a clothing boutique, run a catering business, become a doctor who had love affairs with other doctors around all that sickness and death. Once she even thought about becoming a writer because of the loose hours, but she knew she'd be all the torture without any of the talent.

She'd latch onto these new ideas with adolescent intensity but no follow-through when it became clear that these careers lacked the effortlessness and polish that they do on TV.

She'd go back to doing what she always did—living off her past success, drinking, spending money on things that gave her a short thrill, sometimes watching herself on YouTube until her skin started to prickle and aimlessness rolled over her like a panic attack.

So when her brother's fiancée started going on about a wellness retreat up in the Catskills, especially one that was legally allowed to administer ayahuasca ceremonies because the guru running it was an ordained shaman—well, why wouldn't she go?

Why wouldn't she want a complete overhaul of her shitty self over a single weekend?

A month ago, Katie wouldn't have been interested in a retreat. She would have been panicky-pissed for even being asked. It was too much like an intervention. But her life had gotten especially messy lately.

Her last boyfriend had cheated on her; she'd intercepted a text with *A souvenir, so you'll always remember last night.* Attached was the female equivalent of a dick pic—a headless torso with a mannequin-thin waist inside Walker's grungy bathroom.

Hey, cheating assholes of the world, don't eat greasy, sauce-laden chicken wings and swipe your passcode if you don't want to leave a traceable outline that your girlfriend can use to break into your phone.

After finding this out, Katie had fled to Nate's apartment downstairs. Her brother was always good about putting her up when she was feeling especially histrionic. His fiancée, Ellie-Rose (yes, she'd introduced herself that way, pretentious hyphen and all—Katie was certain that set the unfriendly tone between them), attempted to whip up some late night comfort food consisting of kale and brown rice soup. Katie ended up drinking all the red wine instead.

She could only piece together that, for unknown reasons, she felt compelled to use her last lucid moment before passing out on her brother's couch to tweet a bad joke about lesbians. The tweet put her in a virtual pillory, and the masses came out with an especially gleeful hatred reserved only for spoiled, self-piteous ex–child stars. This sudden thrust back into the limelight also resurrected her old stalker, who drew shaky portraits of her like he was masturbating with his free hand. She was always in her signature Spade fedora, naked, and restrained with a bizarre patchwork of ropes. Now in addition to being depressed, Katie was also disturbed.

Profoundly disturbed.

So a retreat was an easy sell. All Ellie had to say was that ayahuasca tea was like ten years of therapy in a single cup—and she would know because she'd tried it before—and, well, Katie loved a good shortcut. Tip back a cup of cure-all tea, hallucinate, let your life play out like a film before your dilated pupils, check off exactly those places where things went wrong, and *bang*, you have all the answers for what to do next. A full mindscape. Or something like that—either way, it wouldn't be the first time she'd felt like the answer was at the bottom of a glass.

She immediately called on her old college besties. Their attempts at having annual reunions were getting increasingly difficult (*Everyone is so busy but me*), so there was no better time to force one on them because it was Memorial Day weekend and there was no way she was going to have a good time with just *Ellie-Rose*. She downloaded some Enya songs to get into the mood for a new age retreat. She bought a ridiculous amount of Lycra, which she was now finishing packing. Facecloths. Her pillow. She needed to bring her own. She couldn't bring herself to use hotel-issued facecloths or pillows; it had something to do with the scar on her cheek, an irrational fear that she could get an infection—as if it were still an open wound.

Katie showered, dressed, zipped up her suitcase, put it by the front door, and looked at it with a flash of satisfaction at her organizational skills, like she'd just completed the blueprints to a highrise, before grabbing it again and clomping down the steps to her brother's place.

Katie's only sound financial investment was buying her Brooklyn townhouse. She'd it converted it into two self-contained units. The third and fourth floors were hers, while Nate had the main and garden levels. He paid a nominal amount of rent, which Katie accepted because it made her brother feel better about himself, but now that he'd moved his girlfriend in, she was having second thoughts. Ellie had taken over the garden level for her jewelry-making hobby, which wasn't really a hobby since she sold her wares on Etsy, and yet as far as she could tell Ellie wasn't even helping pay part of the "nominal" rent.

Her usual hostility, whenever she suspected she was being used, fizzed bitter on her tongue like aspirin. But Katie had to swallow it down since she was about to spend the weekend with Ellie.

As she reached the final bend in the banister, she had that frequent childish urge to slide down it, to please an audience that no longer existed. "Yes, way, we're going on va-cay!" Katie hollered, doing her little shoulder dance as she barged her way through her brother's unlocked door. If storm clouds hovered over her when she was alone, they turned into cannons popping confetti when she wasn't. She put down her suitcase and handed her brother instructions on how to take care of her cat—no easy feat because Mr. Dick Wolf needed his daily hairless-cat version of body butter and at least one sweater change, which usually left her with a few bleeding scratches. He was not a nice cat, but what could she say? She had a soft spot for ugly, misunderstood animals.

"You're forty minutes late, Katie. Ellie texted you three times. I knocked on your door twice." Nate was standing there in a crisply ironed, checkered button-down shirt and beige Dockers. Since meeting Ellie, his style had shifted from jeans and ironic T-shirts to something a preschooler wore on picture day.

"Really? I didn't hear you or my phone." Not true, but Katie hated being rushed. It made her anxious. She moved into the kitchen, grabbed a pancake off a tinfoil-covered plate, took a bite, and immediately spit it out into the garbage. "Oh my god, this is awful! Seriously, how can pancakes be gluten-free? It's like taking water out of clouds."

He gave her a *you're ridiculous* shake of the head and dropped his voice. "Listen, Katie, be nice, okay? Just try to get along with Ellie."

"What the fuck? I'm always nice to Ellie." She hated that her future sister-in-law set her brother on her like this. They'd have a single exchange—Katie would maybe say hello or something—and somehow Ellie would twist it all up and Nate would call her and ask, "What did you say to Ellie? She thinks you hate her." They just had nothing in common. Ellie completely lacked any sense of humor. Or at least Katie's brand of it. Whenever they talked, it was all jagged edges, and Katie could always sense how hard Ellie was *trying to be nice.*

"You know what I mean. Just tone it down a bit. Get to know her. She isn't going anywhere. You know that, right?"

"I do, yes." Katie softened at the sight of how in love her brother was with Ellie. "I am going to some flaky, guru-led retreat, Nate, to get to know your fiancée better. You can't say I'm *not* trying. Hopefully when we return, we will be bonded and totally zenith like the TV made out of fake wood in Grandma's basement."

Nate rolled his eyes. "You're not as funny as you think you are."

"Probably not, and that explains why your fiancée always says, 'That's so funny,' in lieu of just, y'know, laughing." Then Katie imitated Ellie's nasally puff of air that she passed off as laughter.

"Katie." Nate's voice went up.

"Just kidding, Nate. I will make sure Ellie has a wonderful weekend, and I will woo her like she comes with a dowry, 'kay?"

"Thank you." Nate reached over and squeezed her shoulder. Katie patted his hand, then grabbed some milk out of the fridge, saw that it was coconut milk, and put it back. "I really hope this experience brings you two closer."

"Me too. Now don't you have any real food in your place?"

"You're here. Finally." Ellie emerged from the back bedroom, and immediately Katie felt like a garden gnome next to Ellie's runway-model height. Katie was just brushing up against five foot two like her own body stopped growing when she was twelve to extend the shelf life of her child-actor cuteness.

· Worse, Ellie also made her feel childish with her cool self-control. Even now, Ellie looked perfect, as usual. It was as if she'd walked off an Anthropologie billboard. Summer scarf, tights, and a belted tunic. Her butterscotch hair tumbled over her shoulders in wavy curls meant to look natural but that had to be premeditated and shellacked into place. When she wasn't this perfect version of artsy college student, then she was the perfect sexy coed, always in oversized Columbia sweatshirts and shorts so short, Katie could only guess she had them on. It was too affected. It reminded Katie of pulling outfits from the *Spade* wardrobe: the nerdy girl wears glasses, the mean girl a cheerleader's outfit, and an Anthropologie getup for a wellness retreat. Katie didn't trust it. Her wariness only deepened when their mother loved Ellie on sight because she was so "marketably" beautiful. Lucy was always mentally plotting a family reality series that she had yet to convince Katie to do.

This would be the first time Katie would spend any time alone with her future sister-in-law. This girl who disappeared while they drank beer and watched a Rangers game to work on her jewelry line; hunks of wood and resin, glass baubles filled with something plucked out of a field, all inspired by the environment. She drank herbal teas all day long, wore dresses as her *comfy home clothes*, went to yoga (and here she'd once corrected Katie—one does not *do yoga*, or *go to* yoga; one *practices* it), and talked about gluten like it was a terrorist. Her skin was so perfect, Katie fought the urge to jab her to check it wasn't latex. She'd been watching her brother float after Ellie like she had a golden lasso wrapped around his dick. But how well did he know her? She was a complete stranger eight months ago, and now he wanted to *marry* her?

It was another reason Katie agreed to the trip; she was going to be Nate's sober second thought.

"Are you ready?"

Katie smiled hard at her. "Ready as I'll ever be."

ELLIE

Ellie planted one last, lingering goodbye kiss on Nate's velvety lips. This would be their first weekend apart. "Ew, gross. Get a room or let's go! We're late." Katie, clearly squeamish, gave a stage-effect groan and drummed on the dash. *This from the girl who'd made them late.*

"All right, you two, have fun. But not too much fun." Nate gave his sister an Old West squint. "You. Don't get my fiancée into any trouble."

"Oh, Nate," Ellie said in her twinkly English accent as she ran her hand over his forearm before pulling away from the curb, veering a little too far into the other lane, which yielded rapid-fire honking from an irate cab driver.

Katie leaned out the window, hand cupped to mouth, and shouted, "She's British, not deaf, asshole!" She plopped down into her seat, almost losing her oversize sunhat that took up her entire side of the vehicle. "Wait, you know what side to drive on, right?" Katie liked to make jabs at Ellie's Britishness.

Ellie smiled tightly at her sister-in-law-to-be. "Of course; I just didn't expect that you'd get something so big." For some reason, Katie had thought it would be prudent to lease a mammoth black Escalade to go up to a retreat that bragged about its eco-sustainability. She'd arranged to have it dropped off and now Ellie was driving because Katie, for some inexplicable reason, hadn't been able to get to the DMV to renew her license, which expired the day after she leased this monster. No excuse or apology was offered unless you counted a deadpan *I forgot*. Good thing Nate was there to sign for it.

"So we'll head right to LaGuardia first," Katie said, all nonchalant, then snapped her gum. She slid on some mirrored sunglasses to go along with her ridiculous hat.

"What? Why?"

"To pick up Ariel. Then we'll get Carmen."

Ellie had no idea what she was talking about. "Are you giving them a ride somewhere?"

"Yeah, to the retreat."

"You invited your friends?" Ellie's mouth gaped with outrage.

Katie looked at her as if she were senile. "I told you that."

"No, you certainly did not."

"I swear I did."

"No. I would have remembered that. I'd thought this was going to be just us." Ellie felt sucker punched. This changed everything she'd planned for the weekend. Their weekend. Rather than apologizing for this rude intrusion, Katie just kept repeating that she was *sooo sure* she'd told Ellie, as if through sheer repetition she could make something true.

"It's just Ariel and Carmen," Katie finally added, like it mattered.

But of course, Ellie thought. Of course Katie had to invite along members of what she referred to as her *girl squad*—an ever-changing ragtag group of other daytime drinkers and hangers-on—because she didn't want to be alone with Ellie. It confirmed what Ellie had long known, something she'd complained to Nate about. *Your sister doesn't like me.*

"I went to college with them," Katie said because she frequently liked to reiterate that she'd briefly attended college—as if a year of theater compared to Ellie's graduate studies in environmental sciences.

Ariel. Ellie knew that name. Katie said it a lot around Nate, making his neck burn bright red, which made Ellie fairly certain Nate must have slept with this Ariel at some point.

Unbelievable. What are we, five minutes into this trip? And already the Katie Manning circus has taken hold.

She should turn around, run back to her fiancé. Katie probably expected her to do just that. Hightail it back to a very disappointed Nate so Katie could put her arms up over her head and claim that she'd tried but that Ellie was the one who'd *bailed.*

Whenever Ellie felt like she couldn't take Nate's sister for another second, she thought of her as that slightly bewildered-looking girl playing Shelby Spade, and she could pull it together. Adapt. Ellie knew going into it that it wasn't going to be easy this weekend. She gripped the wheel harder. "LaGuardia, you said?"

Nate had waited for his second date with Ellie to reveal the identity of his sister, and he'd told her with the same gravitas as if he were telling her he was HIV positive. Apparently, Nate had put up with a whole stable of ex-girlfriends who'd wanted nothing more than to hang out with their preteen hero Shelby Spade and enjoy the accompanying fringe benefits of being friends with a celebrity (to which Ellie could personally attest was not much). When she'd told him her mother wasn't keen about owning a television, and she had no idea who he was talking about, well, Ellie believed that sealed the deal with him right then and there.

Their first date hadn't really been a first date but an interview—then again, was there really a difference between the two? Ellie had walked in with her résumé for a waitressing job at Nate Manning's new restaurant and had left with a boyfriend. Or least that was how she loved to answer the "how did you meet" question.

It was September and she'd been in New York exactly forty-eight hours. She had her hair up in her best artsy blond bun and was wearing a sleek, sleeveless black jumpsuit with just the right amount of plunge in the neck. Not too desperate but enough to offset the glasses. She softened her startling blue eyes with sexy reading glasses she picked up last minute at CVS. And yes, she referred to her own shade of blue eyes as *startling*. What could she say? She knew what she looked like.

The restaurant was a week away from its grand opening, and the flooring was still being installed. It was an upscale gastropub jammed with flat-screens, a mix of cozy booths and round tables, exposed brick, and twenty-two-foot ceilings. She sat at the bar while Nate stood behind it, glancing over her résumé.

He asked her the usual interview questions over the intermittent buzz of a circular saw and random hammering. She drew his attention first to her brief stint as a runway model, telling him that while she did not have any direct waitressing experience, she did have impeccable balance.

He liked this. Then she made sure to tell Nate she was never serious about modeling but making the world a better place, and that's why she was finishing her graduate degree at Columbia. Her focus area was human impact on the environment. Nate looked genuinely impressed. Beautiful with substance—if she ever started a perfume line, she'd call it that. Nate asked her more questions about her studies, and she was ready with a bouquet of less sanctimonious-sounding answers.

"So if I hire you, am I really helping out the world at large?"

"I think that's an accurate statement. And if you hire me, I'll bring major composting skills to the position." Ellie smiled, and took off her glasses.

Nate flicked his eyebrows and smiled. Oh, that smile, with its slight gap in the front teeth, a smile that had been goofy when he was younger but now gave him a slightly dangerous look. She'd go so far as to call it disarming, that gap.

She'd later tell him that he looked much better now than he did in those old *Tiger Beat* pictures, and she meant it. She'd done her research on him. Nate was the pinup who was probably never pinned up much. The guy who balanced a basketball on his index finger in a good-guy pose because he wasn't good looking enough to be broody—he was too happy, too open-faced, too jug-eared, not that she said this to him. For a while, like other siblings of established child actors, Nate scored a few guest spots on *Shelby Spade*, but it didn't go anywhere for him; his restaurant was aptly named Underdogs. All that remained of his stunted glory days were those *Tiger Beat* shots and a few archived online questionnaires about what he wanted in a girl.

Your fave food: Anything Italian. (Check. Ellie made a mean lasagna.)

What you like in a girl: A good sense of humor (Didn't they all say that?), *a nice smile. I have a soft spot for blondes and English accents.* (Ellie had just highlighted her hair and spoke with a crisp London accent, so check and check!) *And someone who cares about making the world a better place.* (Check! Check! Check!)

"So should I expect a call, or are you saying I'm hired on the spot?" Ellie tucked a strand of blond hair behind her ear, never breaking eye contact. The interview was going so much better than she could have ever expected.

"It depends." Nate looked away first. Another glance at her résumé. Then he made a proposition: if she could start working right then, she was hired. See, he needed someone to taste test some cocktails, because, he said, every good restaurant needed a signature cocktail you couldn't get anywhere else.

So Ellie stayed and taste tested a gag-worthy fleet of neon cocktails that were either too bitter, too tart, or too sickly sweet. Nate worked behind the bar like a frenzied chemist until he finally handed her something good. Really good. When she told him so, he looked stricken. He'd forgotten exactly what he'd put in it. Nate tried another three or four mixes but didn't get it exactly right, and so she got up and joined him behind the bar.

The work crew left, and they spent the rest of the night trying to replicate whatever Nate had made, getting messy drunk in the process—one of those rare occasions Ellie let herself drink too much. It wasn't until the sun started to come up and shot into the restaurant, lighting up one side of their faces like phantom masks, that Nate grabbed her and kissed her, his lips tasting of sugar rim and whiskey. He pulled back and looked at her. "Who are you?"

Ellie could have easily answered, *I'm the girl you described in* Tiger Beat; *I'm the girl of your dreams*, but she instead kissed him back, and he cleared the bar of shot glasses and lime wedges. A bottle of bourbon shattered on the ground. He lifted her up and parted her knees.

Afterward, she wanted to call someone. Her mom or her sister. Let the details spill out of her like a schoolgirl. Her stomach tripping over itself.

And then Ellie met Katie.

The worst thing about Nate was his sister.

They didn't actually get on the road until the afternoon. *Four and a half hours* after they'd left the apartment, all because Katie could not make adequate arrangements to meet her friends. She did not check airport arrival times, so they had to wait inside LaGuardia, wilting in its soupy, warm, Cinnabon-flavored air that tickled the back of Ellie's throat.

When they returned to the parking lot, Ariel tossed in her suitcases and cooed over the Cadillac SUV, and it was suddenly clear Katie had rented this tank just to spark envy.

They had to fight traffic back to pick up Carmen at a client's apartment. When she parked, Ellie went to turn off the car, but Katie insisted they keep the missile of an engine running to unnecessarily pump out its noxious pollutants, just to keep the AC going.

"How is Carmen?" Ariel asked gravely from the back seat.

"I don't know; I hardly see her anymore. I mean, she has like four kids now."

"Your friend has four children?" Ellie asked. She couldn't picture Katie having a friend with that much responsibility, who couldn't go out and party with her every night, or Katie enduring all the mundane details mothers shared about their children. Unless the friend wasn't a very good mother.

"No, no. They're her siblings, but she's practically their mother." In the fifteen minutes they waited for Carmen, Katie explained how Carmen had been in her last year at NYU and already armed with a scholarship to attend med school at Dartmouth when her hard-partying, bipolar mom walked out for a plumber and hadn't paid a dime of child support since. Carmen was forced to defer school for a year to work and help out, but she never went back to finish her undergrad degree and lost out on her scholarship. Now Carmen was a home-care worker, caring for her siblings and her Parkinson's-afflicted dad, crammed into a crumbling three-bedroom duplex on Staten Island.

Ariel made a sad clicking noise. "It's the cycle of poverty," she said just as Carmen came hustling out of the apartment building, still in her scrubs and peeling off latex gloves, which she tossed in a garbage bin. Ariel and Katie jumped out of the SUV and greeted their friend with a round of screechy "missed you so much" that went on for several minutes. Ellie turned the music up, then cranked it back down when they got back into the car. "Did not want to spend a second longer in there than I had to," Carmen said without explanation as she jumped into the back seat and placed a wrist full of colorful reusable grocery totes at her feet that were obviously doubling as luggage.

But now, finally, finally, finally, they were jostling along on the highway, a car full of four instead of two, Ellie feeling like a chauffeur as Katie fiddled with the console's buttons, yanking the volume up and down on some yodeling electronica they were listening to.

"It's just so nice we're all together again. Woot! Girls' weekend!" This was the third time Ariel had said some version of this in the last five minutes.

Ellie kept catching Ariel's eyes on her in the rearview mirror. Like Ariel was studying her face and probably realizing she'd never stood a chance with Nate.

Ellie felt better now that she'd seen her. She was a chubby, eager-to-please girl attired in a matronly floral-patterned dress who laughed way too much and way too hard. She was from some Midwest town where middle school pregnancy pacts and deep-fried Mars bars were probably made with equal zeal. She overly used the banal word *weird* and said things like *geez Louise* and *holy mackerel.*

If Nate had slept with her, it had to have been out of sheer laziness. Some drunken encounter at one of Katie's parties.

"I'm excited for the massages," Carmen added as she changed out of her scrubs in the back seat and pulled on frayed jean shorts and a stringy tank top. She pulled her brown hair up in a bun so high it nearly grazed the roof of the SUV. How many blind spots was Ellie going to have to contend with?

"Yeah, but check out these workshops." Katie read from her phone. "'Unleash your inner warrior and create the life you've always wanted by tapping into your true potential.' And here we've got your usual buffet of yoga, meditation, hypnosis, art therapy, aura readings, breath-work and an adventure course—whatever that means. All brought to you by an integrated psychiatrist-shaman named Dr. Dave, ordained by the Church of Brazil, and his wife, Naomi, who is a creative nutritionist. Again, whatever either of those things mean."

Katie was playacting right now, pretending this whole trip was a lark Ellie had talked her into, when really she was probably mentally pleading that the retreat would work. That she would return a completely different person. Surely her friends knew too that she wouldn't be there if she didn't want to be.

No one could make Katie do anything she didn't want to do; otherwise, she'd have a job or some semblance of responsibility. Ellie had planted the seed, yes, had even nudged Nate to nudge Katie with a dire warning that her lifestyle of binge drinking and promiscuity was going to get her killed. Ellie stayed in the other room and eavesdropped on Katie's tear-filled acknowledgment that she was a former child star with nothing left, that everyone hated her after her Twitter bomb, and she would do anything to be different. So Katie could act as if she were on board just to trip out on a psychedelic tea, but Ellie knew better. Deep down, Katie was hoping for a transformation.

"The Sanctuary has mainly four- and five-star reviews on Trip-Advisor, and most of the comments were people saying how life-changing their experiences were and that they couldn't wait to go back," Ellie added, hoping it would help Katie out of her little act of reluctant attendance.

"Well, I have done my own research into the retreat," Ariel said with a certain amount of intrigue, and Ellie waited for her to reveal something seedy or damning about the retreat. "And oh my goodness, Dr. Dave is sooo hot," the girl gushed, her entire body twitching like she'd inserted a vibrator.

"I mean, yeah, the dude's attractive. That's kind of a prerequisite for a guru, yeah? But seriously, that Instagram account of his? What is up with people's victory posturing? Like, what?" Carmen said as her fingers danced over the screen of her own phone. "Like, look at this." She wagged her phone back and forth. "Did Dr. Dave just win a Nobel Peace Prize? Did he cure cancer? Did he finish a marathon? Nope. Just got up, picked out hipster-chic workout clothes for the day, and walked down to the beach with a camera. It's so narcissistic. And, like, how serene, living-in-the moment are you if you're pausing to take a selfie?"

"I just want to trip out on the magical tea," Katie said when she was finished laughing at Carmen's tirade like she didn't post her own victory poses, like that one time she'd organized her closet. "Ellie drank the tea and had a fab experience." And like that, Katie handed the conversation baton over to Ellie.

Ellie was surprised; she didn't think Katie had been listening when she'd told her the very true story of when she'd backpacked with a friend in Peru and experienced the tea with a real shaman. How she'd hallucinated and purged—emotionally and physically—until it felt like her guts were splitting. Yet when it was over, her life path emerged like a yellow brick road. "Ayahuasca is completely life-changing." Ellie took another breath, trying to put words to an experience that transcended language.

"*Oh my god*, pull over!" Katie screeched, cutting her off. Ellie swerved, thinking she was about to hit something, but Katie had her phone out—not that she ever put it away. "We need to get a picture of us with that!" Katie pointed at a giant roadside advertisement.

Ellie waved them on, refusing to join in—she *said* in case a car came and she had to move the Escalade. Really, she felt like a mic had been ripped from her hands as she watched the trio of these woo-girls pose with Big Dick's Landscaping.

They piled back in, and for the next three hours Ellie tried to follow along the tangle of inside jokes and old college memories passed among Ariel and Carmen and Katie, but she ended up spending the entire road trip with a perma-grin on her face while having no idea what they were talking about.

The only other time Katie tried to include her in the conversation was when she asked her to say *zebra*.

Ellie shrugged and pronounced it the British way, "ZEB-ra."

"Now say *cocksucker*."

"I'm not saying that."

"Pleeease, it's so funny with your accent. Listen to this. C'mon, Ellie-Rose, just do it! Say *cocksucker*."

Ellie gave in and said it. A round of laughter. Katie loved to pretend Ellie's accent was adorable so she could openly mock it. Apparently, the same could be said about her full hyphenated name, since this was the first time she'd heard Katie use it.

Katie then requested for her to say out loud:

Tit-fucking.

Hairy balls.

That zebra cocksucker just tit-fucked me with his hairy zebra balls.

"Wow, and it still sounds like you've just asked me to tea." Followed by a genuine squeal of teary-eyed laughter. She also called Ellie Down*town* Abby, and Ellie never corrected her. There's a reason stand-up comedians do thirty-minute sets; they're exhausting after that.

The GPS directed them through a series of turns and winding roads until the road that led to the Sanctuary lolled out of the thick, dark trees like a tongue. Once they'd turned onto the driveway, it took a full minute to reach the lodge.

It was a massive, chalet-style lodge with a stone façade and dark blue trim, perched on 160 acres of wooded lakefront land. It blended so perfectly with its surroundings that it almost seemed to be outfitted with camouflage.

There was also a smaller guest cottage on the opposite side of the barn that Katie had complained was already booked when she'd reserved their room. At the time, Ellie had thought the guest honeymoon cottage was a bit much just for the two of them, but now it made sense since Katie had been booking for four.

They pulled into the circular flagstone driveway and parked.

The girls slid out of the Escalade, slammed their doors shut, and stretched. Finally able to breathe real air and not the fuzzy scent of a Glade clip-on, Ellie took a deep breath. She basked for a second in the gentle tinkling of wind chimes and other whistling and moaning wind contraptions—of which there sounded to be plenty—a balm to her ears after listening to blasted music and shrill voices. "Aw, look at you; you're meditating already." Katie clucked her tongue, and then before Ellie could avoid it, Katie pounced and took a group shot. *Tap, tap, tap,* and she was loading it to her freshly reactivated Instagram account. "It's like a show of bravery to reactivate," she told her friends. Of course, it also looked good for Katie Manning to appear so reticent, that her first post-tweet pic was of her at a wellness retreat.

Ellie tried to tamp down her anger at being displayed online without her permission. Up until then, she'd managed to evade any association with Katie's social media.

They grabbed their bags from the trunk, bumping and dragging their oversize suitcases—except Carmen, who looked downright spry, bags swinging at her wrists—up the driveway and onto the porch. The lake was shining under the afternoon sun like tinfoil. On the dock was a girl doing a headstand on a yoga mat. Her bloodred face matched her red headband and was aimed toward the house like she was waiting for someone to notice her. Her Cancun-style braids dangled from her head like Medusa snakes, and her substantial armpit hair rustled in the wind. The girl lifted up one hand and stayed like that for a few seconds, showing off her strength before flipping down onto her feet. She made a heart shape with her hands.

"Oh, wow, I can smell the patchouli from here," Katie wisecracked. Ariel laughed again, harder than the joke warranted. Ellie got the feeling that Ariel acted as a portable version of canned laughter for Katie. An unpaid ego groomer. Or maybe paid, considering Katie did foot the bill for both her friends to be there. Airfare and all. Ellie knew this, because her friends kept thanking her for the trip. Katie brushed it off as no big deal, but Ellie knew that she was blowing through her money.

Nate told her so.

He kept a careful watch over Katie's finances.

Now Ellie felt her skin prickle with another wave of defensiveness, but just as quickly, she shook it off. If Katie wanted to spend the weekend belittling the retreat, there was nothing she could do about it. Katie was there. It was a first step in what Ellie had lately abbreviated to Project Katie. That was all that mattered.

ARIEL

Under a haze of unrelenting giddiness, Ariel was still laughing about the patchouli comment when the door to the lodge opened. Standing there were the owners, operators, and married couple, Naomi and Dr. Dave Lundgren. Both were sun-kissed and dressed in long, white, flowy collarless shirts.

"Welcome, welcome." Dr. Dave held the door, and he was so tall that Ariel easily passed under his arm. Always an awkward thing for a grown woman to do—pass under a man's armpit to enter a place.

"We're so honored to have you here." Naomi smiled with preternaturally white teeth marred only by a black fleck between her front two teeth that Ariel guessed was a chia seed. She clasped her hands in front of her, pressed her bare feet together, and offered an Eastern bow. Her hair fluttered forward like a cascading waterfall; it was styled in what Ariel knew only as a bowl cut.

Katie stepped inside, tried returning Naomi's bow, and broke out into a new round of laughter when they bumped heads on the way down.

"I admire your energy, girls," Dr. Dave said about their little slapstick routine. Ariel would have bristled at *girls* like she always did when a man called her one, but not with Dr. Dave. Maybe it was because he was younger than his wife by at least a decade; he was maybe in his late thirties. Early forties at the most. Somehow that made it okay. Or maybe it was because Ariel felt smitten.

It was *weird* to see Dr. Dave in real life after watching hours of him talking on his YouTube channel. It was the same way she'd felt about Katie when she'd seen her for the first time in real life. There was something surreal about it, like animation that had been superimposed into the real world. Back in college, it had taken a long while to not view Katie as a hypercolored, flawless celebrity. She would just look at her with complete wonder until Katie would grow surly and tell her she was creeping her out.

At first, Ariel only clicked through the videos so she could better see where she was going—Dr. Dave recorded himself in different parts of the retreat—and to understand why Katie had wanted to come to this place. But he was easy to watch, with his chiseled jawline and his Nordic ice-blue eyes and that deep, throbbing voice that kind of put her in a lull.

Of course, this was before Ariel learned they were attending this retreat *ironically*. That Katie wasn't taking it seriously at all, only pretending to so she could make fun of Ellie's new age beliefs before the marriage—which Ariel couldn't hear about without her stomach going eely.

"It is so wonderful," Naomi said, her eyes going dewy. She had all the perkiness of a Zumba instructor. Ariel would know, because she'd spent the last year thinking Zumba was the answer to her extra weight. *It wasn't.*

Then Naomi went in for a hug, like the bow wasn't enough.

Ariel was *not* a hugger. A lot of people assumed otherwise, she knew, because rather than *resting bitch face*, Ariel suffered from *resting super-approachable face*. She came across like a jolly fat girl, but she didn't like to be touched unless she explicitly invited it. However, being Minnesotan, Ariel was polite more than anything, and so she hugged back. "Thank you, and I admire your welcoming techniques," Ariel said awkwardly, giving Naomi a hard, drumming back pat, which was universal code for the hug to end.

Dr. Dave then swooped in for his own hug. A button on his shirt scraped against her cheek and nose. Ariel started laughing again.

Really laughing. She thought she was going to lose control for a second and just drop to the floor, giggling, because it was her reaction any time she felt awkward. She would picture herself being mugged or being held at knifepoint by a rapist and start to titter away, her entire body vibrating with nervous laughter. *"You think this is funny, bitch?"* And her throat would be slit just to shut her up, and she'd be murdered with some idiotic grin on her face.

Ariel touched her cheek and tucked her hair behind her ears.

She took a moment to look around while Dr. Dave and Naomi made the rounds, hugging Carmen and Ellie tightly as if they were long-lost family members who they were generously putting up for the weekend. It rang a little false, considering how much the rooms cost. Before Katie was even done asking Ariel if she wanted to come to a retreat in upstate New York, Ariel was googling it, looking at the room rates, enlarging the aerial views of the sprawling 160 acres of lush green, the fruit trees and vegetable garden, the charming wood swings and hammocks.

It looked like an exclusive country club.

This was the perk of being best friends with a celebrity.

Ariel missed Katie. The whirlwind quality of her. Her fairy godmother–ness. One minute she'd be standing in her boxy apartment trying to overpower the fried smell of Shakopee's only Boston Pizza with Febreze, and the next thing, Katie called and she was twirling around like she'd just won some sweepstakes contest.

She missed Carmen too, even if they weren't as easy around one another without Katie sandwiched between them. She missed their little threesome. She missed college, when they were still sky-high on their potential. On their special-ness. When they had yet to open that first nesting doll of adult disappointment and failure.

Ariel didn't make it in New York past that first summer after graduation. She couldn't afford the necessary rounds of unpaid or insultingly underpaid internships to get hired by a decent advertising agency. Her parents called and checked on her as if she were a plummeting investment; they were so baffled that college graduates weren't rewarded with jobs once they graduated.

So she went home, tail between her legs, and eventually got a job as an event planner at a Holiday Inn—it was as glamorous as it sounded—with the goal to save up and return to the Big Apple. That was five years ago, and now she didn't even have the Holiday Inn job to show for it.

She knew she was too young to already be living in the past, but she was anyway.

While all the hugging was going on, Ariel peeked into the living room and had to stop a squeal from bubbling up in her throat. It looked even better than it had online—the high ceiling crisscrossed with exposed beams. The dark, shiny wood. The way the room stretched on and on into a dining room with a wall of windows to gaze through at the lake, so sparkly that unicorns could drink from it.

It was beautifully decorated. A rustic coffee table with a stack of three leather-bound books topped with a seashell. A knee-high bronze horse sculpture next to the fireplace. A dark-and-stormy-night oil painting hanging on the mantel. Four chairs with ornate, rolling wood backs. And the pillows! So many throw pillows! Blues and reds and herringbone all arranged just so on the couches, a combination of colors and patterns and fabrics that shouldn't make sense but somehow did, a big middle finger to the simple plebeian tastes of purchasing furniture in matching sets. Ariel was always awed by interior design that didn't match.

She inched farther inside the room. It looked like it'd been ripped from her Pinterest Bohemian Dream Room board. A pinned Williams-Sonoma advertisement. Ariel's insides quivered like they always did around nice things. *It's Pinterest perfect.*

A middle-aged woman with gray-brown hair with one of those

zany stripes of purple meant to announce a lingering youthful wild streak was sitting down on the floor in front of the coffee table. Ariel almost didn't notice her. She was gripping a canary-yellow colored pencil and pressing it hard onto a page. "Helloooo. Oh, coloring, nice." It was all Ariel could think of, because what did you say about coloring? The woman's head snapped up, and now Ariel could see her face. It was a contorted mask of grief. The woman looked like she was crying, *weeping* on mute. Her mouth, opened and puffy, emitted an airy sound. Almost soundless, like air being let out of a tire.

"Sorry." It was all Ariel could say as she backed out of the room.

"Let's show you all to your rooms so you can get settled. Orientation starts at 5:30 sharp in the main room." Dr. Dave did not offer to carry anyone's bags as he led them up a wide, creaky staircase.

It was much warmer on the second floor. Too warm. As if the air-conditioning couldn't make it up there. Dr. Dave flung open the doors to two side-by-side rooms. "I call them the Blue Bliss Room and the Green Serenity Room," he said with a schmaltzy flourish, as if he were presenting the penthouse suite of some Las Vegas tower. The girls shuffled forward and looked in each room. Ariel sensed Ellie behind her—or really over her; she was so damn tall.

So this was Ellie. The bride-to-be was finally unveiled. How many hours had Ariel scoured the internet for a picture of her just out of curiosity? She was pretty, if you were into perfect, heart-shaped faces devoid of any character.

Her stomach was knotted the entire drive up. She'd always been holding out hope that maybe on the handful of weekend trips to New York City she'd made since college, something would happen again between her and Nate. Not sloppy drunk sex but something sober and real. And then it would be Ariel living with Nate, right below Katie, and they would be one big happy family.

She couldn't picture Nate happy with Ellie. She was snooty. She didn't try to engage with them even though Katie kept trying to include her in the conversation.

Ariel had stared at Ellie on the ride up and wondered if she knew about her and Nate, until Ellie caught her in the rearview mirror and aggressively held her gaze until Ariel looked away.

"Oh, I love these rooms," Katie gushed. "It kind of feels like you're staying with some old eccentric English aunt, hey, Ellie-Rose? I am gonna take the Blue Bliss one because it sounds like a fun cocktail."

Ellie smiled. "Not my aunt, she likes her knickknacks. But spartan surroundings certainly help to declutter the mind."

Dr. Dave nodded. "That's the idea, all right."

Ariel rolled her eyes. She thought the rooms were too bare. Though she'd studied the pictures online, she'd just assumed that certain amenities had been left out on purpose, as part of the "unplug and relax" Valencia-filtered marketing scheme and that just outside the frame was a flat screen and minibar. But the rooms were much plainer than she'd expected. Almost stark with two twin beds and mismatching blue homemade quilts. A blue vase with a daisy. A water pitcher on a gold embossed plate. All shabby chic and quaint but practically empty.

Her phone suddenly jingled. She pulled it out of her purse. Dr. Dave made an audible sigh.

It was her dad calling. She hit Silent.

"Then I guess this is our room," Ellie said cheerily and followed Katie into the room, brushing too hard against Ariel to be an accident.

"Oh, I thought . . ." Ariel's voice went sticky in the back of her throat. She'd thought she'd be sharing with Katie. They were *best friends*. She hadn't seen Katie in over a *year*!

Ariel stood there a second too long, about to push her way inside and cut off Ellie's confident toss of her suitcase onto her bed, when her phone lit up again. Her dad. Ariel dismissed the call.

Then she received a text before she could even put her phone back in her bag. Her dad had never texted her before.

THE POLICE JUST LEFT HERE! WHAT HAVE YOU DONE ARIEL!!? CALL HOME NOW!

Ariel's heart did a panicky hiccup out of her chest. The air went clammy.

Carmen bumped canvas bags past her. "Guess that makes us green and serene."

Ariel turned her phone off, slipped it back into her bag, and followed Carmen to the other room.

"Good! I'm glad the room speaks to you. Sometimes, I feel the rooms themselves pick their guests." Dr. Dave tipped his head back like he was mind-blown, and Carmen whispered in Ariel's ear that she got the feeling *Dave* was mind-blown a lot.

CARMEN

Twenty minutes later, they were all tumbling down the stairs into a living room that reminded Carmen of some kind of lodge, where a secret society of powerful men with goblets of brandy in hand met to make decisions for the rest of society. Maybe it was the antler chandelier hanging over the dining room table or the massive stone fireplace, where evidence of some despicable act could easily be burned to ash. Either way, there was something about this place she already didn't like. Maybe it was her ingrained suspicion of people with money. Maybe she just distrusted unbridled displays of happiness without the obvious help of pills or alcohol.

How am I even here?

How many times did she say no, no, no to Katie's zany, psychotropic tea–drinking adventure? To her onslaught of GIFs with dancing teapots and psychedelic twirling tunnels? (Katie once wrote an essay broken up with GIFs and still wondered why college didn't work out for her.) Katie finally resorted to guilting her with, "Remember that car I bought you?"

The Mustang. When Carmen was forced to drop out of school, Katie rushed out and bought her a flashy orange Mustang to take her dad to his doctor's appointments or her siblings to school. It was such a generous, bighearted gift but oh so misguided. Carmen couldn't afford to pay for insurance, parking, and oil changes when she was scrambling to feed and clothe her four siblings and pay for her dad's meds. Plus the car itself was way too low to the ground for her dad to get comfortably in and out of. A car was a luxury she didn't need. She was forced to sell the Mustang behind Katie's back, telling her it was stolen, which it would have been eventually in Carmen's neighborhood.

Carmen was flooded with that same bewildered feeling she'd gotten in college when she found herself doing things she normally wouldn't because it was impossible to say no to Katie. Then she felt a pluck of real guilt for leaving Dad for an entire weekend to be watched over by her siblings, who were either too young or too self-centered to do a good job.

"How can you go after that tweet? I mean, you're a lesbian!" Carmen's eleven-year-old sister had looked at her like she was a traitor then recited the tweet, including the laundry list of offensive hashtags, verbatim with Katie's nasal grind.

"Heartbroken emoji. I could become a lesbian, but I think I'd rather kill myself. #mensuck #sorrygirlsbutilikeshavingmylegs #flanneldoesntsuitme #comfortablefootwareisugly #cheatersalwayslose."

In a single post, Katie had declared suicide was a better option than lesbianism. She was annihilated on Twitter for equating those two things, but Carmen knew Katie wasn't even the slightest bit homophobic. The first night they met, Katie had tried to have her college lesbian experience, and Carmen had laughed her off. Insensitive, ignorant, and idiotic, yes, but not homophobic. It was her shtick to be outrageous; there were things Katie said that Carmen laughed at when she shouldn't have. She was guilty too, so she couldn't turn around and act *sensitive* when the joke was on her. That was just hypocritical.

But still, she couldn't help it; the tweet had nagged at her. Until she realized she could hang it over Katie's head by acting more offended than she really was, and then maybe it would be easier to ask her for a loan.

The things she did for money.

* * *

Six other guests were already seated in the living room, stiff and silent on the chairs and couches. It was the atmosphere of a walk-in clinic waiting room. Carmen sat down next to Ariel on an open love seat. Katie and Ellie took hard-backed chairs, and for no good reason, Naomi looked at them and said, "Amazing," with glistening eyes and flushed cheeks, then handed each of them a pamphlet. Carmen was sure the pamphlets were going to be about the perks of mass suicide; instead, it was the weekend itinerary. Maybe it was their matching blousy shirts that were making her feel twitchy—she couldn't decide if Dr. Dave and Naomi looked more like cult members or guests on a cruise ship. It was a thin line. Carmen flipped the pamphlet open and glanced at three days worth of yoga, journal writing, circle drumming, and other vague things like *group exercise* and *solitude*.

"Before going over the itinerary, let's do introductions so everyone can get to know each other's beautiful souls. First, just a quick bit about me." Dr. Dave put his foot up on the coffee table in what Carmen considered to be the cool-youth-pastor pose and cast his blue lashy eyes around the room. "I'm a psychiatrist who spent years treating my patients with pills. One unfortunate day, a particular patient I thought was making progress attacked me with my pen." Dr. Dave lowered his collar to show off what looked like a series of old cigarette burns. "It missed all the important veins, but that didn't matter. I'd had a near-death experience. Everything changed for me that day. I could see more clearly and realized that I was only managing symptoms, not really curing people. I began searching for something better, something more holistic so I could help others. I quit my practice and traveled."

Dr. Dave's travelogue was what was to be expected. First there was India, then a stay with monks in Tibet, then a few months in Thailand, as if these places only existed to teach Dr. Dave about happiness, peace, and self-realization. He somehow found himself outside the city of Iquitos (Carmen rolled her eyes; like Dr. Dave hadn't gone online and arranged a flight before finding himself suddenly in Peru) somewhere in the jungle sipping ayahuasca tea and Dr. Dave felt all things he was now promising. "Utter transcendence."

He had decided to bring the tea back to the state of New York and couple it with a program he developed to treat his most difficult patients, which Carmen thought probably hit on something deeply unethical. "I just might be big pharma's number one enemy, because their transformation was nothing short of miraculous."

"It really was," Naomi piped up. She closed her eyes, and gave a swaying nod like she was enjoying a florid hallucinogenic flashback.

Carmen tuned out the rest of their backstory that was just one victorious insight after another. She didn't see how DMT in the ayahuasca tea and self-help were that far off from what he had been doing with therapy and drugs. She let out a bored sigh and thought how much better it would have been if Katie had just given her the money she'd spent on this weekend. That would have made an actual difference in her life, instead of this mamsy-pamsy spiritual stuff with a heavy dose of cultural appropriation as the cherry on top.

"And so by the end of the weekend, each of you will be able to manifest your dreams into reality. You really can have everything you want. Now please, my guests, introduce yourselves. Just your name and what brought you here," Dr. Dave said, followed by more nods and crinkly-eyed smiles.

The introductions were short and stiff. There was a handsome French Canadian couple named Simon and Marie. Both college professors who said they were on the brink of retirement but looked too young for it. They were repeat customers because Dr. Dave's brand of enlightenment spoke to them. "We come so often, the border patrol practically waves us through," Simon said with a studded accent and a warm chuckle.

Paula went next. "I'm also part of the repeat customer group," she gushed. Carmen's eyes kept being drawn to the tattoo of a dog with dead eyes gazing out from Paula's meaty arm. "I guess I'm here this time for a tune-up." She described herself as divorced and in her midfifties. "Just learning who I am all over again." Carmen noticed Paula still wore a wedding ring.

Dr. Dave and Naomi made gentle *ooh*ing and *ahh*ing noises.

Then there was Anthony—early thirties with a Three Musketeers goatee—a paunchy, creatively blocked video game designer attending the retreat to hopefully get unblocked. Simple as that.

Then Max, who joked about being the only black dude there before his face turned sad and serious. He was a paramedic on leave, and he'd heard ayahuasca tea could help with PTSD.

It was Carmen's turn. She felt flimsy and shallow going after everyone else, especially the paramedic. The patients Carmen dealt with had long accepted their impending death, and Carmen was mostly there to clean them up and fix their televisions by pressing the right input on their remote controls. She'd expected there would be more guests, not this intimate, boutique-style retreat. It was now going to be so much harder to lurk under the radar of all the guru-led hocus-pocus, which she had no plan to take part in.

"I am here to spend time with my friends," she offered as her reason for being there with a big smile. No sense lying. Naomi's mouth twitched, and Dr. Dave gave her a tight smile like they could sense she was there for all the wrong reasons—which she was—and so she added, "And to destress and refocus. I'm in the medical field as well."

Dr. Dave shifted his focus to Ariel.

"Hi, I'm Ariel," she said with the bubbliness of a diner waitress. "I'm just going to say ditto to what my friend Carmen here said."

Katie offered similar reasons for being there but added wanting to get out of her comfort zone and that she was also *really, really, really* looking forward to the tea.

Ellie's answer was just as trite but better articulated. She wanted to bring more "mindfulness into her life and increase her physical flexibility."

The feral-looking hippie girl, who'd greeted them with a finger heart, went last. Her name was Lily. She was there "to have my mind blown, y'know, just *boosh*," she said while miming her head exploding.

"And that you will, girl." Naomi reached over and touched Lily's slender shoulder. "You will." Lily responded with a smoker's cackle.

Dr. Dave grinned and nodded with agreement. He put his hands on his slender hips. "This weekend will be transformative. None of you will leave here the same person you are right now."

"Oh, Dr. Dave, I'm so excited." Paula's shoulders jiggled up and down.

"Good thing, Paula, because this weekend is going to get you all out of your comfort zones so you can alter your outlook, alter how you see yourselves—because what do I always say, Paula?"

"What you see is what tends to be," Paula answered rotely.

"That's right. I truly believe you can change everything about yourself in a single weekend." Dr. Dave then started to expound on the fairy-tale properties of ayahuasca tea, and Carmen tuned out.

She noticed some strands of Ariel's reddish hair on her black tights, and her stomach turned. Upstairs in their room, when Ariel had bent down to unzip her suitcase, her hair had parted in just the right way to reveal a shiny white patch of scalp on the back of her head. Like a third, blind eye. Carmen startled, her mouth went dry, and when Ariel turned back around and offered up that Keebler elf smile of hers, Carmen had to look away. Ariel was pulling out her own hair again. It had happened once before, during first-year exams when Carmen noticed a little patch of skin behind Ariel's left ear, which Ariel laughed off as a nervous tic. But this, now on the back of her head, was bigger than a quarter. There was something very disturbing about it.

Dr. Dave was now instructing everyone to close their eyes. "I want everyone in the room to take a deep breath, relax your minds, and try not to think for thirty seconds. Thirty seconds. That's all. Just let your thoughts, *whoosh*, go right out of you." Everyone closed their eyes. Carmen shifted awkwardly. *Isn't this where indoctrination starts? When the gurus tell you not to think?* Carmen closed her eyes anyway.

"Do you feel that? Do you feel your pure, undiluted self? How infinite your presence is? You're all here because you're meant to be here. Once you accept this, you can accept everything else we have to offer. You can have the full experience. But first! First! You all need to take the proper steps. You need to get ready, prepare for the journey into yourself so when you leave here, you can follow your bliss."

Carmen sputter-laughed. She pressed the back of her hand to her mouth to stifle it, but it was too late. Everyone's eyes were open and on her.

"Carmen? Do you have something to say?" Dr. Dave came over. He moved in this slow, languid way with the confidence of a man who knew how good looking he was, and had never been told that whatever he was saying wasn't completely fascinating.

He placed his hand on Carmen's shoulder and gave it a squeeze, then left his hand there. His smile was smug and his palm was cold.

"I am sorry; I just feel that the whole *follow your bliss* thing is a bunch of bullshit elitist rhetoric."

"How so, Carmen?" Dr. Dave said her name again.

"Well, all it really means is that people enjoy the gratifying feeling they get when they indulge in their personal pleasures." Everyone in the room was now looking at her as if she were a sad outcast. "But I can absolutely respect everyone else's journey here . . , it's just probably me. I . . . yeah." Carmen's voice trailed off.

"We don't mind tough customers, do we, Naomi?" Dr. Dave chuckled and released Carmen's shoulder.

"Not at all; in fact, we love the challenge. You'll see," Naomi said in a singsong voice. Rubbed her hands together and gave her a honeyed smile.

Oh no, Carmen thought. What had she done? She didn't want to be their challenge, their tough nut they had to crack to prove something.

"By the end of the weekend, Carmen, you will come to understand that bliss is not bullshit but a deep sense of being present. Of doing what you must absolutely do to be your most authentic self." Dr. Dave used a condescending tone that made Carmen's skin prickle. "And so now, who is ready to take the first step?" he asked.

Paula started opening her purse, and immediately Carmen's mind went to the donation basket they passed around in church when she was younger. The one her mom would pretend to add to but really snatch out a handful of bills from, later explaining that she was just cutting out the middleman because they were the fucking needy.

"The first one is probably the most painful, and you'd all better brace yourselves." Dr. Dave sucked in air through his teeth, stroked his chin, and gave the room one of those assessing looks that asked, *Can you handle it?* "You need to give up all of your devices. Now don't panic!" A warm chuckle. "The Sanctuary is outfitted with full internet and phone service, okay? So if you can't handle it and need to plug yourself back in, then you can, but I strongly recommend you don't. So if you truly want this to be the life-changing weekend it's meant to be, then this is the first step. If you don't really want to change, then keep your phones." Dr. Dave handed Naomi a wicker basket, and she went around and collected everyone's phones. Carmen blew out a lungful of relief. She was fine with that.

It was better than fielding calls all weekend from Megan.

When Naomi got to Anthony, he looked like he was in physical pain as he dropped in his Apple watch, then his phone, and promised to add his iPad and laptop later once they were in their protective sleeves.

Carmen tossed in her phone and watched as Katie reluctantly added her own phone, asked Naomi a question, and then drew her phone back out with a sleight of hand Carmen's mother would hove envied.

"I know." Dr. Dave gave the room an empathetic wince. "It hurts, but the other four steps will be easier without that little devil of distractions in your pockets. Step two—please read."

Naomi locked the phones up in a china cabinet, then passed out another round of paper. This time it was bullet-point instructions on how to prepare for "Your Spiritual Journey," followed by a waiver that absolved the Sanctuary of any legal responsibility for any and all injuries or damages occurring for any reason during the ayahuasca ceremony.

Not shifty at all.

Carmen had no intention of drinking the magical tea.

She couldn't risk her golden eggs. Eggs that were going to go on to be fertilized by a stranger's sperm, then placed in another stranger's uterus. Maybe then given over to completely different parents.

She'd started donating her eggs in her second term at NYU when she realized that her financial-aid package, even with a scholarship, fell short of covering all of her tuition.

She had tried working as a bartender, but the late nights caused her grades to slip, and her partial scholarship was threatened. She was in danger of not being able to finish out the year. She would have had to drop out, left with nothing but crippling debt to show for it (which eventually happened anyway).

Enter Darla Gibbins from ReproGen. She'd solicited Carmen in the student commons, stepping out in front of her as if she were selling hand lotion in a mall. Darla looked like either a madam or a television evangelist. Chubby and virtually chinless, her fake thick lashes wagged from her eyelids like butterflies stuck in glittery grease. "What's a little discomfort for a couple of weeks if it puts up to $10,000 in your pocket? Easy money."

Ten thousand turned out to be seven thousand. But the egg donation was easy, and she could study in the waiting room. She was hooked.

Now Carmen was on her fourth donation because clearly she

came from especially fecund stock, and the money was just covering the little extras like clothes and replacing the busted picture
window because they couldn't go another winter with cardboard
as their only protection. Her thirteen-year-old brother, the shithead,
had gone on a Banksy-inspired vandalism spree and now Carmen
was stuck paying off his fines to keep him out of juvie. Then to top
it off, the hot water tank just went.

She told herself it was her last donation, but even she didn't believe it. She felt hooked. It wasn't the easiest way to make money,
but out of all the ways to make money, it wasn't the worst either.

Carmen felt she was nine years old and back in the free swimming class offered to low-income families. The instructor had called
the kids who'd passed to stand on the side and left the failures in
the pool, half treading water, half drowning, looking up at them,
chlorinated water burning up their noses and eyes. Carmen did
everything right to escape that pool, but there she was anyway. Poverty was like a serial killer at the end of a horror movie; just when
she thought she'd gotten away, it popped up stronger, yielding an
electric bill like a machete.

She still skimmed the release of liability waiver and signed it
anyway. She planned on backing out at the last minute to avoid
Katie's inevitable wheedling that would last the entire weekend.
Carmen's contract specifically stated she not partake in any drugs or
alcohol, yet she couldn't deny her interest was piqued. She'd love to
drink some magical tea, morph into her spirit animal or whatever,
and gallop around in some rainbow-drenched, unicorn-laden alter-
nate universe for an hour or eight. Her life was *hard*. It'd be nice to
sink into oblivion for a while. It was what she'd always liked about
Katie; she brought out Carmen's risk-taking side. She slayed her
type A. Got her to loosen up, drink too much, have fun, take off her
glasses, let her hair fall loose like the schoolmarm in some old-
school rock video who suddenly gave in to all her seething impulses.
Katie was her bad influence. Someone she could blame for doing
what she really wanted to do.

KATIE

After the orientation, Naomi led them on a tour of the grounds and pointed out all the pleasant nooks and crannies where guests could sit and reflect. Or stretch. Or breathe. There was going to be a whole lot of stretching and breathing going down this weekend.

She showed off her healing room, which had the humid atmosphere of an evil botanist's lair with a massage table. She led them outside to the barn, which still looked like a barn from the outside, but it had been converted into a spa. There was a hot tub just outside of it, flanked by two large frond plants. "This holds the same ancient medicinal formulas found in healing springs worldwide." Naomi gestured to what appeared to be an ordinary hot tub to Katie.

Inside, the stalls had been converted into treatment rooms and guests could choose treatments ranging from stone massages to mud scrubs to full oxidation with Himalayan salts. None of which sounded too appealing to Katie. The place smelled heavily of essential oils that all seemed to blend into something that reminded her of cough syrup, or maybe it was Vicks VapoRub, and it made her a little queasy. It was always AJ and rarely Lucy who made sure to apply a glaze of the stuff on her chest back when she was sick.

"The sign-up sheet is here." Naomi made a reaching motion and on cue, a young female staff member dressed in a starchy white outfit much like scrubs worn at a psychiatric hospital stepped out from one of the "stalls" holding a clipboard with a tethered pen swinging like a pendulum. The clipboard was passed around, and then returned to the girl, who retreated back into the treatment room.

The tour ended with the group shuffling into the kitchen, where Naomi listed all the forbidden foods on the opposite side of a long butcher-block island, the top of her head almost grazing the pots and pans dangling from the exposed rack—something to do with MAOI inhibiters and gluten and how it interfered with the tea— with big-eyed zeal. "Absolutely nothing pickled." She held up a jar of sauerkraut. The lecture seemed so pointless considering the retreat provided meals for its guests but Naomi used it as an oppor- tunity to sell her online integrative nutrition courses (only $599 per course and a lifetime of good health!).

Katie's eyes glazed over until Naomi said there was no alcohol or caffeine anywhere on the premises, and then she felt zapped back awake. Katie struggled with her sleep; she badly needed a drink before bed. It was medicinal.

She hadn't read a ban on alcohol anywhere on the site, which she was now realizing was more than a little misleading. Katie had thought everything preceding the tea was going to be an ex- tension of Keep Calm and Carry On, with umbrella drinks. Not this free-labor, boot-camp vibe.

"Are you kidding me?" Katie groaned, and Ariel echoed her. El- lie shot Katie one of her fixed little smiles that meant she felt sorry for her lack of self-discipline. *It's only three days.* Katie got that cunt- ish smile from Ellie a lot.

"I know, I know." Naomi put her hands up.

"Once upon a time, I would have felt the same way, but *trust me* when I tell you it will all be worth it. You will all be leaving here Mon- day morning as the beautiful warriors you are meant to be, ready to create the lives you've always wanted. You will remember this week- end as nothing short of *epic*." She pressed her hands together into prayer mode, her muscles popping in her ridiculously sculpted arms.

"Not like that; you're wasting half the apple," Naomi suddenly snapped at her kitchen staff peeling apples next to the country sink.

Katie had hardly noticed her. She was in the same white outfit as the staff in the spa. Both were young women, very early twenties with pretty, averted faces. "Like this, remember?" Naomi corrected the girl's apple-coring technique, and the girl practically curtseyed and went back to work. "Sorry about that. Now please follow me." Naomi led the group out the garden doors, into an outdoor dining area covered with a pergola coated in flowery vines, then down the steps of the deck. "We're going to play a game of garden bingo." She made a sweeping gesture toward a patch of land enclosed with rabbit-wire fencing.

"Garden bingo? What is that?" Anthony asked, his hand raised.

Naomi looked around, amused at everyone's confusion. "Come on, no one's played it before?" She did a mock dropped-chin look of surprise. "It's when you go outside and randomly unearth some veggies in the garden and then we come up with tomorrow night's dinner plan using what you picked." Naomi clapped twice, then rubbed her hands together. "It's so fun. Now go on. I can't wait to see what you bring back—what you excavate is so telling about your personalities." Naomi slid back through the garden doors and into the kitchen. "Of course it is, *Naomi*," Katie quipped under her breath and got a smile out of her friends. Katie now felt bad for roping Ariel and Carmen into this—she'd had to practically beg Carmen—but only for a second, because she couldn't imagine being there without them. It'd be twice as boring.

Ellie said she wanted to get some vegan menu ideas for the wedding, and followed Naomi inside. Yet another part of the wedding plans that Katie was cut out of.

Katie wasn't going to wait for her, instead ushering her friends down the steps and away from the house.

"This is all so, um, different," Ariel said as they made their way toward a huge garden.

Katie took this as Ariel's polite way of saying that the weekend was going to suck, and she suddenly felt the need to loosen things up. Get everyone back in a good mood. At her core, Katie was a people pleaser. A performer. She was not above fake-tripping over something to get a laugh, to put the room at ease. She was always at the ready to sacrifice herself to some stupid act.

"C'mon, Ariel. We'll have fun; at the very least, this is something we'll be able to laugh at for like a decade."

"There's *no caffeine or vodka here.* How are we going to have any fun?"

"That's the point. Like, it'll be *remember that weekend when we remembered everything about the weekend.* Ha! We're going to have some good, clean-living fun. Don't you want to be transformed?"

Ariel's nose scrunched, and her head wobbled. "Are you saying I *need* to be transformed?"

Katie gave Ariel an exaggerated eye roll. "Noooo. I'm not saying that at all. I didn't want to come here alone, with just *her*. This place was *her idea*, and my brother wants me and his fiancée to be friends, so here I am." Not exactly the whole story, but Katie didn't want to reveal she'd wanted to come to the retreat—not now. "I need some kind of advent calendar, counting down to my brother's divorce. Whiskey instead of chocolate, of course."

"They're not even married yet," Ariel was quick to point out. And again, Katie thought it was too bad her brother didn't want Ariel. She'd pushed Ariel so hard on Nate, and nothing. Just a single night of drunken sex that made Ariel turn into a stalker for five straight weeks until finally she dropped it. Katie knew Ariel probably still wanted her brother. Maybe not actively, but it was like a dormant virus lurking in her somewhere.

"Maybe you can stop it? Tell her that Nate has a dark side." Carmen grinned.

Katie flashed to some rom-com scenario that had her planting ideas in Ellie's head. "Good idea. I'll tell her that Nate once killed a kitten 'just to see how it feels.'"

"Or say he has a rare skin condition called 'disappearing penis' in which his junk hibernates for months in folds of his skin," Carmen added.

"Ew, good one, but let's not talk about my brother's junk." Katie laughed.

"All right, but I do have to say, I'm surprised too, Katie. This place just doesn't really seem like you," Carmen added.

"I know. I know." Katie sucked in her bottom lip. "But what if it does work? The tea?"

"What do you want it to do? The tea?" Carmen visored her eyes and gave her a look of concern, but it wasn't as sincere as it could have been. Katie suspected Carmen was still resentful about the tweet. A tweet she didn't even remember sending, and was deeply embarrassed about, but come on. She wasn't a bad person. Carmen knew her better than that.

Ariel stopped walking, turned, and grabbed Katie's hands in a motherly gesture. "Are you okay, Katie? You'd tell me if you weren't okay?" Ariel's eyes searched her face. Katie shook her off.

"So we're all skeptics. It actually makes this whole weekend more fun. We should actually take bets right now on who comes out of this a crystal-loving, gluten-free, spiritual person." Katie air-quoted *spiritual*. "I am going to put my money on Carmen, because lesbians are known to—"

Carmen gave her a tight smile. "Don't. Just don't."

"Too soon?" Katie asked her, and Carmen nodded. So it was definitely not her imagination; the tweet still dangled there between them. Katie could no longer tease her with lesbian stereotypes; something was now off-limits between them.

"Seriously, Katie. I just . . . I can't believe you of all people want to—" Ariel cut herself off.

"Want to what? Better myself? Not party so much? I'm kind of floundering, if you haven't noticed." Her voice came out too loud, too sad even. Ariel and Carmen gave her sympathetic looks, but neither tried to argue with her. Katie wanted to hear, "Whaddya talking about? Nooo. You're doing great."

Instead, Ariel clicked her tongue and started to say something about coming to stay with her for a little while, so Katie cut her off. Being pitied made her gut swirl with acid.

Fun. They needed to start having some fun. Her inner director started commanding her to loosen up, smile. Flash those dimples. "So I want to transform like Optimus freakin' Prime." Katie stopped walking, did a goofy robot dance. Let her forearm dangle from her elbow.

Her reference to a child's toy was pathetic and cheesy, but her friends gave her a gratuitous round of laughs anyway.

Sweet release.

God, it was so nice to just be with them again, Ariel and Carmen. They were like a cross between an old comfortable sweater and an all-star improv group. She was glad Ellie was still talking to Naomi. It was so much easier without her. They could just let themselves go.

Next to the garden's entrance was an oversize tub with a sign that read GARDEN TOOLS, which was a tad insulting. They each grabbed something from the tub, picked out their little plots of land, and started jabbing at the dirt.

Katie was plucking out a carrot when a shadow crept over her, cooling her skin. She looked up to see Lily standing above her, hands out like she was about touch Katie's hair. "I knew it was you! I knew it." A girlish squeal. She snatched back her hand and beamed a toothy smile so big it looked like it hurt. "*Shelby Spade.* Holy shit! I can't believe I'm here with Shelby Spade. Like, that's so crazy. I was your biggest fan." So the heart-fingers were aimed at Katie, or really, Shelby Spade.

"Oh, why, thank you. I appreciate that." Katie had mixed feelings about being recognized. Most of the time, she was annoyed when people didn't know who she was, but lately, she couldn't stand the inevitable question of what she was up to now when she had nothing to offer. Sometimes she'd lie and say she was doing a lot of voice-over work, because it would be harder to prove she wasn't. But it did make her feel like a washed-up D-lister.

"No, seriously, I had the Shelby Spade comforter, lunch box, the doll. Actually, I had two dolls, one for playing with—" Lily took a big, sputtering gasp of breath "—and another I kept in the package in case it became a collectible."

The Spade dolls never ended up being worth much. Katie shifted uncomfortably, glanced at Lily's bare legs, and noticed she had some kind of skin condition: splotches of round scabs the size of cigar burns peppered her legs.

"It's always so great to meet a fan of Shelby Spade," Katie said again, catching amused looks from her friends, hoping to wrap it up, but Lily lingered.

"I headed an official fan club. Once you wrote me back. Do you remember that?"

Katie thought about the piles of fan letters, so lovingly decorated and stuffed with glitter, tossed unopened into a recycling bin. Only the return addresses were recorded by whoever did those things for her, and then the fan would receive a form letter on what looked like personal stationery and a printed signature. Of course, Katie claimed to have read every single letter. *I love my fans so much; they mean everything to me.* The novelty of opening those huge piles of mail lasted two seasons, then Katie lost interest and fan mail became an administrative burden someone else dealt with.

"Oh, of course you don't." Lily gave a croaky laugh. Her eyes slid over Katie's scar.

"Thank you. Really. I appreciate it," Katie repeated in an even more heartfelt way, clasping her hands together to show how grateful she was for the praise. She picked up her garden shovel, hoping Lily would move on, but Lily kept talking.

"I made my mom take me all the way to Portland for one of your mall appearances. Actually, I made her take me to a few, it was, like, the highlight of my middle school experience. It's so weird; I just always felt if you met me, we'd be friends," Lily said and took a small step toward her. Now Katie was catching a hard whiff of mental instability.

"Huh," Katie said, heard her friends swallow down laughter. Again Katie was going to offer up another conclusive "nice to meet you" statement, but Lily was now motormouthing along, not blinking.

"Lacey Evans was the *worst*. I had someone like her, the typical mean girl in my school; she did something really horrible to me. I actually had to leave eighth grade but I soooo got her back—"

Katie caught sight of Ellie making her way down to the garden, and because she couldn't figure out a way to end Lily's relentless chatter, she turned her back on her, grabbed a rogue baby potato, yelled, "Yo, Ellie, think fast!" and flung it at her.

The potato nailed Ellie in the chest and left a muddy streak over her left boob.

"Oh no, I am so sorry, Ellie! I thought you'd catch it." Katie put her hand over her mouth because it was funny and she couldn't help laughing out loud. *See, this is why your brother's fiancée doesn't like you*. Ellie wiped at the mud, then looked at Katie and her friends, who were also laughing, and kept the potato in her hand when she should be hurling it back at Katie. That was how these things worked. It was what a good-natured person would do. Katie looked back over her shoulder; Lily was still standing there.

"Funny," Ellie said with that impenetrable smile.

"Heeee-il-ar-ious!" Lily folded over at the hips and let out a hee-haw that erupted into a rattling cough. Katie ignored her.

"You can hit me back; seriously, just fastball that thing right at my head. I won't even duck. Organic food fight?" Katie waved her arms jokingly and moved farther away from Lily. But Ellie just shook her head as if that was an unthinkable response and placed the potato in one of the wicker baskets, knelt at some sprouts, and started to unearth them with her bare hands. *Okay, then*. Katie felt something stiffen in her chest. Ariel lobbed a clump of roots at her to be nice, but it fell short of hitting her and the moment passed. Now Lily was in her spot, using the spade she'd just been using to jab where Katie had just been digging.

Katie shuffled over to Carmen's plot and crouched down next to her. "Dig up anything interesting?"

"Seems like you made a new friend." Carmen flicked her eyes at Lily and made an amused face. "The treachery of fame, huh?"

"It's like I had one last superfan, and she just happened to be here," Katie whispered. Lily tossed her a hopeful *pet me* look.

"Well, when you have a houseful of people who all have something they want to purge, someone is bound to be unstable," Carmen said.

"Hey, can anyone tell me what this is?" It was Max, the PTSD paramedic, cradling something in two hands like it was a newborn. He lifted it up, a flesh-colored thing with an antenna sprouting up the top.

"I think it's a ham," Katie called out, snorting at her own joke.

Max laughed. "So you're sayin' I just dug up a dead pig?"

"It's a turnip," Ellie corrected Katie. Max smiled at her, and turned to dump his turnip into the community basket they were supposed to bring back to Naomi.

"Oh, wait, do you mind taking a picture of us?" Katie handed her phone to Max. "I know I'm asking you to handle contraband here, but I just couldn't part with my baby. It's still breastfeeding."

Max scrunched up his nose, laughed. Dimples flashing. "Hey, I'm not telling on you, funny girl."

Lily sprang up and rushed over, crushing a row of greeny shoots.

"I can do it. I would love to get a picture with you. I was just thinking how badly I wish I had my phone—"

"That's okay, Lily. Max can do it," Katie said with more snap in her voice than she intended, but this girl just wasn't taking a hint. Lily made a wounded "Oh," but still hung about watching.

Katie reached over for the panama hat and shades she'd been carrying around since she'd left her room and, in her best flirty voice, said to Max, "It's not, like, hooked up—the phone. I just brought it for the camera."

"It doesn't matter to me. I don't work here." Max shrugged and laughed it off. A nice smile with broody eyes. He was cute. The kind of guy Katie would like to talk to again. She started to pose with her garden rake and then posed again, pretending to yank things out of the garden. "Which of these things are hoes? We could pose with them; we'll each hold one, and then we'll, like, post, 'Me and my hoes.'"

Carmen reminded her with air quotes that her phone was out of service.

"Come on, Ellie." Katie tried to lure Ellie into the picture, but of course she refused. It was like Ellie couldn't even stand to be seen with her.

"No, no. I'll take the pictures, though." She took Katie's phone from Max. *Of course.* She was so clueless. Max flicked his eyebrows up at them and went back to gardening.

Katie set up a shot that made it look like Carmen was going to hit them with the rake, and then they took turns posing with various garden tools, forgetting all about actually digging up vegetables and Lily's burrowing eyes.

ELLIE

The dining room table was decked out in boho chic with cheery, mismatched place settings, wildflowers in mason jars, and several beeswax candles that made the air honey-fragranced.

Dr. Dave and Naomi were standing at the respective heads of the table, waiting for their guests. They had placed cards on the dinner plates that instructed everyone where to sit. "I like to even out everyone's energy," Dr. Dave explained. Ellie was seated between Dr. Dave and watery-eyed Paula. Katie and company were also broken up, with Katie placed right beside Lily.

How perfect.

Ellie watched as Katie gave Lily a polite smile that dropped as soon she sat down. But Lily was beaming and made sure to slide her chair ever so slightly toward Katie.

It was getting a tad heavy-handed, this fangirling over Katie. Lily's room also happened to be down the hall from theirs, and once they'd finished washing up and changing for dinner, Lily slipped out of her own room and into the hallway with unabashed schoolgirl clinginess. "I'll walk down with you, Katie."

Right now, in this soft lighting, Lily almost looked like Ellie's dead sister. She hadn't seen it at first, but she could now—maybe it was her heart-shaped face, or how slight-boned Lily was, and that childlike unfettered admiration of her idol.

Nate had a wayward sister, and Ellie had a dead one.

He also had a white-knight complex. When Nate learned about Violet, he yearned to foster a sisterly relationship between Ellie and

Katie. That's why he pushed Katie so hard in her direction, but he'd gravely misinterpreted Ellie's feelings toward Katie.

Katie could never make up for Violet's absence.

Even now, it was jarring to see a proxy of what her sister might have looked like if she'd made it to adulthood, and Ellie had to look away because it made her queasy with loss. She pressed her thumb into a fork tine until the pressure in her throat stopped fluttering.

The food came, delivered to the table by the starchy staff and then passed around family-style. Ellie spooned up different grilled vegetables, oily salads, and a patty made of quinoa.

Dr. Dave kept the conversation afloat with questions that were probably pre-prepared, but he managed to sound genuinely interested. "So, Max, have you always lived in New York?"

Max was originally from Atlanta but had been in New York for ten years now.

"What subjects do you teach, Marie and Simon?"

Marie taught art history, and Simon taught political science. "Let's just say, we could make interesting political cartoons for *The Globe and Mail*," Simon said, and Marie rewarded him with rote-sounding laughter that made it clear it was a joke Simon made a lot.

"What is the video game you're creating, Anthony?"

"Well, it's an epic medieval-themed journey to—what else?—get the girl and rule the world." He could've stopped there, but then Anthony went into a lengthy, twisty, mind-numbing description of how the character progressed through all levels of the game and the trouble with coming up with unique weaponry. "Maybe I should just go retro with fireballs?"

"If that's what's speaking to you, then I would say yes, because you should always follow that which excites you," Dr. Dave answered. Anthony blinked and nodded like he'd just heard something profound.

"And Paula, how was the move into your new condo?"

Paula complained about fees and her new neighbors. The pinch in her forehead made it clear she was the kind of woman who wasn't happy, even when she got exactly what she'd said she wanted.

"Lily, what kind of work are you in?" Ellie turned and watched her answer.

"I'm an artist."

"And what kind of art do you do?"

"I do everything, man. Ask me what I don't do." A sharp rasp of laughter, and Ellie noticed her teeth. Something lurched inside of her at the sight of her poor oral hygiene. Violet would have never let her teeth get like that.

Dr. Dave asked her a question about murals, and Lily listed a few she'd done that all sounded more like under-a-bridge graffiti. Naomi interjected and said that going by an art therapy canvas Lily had just started, she was a brilliant *artiste*. Lily beamed and scratched at her arm under the table.

Dr. Dave moved on. "Katie? What was the most rewarding aspect of your career on television?"

"Oh, that's easy. The fans, of course." Katie amped up the charm. Any mention of her previous stardom and it was like the flip of a switch. Even her body language changed into something giggly and girlish, but in a rote way. Ellie balled her hands into fists under the table. "I loved visiting fans in the hospital. Just to be able to cheer up those kids was amazing."

Lily sat up, looking eager to get another serving of Katie's self-aggrandizing bullshit. "I think you're amazing," she huffed.

Dr. Dave shuffled the conversation to Ariel, who wouldn't shut up, and then Carmen, who was aggressively reticent about the details of her life and gave him very little. Still, Dr. Dave kept his elbows on the table, leaning forward like everything everyone said was the most interesting thing he'd ever heard. A perfect host. Two buttons undone around the collar. He swirled his apple cider in his wineglass. Dr. Dave was an attractive man. Ellie wondered if he wore eyeliner or if was he was one of those men who just looked like he did. Naomi made curly little active-listening sounds in her throat. For a second, Ellie pictured how they had sex and then pushed the image away.

Slowly, natural conversation built up, and the table was full of cross talk and chatter. It was an admirable guru trick to put people who were strangers hours earlier at ease like this.

Ellie could feel Dr. Dave's eyes sliding toward her. "And you, I saved you for last. What's your story, Ellie?" he asked in a lowered voice.

"My story?" Ellie hated this question. It was so open-ended and directionless, and it put all the work on the person answering. What story was he referring to? The story that made for palatable dinner talk, the one that scored her a nice, successful fiancé? Or the whole story, one so ugly and sad she hadn't told it since meeting Nate—no one wants to be the bellboy for that much baggage. For a second, she had an urge to blurt it out. Much in the same way she'd occasionally played out social experiments in her head. *What would happen if I licked that painting in the MoMA? If I hurled my plate of food across the restaurant like a Frisbee? If I pushed that person onto the subway tracks?*

Mother made sure to tell me that it was my fault Violet died, even before the breathing tube was pulled from her lifeless body. There's never been a day that I haven't felt the suffocating sadness of her absence. It's almost like a physical presence, like a dead Siamese twin still attached to my body. In a way, she's more with me now than if she'd lived.

"Well, I recently moved to New York, and I'm engaged. To Katie's brother." Ellie smiled and motioned toward Katie, who was leaning forward on her elbow, her finger pressed on her bottom lip as she chatted up Max, giving the back of her head to Lily.

"And what does this fiancé do?"

Ellie thought it was irksome Dr. Dave didn't ask about her career first, but then she didn't really have one. "He owns a restaurant." Technically, Katie owned it, because she gave him the money to buy it. Nate had such big plans for it, but every month, earnings fell short of his soaring expectations. To make matters worse, he also had a sticky-fingered employee he couldn't quite nail in the act. Ellie would try to remind him how hard it was to make a restaurant work in Brooklyn or anywhere, that he had to expect a loss for the first two years, and Nate would say, "I know, I know, but still." He wanted so badly for the restaurant to turn into a thriving success. To get off the allowance his sister gave him; he thought Ellie didn't know, but she'd seen his bank statements. To finally step out from Katie's long Nickelodeon shadow and be his own man.

"So he's a chef?"

"No, not exactly. He bought the restaurant, and now he manages it."

"What sort of restaurant is it?" Paula cut in, and Ellie said it was a gastropub.

"Oh, I see. Gastropub? What is that, a glorified Applebee's?" Dr. Dave smirked. "I'm kidding. So he's just the money guy, your fiancé?" Dr. Dave said it in a way that indicated he was slightly disappointed to hear she was with someone who didn't have a tangible talent for anything.

"I guess he is, yes." She pressed a cloth napkin to her lips.

"Nice, very nice. But what's *your* story? Before New York, before the fiancé."

Ellie recited her made-up biography. Her tea-sipping mother living in London who suffered bouts of agoraphobia. Her unreachable, tumbleweed father now running an exotic animal rescue in Madagascar. Her recent South American travels and her final move to the United States to go to school.

"How nice," Paula cheered, waited half a beat before trying to draw Dr. Dave's focus back on her. "Has Nikki been back? I expected to see her this weekend."

Dr. Dave's eyes snapped toward Paula, something dark passing over his face. It was Naomi who answered from across the table. Apparently, she had good hearing.

"Unfortunately, it seems Nikki has moved on. We haven't heard from her. Sadly, she isn't doing well."

Ellie wondered at the contradiction in that sentence. *We haven't heard from her. She isn't doing well.* How did they know that this Nikki person wasn't doing well if they hadn't heard from her? Or maybe that was Naomi's assumption—that if someone stopped attending their retreat, they couldn't be doing well.

"So you're well-traveled then?" Dr. Dave was looking at her again. He rested his chin on his fist. For a second, Ellie felt drawn into his stare and had to look away. He was a beautiful man.

"Oh, I don't know about that; I traveled a lot as a child before my parents divorced but there are still lots of places I want to see." Ellie looked down at her plate and speared some of the patty with her fork. Dr. Dave's intensity was making her uncomfortable. "Paula, your new condo, is it on the top floor?"

"It is. It has a wonderful view. And Dr. Dave, I have to thank you; your Rule of Five techniques from your guidebook were just so helpful." Five minutes sitting between Paula and Dr. Dave and it was clear the divorcée was in codependent love with her guru.

"That's lovely, Paula, but give me just a moment here to focus on Ellie's story."

Paula gave a little huff of disappointment. Ellie shifted uncomfortably in her chair, looked around the table, and caught a pointed look from Naomi, who quickly looked away. "There's something about you. I saw it when you first walked in. You're a layered soul, aren't you, Ellie? Tell me about your layers."

"I haven't really thought about it." Ellie tried to laugh it off, but Dr. Dave was looking at her so intensely. "I mean, everyone has their layers, there's nothing special about mine."

"Well, that's not true. You certainly have a beautiful top layer." She felt a hand on her thigh. Warm and dry, squeezing her under the table. Dr. Dave's face remained cool and impassive. She fought the urge to jump up. Was this really happening? Was Dr. Dave hitting on her, right in front of his wife? His other guests? Like she was just another dish on the table he was free to sample? He let her thigh go. "And I know that can be distracting. Constricting, even. Those inner layers get neglected. I hope your fiancé doesn't stop there, satisfied with just the outside. I sense tightness in you, Ellie, like you're bracing yourself for something."

Ellie dropped her napkin onto her plate and shifted her chair over in an obvious way, but Dr. Dave acted as if he didn't notice. This was going to be a long weekend. The worst part was that Dr. Dave wasn't wrong. She *was* bracing herself.

ARIEL

She shouldn't be there. It kept coming at her in thick, panicky waves how much she shouldn't be there. How many times had her dad called? Had the police called her too? How many times had her phone lit up in that basket of phones? Locked away in that cabinet, going unanswered. Each missed call like a shovelful of dirt, digging Ariel in deeper. Her chest was tight, her throat narrowing. She was smiling and laughing, but a panic attack was churning inside of her. *What did I do?*

They were moving from the dining room to the beach for what Dr. Dave called their first challenge, crossing the long, rolling stretch of carefully clipped green grass that segued to sandy beach. The sun was a cheery pink lozenge hovering over the lake.

"Nothing makes you feel more capable, more empowered, than starting a fire. It's a deeply primal thing, and sometimes you have to go back to advance. You have to regress to progress." Dr. Dave made a clever analogy to finding oneself in the belly of a slingshot, of being drawn back and then held down until one learned to break free and soar forward.

Ariel heard the tickle of laughter Carmen was trying to swallow, and she couldn't help feeling belittled by her.

"But the catch is, you need to start a fire with only the tools nature provides: flint, wood, and, out of kindness, I threw in a pocket knife too." Dr. Dave quipped that he was popping their "self-reliant" cherries right off the top, then divided the guests into two groups of five. Ariel felt buoyed that she was with Katie and that Ellie was on the other team.

Just as Dr. Dave was reciting, "On your mark, get set . . . ," Ariel caught a look from Ellie she didn't like. She'd seen it earlier in the drive up, then over dinner when Ariel asked if there was a meat option for dinner. It was this unkind, just-ate-the-canary smirk. A violent urge to wipe it off her face pulsed through Ariel.

She felt a sudden, urgent need to win the challenge.

When Dr. Dave yelled, "Go!" she sprinted toward one of the two crude-looking firepits made with rocks.

Ariel's ten years of Girl Scout training kicked into high gear. "Okay, so first we need some kindling. Small dry sticks or leaves. They just need to be dried out enough to catch a spark."

"Duh." Lily rolled her eyes.

Ariel ignored her. Max and Katie strolled up to the firepit like they were on a Sunday walk at that park and this wasn't a timed challenge. She overheard Max comment, "Whoa, your friend is really serious about fire."

"I didn't do this exercise last year," Paula said, looking slightly bewildered.

"But why do this? Because, y'know—matches and lighters?" Katie gibed. Max said something to her, and she rewarded him with a flirty giggle. Ariel immediately slipped into her matchmaker role with Katie with the same ease as stepping into a warm bath. "You and Max go together to look for driftwood along the beach. Paula, Lily, and I will split up and go into the woods." She clapped her hands once, but stopped herself from saying, "And break."

No one listened to her. Instead Paula started yammering about the beautiful fireplace she had in the house she'd once shared with her husband. "But it was gas!"

Lily wandered after Katie and Max, picking up inflammable things like rocks and tossing them into the lake.

The other team had already dispersed. Ariel watched as Ellie leaned into Carmen, then pointed toward a woodpile next to the barn.

So it was up to Ariel to win this for her team. She moved off the beach and was about to start up a path into the woods when she had a better idea. The quickest, most surefire way to start a fire was with dryer lint. Just a little Girl Scout secret. Never go hiking or camping without it. So, rather than follow her own instructions, she decided to head toward the house and raid the dryer.

She jogged back up to the house and looked on the main floor in case she'd missed a washer and dryer during the tour. She peeked into the kitchen. A twiggy blonde was standing at the sink, scrubbing big pots and charred-looking frying pans. She was dressed in the same crisp white Sanctuary uniform, but with an apron that had *Namaste* written in a splashy font across the front. Ariel watched her reflection through the window over the sink. Her hair was tied up into a high bun, and it shook as she scrubbed. Ariel waited for her to turn on the water to block out the noise of opening the basement door, which she had just spotted.

The door to the basement was at the back of the house. There was no light switch. The stairs were rickety and shallow, and Ariel had to go down sideways because she was afraid she'd fall.

There was a light switch at the bottom. When she flipped it up, an overhead, buzzing fluorescent light flickered on to operating-room brightness. The basement was L-shaped, clean, and cold. The stone-foundation walls were lined with shelving filled mostly with root vegetables.

Ariel stepped around the potatoes, passing a rusted bike and a couple of wooden barrels. As clean as it was, the air was full of rot. Like some rogue potato had rolled under the hot water tank and had been long decomposing.

She rounded the corner and saw an industrial-size washer and dryer. She flung open the dryer, pulled out the lint screen, and pocketed its ample woolly contents. She slammed the dryer door shut and turned to leave.

That's when she noticed a slatted room divider set up on the far side of the basement. It took a second for Ariel to see it, but there was a rope tied to a beam, gently swaying back and forth. Whatever was on the end of it was hidden behind the divider.

Blood drained to her legs, making her feel dizzy.

Ariel batted away a spiderweb as she made her way over. She touched the divider, pulled one of the panels back. The hinges creaked.

She suddenly reared back as if a lead pipe had hit her in the face, knocking down the entire room divider. She let out a shriek, stumbled over her own watery legs. Her backside hit the concrete floor hard. Pain throbbed up her tailbone and right into her spine.

There was a body, hanging, twisting slowly around.

Like a child, she immediately clamped her eyes shut, her heart twitching away in her chest. *I can't look. I can't.*

She'd never seen a body before.

She turned away and stood up. *Don't look, don't look.*

But then, as if she couldn't help it, she turned around and looked.

Ariel let out a bubble of laughter.

It's a mannequin.

Dressed in a powder room–blue turtleneck and pressed slacks. Its brown wig was on sideways and hung into its blank face.

There was a sign tied around its neck that read, MY OLD SELF.

Ariel got up to take a closer look.

Behind it was a vision board that ran half the length of the wall. The wall was layered in cutouts from magazines—pictures of fit women in a variety of yoga poses, on paddleboards. There were hundreds of them. It echoed Ariel's own vision board, but this was so much more excessive—the perfect body repeating over and over.

On a small tea trolley shoved into the corner was a framed family photo. The unimaginative kind of family picture taken at a portrait studio with the usual cloudy, gray-blue background that looked like brewing storm clouds. A man, woman, two children, all dressed in matching shades of late-'90s denim. The woman's face was scratched out. Ariel looked closer. If Naomi was the mom in this photo, then she was much older than Ariel had assumed.

Ariel put the divider upright. She couldn't get out of there fast enough. It sent a chill over her. This idea of perfection trapped down there, in a basement, among rotting potatoes. She was starting up the stairs when the dishwasher, her hands raw looking and dripping, appeared at the top of the steps. "What're you doing down there?" She glared down at Ariel.

"I was just looking for something to eat." Ariel had no idea why she'd lied. Sometimes she did that—lied for no good reason—but she didn't want to be thought of as a cheater, using dryer lint. Which she now regretted doing anyway.

"There is a fruit bowl out on the dining room table. You can't eat just *anything* between meals." The blonde's eyes swept over her body disapprovingly. "The basement is off-limits to guests."

"Good to know." Ariel brushed past the dishwasher and left the house. As she hustled back to the beach, she realized she'd forgotten about her plan to try to pick the flimsy-looking lock on the china cabinet and get her phone back—her other reason for going up to the house.

She'd been feeling guilty about not calling her dad back. She started to picture her parents, standing and staring out the back window in the same bungalow Ariel grew up in. The same window they always looked out when they worried. They'd have their arms wrapped around each other as they pondered where they went wrong with their daughter after modeling such a perfect marriage.

It was her dad who made Ariel's chest hiccup with bursts of remorse. He was a gentle, quiet, church-attending man who took her to daddy-daughter balls to exemplify the sort of man she should want to marry. He would never understand how Ariel let her emotions get away from her like that. All of her life, her dad would caution Ariel, "Self-pity is the gateway drug to all evils."

He was right. Ariel had been feeling sorry for herself.

Her dad would then only hear that she was the other woman. Not a mistress who was whisked away on tropical holidays or had her rent paid. It was much worse. Just a woman for quickies squeezed in on lunch breaks. He'd compare her to her older sister, Amy, who'd already been married a decade to a mortgage broker and had four perfect children and a tiny waist.

He would be so disappointed in her. Ariel's vision blurred with tears as she walked back toward the lake. She was suddenly glad she didn't get her phone. She didn't want to know.

The other team was still chipping away at the flint with the knife, unable to get much of a fire going beyond some puffs of smoke.

Naomi and Dr. Dave stood together at the top of the beach, where sand abruptly turned into the Sanctuary's emerald-green grass, watching.

Dr. Dave let out a chuckle when he saw Ariel. "You get what you need?"

Naomi's white blouse billowed in the wind.

Ariel nodded. She pushed her way through her team, who were failing miserably at getting anything to catch fire. She took the flint and knife from Max and huddled in close. She dropped her handful of lint into the pit, angled the flint into it, and started hitting it with the knife.

Just as she'd thought, a few hard strikes of the knife and the lint caught the spark. She slowly dumped a few sticks onto it, and they caught fire. Katie wooted.

Suddenly, there was a strange squirting noise and the tiny flicker of flame exploded into a flash fire. Ariel lurched back. Her face was burning. She had to feel her eyebrows to make sure they weren't seared off.

Lily let out a churlish laugh. She waved a small canister of lighter fluid. "Look what I found by the barbecue. Now *there's* a fire."

CARMEN

"That nut job almost burned my face off!" Ariel said again.

They were now on a meditative hike. Dr. Dave had cheerfully prescribed it as he'd dumped a bucket of water on both fires and declared Carmen's team the winner, a smile frozen on his face as if one of the guests did not just try to blow up the beach.

"Do you think she did it on purpose? Who doesn't tell someone to back up?"

"I don't think she realized what she was doing, Ariel. I don't," Carmen tried to console her. Ariel had a tendency to take things personally. "I mean, clearly the girl isn't all there, right? I think she was just trying to impress Katie." Lily had immediately looked to Katie afterward with an expectant expression on her face like she was waiting for some kind of reward.

"I have something that might help," Katie said in a singsong and pulled out a joint.

Ellie's eyes went big, and she shook her head. "You really shouldn't. It could affect how the tea will work. It says so in the pamphlet." But of course Katie ignored her, lit up, and passed it to Ariel, who took a long, hard pull, then passed it to Carmen. Ellie strode ahead and away from them.

Carmen's hand reached for it based on pure muscle memory. For a second, she let the joint dangle between her fingers like a cigarette. She shouldn't. Megan would have a fit. Maybe that's what suddenly made her want to do it, same as when a berated, underpaid housekeeper spits in your food. A little act of rebellion driven by economic disparity. Being around Katie, someone with money, someone who could do whatever she wanted to, brought out a certain sullenness in Carmen. She took a long, heavy puff on the joint, and passed it back to Katie.

She really couldn't see how a little weed would negatively impact her eggs anyway. She smoked it all through college when she was donating and as far she knew, the babies born from those batches were just fine. Or so she thought, since they let her keep donating.

Megan was getting into her head.

Maybe she would drink the tea too. What was the worst that could happen? Her eggs would turn into people who believe in the healing power of positive thinking and crystals?

The inspirational messages that the proprietors of the Sanctuary spiked into the ground every few feet like roadside crosses soon became really funny.

YOUR REALITY IS WHAT YOU MAKE OF IT. LITERALLY.

BE YOUR OWN CREATION.

YOUR THOUGHTS REAP WHAT THEY REPEAT.

YOU ARE INFINITE.

BE YOU-NIQUE.

The paths were overlaid with wood chips, and they kept getting stuck between Ariel's toes and under her feet.

"Why did you wear flip-flops?" Katie asked. "Take them off."

Ariel started walking like she were barefoot on hot coals, and this too was hilarious.

With Ariel lagging behind, and Ellie up ahead, this might be one of the few moments alone Carmen had with Katie this weekend. And so in a roundabout way Carmen brought up the busted hot water tank, and her brother's legal troubles.

Katie turned toward her, exhaled, and squinted at her through the smoke. "Do you need money?"

"Just a loan and I swear I'll pay you back as soon as I can." Carmen felt a small part of her soul dying. She hated stretching out her hands and asking for money. Hated that angry pinch in her chest, when she thought about how much money Katie had and the insubstantial way she spent it.

"Yeah, no problem. Come on. That look on your face is killing me. How much do you need?"

"A new hot water tank is about fifteen hundred bucks with installation." Katie passed her the joint. Carmen took a pull and handed it back.

"I'll transfer you three grand, okay?" Katie said, nonchalantly. Like it was nothing. Carmen couldn't tell for a moment if she felt grateful or if that new anger she'd just discovered she had was going to take over. It was bitterness. She could see it in the mirror, etched into her face as an angry V between her eyebrows. More and more she'd found herself scrolling through her friends' or ex-classmates' Instagram accounts and seeing them flush with a doctor's income, vacationing in the Hamptons—living what was supposed to be her life—and this childish feeling of injustice, of "life wasn't fair," lurched through her.

But then she thought of having hot water again, and not those tepid, tea kettle–heated baths they'd been having. Two kids at a time, because it was so much effort to heat it up again and then Carmen running her hair under freezing cold water because the bathwater was too dirty and she was too tired, middle-aged tired. She quelled her bitterness, and just felt grateful. And now, Carmen could finally relax.

Paula speed-walked past them, her nose crinkled at the smell of weed, and she stopped like a cartoon bear trying to locate a picnic lunch. She then waved the air in front of her to clear the scent. She gave them a disappointed tilt of the head. "Oh, girls. If you let your twenties turn into a tsunami, you'll spend decades cleaning up after yourself. Remember that, okay? Because I wish someone had told me." She kept walking, and Katie played up being riveted by Paula's advice.

"Put that on a sign," she called out after Paula, who flicked her hand at them in a *yeah-yeah* gesture. Katie handed the last of the joint back to Carmen, who sucked in the smoke, then blew it out with her head tilted back. Up in a pine tree, something glinted. It was a deflated Mylar balloon, its string snagged around a branch. It looked out of place on the manicured trail. It twisted, and Carmen blurted, "Oh my god!"

"What?" Katie looked up, her face drained. It was an old Shelby Spade balloon. There were Katie's grinning, freckled cheeks smiling down on them. Two fingers on her fedora, tipping it forward. GET WELL SOON, the balloon said. "That's so freaky." Katie shivered.

They stood under the tree in stoned awe until Ariel caught up and Ellie circled back.

"What is it? Oh my. I am sure it's just some old litter that was picked up by the wind," Ellie said unconvincingly.

"Yeah, over-a-decade-old litter just when the real Shelby Spade comes by." Carmen shook her head. "So bizarre."

"Do you think Lily brought it with her?" Ariel asked. It was a serious question, but because they were high and already laughing about everything else, it was suddenly hard not to think of this girl who adored Shelby Spade showing up at a wellness retreat with a thirteen-year-old GET WELL SOON balloon as anything but hilarious.

"Probably!" Katie snorted. "It's just so freaky. Let's get out of the woods."

So now Carmen was going into the partnered breathing workshop half-baked.

Her brain was lathered in THC. It had loosened up the hormones she'd been injecting.

Gone was that tight and anxious feeling, replaced with something fuzzy and soft for the moment. Her bruised, punctured abdomen felt settled. She'd managed an injection right before dinner. She was a seasoned pro with the covert needle to the gut.

The partnered breathing workshop was being held in the solarium, though the sun was setting. Other lighting came from three dim lamps. Colorful yoga mats were spread around the room like islands. Carmen, Katie, Ariel, and Ellie were the last to arrive.

The minute they entered the room, Naomi separated them and paired them with other guests. Dr. Dave moved to pair with Ellie. It was a subtle waving motion that no one else seemed to notice except his wife.

Naomi cut him off and quickly shuffled Ellie over to Simon. Then she ordered an irritated-looking Dr. Dave to pair with Anthony, and put Carmen with Marie. Katie slinked close to Max, and Naomi took her by the elbow and stuck her with Lily. "And, Ariel, you can be my partner." Ariel's mouth dropped as Naomi grabbed her by the hand and pulled her up to the front of the room, looking like that kid in gym class who got partnered with the teacher.

She sat Ariel down then positioned herself so that they were sitting, spread-eagled and heel to heel. "Get yourself in this pose with your partner. Now I want you both to start breathing. Send your breath to the part of your body where your most negative emotions lurk. Let your breath blow your tensions away."

In the first few minutes everything in Carmen's body screamed No! but Marie was so gentle and reassuring that she started to relax. Ariel was struggling to keep her knees straight. Her face turned beet red and pissed looking as Naomi pulled her forward. When it was Ariel's turn, Naomi pressed her head right down to the floor like her spine was made of rubber.

Katie tossed Carmen a panicky expression as Lily gazed at her and tugged her closer in their little teeter-totter exercise. Carmen tried not to laugh. High on weed, she could give herself over to the ridiculousness of the place.

She was even starting to have fun. Let it be some mescaline-in-the-desert thing she did one time (but y'know, tea in upstate New York). "Slowly change positions, with one partner offering their back to the other. Surround your partner with a gentle embrace. Allow a light connection between your bodies as you begin to take deep breaths, not as two people but as one." Ariel's eyes went big and panicky as Naomi started manhandling her.

The shift in positions caused a ripple of nervous laughter in the room, which Naomi tried to smooth over with, "Remember, if you believe you can, you can." She let that little gem of wisdom float into the breathy room. She was most certainly the author of those empty inspirational quotes. This brand of positivity pissed Carmen off. It was both egotistical and cruel to say that people could control what happened to them. If all anyone had to do was wish something with a positive thought, then she'd be a doctor, not stuck in a dilapidated house, breathing in the fumes from the city dump.

Marie pulled her in tighter; she was straddled in so tight behind her that Carmen could feel her pelvic bone. Marie's mouth went to her ear. "You're not here; you're thinking too much." She said it in her thick French accent that made Carmen's stomach flutter.

She mumbled back, "Yep, sorry." Carmen leaned back into Marie. She *wanted* to lean into Marie. What was happening here? There probably could not be a more intense icebreaker than going into various embracing positions with a complete stranger.

Naomi instructed the group to turn and face their partner, looping their legs over one another's hips.

Marie grabbed on to Carmen's arms again, and they both started breathing. Matching their inhales and exhales as Naomi was telling them to do. Again, unwavering eye contact.

The door to the solarium thumped against the wall. Katie had suddenly gotten up and left.

Lily looked forlorn. Naomi untangled herself from Ariel to go after Katie. Realizing at the last moment that she was leaving Ariel on her own to breathe, she tried to pair her up with Lily but Ariel recoiled. Instead she flopped down and closed her eyes, like she was going to go to sleep.

"Look at me," Marie urged, and Carmen shifted back to her. There was something mesmerizing about staring into the face of a stranger. Having them stare back at you. Something about it that made you feel your own blankness. Without speaking, giving up all control of how you were seen.

Carmen took in Marie's pretty face. She was the older woman hocking beauty creams in commercials until her features seemed to move. She was about the same age as Megan, the woman who was going to receive Carmen's eggs. Midforties. When Carmen told Megan she was going away for the weekend, she could hear the clickety-clack of a keyboard in the background.

"The Sanctuary, you said? In the Catskills? Huh. Oh, well, that looks like a nice place." More clicking and clacking. "Probably be good for you to have some downtime before you constantly have to be at the clinic for monitoring." Right now, Carmen was technically in a drug-induced menopause. The drug Lupron was turning her sex organs off so she could hyperstimulate them a week from now, and then she'd spend her mornings in the clinic, hoping to see her ovaries swelling with eggs like two satchels of gold coins.

Then Megan's voice went suddenly shrill, the tapping on her keyboard more frenzied. "What's this? You're not going to drink that tea, are you? It's a Schedule I substance—you do know that, right? Same as ecstasy and heroin! You can't take it! Oh no, no, no, Carmen." She could picture that same shrill voice fueling a child with anxiety, swiping a box of Skittles out of their hands due to carcinogenic dyes and rotted teeth. She could only ever see Megan's child in a navy-blue school uniform with severely parted hair, fingers pulpy from violin lessons.

They had met in person only once at a café, where Megan thrust an impersonal gift bag full of bath salts and scented candles at her (because what were you supposed to give someone who was gifting you a child?); then she worried Carmen would have a bath and it would be too hot and wreck her eggs. Ever since, she'd bombarded Carmen with anxious phone calls and emails. Megan was a lawyer who'd waited too long. Carmen wondered if she'd be in the exact same position one day. She planned to go back to med school someday, and here she inwardly cringed. *Someday* was a loser's measurement of time, but *if, if, if,* she ever got back to med school, she would probably be in the exact same position as Megan by the time she was finished with her medical degree, followed by a few years of actually being a doctor. She should set some of her eggs aside for herself, but she couldn't afford to.

"You're leaving me again," Marie said, snapping Carmen back to the solarium. "Come back. Be present."

Be present.

Carmen was entwined with Marie's body, feeling oddly aroused by this older woman's embrace. Her coaxing voice. There was this seamlessness between their bodies. Like they'd known each longer than a few hours.

She wondered how many of the group would sleep with one another by the end of the weekend. Dr. Dave was casting Ellie a hungry gaze from across the room, over Paula's clingy arms. Katie had been tossing Max flirty eyes whenever she could, before she'd suddenly gotten up and left. Carmen wondered if that was not the point of all this intimacy.

And then Carmen really did stop thinking. She focused only on her own clear breathing, on Marie's dark tousled beauty and the inflections in her voice that made everything she said more lively and exotic. It made Carmen feel outside of herself. Looking at Marie, she thought getting old wasn't something to worry about. Not that she worried about things like that. Men were more obsessed with youth than women were—one good point about being a lesbian.

"You're still thinking." Marie reached over and caressed her cheek.

Carmen arched toward her and tried to stop thinking again, focusing only on breathing and Marie.

Time fell away into nothing until Dr. Dave spoke; his voice felt as if it were shaking the room awake. "Okay, okay, everyone. Let's disengage from our partners. What we're going to do next is what I call the 'declare your pain' circle." Dr. Dave then ushered everyone into a circle. Katie sat across from her. Carmen never noticed her return. "What I want is for anyone who feels like it to unburden themselves; just spew out whatever it is that's making your heart heavy. There is nothing quite like having your pain heard by other people. And I want you to think of the circle of people around you as sponges who can absorb some of your pain. I want you to scream and shout and be as ugly as you need to be. It's completely voluntary. Now who wants to go first?"

Paula was the only one who put her hand up.

"All right, Paula, go ahead." Dr. Dave motioned for her to sit in the center.

Paula delivered a long, weepy screed against her ex-husband: how he'd cheated on her, how her adult children were taking his side, and then she howled for five straight minutes. *This is like being plunged into ice water after a hot tub*, Carmen thought.

Lily popped her hand up next, wiggling around like a kid who'd had too much sugar. Inside the circle, she took some time to look around before saying in her gravelly voice, "I don't have many grievances, actually. Just one really." She tossed her head back. "Why? Why? Why are there so many fucking shitty people in the world?" When she snapped forward, though it was dark, it was obvious she was staring at Katie. "I mean, all I have is love and admiration to give, and people turn their backs on me like I'm nothing, and they think I don't notice. Well, I do notice, and it hurts, man. It hurts." There was a long stretch of silence before Lily just shrugged and went back to her spot.

Katie shifted uncomfortably and leaned back on her hands.

Max volunteered next. He sat down cross-legged, rested his hands on his knees. "The carpet. I always see the carpet. It was some paisley print—like swirls. I can be doing something, not even thinking about anything, and that print just sears into my eyes.

That's what they gave him—a carpet tile. And I always wonder if that made them feel better? Kind?" Max shook his head, his eyes fixed on something beyond the circle. "He was a ghost child. That's what the people in the building called him because they heard him but didn't see him. The superintendent had to go in because of leaking pipes. He was nine years old but the weight of a two-year-old. His parents kept him locked in a kennel inside the storage closet. With a fucking carpet tile for a mattress and a blanket."

Carmen's chest started to tighten. The poor child. Her mind flickered to Megan. She hadn't met her husband. Before Megan, she hadn't met any of her egg recipients. Who were they? What kind of parents were they?

"When I picked him up, he was so light. So, so light. Like he never existed. But he did. They gave him a name; that has to mean something, right? He had a baby book; the first year was filled out. What happened?" Max's eyes refocused, and he looked around the circle, not for an answer but begging for acknowledgment that there wasn't one.

A long stretch of silence followed until Dr. Dave spoke up. "Thank you for sharing, Max. I want you to stand up now, okay?"

Max stood up, his eyes openly flowing with tears.

"I want you to scream, okay, Max? Just scream. We're here for you, Max, and we're going to listen. Scream, Max. Get that shit out of you."

"Nah, I don't need to scream or anything like that." Max made a face. Shook his head.

"Just try it, Max; it's so powerful and cleansing to just hurl your voice at other people," Dr. Dave urged.

"You will feel so much release, Max. Just do it." Naomi leaned forward.

And like that, Lily emitted a shrill, open-mouthed shriek that seemed to go on for a full minute. When she stopped, she looked at Max with a half-smile. "See? It's easy."

"All right." He nodded, put his head down, pinched the bridge of his nose, shook his head, and blew out a big gust of air. The room went quiet. He loosened up his neck. A light rain started to *tick, tick, tick* against the glass roof of the solarium. Suddenly, Max threw his arms out, arched his back, and emitted a long, high-pitched growl so full of anguish that Carmen felt it go up her spine, sharp as a fingernail.

Everyone stood up. Carmen did really feel physically heavier. And as if the circle were a single collective body, they each took a step in, then another one. Max screamed again, this time so pitched with horror Carmen just wanted to hug him. She found herself reaching out for him, touching his shoulder.

And then Paula let out an angry, strangled cry. The next thing Carmen knew, the entire circle was screaming, their voices condensed into a furious choir.

It felt so good to feel her own voice come up like a freight train, tearing up her windpipe and bleeding into the other voices. It had to be some primitive, tribal thing to want to collectively spew emotion without needing to rely on words. She couldn't say how long the screaming lasted, but when it ended, there was a round of loose laughter. The way people laughed at funerals to deflate heightened emotion.

And like a funeral, everyone seemed glad to move away from one another now that it was over.

SATURDAY

KATIE

The house, despite its makeover, showed its real age at night, creaking and popping like a Botoxed arthritic. Katie tossed and turned, wishing she'd brought her sound machine. Sleep never came easily for her. She naturally fought it, so it had to happen to her incidentally while she was doing anything but trying to sleep—watching TV, reading, scrolling through her phone—until sleep just overtook her. Reaper-style. And once she was out, she slept like the dead. But there was nothing else to do but wait for it.

She was feeling uneasy about being at the retreat.

It was Lily.

The way she looked at Katie when she'd squirted lighter fluid on the fire like it was supposed to impress her.

The weirdo breathing exercise.

How Lily kept hissing out her favorite episodes of *Shelby Spade*, and what she thought might have happened to some of her "classmates," like they were real people and not actors. Then there was the way she had pulled Katie in, wrapping her body around hers; it was too hungry. All Katie could notice were her unshaven legs, the black filth on the bottoms of her calloused feet, and the newish-looking tattoo on her inner arm of some swirly design that looked chosen to cover up scars. She smelled like body odor and campfire. Katie felt like she couldn't breathe. Lily had panted her hot breath on her cheek and neck. "Remember when Lacey Evans accidentally killed the class hamster and then Josh Jones took the crown from Lacey and placed it on you to be his homecoming queen? Josh was, like, the first guy I ever masturbated to. I'd, like, pause it on his face, lick my fingers, and go south."

Katie almost threw up. She mumbled something about being too hot and shook Lily off more roughly than she'd meant to, knocking her backward. But she couldn't take another second of Lily's suffocating body touching hers. She speed-walked out to the porch, gripped the railing, and took big gulps of fresh air.

"Is something wrong?" It was Naomi. Katie hadn't heard her creep up behind her in her spongy cork sandals.

"What? No. I just wanted some fresh air. It's, uh, stuffy in there—that's all."

"Huh," Naomi said in a way that made it clear she didn't believe her. Katie had hoped she'd go away, but of course she didn't. "Well, you're the only one who left."

"Okay, well, truthfully, Lily was making me a little uncomfortable."

"Is that it?" Naomi's voice had dropped into a baby-voiced taunting wheedle. "Katie Manning was made to feel a tad uncomfortable, so she quit?"

"What? You don't have to . . . whatever you're trying to do, give me a pep talk. I get it. It's fine."

"You know what? I do, Katie. It's my job to get you out of your comfort zone. Isn't that what you said you wanted out of the weekend yesterday at orientation? To get out of your comfort zone? Well, my husband and I have dedicated our lives to helping people do just that so they can become conscious of their negative behavior patterns. It's the only way to break free of them. So are you a quitter, Katie?" Naomi had dropped the taunt and went serious. She jutted her chin and moved her hands to her hips in some boot-camp stance. Her white blouse was glowing.

"I'm not a quitter. I just—" Everything started to stiffen in Katie, and an angry ball of outrage over being criticized for something she already knew to be true was building in her chest.

"Exactly!" Naomi's voice switched again into something resembling a bubbly cheerleader's, and she clapped her hands. "I *know* you're not a quitter, but do you know it? C'mon, now; let's get back in there."

Now the bright, angry sun was hitting Katie's face through the lacy curtains. Her eyelids lifted, then drooped back down, lifted, drooped. Too harsh to be her night-light. It wasn't Katie's best-kept secret—as if she had one—that she didn't like the dark. A childish fear. But last night, Ellie clicked the lamp switch and the room went inky dark, and Katie was too proud to turn it back on. All she could do was stare at the shadowy outline of the doorknob with its quaint and simple lock (another thing she did each night—checked the locks) and listen to the wheezy house and the chirping, hooting, and those scuttling noises going across the roof as if all the outside were trying to get in.

Now Katie's body was fighting to stay asleep.

She reached out mindlessly for a pillow, a blanket, anything to block the bright sunlight. Her hand grazed something hard and sharp. She blinked her eyes open. A long moment of disorientation. She couldn't tell what she was seeing, it was so out place. The shape of it; the grinning serrated edge looked rusted and old.

It was like a dream. She couldn't be awake.

A knife. A bloodied knife.

It was right in front of her, practically sharing her pillow like a rose left behind by a romantic one-night stand.

But she *was* awake. She bolted upright. Instinctively, she picked up the knife. She saw streaks of blood on her hands and up and down her forearms. Katie leaped from the bed and rushed into the bathroom, the knife still dangling from her hand. She dropped it in the sink with a clatter and gaped at herself in the mirror. A red handprint blazed across the front of her tank top. Her heart started to flip.

What the fuck? What the fuck? What the fuck?

She'd cut herself. She had to have somehow cut herself. Her hand went to her cheek. There was more blood on her face. Same side as her scar. Two smeared thin strips of it, like half a claw mark. Maybe her scar had split open somehow. That had to be it; it had reopened and oozed while she was asleep. It was something she deeply feared; it was why she brought her own facecloths and her own pillow. As if everything that came in contact with her face held the capacity to slice it back open even though the Incident had been twelve years ago.

Katie turned on the tap, cupped some water, and splashed it across her face, then used one of her washcloths from home to dry her cheek.

Her scar was still a tightly sealed, shiny line.

She pulled off her tank top and pajama bottoms and examined her entire body to see if she'd cut herself somewhere else, but there was nothing. No cuts. Not even little nicks that she might have slept through, no cracked scabs, no scabs at all. Her gut twisted. If the blood didn't come from her, where did it come from?

Ellie. Something happened to Ellie?

She was too afraid to look, but she knew she had to. Katie inched toward the door she hadn't closed all the way and bent slightly forward to peer out into the room at Ellie's bed.

It was unmade and empty.

Her heart jumped up into her throat. She couldn't get enough oxygen into her lungs.

Fuck no, no, no.

She stepped back into the bathroom, gripped the edge of the sink. Her head was racing with thoughts of calling Nate to explain his fiancée was missing and that, in unrelated news, she'd woken up with a bloodied knife.

The door to the room suddenly creaked open. Katie sucked in a breath, held it until it ballooned in her chest so hard her ribs strained. What if there was a serial killer in the house? And he was back because he'd forgotten his knife?

Katie slammed the bathroom door shut, twisting the lock. She pressed her shoulder against the door, bracing her legs like it was about to be kicked down.

The opening of a drawer. A sigh that sounded like Ellie's usual uptight sighing. So her soon-to-be sister-in-law was alive and well. Katie pressed her forehead into the door and let out a gusty breath. She turned her back against the door and peered again into the sink at the bloodied knife, like it was a live, dangerous thing that could leap at her and start stabbing her on its own. She felt disoriented, like she was trapped in a bad dream and couldn't wake up.

"Katie? You all right?" Ellie was outside the door. "There's blood on your pillow."

"Yeah, I'm fine," Katie said, her voice weak and bubbly sounding. "It was just a bloody nose." Why was she even lying? *Because something bad had happened.*

"You don't sound fine."

The bathroom was closing in on her. Bile started rising up the back of her throat. She rushed for the toilet and spit it up.

Ellie tried the knob. "Could you let me in, please?" A pause, then the dinging of something metal going into the bathroom's doorknob. Ellie picked the lock and opened the door. Her eyes went saucer-big as she took in the scene. She gasped at the sight of blood remaining on Katie's cheek and arms. Then she spotted the knife in the sink. A pinkish spattering now lined the basin from blood mixing with water from the faucet, making it look worse. Bloodier. A second passed where Ellie looked as if she were deciding whether to flee or not. "What happened?"

Katie, still half-bent over the toilet, pushed the lid closed and faced Ellie. Her blood-streaked arms came up in some clownish *I dunno* gesture, and this made Ellie's expression turn panicky.

"Are you hurt?"

Katie shook her head.

"Then why is there a knife? Is that your blood?"

Again, Katie shook her head.

What did you do? Katie, what did you do?"

"Nothing! I didn't do anything." Katie let out a hot, blubbery sob. She pressed her hands into her shaking head. "I don't know, I don't know."

"Where did you get the knife?"

Katie's eyes just bulged. "I don't know. Did you see me this morning? With it?"

"I don't understand."

"Did you see me with the knife?"

Ellie cocked her head. "Are you a cutter, Katie? Did you cut yourself?" She moved in closer.

"No, I don't cut myself. I don't."

"Why do you have a knife?"

"I don't know." Katie gasped, and her hands shot up.

"Well, where did you go last night?"

"What? Nowhere. I just went to sleep."

"I saw you."

"Saw me what?"

"Leaving."

"I went somewhere? What are you talking about? I went somewhere?"

"You left. I thought you were going to Carmen and Ariel's room."

"I didn't leave."

"You did. I saw you."

"You saw me?" Katie felt a watery rush of panic fill her ears. She'd been sleepwalking since her teen years. It had started right after the slice and dice of her face. She'd been given a garden variety of diagnoses for its cause. A psychiatrist told her it was "neurosis manifested" and gave her a prescription for Zoloft; another said it was just extreme restless legs syndrome and gave her a prescription for Mirapex. She didn't put much stock in their diagnoses and didn't bother taking either medication after figuring out they didn't offer much of a high.

"Ellie, you know I fucking sleepwalk. Why wouldn't you stop

me? Nate locks me in every night! If you saw me up walking, why wouldn't you at least check that I wasn't sleepwalking? Especially after what happened last time?"

When she was younger, Katie woke up in all sorts of alarming spots like she were hiding in her sleep. In the crawl space under the stairs in their California house, in the back seat of Lucy's BMW, under her bed. Right before they moved to New York at the suggestion of her latest agent to do theater or attend NYU (where she was treated like a privileged moron; these were serious theater students who made sure to let her know that Katie's Nickelodeon honing of the craft of shout-talking was outright offensive), she somehow let her white Pomeranian outside, and it was hit by a car. She woke to Nate gently shaking her as she held her dog, which looked like an oversize bloodied cotton ball, in her lap.

She had been a New Yorker for all of three months when she woke up on a frigid night, barefoot in sludgy ice. Sleep had become a dark, dangerous terrain she had to cross over. She was always afraid of where she might wake up. In her late teens, she realized that alcohol was the perfect antidote to sleepwalking. She didn't sleepwalk when she went to bed wasted.

Nate kept Katie corralled inside the town house with a bunch of babyproofing things like gates and doorknob covers. None of which worked as well as booze at keeping her flat-out on her back through a night. Sleepwalkers can still perform complex tasks. So Nate installed a keyed deadbolt and kept the key on him overnight. That way Katie could still safely amble about the town house.

Then Ellie moved in, and in the first week, she forgot to lock the front door, and Katie wandered outside, straight into traffic, almost ending up like her little white dog.

"That was an accident, Katie. I've apologized a thousand times for that. But last night, what happened *last night*? You didn't look like you were sleepwalking. And it's not like we're talking about a few bruises and a close call; you're practically covered in blood! There's a knife in our room! This is just so disturbing." Ellie peered into the sink at the knife. Water dripped from the tap, hitting the blade with microsplashes.

The black-and-white tiled floor started to sway under Katie's feet. "Oh my god." Katie slumped down onto the toilet, putting her hand on the wall to steady herself. "Why would I have a knife? Why? Maybe I went to make a sandwich?" Katie said hopefully, but she knew there was no bread on the premises, and it still didn't explain the blood. Ellie sat down on the edge of the claw-foot tub, across from her. She had a watchful look on her face that was making Katie even more unnerved. "What? Why are you looking at me like that? You think I did something? That's what you think?" Her voice went pitchy. Tears started to slide down her face. "What could I have possibly done? Run outside and tried to eat a forest animal? I've never hurt anything or anyone."

Ellie's eyes immediately flickered away, about to say something, then changed her mind. "Stop. We don't know if anything has even happened, so just pull yourself together. Stop panicking." Ellie took hold of her wrists. "What we need to do is go downstairs together and see what's happening. So get in the shower and clean yourself up." Ellie leaned back and turned on the shower. She grabbed a fresh towel off the rack, which Katie thought she was going to hand off to her, but instead Ellie said, "I'll take care of this for now. Get in the shower."

Ellie gingerly picked the knife out of the sink, wrapped it in the towel, and carefully placed it in the dresser on her side of the room.

Katie dragged herself into the shower. She turned the water so hot it seared into her skin, and she scrubbed herself, watching the mystery blood go down the drain. She looked over her skin again to see if there were even the slightest hints of injury, hoping to see some gash, even to have her period or some other way to pull together a shaky explanation—but there was nothing.

Ellie waited for her, sitting ramrod straight on the edge of her bed, an unreadable expression on her face. Katie pulled on shorts and a T-shirt, and with her hair still wet, they left the room together.

In the hallway, Katie started toward Ariel and Carmen's room, but Ellie put a hand on her shoulder. "I wouldn't. Let's go down first."

Katie nodded like this made sense, but she wasn't sure it did.

With each step she took down the stairs, her heart drummed harder. Her throat tightened. Her breath felt shuttered up tight in her chest, and she had a sick, anxious feeling that any second she was going to glimpse yellow police tape, or hear the fuzzy belch of a walkie-talkie and the jingle of handcuffs twirling on a finger as a police officer waited for her.

But the front foyer was empty, and breakfast smells filled the lower half of the house. If something bad had happened, surely breakfast wouldn't be served. Katie felt herself calm down a notch. She followed Ellie into the kitchen. It was a buffet-style breakfast on the kitchen island.

"We should eat." Ellie took a plate from a stack and handed her one.

"Good morning." Carmen stepped inside the garden doors, her cheeks rosy, eyes glowing like she'd just been laughing at something. Katie was so relieved to see her, the plate almost slipped from her sweaty hands.

"Where's Ariel?"

"She's on the patio. It was next to impossible to wake her up. 'It's not a vacation if your day starts before 10:00 a.m.'" She mimicked Ariel's voice. "But you're the only one who missed the meditation and yoga," Carmen pointed out.

The only one.

Katie let out the breath she'd been holding.

They went out through the garden doors and sat with Ariel at one of the small bistro tables spread out like a restaurant patio. As Katie picked through her food, she continued to calm down. Simon and Marie were there. Paula was sipping from a mug and writing in what looked like a journal. Max and Anthony were sitting together. How twisted was it that she was doing a head count to make sure she hadn't stuck a knife into anyone? Max gave her a sunny smile and waved at her, a spoon flapping between his knuckles.

"So cute, and I think he *liiiikes* you," Ariel trilled with enough volume to be sure Max overheard.

Max's ordinary, goofy wave immediately put Katie at ease. People didn't wave at one another like that if there'd been a stabbing. Everything was normal. All good. The sun was streaming through the vined pergola. *I was the only one missing from yoga and meditation.*

Katie almost laughed right then. What was she thinking? If she was going to get technical about it, she wasn't exactly fit enough to take down anyone at the retreat. Especially not while she was sleeping. Sure, she did some yoga, but just how normal people did yoga—for the clothes and some flexibility to impress the dudes. She performed yoga, she didn't *practice* it. She could almost picture the day when this exact moment would be relegated to the list of zany Katie stories. *Did I ever tell you about the time I woke up next to a bloody knife at a wellness retreat? Ha ha.*

Her panic started to flatten.

She waved back at Max, and he motioned if he could join their table. Everyone on the patio shuffled their tables closer, and breakfast passed with easy small talk.

Katie was totally convinced that the likeliest scenario for the knife was that she'd sleepwalked her way down to the kitchen, nicked herself somewhere, and the blood was the same as a razor cut when shaving her legs in the shower—worse than it looked.

"What do you think this obstacle course is all about?" Anthony turned the itinerary he was holding around on the table.

"Oh, an obstacle course? I'm going to have to miss that one, because I have a headache?" Ariel's voice tipped up as if she were asking a question. She pressed her hand to her head the way people did in Advil commercials. She was such a bad liar.

Naomi swooped in. "You have a headache?"

"Yes. I think it's best if I catch up with everyone in a little bit. I'll just grab some, uh, Tylenol and lie down."

"Tylenol? Are you kidding me? That's one of the most dangerous drugs on the market today." Naomi's voice squealed toward outrage. "Come with me to my treatment room. I can heal you."

"Oh, no, that's okay; maybe a walk will help." Ariel's eyes went wide and pleading, which Katie and Carmen couldn't help laughing at.

"No, headaches can be serious, Ariel. You should let Naomi help you." Carmen kicked Katie under the table.

"Yes, and Carmen would know. She's practically a doctor," Katie added solemnly.

"It's true that acetaminophen would never be approved by the FDA today." Carmen shook her head and poured some coconut milk into dirty-colored tea.

Ariel mouthed, *What are you doing?* at them as Naomi led her away.

The flutter in Katie's gut had stopped.

"I'm intrigued. What do you think Naomi will do to her?" Carmen arched an eyebrow at the table. Anthony started to share his own struggles with migraines. Dr. Dave strolled onto the patio. He touched Paula's shoulder as he passed by, chuckled at something Simon said as he made the rounds.

Katie noticed that Ellie's eyes were zigzagging around the patio. "Where's Lily?" she asked.

The question hit Katie like a dropped anvil.

ELLIE

"Unfortunately, Lily has left us rather abruptly." Dr. Dave had been looming and was now answering Ellie's question.

The blood in Katie's face drained.

Paula gasped across the patio. "Oh no."

"Yes, it's too bad, but Lily needs to pursue her own spiritual path, and if the Sanctuary isn't it, that's well and fine," Dr. Dave said congenially enough. Like Lily's absence was the equivalent of a bad online review.

"When did she leave?" Katie asked, her voice quivering.

"Did she even really arrive?" A dark look passed over Dr. Dave's face quicker than the jolt of a reflex. "The Sanctuary isn't for everyone. I like to think the Sanctuary is only for the spiritually hearty." Each time he said *the Sanctuary*, it had the same effect as referring to oneself in the third person.

Paula inexplicably started weeping. She was clearly histrionic. Dr. Dave went over and rubbed her back.

"'Scuse me." Katie jumped up from the table, knocked into it so that water and tea splashed over cups.

"What's up with her?" Carmen moved to go after Katie.

Ellie cut her off. "I think I know. I can deal with it." She let out a flustered sigh as she got up. "I think it probably still has to do with the tweet. I can't tell you how many times she does this at home. It just hits her in waves like this. Katie just can't stand not being liked."

Max made a face, and as Ellie left, she heard Carmen filling him in.

* * *

Katie pounced on Ellie the second she stepped into their room. "Lily was there this morning, right? At meditation or whatever the fuck?"

"Well, actually, no, she wasn't." Ellie took in a deep, steadying breath. Katie was in full panic mode. "But that doesn't mean anything. You weren't there either."

"How could you not tell me that?" Katie shot her a blameful look.

"I just didn't think."

Katie rushed over to Ellie's dresser. She yanked opened drawers, tossing aside folded underwear, until she found the knife.

"What are you doing?" Ellie needed to de-escalate this.

"Lily isn't here! She's gone. And there's this knife . . ." She unfolded the hand towel, set the knife down on the bed, and stared at it like it would give her all the answers.

"And Dr. Dave just said she left to pursue her own journey. Please, Katie, calm down. You're acting very erratically." Ellie wasn't sure exactly how to play this. The knife wasn't something she could just let Katie pretend wasn't serious. Katie could do that, disconnect from worrying events. From her own despicable actions. The child star in Katie also couldn't handle blame or responsibility, so Ellie was going to have to seesaw along with her. If she pushed Katie too hard in any one direction, she would become unpredictable.

Plus there was no body.

"But we don't know she really left. No one saw her leaving." Katie was pacing back and forth between their twin beds. Her hair, still damp from her shower, had turned stringy and fell over her buggy eyes in a way that made her look like a newly admitted psychiatric patient.

"Again, it doesn't mean anything." Of course, Ellie couldn't say that with any real conviction in her voice.

"It's just . . . I fell asleep thinking about her, about Lily and how much she grossed me out. I just wanted her to leave me alone yesterday, to go away. And now she's gone, and there's a knife in my bed. What did I do?"

Ellie felt a small thrill at seeing Katie get this worked up about something other than her petty little problems like getting her winter clothes out of storage or cleaning her cat's litter box. These were her usual hardships. "You're jumping to the worst possible conclusion here, Katie."

"Am I?"

"Well, what's the last thing you remember?"

Katie stopped and looked at her. "I just . . . I can't figure it out." She brought her palms up to her temples as if she could squeeze out a different answer to a question she couldn't bring herself to ask. "I didn't have the dream last night. I call it a dream, but it's not really a dream—more like an auditory hallucination, but then that's not exactly right either. Maybe it's a dream with sound, but it's music."

"What are you talking about, Katie?"

"The last thing I remember when I sleepwalk is always the same. It's always music, and I think what happens in my sleep is I have to go toward the music, like it's the saving white light of heaven or something, or maybe it's more literal, like I have to go and face the music. I don't know how to explain a dream. But it's always the last thing I remember, and I didn't hear music last night. I just . . . I don't feel like I was sleepwalking."

"But, Katie, you never remember your sleepwalking episodes." It was true. If someone told Katie that she did anything while she was sleepwalking, it would just be a blank space for her. One night, when Ellie and Nate had just finished having sex, Ellie—still naked—got up to use the bathroom and practically ran right into Katie. It was dark; she didn't even see her. Her nipple actually grazed Katie's arm. *Her nipple.* Ellie let out a yelp, waking Katie, who then started screaming herself. A *where-am-I* shrieking at the top of her lungs, over and over like a siren. What a scene. It was like a sitcom-level circus after that, with Nate scrambling into his boxers, then trying to lead his stunned sister out of the room.

It was by far the creepiest thing that had ever happened to her. When Nate came back into the room, Ellie started yelling at him. "How long has she been standing there? She saw us having sex!" Nate calmed her down by telling her not to worry, that Katie would never remember any of it. And she didn't. There really was just nothing. No memory at all.

"Oh god, oh god." Katie stopped moving, wrapped her arms around herself. Her eyes flickered back and forth like those of a cat following a laser pointer. The idea had to be soldering into her skull. Ellie held her breath. "What am I going to do? What could I have done anyway? I just . . . I don't hurt people. I've never hurt anyone."

Ellie nodded at the knife. "Let's put that away." She stood and bundled it up again in the towel and placed it back in her top drawer.

"All I ever do is walk. I literally sleepwalk. That's it. Walk. I don't wake up with bloodied clothes. I've never been violent. Ever. That's what I'm trying to say." Katie started pacing again. Twisting and untwisting her hands.

"Except—" Ellie winced. Sucked in her breath and pressed her lips together.

"Except what?" Katie looked like she were about to pounce on her. Ellie automatically braced herself.

"Nothing. I didn't mean to . . . shouldn't . . . have said anything," Ellie stammered.

"Tell me." A growl.

"I can't. Nate would be so angry if I told you."

Katie's eyes narrowed to slits. "Tell me right now."

Ellie sat there a few beats, not sure how to word it. She had to tell her gently. "Your dog. The one you have pictures of in your apartment?"

"Richard?"

"Yes, Richard."

"He was hit by a car." Katie looked totally baffled.

"That's the thing. Nate told me . . ." Again Ellie tapered off. *Tread carefully.* She didn't know how Katie was going to react. She was glad the knife was put away and that if something were to shift, she would be able to reach it first. She'd never been certain with Katie where the divide was between moody and instability.

"Go on."

"Richard wasn't hit by a car." Ellie let that dangle midair to ease Katie into what she was going to say next.

"Yes, he was."

"No. You . . . there's no easy way to say this, but you killed him. In your sleep. Nate said you didn't mean to. You had no idea what you were doing, but you must have been having a really bad dream. When he found you with the dog, he told you it was run over because he knew you would—"

"What?" Katie was shaking her head wildly. "No. Oh my god. I loved that dog. You're lying to me."

"No. Nate was the one lying to you." Ellie kept her voice firm.

"But how? How did I kill my dog?"

"You stabbed it. Nate took the knife out of your hand and covered the dog with a towel so you wouldn't see, before waking you up."

Katie stood there, stunned, her freckles blazing like a bad rash. She remembered the towel, the way it was soaked through with blood.

"Richard!" she cried out and sank onto the desk chair. "No, no, no." She started a few sentences with "I would never" and "I couldn't" and ended with broken sobs.

"Katie, I think the positive to this story is that you didn't try to hide Richard or cover it up. If you hurt Lily while sleeping, then where is she? It's a little far-fetched, isn't it? To kill someone, then cover it up while you're sleeping?" Katie was zoning out.

"I need a fucking drink."

"What you need to do is think. What did you do last night?

Where did you go?" Ellie took hold of Katie's hands and squeezed hard. "Focus."

"I don't know. I don't remember. I don't remember sleepwalking. I don't remember anything." Katie tore her hands away and fisted her hair so hard her skin seemed to lift off her face into some grotesque thing out of a wax museum.

"You have to try."

"I *am* fucking trying! I don't remember. I didn't have the dream last night. If I did, I don't even remember that," Katie sniveled. Her lips were puffed out. She had a dazed look on her face, and her upper body swayed like she was drunk.

"It's okay. We'll figure this out." Ellie took Katie into her arms. Even under the circumstances, the intimacy felt strange and awkward. Katie let out a sob, her body shaking. "Look, why don't I just go back downstairs and ask Dr. Dave for more details about how or when Lily left. I am sure there's a reasonable explanation —"

"No, don't," Katie snapped.

"No? Why not?"

"Because what if I did it? I'm scared."

"Even if you did, Katie, you were sleepwalking; it wasn't your fault." Ellie rubbed her back. "It's not your fault. The first thing we need to do is get rid of the knife."

ARIEL

"Please undress and lie down there. Here's a towel." Ariel felt a small flutter of relief at the sight of a massage table. The entire walk from the patio to this room, Ariel had felt twitchy and nervous about being alone with this woman who'd symbolically hanged herself in the basement.

Naomi's treatment room had an earthy odor despite an onion-shaped infuser on a floating shelf, spewing eucalyptus steam. On the wall hung a large periodic table for healing crystals. And then there were the plants. So many scrawny potted plants.

Behind a bamboo partition, Ariel took off her clothes down to her underwear and wrapped herself in the towel. She stepped out from behind the partition—a little like the one in the basement—feeling very self-conscious; her body type had to give Naomi nightmares.

Naomi squirted something on her hands and motioned again at the table. Once Ariel was facedown on the table, Naomi asked if she was ready.

"Yes." Ariel closed her eyes and waited for the warm feeling of essential oils to come streaming down her freckled back.

Nothing happened.

"Do you feel that?" Naomi grunted softly.

"No, can't say that I feel anything." Ariel emitted a nervous giggle.

"I'm surprised. I can feel how bunged up your crown chakra is."

Ariel's hand automatically went to the bare spot on her head, making sure to keep it covered with her hair. She felt a tremor of disappointment in herself for falling back on an old habit—*habit* sounded better than *compulsion*—mixed with an urge to take out a few strands and feel the immediate calm it brought.

Ariel lifted her head and saw that Naomi was swirling her hands a couple of inches above Ariel's body like a witch over a stewing cauldron. "I once unblocked a woman's fallopian tube." Naomi flicked her eyebrows at her with surprising cockiness. "She was pregnant six months later."

"Oh. I get it now. Okay." Ariel dropped her head back down and wondered what an acceptable amount of time would be before she could claim to be cured of her headache. Five minutes? Eight? So there was going to be no kneading of tense, knotty muscles.

And what if she did have a headache? She was pretty sure there wasn't an Advil or Tylenol in sight! Did they even have a first aid kit? Or would Naomi try to cure an open, gushing wound with her mind too?

"Your friends seem really fun. The English one, Ellie, she's very pretty."

"Hmm." Ariel again felt insecure at her own near-naked body in front of a woman who valued perfection.

"Yes, they are. I actually just met Ellie for the first time."

"Huh." A few beats passed, and Ariel was starting to feel uncomfortable by this silent miming of a massage.

"So how did you meet Dr. Dave?"

"I was his patient."

"Aren't there, um, rules against that?"

"Yes, there are. Definitely."

Ariel waited for her to say something more about it, maybe how she stopped being Dr. Dave's patient so they could officially begin a relationship, but nothing. Just silence.

"Well, I know what it's like to have an inappropriate work relationship. I was dating the hospitality manager at the Holiday Inn back home. We had to sneak around in the unoccupied guest rooms." How many rooms did she and Rob have sex in? How many times did she gaze at those dusty, paisley-patterned curtains that hadn't been updated since the '90s? In lighting purposely set to dim to make the rooms look nicer. Felt the bleach-stiff sheets scratching her back as Rob explained that his five-year-old marriage was over. They'd married too young—though Ariel didn't think twenty-eight counted as *too young*—and had grown apart. Rob had sold Ariel on the fantasy that once he was officially divorced, he was going work it out with corporate so they could be transferred together to New York.

He was just waiting for the right time to tell his wife—of course—and if she weren't so gosh-darn prone to depression, he would already have ended it—of course. He couldn't live with it if, heaven forbid, his wife hurt herself. It was, again, all about timing. So Ariel waited eighteen months for Rob to find the right time, making the most ancient of womanly mistakes—believing a cheat and a liar.

Whenever Rob's wife had shown up at the Holiday Inn, Rob always sent Ariel a text to warn her and then Ariel would hide out in the break room or a conference room or the two-treadmill gym. Rob would do this because of course Ariel wouldn't want to see Bridget. He even passed himself off as being *sensitive to Ariel's needs*. Once or twice, Ariel had met his wife before the affair started, and Bridget seemed happy enough, but it'd been months since Ariel had seen her.

Until three weeks ago, when his wife had come waddling in at noon with a Subway sandwich tucked under her arm—the equivalent of a romantic picnic basket in Shakopee—for Rob and a very noticeable baby bump.

Ariel's boyfriend was going to have a baby.

With his wife.

She was always going to be his side piece because there was no better place to have a workplace affair than at a hotel.

What did Ariel do with this information?

Nothing.

She had smiled her way through the day and started yanking at her hair as soon as she walked out.

She had driven by Rob's house at night. Watched through the window as they painted the baby's room pink—so trite—and realized right then she was probably in love with him.

Naomi's breathing suddenly became more labored. "Can you feel it now? The release?"

"I can, yes. Thank you. My headache is officially gone," Ariel said with the cheery falseness of an audience volunteer in an infomercial. When Ariel tried to get up, Naomi snapped at her to stay still.

"You need to stay lying down for another twenty minutes for circulation purposes." Naomi dabbed her own forehead with a towel.

"Okay." Ariel stared down at the tile and circulated.

CARMEN

The obstacle course was a mix of climbing nets, suspended bridges, and swinging logs thirty feet off the ground. And now that it was over, every little muscle in Carmen's body was tweaked and humming.

Dr. Dave had prefaced the course with the same lecture he was delivering now—some shit about positivity and overcoming obstacles. Finally, he instructed everyone to take a *solitary walk of reflection*—not just a walk or a hike but a *solitary walk of reflection*—to ponder his wisdom.

"The course was surprisingly fun," Ellie said brightly.

"It really was." Carmen nodded, and wondered why Katie was looking so sour. "Definitely feeling like I could do some *American Ninja* right about now," Carmen joked, adding a little ninja kick.

Katie gave her a weak smile in response, mumbled that she was going to take that *walk of solitaire*, she said it just like that, like the card game instead of solitude, and strode away on her own as if something were chasing her. Ellie went after her. Carmen watched. It looked like they were headed toward the house, not a hike.

What was wrong with Katie? She'd been quiet ever since she'd fled the table at breakfast and hadn't taken off those damn sunglasses since. She didn't believe the whole PR-sounding excuse about how Katie still got upset about her careless tweet.

Once Katie was finished feeling bad about something, like her tweet, she was done. The girl could compartmentalize like a sociopath. No way she was going to get all moody over something that had happened a month ago. It was one of the things Carmen admired about the girl—her lack of turmoil.

Dramatic, yes, but genuine angst, not Katie.

Carmen suddenly realized she wasn't even sure she cared. Her skin was slick with sweat, and her nose was running. She pulled out the itinerary from her backpack. The rest of the day was full of workshops on self-hypnosis, wood chopping, drumming, and stand-up paddleboarding.

Maybe this weekend was like some farewell tour of the girl group they once were in college. What was the five-year survival rate of college friendships? She couldn't party with Katie anymore with a houseful of kids depending on her, and she could never really relate to Ariel's scrapbooking mentality and dreamy aspirations— Ariel was the first person she'd heard use the term *hope chest*—and the way she wanted what other people had, just to have it.

Carmen felt a decade older than both of them.

What did they have in common anymore?

She took in a deep, pine-scented breath, and it hit her like a gleeful smack in the face—she was alone. Right now, she was enjoying the freedom to go for a long, guiltless walk. There was no crying or fighting, no school lunches to be made or adult diapers to be changed. This morning, Carmen had even had a full bowel movement with no one else needing the bathroom. It was a complete luxury to be outside in all this open space with the sun beating down on her. A beautiful infusion of vitamin D seared into her pasty indoor skin.

She decided to aimlessly drift down a path.

Her, doing nothing.

Before, when she was the type A scholarship student, this would have bothered her to no end, the pointlessness of walking just for the sake of walking. With no end point in mind. No claim to be made at the end of having climbed some rocky surface or hiked x number of miles. Instead, she just took in the chirping birds, the gently lapping lake, and the way the sun made all the trees sparkle.

She'd only been about fifteen minutes up one of the trails when she came across a leg sticking out at the edge of the path. The foot flopped over at a nasty angle.

Marie was on the ground, propped against a tree.

Marie waved at Carmen in a shooing way that made it look like she was embarrassed. Her cheeks were pink.

"Oh no! What happened?" Carmen took off her backpack and set it down.

"You will never believe it. After climbing all over that rope course, I go for a walk and trip on nothing and roll my ankle." Marie let out a twinkle of laughter. "I was hoping my husband would come by and help me back to the house."

"Let's see." Carmen hunched down and took a look at Marie's ankle, comparing it to the other foot. She slowly moved the injured foot, and Marie winced in pain. "It could be sprained. We need to get this elevated and put some ice on it."

She helped Marie hobble down the path. Simon and Marie were staying in the guest cottage. It looked like a cute, miniature version of the house. They struggled up the four steps to a small porch. Marie laughed as she unlocked the door. "My husband is always telling me I am too clumsy. A klutz, he calls me. He will never let me live this down."

Carmen took more of her weight as they shambled inside. The guest cottage was very much a honeymoon suite with its large canopied bed angled toward a stone fireplace that came with a real-looking bearskin rug sprawled out in front of it.

Carmen led Marie to the bed, set her down, and then lifted her leg up slowly. Marie leaned back onto the stack of pillows in a seated position. "Keep it elevated." Carmen looked around the room for something to prop Marie's leg up since Marie was already leaning against both pillows on the bed. "Do you want me to take one of those pillows and put it under your leg?"

"No, no. I am fine." Marie waved her away. "Plus I need them for my back. Ah, it is tough getting old."

"You're not old. And ice. I'll go and find an ice pack."

"Do not worry about it. All I need is rest and Advil. There is a bottle in the bathroom; if you could get it for me, *s'il vous plaît*?"

The bathroom was down a hallway and to the left; as far away from the honeymoon bed as possible. The bathroom in the cottage was three times the size of the one in Carmen's room. The claw-foot tub was massive and there was a separate shower with so many body sprays it looked like a mini car wash. A skylight lit up the entire space.

Carmen glanced around for the Advil. The vanity was covered with several travel-size bottles and tubes of sunscreen, face cream, body wash, and Voltaren. Spilling from two toiletry cases was an electric shaver, orange prescription bottles that she checked the labels of out of habit, tweezers, a palette of beige-y eye shadows, and a contouring brush, but no Advil.

"Did you find it?" Marie shouted from the bed.

"No, not yet."

"It's there somewhere, next to the sink."

Carmen checked over the rest of the bathroom. She still didn't spot any Advil. She opened the cupboard door under the sink. Empty, aside from a large black duffel bag. Without dragging it out, she crouched down and unzipped it just a little to see if there were more toiletries and if maybe Marie's Advil hadn't been unpacked.

Inside were cheery lime-green Styrofoam yoga blocks. There were about a dozen blocks, which seemed a tad excessive in Carmen's opinion. But the block was perfect. If Marie kept her foot up, even just a little, she would keep the swelling down.

Carmen pulled a block out, and then nearly dropped it because it was much heavier than it looked to be. She caught it before it hit the floor.

It was as heavy as a hand weight. Then she noticed an almost invisible line around the block. Foam shouldn't have seams. It was razor thin, like it had been opened with a carpenter's knife and

then resealed with clear glue; she spotted the slightest dried dribble of it at the corner. These were shoddily made blocks. Why bring
yoga blocks at all when the retreat provided their own? Simon and
Marie said they attended the Sanctuary often, so they would know
that. And come to think of it, Carmen hadn't noticed Simon or
Marie using any blocks at all during yoga that morning. A warning
went off inside of her.

"Oh never mind!" Marie called out, and Carmen jumped. "The
Advil is right here, in my nightstand. Oh, I swear, I am too forget-
ful these days!"

"Oh okay, glad you found it. Mind if I use your bathroom while
I'm in here?"

"Of course," Marie shouted back.

Carmen pushed the door closed and locked it. She moved to
the toilet, set the heavy yoga block on her lap, and tried to pry it
apart but couldn't. She tried to burrow her finger through the
glued seam opening but couldn't. She grabbed some nail clippers
and used the filer like a crowbar to pry the block apart, but it was
too short and stubby. It wasn't working.

Why did she care? Why did she have to know what was inside
the yoga block? She should put it back. It had nothing to do with
her. And yet she didn't want to. She was curious now and wanted
to know for the sake of knowing. Carmen was just that type of
person; if she came across a box that said DO NOT OPEN, the first
thing she would do was open it.

She looked around the bathroom vanity for something. She
flushed the toilet, hoping the noise would cover her rummaging
through the black shaving bag. There was a small pair of scissors
that Simon probably used to trim his nose hairs with. She jabbed
the scissors into the block and whittled her way through the glue.
The block started to open.

Holy fuck.

KATIE

Ellie didn't listen to her and went asking Dr. Dave for more details about Lily while Katie showered and dressed. When Katie came back out of the bathroom, Ellie was waiting for her with a solemn expression. "Dr. Dave didn't have much more to say, only that Naomi sensed something was off. This morning they discovered that the china cabinet had been pried open. A phone was gone, which they obviously now know was Lily's phone. Dr. Dave didn't seem overly concerned, and even thinks she'll realize her mistake checking out early and possibly come back."

Katie kept her arms tight at her sides, braced for whatever Ellie was going to say next. She could tell by her face that there was more to tell.

"So at first I thought that was good news that Lily decided to check out at such an odd time so she could filch a few things from the Sanctuary, but then." Ellie paused, licked her lips. The building tension burned like a rash across Katie's chest.

"As I was leaving the patio, Anthony overheard and stopped me to let me know that he woke up in the middle of night because he heard shouting. I asked what voices he'd heard, and he said two women and neither had a French or British accent. Again, this doesn't necessarily mean anything."

But that wasn't true. It meant something. Of course it did. Now they were whipping down the highway. It had been Katie's idea to go looking for Lily because she felt helpless and couldn't stand not doing anything.

Katie sat there, unblinking, in the passenger seat. Zombified by terror. *Am I a murderer?* Her head was filled with a panicky, high-pitched static. Her thoughts kept turning in on themselves. Then, just as she was about to claw out of her own skin, she'd feel a welcome gust of denial. *There's no way. No way.* She wasn't capable of hurting anything. *A person. I couldn't. I couldn't stab. Yeah, right.* She could almost laugh out loud at the idea of it. There were things you just knew about yourself.

But wasn't that why she was out in the middle of nowhere? To figure herself out? What did she know about herself, really? She'd been *100 fucking percent* sure she would never hurt an animal until that morning—and never a dog she loved. She'd been sure that while her sleepwalking made her anxious, it was mostly just a benign annoyance as long as Nate kept the doors locked. All this time, she'd thought he was protecting her, but maybe he was locking her in to protect everyone else.

Am I a murderer? How would I know? I was asleep; I wasn't even there for it.

Lily was caught in the background of the picture taken when they first arrived. That's what you did when people went missing: you went around flashing their picture. It's what Shelby Spade would do. Plus she wanted to buy booze—no, she *needed* booze—if she was going to spend another night at the Sanctuary. It was the only way to keep everyone else safe.

They would find Lily, see she was alive and well, and then go back to enjoying their weekend. She was grateful she didn't have a valid driver's license and that Ellie was driving, because all she seemed capable of was rocking back and forth in the passenger seat. She was not calm in times of crisis.

Ellie leaned over, put her hand on Katie's leg, and squeezed. "It'll be all right." But they both knew it could just as easily not be all right. Just do the fucking math: *Blood + knife + a middle of the night argument between two women.* There were only six women including Naomi left at the retreat, two had accents and there was only one sleepwalker. And oh, multiply that now by a sleepwalker with a history of violence, of somnolent stabbing. Of murdering her own dog, and again, her dog's name came out of her like a dying gasp.

Ellie gave her a sidelong glance, and once more Katie could feel her daggers of resentment; the entire SUV was humming with blame and something else. There were creases of worry in Ellie's forehead. She was either afraid *of* Katie or *for* her. Neither was good.

"Pull in there." Katie pointed to a green warehouse-looking building with a four-leaf clover on the sign.

"Really? Happy Harry's Liquor Mart?"

"We have to start somewhere," Katie whined at Ellie and told her to wait in the car. In the store, she grabbed a bottle of vodka, then a second one. At the checkout, she pulled out her phone and zoomed in on Lily. While her face blurred somewhat, her features were clear enough. "Have you seen this person? Anywhere?"

The cashier leaned over, his ample gut nearly knocking over a tray of BIC lighters, and looked at the image through thick glasses that magnified his eyes. "No idea, but going by the dreads and bandanna, she looks like one of them tree planters."

"Tree planters?"

"Yeah, at least that's what they call themselves. Bunch of vagrant idiots who showed up a few weeks ago, saying they're gonna plant a tree each time our president calls climate change a Chinese hoax, but mostly they're just junkie troublemakers. There've been a bunch more break-ins this summer, and whenever they come in here, they're stoned as hell. Plus they started planting trees in early July when any half-wit knows you plant trees in the fall if you want them to actually grow. One even tried to shove a bottle of rye down the front of his pants, but I straightened him out." The man nodded to something behind the counter that Katie supposed was probably a gun. He looked like the sort of man who owned a stockpile of guns and ran survivalist drills whenever there was talk of a new stoplight.

"So where do they live?"

"I dunno. Where do vagrants live?" He raised an eyebrow, stared at her with his goggle-eyes, and smirked, taking a long pause so she could really marinate in the stupidity of her question. "Probably the woods?"

"'Kay, thanks. That narrows it down." She grabbed her vodka off the counter.

"Climate change really is a hoax, though," the man said after her.

"Seriously? I thought you were just asking questions." Ellie rolled her eyes at Katie's jangling plastic bag.

And that's why Katie had wanted Ellie to stay in the car; she couldn't handle being judged right then, and what did it matter? She set the bag down and told her about the tree planters and how the man recognized Lily as possibly one of them. A bit of an embellishment, but Katie needed to keep looking.

"So, now what?"

"We just need to find them."

They stopped at three more places before narrowing down that the tree planters—luckily, everyone in town thought they were assholes and had some grievance against them—were staying at an abandoned summer camp twenty minutes north.

Before hitting the highway again, Ellie pulled into a self-serve Chevron station to get gas, and as she walked into the convenience store to pay, long curls bouncing, a man in the next bay went statue-still while he stared at her, a dribble of gas spilling out of the nozzle. She had *those* looks, the kind that made men go punch-drunk.

Katie pulled out her phone to check for service. She felt an overwhelming need to call someone. She wanted someone to come and smooth things over like they had in the old days.

AJ.

He would have known what to do. AJ would tell her not to worry, that he'd take care of it. He'd hand her an extra dose of her anti-anxiety medication. She could still hear his voice—*Lift your tongue, little one*—as he placed a tiny white pill in her mouth to dissolve. AJ would then send her somewhere to calm down. A spa, or a nail salon, the movies. He'd hire someone to track Lily down, then call later to assure Katie that she did not stab anyone. Even if it wasn't true, he'd make her believe it was.

He'd always swept things under the rug for her before he'd turned into the disgruntled employee fired over missing funds. Before he'd made her an *Entertainment Tonight* tragic news story. Before *The Incident*. Before the slash-and-dash, AJ was all things to her.

Her beloved manager. A stand-in for a father who weaved in and out of her life whenever he needed money. When Lucy was busy peddling the Spade brand and blowing through the Spade money on shopping sprees, vacations, cars, and all of her cosmetic surgeries—and then recovering from those surgeries—AJ had taken care of Katie. Whenever she'd had a problem, she'd gone to him. AJ was the one who'd bought her first package of maxi pads. He showed her how to keep weight off easily. He gave her advice on how to get through her first onstage kiss.

He called her his "work wife" and everyone on set would laugh because Katie was just ten. AJ in his flashy, well-tailored suits. His black-rimmed glasses and spiky brown hair. He was in his late thirties but never seemed old to her.

Katie's phone was blinking. She had three voice mails she'd been ignoring. The first two were stammering messages from her cheating ex-boyfriend, Walker. How did she ever trust a bartender who went by *Walker*? How did she not pick up on that foreshadowing?

Message 1: "Katie. I don't know how to say this, but—"

Message 2: "Call me back. Please. I think you need—"

She immediately deleted both, feeling a brief dusting of pleasure at being able to cut him off midsentence, to shut up his pleading, stumbling voice. Asshole. She didn't want to hear anything else come out of his mouth. She had really thought it was going to work out with Walker.

And if it hadn't been for him, she probably wouldn't even be there. She wouldn't be looking for a maybe-dead girl that she maybe killed. *Oh my god.*

She cracked one of the bottles of vodka and took a long, greedy gulp, her throat burning up.

Listening to the third voice mail, she felt a blast of guilt the minute she heard his voice.

"It's Clive. I have an update for you. Call me back." She looked at Ellie paying for the gas through the store window.

Clive was the private investigator she'd hired months ago. She felt like shit about it at this very moment, seeing how Ellie was helping her . . . what? Cover up a murder she might have committed? Anyone else would have probably called the cops already.

If they found Lily—*when* they found Lily, she corrected herself—this whole side road trip would become the quintessential bonding experience. Katie could picture her wedding speech. *Lemme tell ya, there's no better way to break in your sister-in-law than with a potential homicide.*

But at the time, Katie had just come across a life insurance policy on Nate's kitchen island. For *her life.* Not Nate's. Not Ellie's. *Hers.* She'd gone into Nate's place for something, and there it was, lying right out in the open like he'd wanted her to see it. Of course, Ellie scurried out of her jewelry-making den, scooped up the papers, and hid them away. Katie called Nate at the restaurant, freaking out. "Why the fuck are you taking a life insurance policy out on me?"

"Because of what happened two weeks ago, Katie!" he snapped at her. "You were sleepwalking in the middle of the road!"

"It was your girlfriend's fault, Nate," she roared into the phone.

"Whatever. You can take one out on me too, if you want." But the way he said it, they both knew it was Katie who was most likely to die. *How do sleepwalkers cross the road? They don't. They get hit by a car and die halfway to the other side.*

"I just think it's a little convenient that right after you move your gold-digging girlfriend in, you're taking life insurance out—"

"No, and don't even say it. I was going to talk to you about it, and anyway, I was just looking into it. It's just a pamphlet, Katie." It wasn't just a pamphlet; it was a document, and it was signed.

She wondered what Clive had found out. What update did he have to give her? The only thing he'd emailed her so far was that he couldn't really find out anything about Ellie. There was no evidence of her being a gold-digger—no trail of short-lived marriages to older, unattractive men or an assembly line of pro-athlete ex-boyfriends who grew tired of passing her between teammates—but there wasn't really anything at all. For anyone else, this would be a big, waving red flag, but it just supported Ellie's story that she was raised by wanderlustful parents. That she shunned social media.

Ellie jumped back into the SUV, dumped change in the console, and handed Katie a sweating bottle of water. "Drink this instead of *bloody* vodka," she snapped as she bumped out of the lot.

ELLIE

They drove another twenty-five minutes, passing a sun-bleached wooden sign that read CAMP SUNNYVILLE on the side of the road, almost completely hidden by a tree and leafy vines. Ellie pulled a sharp U-turn, and they veered down a gravel road in a dust haze. The road dwindled until they were driving on grass, dipping up and down rutted mini-hills that scraped against the undercarriage. "Aren't you happy I rented an SUV?" Katie said, her voice flat.

Ellie kept driving until they got as close as they could to what looked like what had been the main cabin. She turned the engine off, and they sat there looking out, the cooling engine ticking.

There was a cluster of picnic tables angled around a pine tree where the grass was patchy. In the distance, a swirl of smoke drifted up behind the cabin.

Ellie undid her seat belt and got out. Katie hesitated. Ellie waited for her and when Katie took another gulp of vodka instead of getting out, she felt a rush of white-hot rage. She was almost senseless with it, like she could grab the tire iron from the back, if there was one, and smash up the Escalade. Of course Katie wanted to dull her senses, cocoon herself in booze so she didn't have to experience her own distress at full throttle. It wasn't fair.

Ellie stalked over to the passenger side, flung the door open, and in her clipped accent said, "Put your big-girl panties on and get out of the car."

Katie obediently slid out of the Escalade. This was what she wanted, for Ellie to take charge. For someone to take care of her; fix up her mistakes.

To their right was a spattering of pup tents and tarps fastened between trees.

"Let's check the cabins first, then the tents." Ellie started walking.

"This place reminds me of the premiere of season 3, 'Shelby Spade solves the Deep Woods Mystery.' There was this supposed forest monster, like bigfoot, who was terrorizing the kids at night and there was a main cabin, exactly like that, but it had, like, marshmallows and bait and all that, and Shelby figured out the camp counselor was the one trying to scare everyone off because—"

"Katie," Ellie snapped, her cheeks flushed bloodred. "Please stop talking."

"Right. Fine. But I'm nervous. No one knows where we are, and how do we know if that guy you asked at the station isn't in on it? That he doesn't always direct lost travelers to this place so these 'tree planters' can have their monthly ritualistic kill?"

"It's fine, Katie. We just want to see if Lily is here. Maybe she is, and then we can just move on. Don't you want that? To move on with the weekend? A bloody knife without a body is just a knife. It's not a weapon."

Katie squeaked out, "Yes." Her mouth felt sandy.

Ellie could see she wanted it more than anything.

They waded through knee-high weeds, each step bringing up a cloud of mosquitoes. As they got closer to the main cabin, Ellie saw they wouldn't need to knock on the door because there wasn't one. She went right inside and took a look, while Katie lingered behind her. If this were a Shelby Spade episode, it would be Katie in front, while her cowering sidekick clung to her shoulders. But right now, it was the opposite.

On the floor was a scattering of leaves, a set of antlers, and some lumps of blankets. A fetid body odor smell loomed under the ashy scent of the blackened-stone fireplace.

NO FUTURE was spray-painted on the wall in red drippy paint.

One of the bundles of blankets suddenly moved. Katie jumped back. A stringy-haired woman popped her head out, her face so sunken, Katie could see the outline of teeth in her cheeks. She was anywhere between twenty and fifty.

She sat straight up like a zombie popping out of a grave. "What the fuck do you want?" she slurred. Her eyes stayed closed.

Ellie stepped forward. "Hello, sorry to bother you but is someone named Lily staying here?"

The woman said nothing. Her eyeballs flickered back and forth behind her eyelids. She was either thinking or falling back to sleep and already mid-dream. Her nails were picking at something on her arm.

"Excuse me?" Ellie tried again. She took another step closer, while Katie stayed close to the entrance.

"Are you fucking kidding me? I'm trying to sleep. I told 'em all to leave me alone. I got cramps. Go ask." The woman's eyelids flicked opened suddenly like a plastic doll's.

"We're just looking for someone. Her name's Lily. She's, um . . . she has dark braided hair. She's just a wisp of a thing. We were told she might be here—"

The woman started laughing; it was a hard, ugly noise. "Lily of the valley, oh, where, oh, where is lily of the valley?" she said in a fake English accent. "What the fuck is that? You ain't from Eng-Land. I been to Eng-Land." The woman sneered, flicked her pinkie up like she was taking a sip of tea.

Ellie threw Katie a look, cleared her throat, and tried again. "Right. Well, so is there a Lily here or not?"

The woman looked past Ellie at Katie. "You! Do you have a tampon? I need tampons. You look like you got tampons." The woman was saying *tampons* like they were Rolex watches.

Katie shook her head. She was inching her way through the doorframe. "This is pointless; we should just leave," she whispered at Ellie. *Coward.*

"I just need a fucking tampon!" The woman's voice suddenly went shrill. She fought with her blankets to sit up, lost the battle, and sunk back down.

"You know what? I think I might have a tampon in the car, but before I give it to you, I want to know if Lily is here," Ellie pressed on.

The woman's eyes drooped again like she was getting drowsy. She reached over and pulled a bottle of Gatorade out of the blankets, took a swig of something too brown to be Gatorade. "Fuck if I know; go ask Colton. He's at the pool." She flicked her hand in the general southern direction. There was a sudden belch of screeching music. "I told 'em to keep it down." The woman shook her head angrily, her lips still moving as she slumped deeper in her cocoon of tattered blankets.

ARIEL

"Welcome to the mother of all obstacle courses, my friend." Dr. Dave waved his arm upward to an elaborate web of ropes, plank bridges, and zip lines strung between trees several feet off the ground.

"Oh, wow," Ariel said without a trace of enthusiasm. She did not want to be there—at the retreat and now especially at this obstacle course. She'd fallen asleep on Naomi's treatment table and had been woken by a chipper, drumroll knock that had ended up being pointless because the door just swung open.

"Are you ready for the obstacle course?" It had been Dr. Dave.

"What? Didn't I miss it?" The whole point of enduring Naomi's treatment was to avoid an activity with *obstacle* in its description.

"Oh, no. I would hate for you to miss out. I'll wait while you get dressed."

Maybe because she'd been still groggy and half-dressed and scrambling to cover her naked body with her towel, she'd blurted, "Yep."

And now she was standing out in the woods looking up at something only a Navy SEAL should attempt.

"'Kay, let's get a helmet on you." He grabbed an egghead helmet. Ariel took it but did not put it on. "Need help with that?"

"No, thank you." She gave him a pursed look and swatted at a mosquito. She was already sweating. It was hot. A muggy, cling-to-your-skin heat. Naomi forbade insect repellant. When she had spotted Ariel about to spray herself down on the porch before following Dr. Dave into the deep woods, she'd grabbed the can of aerosol out of her hands ("The bees!" Naomi had said with the same "What about the children?" alarm), offering instead her own homemade oily concoction of citrus juice and menthol extract, which Ariel had already sweated off.

"No, thank you?" He gave her a false look of confusion, and Ariel knew he was going to try to talk her into it. She felt even hotter.

"I think I'll pass. This isn't really my thing. And my headache is starting to come back." Ariel didn't want to do the obstacle course. She'd gone far enough out of her comfort zone with *The Handmaid's Tale* breathing session with Bony Naomi, and now she was supposed to cross what looked like an oversize cat's cradle?

It all seemed so pointless. She had to return home in two days and face what she'd done. Even if she left the retreat as some newly minted *warrior*—then what? Positive thinking wasn't going to keep her from getting arrested. And Katie wasn't even paying attention to her.

Dr. Dave still wore a bemused smile. "It's not your thing? Why is that?"

"I'm just not into, like, extreme sports." She dropped the helmet.

"The only limits that exist are in your mind," Dr. Dave said with a tap against his temple.

Ariel didn't think that was true. She'd been watching one of Dr. Dave's online videos before going over to Rob's house last week, all pumped up on pushing boundaries and claiming what she wanted, and look where it got her. She couldn't imagine a more limiting place than prison.

"I was very inspired by your YouTube videos and everything you had to say." Dr. Dave looked pleased by this. "But I know I can't do this. I'm just not a fan of heights."

"Tell me about your phobia of heights."

"Oh, it's not exactly a phobia. I just wouldn't want to, like, fall from anything beyond one foot off the ground." Ariel suffered from only a minor fear of heights but didn't need the extra stress right now. Plus, she could never climb a rope in gym class and was certain she'd plummet from any of the ropes that were dangling like vines and break her neck.

Dr. Dave suddenly chuckled like she'd said something funny. "You know what, Ariel?"

"What?"

"You're my favorite kind of client."

"Why is that?" Ariel felt a sudden uplifting swell in her chest. She wasn't usually the sort of person who was singled out and given special attention. He gave her a slow head-to-toe assessing gaze.

"Because simmering just below all of your insecurities and fears, Ariel, is a true warrior." Ariel felt a slight plummeting at the mention of the weekend's theme. Wasn't everyone there to become a so-called warrior?

"That's great," she mumbled.

Dr. Dave leaned against a climbing wall with one knee bent, the sole of his hiking boot against it. Dressed in beige cargo pants and a white tank top, his thumbs hooked into his pockets, his wiry muscles peaking under his skin, he looked like the romantic lead on the cover of a Harlequin novel.

His good looks were so distracting.

"Tell me something, Ariel. How are the relationships in your life?" Dr. Dave's pool-water eyes locked onto hers and wouldn't let go. Ariel couldn't look away. It was suddenly like he could see directly into her brain to all the little fears and anxieties frantically buzzing around inside of her.

"I don't know—I mean, they're not great." Ariel thought about how Rob would apply both of their employee discounts in the Holiday Inn lounge if he wanted to eat or drink before they found a room to have sex in. Why did she always want men who didn't want her back? She was a placeholder for hotter, more glamorous girlfriends—and wives! Men didn't date chubby women for their hearts of gold the way women were expected to with chubby men. Was there a single sitcom on television with a flabby, bumbling woman who burned every dinner, forgot to pick up the kids, and hid out in a lady-cave to drink and obsessively watch HGTV, only to be loved unconditionally by a svelte, long-suffering husband who fixed all her mistakes without damaging her ego in the process? No! Why? Because it was too scary, too unbelievable. Fat women weren't lovable. Instead, Ariel had to sell herself on her utility; she was the first one a man asked for a favor and she was on it. She practically tripped over herself to do it.

"I thought so." Then Dr. Dave reached over and touched the back of her head, right where her bald picking spot was, and rubbed his hand there. Her knees started to buckle. Did Naomi see it and tell him? His eyes were challenging her to make him stop or deny him in some way, but somehow she couldn't. "I get the feeling you recently suffered a trauma."

How did he know? Ariel nodded slowly. "Yes." Though technically it was Rob's wife who really suffered.

"I get the feeling you don't value yourself enough." Ariel continued to nod.

"Yes," she repeated like she was under some kind of spell.

"I get the sense that you like to hide from your problems? Is that true, Ariel?"

"Yes." Again, she answered with a discomfiting amount of honesty. She also liked how he kept saying her name.

Dr. Dave nodded. "You're not one to lead, are you, Ariel?"

"No. I'm not." Ariel was so fearful of being disliked that she always went with the flow. She considered it a compliment to be called "easygoing," but now she realized she was just a dull follower.

"Have you ever been truly fulfilled? Are you happy with the life you have created for yourself?"

"Oh, well, I wanted to live in New York but I couldn't get a paid internship, so I had to move home. And I guess I started off happy at the Holiday Inn but I wouldn't go so far as to say I was fulfilled exactly. Things are especially tense back in Shakopee at the moment and I still want to move to New York but, like, money is a huge factor and, perhaps, legally that will be prohibited—"

"Jesus, you've just got so much fucking static going on in your head, don't you? It's practically emanating off you." Dr. Dave cut her off. Ariel deflated with embarrassment at her sudden stream of consciousness blather.

"Sorry," she murmured.

"You can't even hear yourself think, can you? Because if you could, you'd realize that you're full of bullshit excuses for not living the life you want."

Ariel made a weak *oh* sound.

"But I think I can help you."

Dr. Dave paused, and made a show of thinking by stroking his chin. "I am going to offer you a treatment. It's completely radical, but I think it's something you might benefit from. Our bodies offer the most direct and perfect path to profound spiritual transformation. Your own body, Ariel, is a gateway to connecting with your inherent self-awareness and wakefulness. I can be your conduit for this connection. We can stop anytime. Do you consent?"

Ariel could feel the heat rolling off him. She realized she was leaning into his touch, and only when she nodded did he take his hand off her head.

It was like a magician's trick how quickly he twisted her around so that her back was against the climbing wall, pulled down her shorts, and shifted her leg so that one foot was on a rubber foothold.

A fleeting moment of confusion. "Oh," she said again. Dr. Dave asked again if she consented, and a small part of her wondered if he was recording her answer.

Ariel paused, feeling ridiculous and exposed without anything on from the waist down.

"You know who you are. You know what you want. Repeat it in your mind, like a mantra." And then Dr. Dave's head was between her legs, his tongue driving into her. Ariel arched back, her hands reaching for something, gripping a foothold in each hand.

I know who I am. I know what I want.

Her eyes rolled back. Something raw and intense was overtaking her. Something bigger than herself. *I know who I am. I know what I want.*

It was a sad thing, but Ariel had never had an orgasm before. At least, not when another person was in the room with her. She'd come close, she'd feel the start of an orgasm begin to crest, but she was always too busy thinking about what she looked like, of what she should do next to make it better for him, so she'd get all jammed up. Like a roller coaster stalling out before the big, exciting drop. Dr. Dave didn't give her time to think. A bird circled overhead.

Everything went Tilt-A-Whirl.

And then Ariel shuddered against him, her legs quaking.

When it was over, he picked up a helmet and slapped it on her head. "All right, let's go." He clapped like a gym teacher, his face set in an unreadable expression. Like what had just happened was as casual as helping someone carry groceries to their car.

Ariel nodded enthusiastically, *I know who I am. I know what I want and I want to complete this rope course.* She felt dazed, like she'd been struck in the head, but rather than feeling stunned she suddenly felt more awake. Like she'd been asleep until this very moment.

She moved with a physical ease she hadn't felt before, and with Dr. Dave following behind her—cheering her on, guiding her legs into the right spots as they crossed zigzagging unstable bridges, climbed a giant ladder, and inched their away across a cargo net—Ariel finished the course. At the end, when she zip-lined down from a nerve-fraying height, her eyes went hot with tears because she genuinely felt victorious. Over what, she had no idea, but she decided that it didn't even matter because something had switched on inside her and was glowing. She looked up at Dr. Dave as they walked together back to the Sanctuary. Her gut was always a beehive of emotions, but right now it wasn't churning at all. She felt only one prevailing feeling, and that was gratitude toward Dr. Dave and how much she wanted to be transformed again and again.

CARMEN

Inside the foam block was a neatly condensed package of cocaine. A kilo? That was how cocaine was measured, wasn't it? Or if not a kilo, then just a shit-ton of cocaine.

Carmen turned on the tap, knelt next to the duffel bag, and rummaged through the rest of the blocks. There were ten heavy blocks hidden among other lighter, empty ones.

Her heart dipped into her stomach. *Oh my god.* Simon and Marie were drug dealers. These were not little baggies for personal use. She took the one she'd opened and hid it at the bottom of the bag, hoping they wouldn't notice.

She grabbed a plastic cup, filled it with water then turned the tap off, slowly and carefully. The tap made a metallic squeal. She gripped the edge of the counter, rearranged her features in the mirror so she didn't look so nervous.

When she opened the bathroom door, Marie was weaving down the hallway toward her. Her bad ankle was lifted and she was using the wall as a crutch and moving faster than Carmen would have expected.

She felt frozen as Marie approached. It was suddenly hard for her to breathe. Would she notice that she'd touched the duffel bag? Would she find the yoga block that she'd pried partway open? Carmen blinked and sucked in a breath.

"You shouldn't be up! I have water for you." Carmen put on her best, cheery home-care voice. A voice that would fit right in on Katie's old TV show.

She thrust the cup of water toward Marie at an unnatural distance. As if Marie were some coked-up monster about to snap down on her.

Her face was unreadable as she continued to approach. She looked past Carmen and into the bathroom. The hallway started to close in on Carmen as Marie made a quick assessment of the bathroom.

"*Merci.* I will be out in a moment," she said flatly. Took the cup of water and closed the bathroom door.

Carmen stood there, staring at the closed door. She strained to listen to Marie in the bathroom. The cupboard opened and then slammed shut. Beads of sweat gathered and rolled down her back. What should she do? Should she make a run for it? Nothing would scream *I found your cocaine* more than running away. The toilet flushed.

When the door opened again, Marie looked as if she'd freshened up. Her hair was brushed and there was a slight gloss on her lips that hadn't been there before.

"I waited to help you back to bed," Carmen said smoothly.

"You're making me feel old."

"You're not old. A sprained ankle is a sprained ankle." Marie smiled and leaned into her, and they shuffled toward the bed.

"What I really need is a glass of wine. I know it is early and explicitly forbidden, but what can I say? I'm Quebecoise and we need our wine." Marie gestured to the dresser, where there were a few bottles of red, and smiled.

Carmen walked over to the dresser and grabbed another cup.

"Pour one for yourself too," Marie called from the bed.

"I should probably go." Carmen knew she was acting stiff and awkward as she grabbed a Shiraz and unscrewed the cap, which she dropped. It skittered underneath the dresser. She started to get down on the floor to look for it.

"Oh, Carmen, please do not worry about it. Please, you must have a glass of wine with me. I do not want to drink alone. And you must now anyway, because you have lost the cap."

Act naturally. Deep breaths. Carmen poured a cup of wine for herself and stood near the bed. "Oh, come on, Carmen, sit down." Marie patted the empty space on the bed next to her.

Carmen sat down on the far edge of the bed. Her body practically coiled into a tight ball.

"You seem nervous. You don't have to be nervous with me. Relax for a moment." Marie reached over and touched her back. Carmen looked at her and felt an unsettling billow of attraction. She had always been attracted to dangerous women, and now here was Marie with her sun-bronzed legs—the good one bent at the knee, with a sheet twisted loose and pulled up between her legs. Her hooded eyes and that accent—it was like a fine mist against bare skin.

"Oh, yes, sure. I would like that." Carmen unnecessarily cleared her throat and reclined back onto the bed, stiff as a corpse.

"So, tell me, are you enjoying your girls' weekend?"

"Yes, for sure." Carmen took another sip of wine. It tasted so good after such a long bout of abstaining, which now seemed so pointless. What would Megan say right now? She'd probably start ripping up their contract, demanding the down payment back on Carmen's eggs.

"You are not very convincing."

"Well, it's not what I'd thought it would be." It certainly wasn't, especially now. Carmen was biting the inside of her mouth to stop herself from asking Marie dozens of questions, like an undercover cop gathering intel. She wanted to know how that cocaine ended up at this retreat. Who were Marie and Simon really? Surely they were not college professors with a yen for self-improvement.

"You mean this retreat or your friends?"

"Both. I love my friends, don't get me wrong, but we definitely have different expectations for this weekend."

"And what are your expectations, Carmen?" Marie leaned in closer, her good leg now touching Carmen.

"I don't have any for the retreat, that's the thing. I am here kind of like a support animal for my friend Katie."

Marie rewarded her with a twinkly laugh. "I am sure that's not true. And what about the tea? Are you looking forward to it?"

"No. Not really. I just can't imagine a tea being able to do all the things it claims to do." It couldn't be a coincidence that Marie and Simon were staying at a retreat that served up hallucinogenic tea. Maybe it was exactly the reason they stayed here. Delusional Dr. Dave was an ordained shaman, practicing his religious right to serve up DMT and therefore the Sanctuary was far less likely to be stormed by the DEA. Was that it?

"I think you will be pleasantly surprised." Marie reached out and caressed her cheek, then leaned over to her nightstand, opened the drawer, and pulled out a joint. "You want?" she asked, and wiggled it between her fingers.

"Apparently no one follows the rules about the tea and not mixing drugs and alcohol," Carmen said as she took the joint. Yes, yes. A little bit of weed would smooth her out. It hit her lungs fast and hard. It was much stronger than Katie's joint the previous night.

"I have had the tea a few times, and it never makes any difference what I do beforehand. It is not much of a weekend without wine, weed, and sex, is it?" Marie flicked her eyebrows, took the joint back, and inhaled.

"And an obstacle course," Carmen added, and laughed.

Marie gave her a long, lingering look. "If there's any question, please know my husband is not an obstacle." It hung there between them, this proposition. Smoke streamed from Marie's nose. She handed Carmen the joint again, and Carmen smiled, not sure what to say to that, so she took a long draw.

"You know what I wish I knew when I was your age?" Marie shifted the conversation.

"What?"

"It's that you can have everything you want in this world. You just need to stop at nothing to make it happen."

Carmen's mind shuffled through her problems. Her dad's Parkinson's. Her college dropout status. The end-of-the-month hustling to keep her siblings fed and clothed. The broken hot water tank. Filling the bath with water heated on the stove for her youngest siblings. Once, even taking a shortcut and washing their hair one by one in the stockpot before it cooled down.

"My dad has advanced Parkinson's." It just came out. As if she was holding her dad up as proof that thinking one can control their life with positive thoughts was pure delusion. Then nothing else came out. Her tongue felt thick and dead in her mouth. The room was getting hazy with smoke.

"Oh, I am so sorry about your father." Marie took her hand; her face was etched with sympathy and it was like getting into a warm bubble bath. She was also kind enough not to say anything more. "Do you want more wine?"

"I will get it." Carmen refilled their cups. This time she plopped back down into bed like Marie was an old friend.

"So, Carmen, do you have anyone special in your life?"

"Not currently. I don't have time." Another toke and sip of wine. Carmen's last girlfriend would have fit right into this place. She had actually suggested that Carmen's dad simply needed acupuncture, better vitamins (which she happened to sell), and to cut out gluten. It was a short-lived relationship.

"You should always make time for love." Marie butted out the joint, leaned in even closer, and touched her hair. Marie wanted to be kissed.

Carmen smiled at her. Her gut fluttered. She didn't know if it was the wine or the weed or the can-do teachings of the place, but a thought was taking form in her. She couldn't stop wondering how much that cocaine was worth.

It wouldn't be the worst thing to let this happen. She reached behind Marie's head and gently guided her closer. Her lips were soft and tasted like wine. Marie's hands efficiently roamed up and down Carmen's body. Their kiss intensified.

The jangle of a key. Simon stepped into the cottage. He stopped like he'd walked into a plate-glass window. Carmen broke apart from Marie and jolted out of the bed.

"Bonjour, Simon," Marie greeted her husband as she pulled up the strap of her tank top and pressed the back of her hand to her lips.

"I should go," Carmen said. She nodded hello at Simon, but kept her eyes averted as she tried to rush past him to the door.

"You don't need to run away on my account." He grabbed her by the arm, just above the elbow, a little too roughly for Carmen's liking. He looked her over and licked his lips.

"I have a spa appointment anyway," Carmen said, pointedly looking at Simon's hand. He removed his grip on her.

"Well then, we will see you later." He gave her a hungry smile and winked.

"Yes. See you soon." Carmen forced herself to smile back and keep her voice upbeat even though her instinct was to lunge for the door. As she exited the cottage, she kept a normal pace. *Don't run, don't run, don't run. They might be watching.*

She blinked into the hard sunlight, and sucked in a deep cleansing breath of woodsy air. Her heart stopped jumping and the panicky ringing in her ears disappeared.

By the time Carmen had made it back to her own room, she knew she wanted to steal the cocaine. All of it.

KATIE

Outside, they followed a THIS WAY TO THE POOL sign, hiking through waist-high grass. When they got past a few trees, they stood there for a disoriented moment. A chain-link fence was half-down and swaying in the wind. They could hear the music and echoing voices but the pool itself was nearly completely concealed by the long grass.

A shirtless, heavily tattooed guy popped up like a mole. He was dressed in cargo shorts and a bright red ball cap that had MAKE PLANET EARTH GREAT AGAIN stitched onto the front. He nodded and said, "Yo," as he walked by them like they belonged there.

"Are you Colton?" Katie asked. The shots of vodka she'd managed to suck down had hit her bloodstream and she was feeling braver.

"Nah, Colton's down there." He thumbed over his shoulder, eyed Ellie, then muttered to himself that all the pretty girls want Colton.

They saw the glint of the diving board railings first. Inside the pool, there were fifteen, maybe twenty people lying on towels or reclined on lawn chairs. Nearly every inch of the walls was spray-painted—and these were not penis rocket ships but an actual mural that made it clear there was some fine arts students among them. The music was coming from someone's phone hooked up to a large speaker. A grimy group-orgy feel hovered over the whole pool; a cluster of skinny kids were passing around a glass pipe. Katie scanned the pool looking for any sign of a braided-haired girl with the headband, but so many of them looked like Lily. There were so many headbands and bandannas, you could probably tie them together and successfully escape out of a prison window.

A guy was cooking something that looked—but didn't smell—like hot dogs on a camping stove. It was a never-ending pool party. A girl standing next to him noticed them first and pointed up.

"We're looking for a girl named Lily," Ellie tried, but the guy made it clear he couldn't hear her and waved them to come down. He whistled to another guy, who sat up, spilling the arms of two sleeping women off his chest. He shook his head, rubbed his eyes, looked up at them, and walked over to the ladder with a slow, deliberate swagger.

He waved at them to come down and then stood at the bottom of the ladder like he was going to spot them in case they fell. Katie looked down. Of course they were at the deep end, and without water, there was a big drop between the last rung in the ladder and the bottom of the pool. If they had to get away quickly, it would be next to impossible to get back up. Still, Katie started down the ladder.

The guy vise-gripped Katie's waist to help her off the last rung, even though she kept saying, "It's okay, I got it, I'm fine. Yeah, no, I'm good."

But the guy plopped her down like it was nothing. Under his artistically torn tank top, he had one of those tense, sinewy bodies that looked ready to pounce at any second.

Ellie stood at the edge of the pool. She looked hesitant, and Katie's shoulders tensed. What if Ellie left her down there? What if getting into this grimy pool was a line she wasn't going to cross for Katie? But then she grabbed hold of the railings, and Katie breathed again. Tank Top did the same thing with Ellie, winking at the guy by the Coleman.

"Are you Colton?" Katie asked tentatively, not sure how to approach her line of questioning now that Ellie had gone suddenly quiet. Katie wondered if she were claustrophobic or something.

"I am." He swiveled his head to move some of his foppish hair out of his eyes. He had blue eyes and chiseled cheekbones that gave him a preppy serial-killer look in spite of the grungy tank top. He offered a white, straight smile one could only achieve from being bound up in braces at some point. His parents had probably hoped he would use that winning smile in a boardroom and not to win over the ladies in an empty, spray-painted pool. He was maybe twenty years old, with a wispy attempt at the bushman beard his friends were sporting. "Are you new recruits?"

"Um, no. Actually, we're just wondering if one of your members— her name is Lily—is here?"

"One of our *members*?" He guffawed. His lips curled like burning paper, and he crossed his arms. "Members? I don't like that word. It's elitist. This isn't some country club; this is a movement." He sniffed. This coming from the guy who'd just asked if they were new recruits.

Right. Katie's showbiz childhood had left her with an acute ability to sniff out which people had been raised as too adorable to ever be wrong about anything. Colton would have been a cute baby. He was cute now. "Okay, well, her name is Lily, and we were told she was here."

"Yeah? Lily? Why are you looking for her?" He gave a noncommittal shrug, still flashing those salesman's teeth and those dimples embedded in his cheeks so deeply they looked like quotation marks. That would be hard, thought Katie, to have the sort of dimples that automatically made your smile look false. He shot a look in the direction of the speaker, and the music was cut. The sudden silence was eerie.

"No reason. We're just looking for her," Katie said, trying to sound casual.

"Does this have to do with Tamara?" He eyed them both. *Who is Tamara? What happened to her?*

"No. Just Lily—we're trying to find her."

"Where you ladies coming from anyway?"

"A retreat. Not too far from here." Ellie answered the question.

Colton sneered. "Oh, how privileged of you. And what does that accomplish? Spending your time and all that money on what? Self-reflection? Useless deprivation that results in nothing but to give yourself a pat on your own back? I can tell you both right now why you're not happy and then you can just give me your money."

Katie shrugged, unsure how to respond, and was going to ask about Lily again, but Colton cut her off.

"You're unhappy because *wellness* is a capitalist construct, and you're still trapped in the falsehood that you have time to work on yourself when the world around you is dying. You'll be happier when you're just trying to survive. That'll cost you five hundred bucks." Colton gave them a menacing grin and Katie wasn't sure if he really expected them to pay.

Katie blinked, nodded, and smiled. "Good to know. So, is someone named Lily here?" She started to describe Lily again.

"Why are you looking for her?"

"I don't . . . just because," Katie said before she could come up with something better.

"Pssht. Well, that's fucking sketchy. You don't know why you're looking for this Lily, and yet you want me to tell you where she is?" Two drunk-looking girls toddled toward Colton; one wrapped herself around him, while the other looked put out, pulled on her friend's tank top strap, and whined, "I thought we were going to pee together!"

Before she could stop herself, Katie started doing her nervous Chatty Cathy routine, trying to de-escalate a situation with a zinger. "Well, at least no one pees in the pool," she joked.

"Oh, you think you're funny, don't you? Wait a second. I think I know you. Where do I know you from?" He rested his hand on his chin and stroked his peach fuzz.

Ellie finally piped up. "We don't want any trouble. Lily's our friend, and we just want to make sure she's okay."

"Whoa, what the fuck? What's that supposed to mean? If she's here, she's okay. She's better than okay; she's making a difference. What are you two doing to make the world a better place?" Everyone was listening now. Colton took a step forward, tilting his head down. His eyes flitted between them and then rested on Katie in what she knew from drama class as the Kubrick Stare. "What, no answer? Because if you're not part of the of solution then you're part of the problem." Colton looked like he was just getting started.

"Let's go," Katie whispered to Ellie.

"They have an Escaaaaalaaaaade." It was the shirtless guy they'd passed earlier, bellowing down into the pool like a glee club singer. He dropped down the ladder and smiled at Colton as if they'd just won a raffle.

"It's not mine." Ellie put her hand to her chest. Katie shot her a look. *What the fuck?* Ellie caught herself. "I just meant, it's a rental."

But Shirtless was already moving into the deep end, announcing over and over that they had an Escalade.

Colton nodded, made a mock dropped-jaw face. "An Escalade! Oh my, aren't you a pair of little piggies." And then he snapped his fingers. "Oh my god, I just figured it out. Of course you're a piggy. My older sister went as you one Halloween." Colton pointed right at Katie's face, doubled over with obnoxious haw-haw laughter. "Slutty Shelby Spade."

Katie remembered the year the slutty Shelby Spade costume became popular. In the final season of *Shelby Spade*, her breasts had ballooned out to a D cup and had to be *minimized* (the polite wardrobe lady's word for binding her with a tensor). She'd started to look too porny in her trench coat and pink fedora.

One of the girls on Colton's arms repeated, "Who . . . who is that? Who?"

"Huh, cool," Katie said meekly. "Okay, well, it looks like our friend isn't here. We should get going." She really wanted to leave. It was scalding in the pool without any shade, and any second someone was going to get the idea to do something nasty to her for the notoriety of it or at the very least demand her PIN and then shoot her in the head when they found out she only had a $500 limit on ATM withdrawals.

The shirtless guy was now suddenly shouldering past them again with a small crew behind him. They ran up the side of the pool like they were doing parkour and were up and out in one easy movement.

Katie had a vision of returning to a stripped, undrivable car. She tugged on Ellie. "We'd better go. We need to go." Katie went for the ladder and jumped at the lowest rung and tried to hoist herself up but could not gain any footing on the wall.

Colton let out a nasty squeal of laughter. "Oh my god, look at her. You're so soft. You're a soft piggy."

The girls started to make horrible oinking noises. "Yeah, that's right, run away, piggies."

Ellie came up behind her and heaved her up. Ellie got up easily on her own because she was in better shape and at least half a foot taller than Katie.

When they got back to the SUV, people were rummaging through it. The shirtless guy came out with a box of granola bars that Ariel had left in the back seat, an unopened bag of chips, and the mini chocolate bars Katie thought of as road trip food. Someone else had pocketed the change Ellie had tossed in the console. The woman from the cabin was crawling around the back, looking wild-eyed. They even took their half-finished bottles of water.

"Thanks for the carbon tax." Shirtless flicked his eyebrows at them. Once their vehicle had been picked clean, Katie and Ellie managed to jump inside, and Katie locked the doors.

Ellie's hands jittered around the ignition, finally getting the key in. She pulled into reverse and hit the gas, and they took off.

ELLIE

"What are we gonna do?" Katie squawked as they hit the highway.

Well, at least she was finally worried about Lily now and not keening out *Richard!* at regular intervals. So far, she'd cried more about that damn dog than a *human being*.

Ellie's shoulders were all knotted up, and she had to aim the AC vent at her face.

"What are we going to do?" Katie whined again. *We.* Of course it was *we* now. At this point, wouldn't thanking her be the polite thing for Katie to do? Rather than drawing her further in as an accessory after the fact of her alleged murder? And was Lily really dead?

"There isn't a body," Ellie reminded Katie. This was the biggest glitch in all of this, wasn't it? The reason Ellie didn't go hollering down to Dr. Dave to call the police but instead put the knife in her drawer. A knife that had *her* DNA and *her* fingerprints on it. Katie didn't even see it either, what Ellie had done for her. How she'd incriminated herself—become an accessory after the fact. Not a single thank-you!

Unless Lily's body had been discovered while they were gone. Ellie tightened her grip on the wheel.

"But the *blood*. There was *blood*," Katie moaned. "Why would a knife be in our room? And why would there be blood on it? What if something *did* happen and I hurt Lily, and this girl just hobbled off into the woods somewhere and fucking died? What if I killed someone?" Katie started knocking her head against the back of the headrest—not the window, where it would actually hurt, Ellie noted.

These hand pats and reassuring phrases was getting exhausting. Ellie felt a twinge of pity toward Katie—how tiring performing all the time must have been. She glanced at the dash clock. It was almost two o'clock; there were less than forty-eight hours left in this weekend, and it would all be over. If you're going to go into darkness, do so quickly. None of this had felt quick.

Since meeting Nate, since living so close to Katie, Ellie's life had been a helix of love and hate, pleasure and aggravation, and she couldn't believe how exhausting these wildly disparate emotions could be.

She'd almost lost it when Katie had started prattling on about that *Shelby Spade* episode, her voice like nails on a chalkboard. She'd had to fight the urge to wrap her hands around her neck and scream, *You spoiled, privileged bitch! Look where you are! Take some responsibility for what you've done!* To hear Katie sputtering as she finally, finally shut up for good. Ellie stayed there in this fantasy a tick too long.

Ellie took in a calming breath and tried not to cringe as she reached over and shook Katie's shoulder. Like a marathon runner with the finish line in sight, she conjured up her endurance. "You're thinking the worst right now, when the fact is, we don't know anything. We really don't."

Katie sucked in her bottom lip. "Well, we know that there was a bloody knife in our room." Her voice was so tweaked with fear it could shatter glass.

That was the thing with Katie—tell her what she wanted to hear and she still argued. Not because she wanted you to stop but because she wanted you to reassure her better, harder. It was like having a personal trainer screaming in your face for another sit-up, squeezing it out of you while your muscles shook. Ellie also didn't fail to notice that the knife in Katie's bed was now the knife in *our room*.

"Right, but maybe it wasn't blood. Or maybe it was from meat. A steak? Who knows how many phantom stains I've spotted in hotels and hostels when I traveled with my parents." Ellie knew this was a loose, lame reason, and she simply waited for Katie's shrill reaction, which came spewing out of her right on cue.

"It's a vegan retreat, Ellie!" Katie crossed her arms, looking pissy that Ellie didn't have a better explanation for the blood. "And there was a knife too, which isn't at all like a phantom stain and a rogue used condom."

Ellie sucked in another breath. She knew it was bad, but it was too tempting to jab Katie a bit in her panic button and listen to her manic little heart swirl around in her chest like a trapped bird. *Maybe you shouldn't calm down,* is what she wanted to say. *You should be panicking that you murdered someone, because it certainly looks that way, and yet here you are, wanting me to tell you it's going to be A-OK.* "I'm sorry. Sorry." She rubbed her eyes. "I'm tired. Look, I don't know what else to say or what other comfort I can offer you. Lily was clearly a huge fan of Shelby Spade and you weren't very receptive to her admiration. Maybe that was a factor in her decision?"

"What? Like so unreceptive I killed her?"

Ellie sighed. "You know that's not what I mean. What I am trying to say is that Lily might have left just because she wanted to. The retreat simply wasn't for her and she decided to go home early. She left on her own accord and the knife, the blood, is a separate mystery. If it'll make you feel better, we can continue to look for her in the woods."

"You think so?" Katie sniveled and started to gnaw on her knuckles.

"I do, Katie. I really do." Ellie felt like she were throwing a bowl of spaghetti at the wall to see what stuck so that Katie could keep her wits about her. She couldn't manage her if she was completely freaking out. "I mean, we don't know a thing about this girl. Happy Harry or whoever only assumed she was part of that crew by how she looked. And when you think about it, she hardly said anything personal about herself in our sharing circle."

Ellie could hear Katie's breathing calm. "That's true. You're right." She nodded. "Yeah, I mean, she could be anywhere. And plus, it's not like, if something happened to her, how could I hide a body in my sleep? It's not possible."

"No, it's not," Ellie said back in a voice that was trying too hard to be convincing, but it still seemed to satisfy Katie because she reached over and cranked up some chirpy pop song, and Ellie thought she was finally going to be quiet. That they could drive for a little while and Ellie could have a chance to think about her next move.

"But the *blood*. There was *blood*." Katie switched the radio off again. Ellie's mind flashed to leaning over, opening the passenger side door, and pushing Katie out of the SUV. She'd had enough. She needed some time away from her, before she did something drastic.

"You know, and this is just an idea, but on the itinerary there was a self-hypnosis workshop, so why not ask Dr. Dave to perform hypnosis on you? Or teach you how to do it yourself. Maybe it will help you remember what happened last night."

Katie didn't even consider it. She immediately started shaking her head. "No, thanks. That would seem too much like seeing a shrink, and I fucking hate shrinks. I've been to a few of them already, remember?"

"Yeah, but, Katie, you're not going to feel okay until you know you didn't do anything violent, and I can't think of anything more we can do ourselves other then to look for Lily, unless . . ."

"Unless what?"

"We call the police and have them look into it."

"Do you think we should call the police?" Katie gave her a pleading look. A part of Ellie wanted to say yes. What if they called the police right now? What would happen, exactly? She could see Katie getting dragged from the Sanctuary. Newsfeeds would start churning again, hungry after the Twitter debacle. There'd be a TMZ shot set on repeat of Katie trying to cover her once-adorable face with some kind officer's windbreaker as she was cuffed and shuffled inside the station. Ellie would need to give a statement. Nate would arrive and start pacing as his future bride and his sister were interrogated. Poor, poor Nate.

"I don't think we need to, at least not yet. Not until we know more," Ellie said primly, and before Katie could question what the *more* was that they needed to know, Ellie kept talking. "That's why I suggested letting Dr. Dave pick your brain a bit. I'm just hopeful there is a reasonable explanation for the knife. Something we might even laugh at down the road." A few beats of silence.

Katie's lips flickered. "Right. Okay, I'll talk to Dr. Dave, then. See if he can shake anything loose. But what if I tell him I did do it? What if I confess?" The skin on Katie's too-white legs puckered.

"If that happens, Katie, Dr. Dave can't say anything anyway because of patient-client privilege." Katie wasn't going to make some coherent confession anyway. How could she?

Katie nodded and whispered, "Right, right."

They could hear the frenetic hammering before they even pulled into the driveway. Out on the front lawn, under the heat of the afternoon sun, were all the retreaters, beating on drums.

Katie flung herself out of the vehicle and stalked off to interrupt Dr. Dave, who was standing in the center of the drum circle, shirtless, veins flickering across his chest as he instructed the group on how to whale on a drum.

Dr. Dave nodded, motioned for Naomi to take over, whispering in her ear as he handed over his drumsticks. Ellie wondered if he added that this was his big chance; maybe he could accomplish what even Oprah couldn't with Lindsay Lohan—the spiritual rescue of a dithering child star.

By the time Ellie picked up her own drumsticks, Dr. Dave was giving Katie a warm, shiny smile as he led her back to the Sanctuary.

Ellie flopped down between Paula, who was weeping as she weakly smacked her sticks, and Anthony, who had to keep pausing his jackhammering to push up his smudged glasses that hung just off the tip of his sweaty nose. Ariel popped her head around him to shoot her a cool look. She waved her drumstick hello in return. Naomi gave instructions to "freestyle your emotions."

A few minutes into drumming, a rabid energy took over. Ellie was angry, and to just openly batter something felt intensely therapeutic. She could feel everything loosen up inside of her. She whipped her sticks up and down as a carousel of childhood memories started their slow turn. The more she hammered down, the faster it spun until she started smashing them away. Until her mind went blank and she was completely lost in the frenzy of the discordant noise.

Time passed.

When she looked up again, only she and Anthony were left, and he wasn't drumming anymore. He was just watching her, with a glazed look on his face. "Wow, looks like you worked out some serious shit there."

She was breathless and hot. She wiped at the dripping sweat falling off her forehead with the back of her hand.

Something caught her eye. A moving shadow up on the slope next to the front of the house. The sun was hitting her eyes, and for one dizzying second, she only saw a blob of black. But the shape was wrong. It moved forward. Seemed to look right at her. It took her a second. And then she knew even before her eyes adjusted. She felt sucker punched in the gut. Her body actually bent forward.

Oh my god.

What is he doing here?

ARIEL

Ariel had been feeling as moony as a schoolgirl.

It was lunch, and she'd planned to spill everything that had happened with Dr. Dave at the rope course. Have a classic gabfest, with Katie and Carmen prodding her for details. Ariel would play coy, dole them out slowly, luxuriating in their undivided attention, until they were so worked up they practically forced it out of her. It would have been perfect, since Ellie stayed behind to go ballistic on a drum (*weird*) and she'd have her friends to herself.

But that brimming-with-excitement feeling was gone.

Katie had made a beeline for Dr. Dave the moment the drumming circle started up. She asked for some kind of treatment, and Ariel had to watch as Dr. Dave nodded and touched Katie's shoulder.

They turned and walked back to the house together.

Ariel's gut turned to acid.

Now she was sitting with Carmen, and it wouldn't be the same to tell just her. She would either shrug and say, "Cool," or—worse—go on some tirade that Dr. Dave was abusing his powers and preying on vulnerable women. And then Ariel would have to defend something that was pure and beautiful. Better than any spa treatment. Up until Katie left with Dr. Dave, she felt like she was floating in a bubble. Buoyed by cranked-up self-esteem and renewed feelings of hopefulness. Her life back in Shakopee might be a mess now but there was always room for change. "She's just in one of her moods. I wouldn't worry about it," Carmen said, taking Ariel's inability to eat as a reaction to Katie's absence. "What do you think this patty is made out of?" Carmen waved the piece of compressed vegetables on the end of her fork at Ariel and started doing a mock wine-tasting shtick. "I am tasting hints of elderberry undercut with smoky notes and black tar."

A spindly woman Ariel had never seen before burst through the French doors off the kitchen and onto the patio.

She was dressed in a powder-blue turtleneck, though it was far too hot for it. A gold necklace was arranged over her shirt. She gripped her handbag like someone would yank it off her shoulder. When she spoke, she had the husky voice of a longtime whiskey drinker.

Naomi bounced up out of her chair. Naomi didn't sit; she never leaned all the way against the back of the chair—she perched. Ariel noticed this and wasn't leaning back in her chair either.

"Hellooo?"

"Yes, hello. Are you in charge?"

"No one is *in charge* here." Naomi offered up a serene smile, her eyes shiny.

The woman eyed Naomi for a beat. "Right. Well, I'm here to pick up Rachel. Could you tell me what room she's in? Or where to find her? I'm not getting any answers out of that one." The woman thumbed over her shoulder at a staff member who looked stricken that she'd done something horribly wrong by letting this woman in.

"Rachel? There's no Rachel staying here."

"What do you mean she isn't here? I'm s'pposed to pick her up. She called me last night to come get her." The woman frowned.

"Sorry, we don't have a Rachel staying with us. We had a Lily, but she isn't here either."

The woman stood there, looking lost. When Ariel heard at breakfast that Lily was gone, she was thrilled. There was no way she could have fully relaxed with that loony lurking around.

"Rachel was calling herself *Lily?*" The woman offered a quick description: short, tightly braided hair, usually wearing a bandanna.

"The person you're describing certainly sounds like our Lily."

The woman muttered something under her breath. "Fine. Okay. So where is Lily, then?"

"As I mentioned, Lily decided to leave us." Naomi smiled with all the pleasantness of a flight attendant. A cloud covered the sun and made the patio suddenly go gray.

"Leave you? When? How did she leave? This place is in the middle of nowhere, and she doesn't have a car." The woman scoffed.

"Probably the same way she got here?" Naomi ventured.

"I don't think so. She said a friend paid for her to take an Uber here, and she called for me to pick her up. And I don't at all understand how she is even here. She doesn't have a pot to piss in, never mind being able to afford this place."

"Who are you, exactly?"

"I'm her *sponsor*. She called me in distress last night saying she had to break into a cabinet to get her phone, because you people took it away and locked it up." The woman cast shifty glances at everyone on the patio.

"We didn't take—"

"Look, I find it really hard to believe Rachel would just take off on foot. At least not *willingly*." The woman jutted out her chin.

"What is that supposed to mean?"

"Whaddya call this place again? The Sanctuary? When Rachel called, she said she was afraid. She said this place was a cult! And we all know what happens when people try to leave a cult."

A dark look ran over Naomi's face. She blinked, kept her eyes closed a second too long. Took a deep breath through her nostrils, released it through her mouth. "Do you know that a single ayahuasca ceremony can cure someone's addiction? Unlike years and years in a twelve-step program."

The sponsor squinted at her. "There's no cure for addiction!

Promising a cure sounds exactly like the kind of garbage a cult ped-
dles to vulnerable people."

Naomi's face stayed calm as a pond. If Ariel cracked her skull
open right now, she'd discover that Naomi's brain probably glowed,
and would be emitting "om" at a high-pitched frequency.

Naomi smiled even more brightly at the angry-looking woman.
She spoke in even more measured beats, like she was mentally
hitting a space bar between each word. "We are not a cult. The Sanctuary is an institute of wellness. Lily had nothing to fear beyond
confronting the transformative experience we offer here. She simply
wasn't ready to reset and become her best self, and while we've never
had a guest leave early before, we would never prevent one from
checking out whenever they wanted to. Now, I wish you and Lily all
the best." Naomi pressed her hands together in a prayer pose.

The woman made a scoffing noise. "Yeah, yeah. Look, it makes
no sense that she would leave when she knew I was on my way.
She was upset about something happening here. I am not leaving
without Rachel."

"And if you're really her sponsor, then I'm sure you know that
asking the same thing over and over and expecting a different answer is the definition of insanity. I'm sorry, but Lily or Rachel is not
here."

"You're insane," the woman barked back, crossed her arms. "I
don't believe she just left. Not willingly. Not at night, not in these
woods."

"Well, believe it. For the final time, she checked out. I am sorry
you needlessly made the drive, but Lily must have been picked up
by someone else. Now, I must ask you to leave before you corrupt
the wellness experience for our other guests."

"I am calling the police." The woman's eyes were bugged out
now, and as she whipped around to leave, she bumped into a chair.
Her face was suddenly skittish as she pointed. "I'm calling the police," she repeated before taking off.

"That was weird," Ariel said, not really thinking about it.

Her head was too overrun with images of Dr. Dave and Katie.

What kind of treatment was he offering her?

Was he enjoying it? Was she? Did Dr. Dave like treating Katie more than her?

What were they doing?

CARMEN

Carmen was almost certain, thanks to a certain Netflix show, that each of those bricks was worth at least $30,000. If she had her phone, she could Google it to be sure. But even if she was off by five grand, *even ten grand,* it still translated into a shitload of money. Money that would change her life. Cure her sob story, take her out of the pool of losers. She wouldn't have to hit Katie up for money ever again and then spend days desperately refreshing her bank account over and over, waiting for Katie to get around to transferring it. She could hire someone to look after her brothers and sisters. Pay for her dad's medication to keep his Parkinson's under better control. And best of all, she could quit her job wiping asses and go back to medical school.

And if not med school exactly, then back to her shining, bright future that was supposed to defy those grim statistics for smart, poor kids like herself. In high school, Carmen memorized the stats like they were a minefield. She believed that doing so meant she could defy them all. If one came from poverty, there was a 70 percent chance that person would never be accepted into college; she'd easily leaped past that one. If accepted, there was a 40 percent chance she'd never even show up for the first day; she'd shown up and kept showing up for three full years of undergrad studies in biochemistry. This was followed by a 60 percent chance she'd never graduate and BOOM—that was the statistic that blew her chances of eluding intergenerational poverty. She was facedown in the dirt with less than a year left to go on her undergrad degree. An unfinished degree meant nothing at all.

She'd go get a trade. That's what she'd do. She was over the academic loftiness of her early twenties—now she'd want to see a quicker return on her investment and become a plumber or an electrician. She'd develop some apps.

It was the first time Carmen felt this; something like hope. Aspiration. Like the rest of her life wasn't going to be a closed circuit that looped round and round the same crappy track. Crashing and burning into the same obstacles, over and over because nearly everything about you was determined by the kind of family you were born into, and Carmen was born into a family of thieves. Her earliest memories were of her mother stuffing frozen meat into Carmen's winter parka, which she was usually wearing long out of season. The skin on her back, chest, and stomach would be pockmarked with frostbite, but at least she had a steak to look forward to. In middle school she carried on the tradition and did the usual shoplifting—clothing, sneakers, and copious amounts of makeup from CVS—anything to keep up the appearance that she wasn't poor. In college, it got worse, among all those trust fund kids and Katie Manning, but she never felt bad doing it. She only stole from a *store*, not from *people*. There was a difference.

Things changed when she started working as a home-care aide. Once it was obvious the patient she was caring for wasn't going to live beyond the week, she pocketed their remaining painkillers and sold them to a skeezy guy named Tommy who lived down the street from her. She didn't like to think of herself as a bad person, but a good person driven by circumstance to do bad things.

If she did manage to steal the cocaine (and it was a big *if*), sell it (Tommy would know how to move it), and have all that money, this would be some wellness journey.

She had watched Simon and Marie's faces when Lily's sponsor was demanding to see her, but they were unreadable. Of course it had to be a *sponsor*. Of course Lily had to be a recovering addict.

Carmen had to think that maybe Simon and Marie had Lily in their cottage as well. That Lily also discovered the cocaine and tried to make off with it, and they murdered her.

Because clearly, Simon and Marie were not average drug mules, haphazardly smuggling condoms full of drugs up their orifices. Their cover was smart and systematic, and if they were acting, they never broke character. They sailed back and forth over the border by flashing receipts of their stay at the retreat, their glowing skin, and their "live, laugh, love" demeanor. Simon even said so during orientation, that the border patrol just waved them through. (Which now sounded like bragging.)

"I wonder what Katie needed to talk to Dr. Dave about," Ariel huffed.

"I am going to take a wild guess here, and say it's probably something to do with her wellness journey," Carmen said, trying to be funny. But for some reason this made Ariel's bottom lip droop.

"How many of Dr. Dave's videos did you really watch before you came here?"

Carmen eyed her, glimpsing a fervor that hadn't been there yesterday.

Ariel aggressively stirred her water. The lemon wedge swirled like something caught in a tornado. "You know, Dr. Dave really does have some positive messages."

"What is he saying that I can't buy on a fake weathered plaque at Urban Barn?" Ariel flinched, and Carmen wished she hadn't said it.

"You're so close-minded. There are gateways in our bodies, y'know." Ariel took in a big gulp of breath that meant she was gearing up for a big spiel that Carmen wasn't in the mood to listen to, so she reached over and squeezed her friend's hand.

"Ariel, I think it's wonderful that you're getting something out this place and when Monday comes, if you can manifest your thoughts into reality, then all power to you." Wasn't that what any successful person had to do? Think about something, come up with a plan, and then put it into action? Even making breakfast required those same steps.

"I appreciate that." Ariel sniffed. Carmen let her hand go and changed the subject.

"So what do you think happened to Lily or Rachel—what do you think her real name is?"

"Who cares? She gave me bad vibes the first time I saw her." Ariel carefully sipped her water. Carmen had never heard Ariel talk about *vibes* before. She gave her friend a closer look. There was something different about her. She was pink-cheeked, almost feverish and anxious looking. It was the same unsettling look she got when she fell in "love." It was like her world halted. Her vision seemed to narrow to a pinprick, fixed only on the object of her affection.

"So much drama." Marie rolled the *r* in drama. She stopped at their table as she passed with Simon, bending down and giving Carmen a dewy peck on her cheek. "Thank you again, my savior, my nurse."

Carmen's cheeks went hot. She glanced over quickly at Ariel to see if she was noticing and it was clear that she was by her questioning look. "How is your ankle?" Carmen asked.

"Getting better each minute, thanks to you. Naomi said she will do some Reiki for me later, so I will hopefully be healed by the end of the day." Marie was looking glazed, like she'd maintained her buzz from this morning.

"Well, I wouldn't hold my breath on that," Ariel muttered.

Simon and Marie sat down without asking, with all the confidence of the cool kids in a high school cafeteria. Simon was wearing a fitted black-and-white-striped cotton shirt; they checked off what the French looked like in Carmen's head. He looked more like an aging rock star than a professor, or did her perception just change now that she knew what was in his cottage?

Simon nuzzled his wife, but his eyes drifted to Carmen. "This one. I have to watch her. She's a klutz." Marie responded in French and they laughed before moving on to talk about a house they were building just south of Montreal.

"I wanted something rustic and quaint, but my husband here has been carried away, and now we're building a mansion. Men! They always need it to be bigger."

Simon grinned and squeezed her arm. "You'll enjoy it once it's done, *ma poussinette*. Our friends would call us wellness junkies, but look at us now. It was always our dream to live in the countryside and it's *manifesting*."

Carmen forced herself to smile. *I think you're both leaving out a few illegal steps of your mental manifestation of a country home.* A country home! It sounded so ostentatious. All Carmen wanted was a working water heater, a front window, and meds for her dad.

"That sounds wonderful." Carmen shook her head with fake wonder.

"And how was your spa treatment?" Marie asked.

"You went to the spa without me?" Ariel, clamping her hand down on her chest, sounded outraged. Carmen almost winced, her mind screaming, *Shut up, Ariel!*

"I did, but then I realized I'd mixed up the time." Ariel tried to say something but Carmen blatantly talked over her. "It's so hard without a phone to keep everything straight, y'know? I didn't realize how dependent I was on it. How are you all coping?" She aimed the question at Simon and Marie.

"We aren't dependent on phones at all, we're a different generation. We talk around the dinner table and tell each other about our day. We try to remember things with our minds or write them down with pen and paper. And I would never forget a spa appointment, it's too important!" Marie waved her hands up in the air dramatically and laughed.

Simon glanced down at this watch. "Speaking of, we have an appointment soon."

"What time are you going?" Carmen asked, speaking way too

rapidly. "I just meant, are you having a couple's massage because it seems like there's only one masseuse and I was thinking of going—" All Carmen wanted to know was when Simon and Marie would be out of their cottage.

Simon studied Carmen with a certain amount of amusement. *He thinks he's the one making me nervous, like I'm a little ball of repressed sexual desire and that's why I ran away from his offer. For once this kind of masculine delusion was working in my favor.* She looked down and shifted uncomfortably in her seat.

"I thought we could all do the hot tub as soon as Katie is done with Dr. Dave. I wonder what's taking so long?" Ariel craned her neck, like she expected Katie to show up on the patio any moment. Or was willing her to.

"Yes, the hot tub is luxurious. I recommend the deep tissue massage and the salt rub treatment. I always get both when I come to the Sanctuary and my skin never feels softer. Feel my skin." Marie reached out and Carmen ran her fingers up her forearm.

"So soft," Carmen muttered and as she drew her hand back, she knocked over her nearly empty glass of water. "Oh, shoot." Carmen set the glass upright, and sopped up the little puddle on the table with a cloth napkin.

"You seem anxious." Marie stared at her through her cat's-eye sunglasses.

"I do? Oh, no, well, I guess that woman showing up here was a little unsettling," Carmen stammered.

"You don't think we all inadvertently joined a cult, do you?" Simon flicked his eyebrows at her and chuckled.

A loud thwacking noise suddenly filled the air. Dr. Dave had referred several times to the cathartic therapy of "hacking shit up," and it looked like Max was taking his turn with the ax. He stood, legs wide, lined the ax up to a log, and then brought it down fast and angrily like he was hitting the strongman tower at a carnival, the log splitting with a furious crack, its pieces flying in different directions.

"No." Carmen rolled her eyes. "It is odd, though, that Lily would just leave so suddenly." She watched Simon and Marie's faces very closely, looking for a flicker of guilt or even murderous glee. But if they were sociopaths, they'd show no emotion. Didn't she read something once that sociopaths blink less than the average person? Or was it more? She couldn't remember.

"She must have been picked up," Marie chimed optimistically. "There's no way she would have walked out of here, even to meet her ride by the highway."

"Yes, many bad things can happen in the woods." Simon sighed, like the topic was boring him. He didn't blink once. He stood to leave.

"Well, we all know she can start a fire, so I think she'll be just fine," Ariel sniped.

KATIE

"Come on down to my office; we can talk there." Dr. Dave led Katie down a hall just off the kitchen.

Here everything was dark walnut paneling. The floors were scuffed and scratched. There was a wall of built-in bookshelves, the kind one could easily imagine sliding open to hidden passageways.

A fireplace, blackened with ash. On the mantel was a display of all Dr. Dave's diplomas and certificates; front and center was his shaman certificate, issued by a Brazilian church in Brooklyn.

"I guess you could say this is my man cave." Dr. Dave forced out a chuckle and flicked on the light, a dim but elaborate chandelier in the middle of a jaundice-stippled ceiling, the sort that shook in movies when a poltergeist wanted to be noticed. Why was she feeling like she was on a stage set?

"It's nice. Very, um, Sigmund Freud." Katie smiled hard. She was getting the same fast heartbeats she always did before a pap test or anything to do with doctors. She was nervous. An anxiety attack was budding in her throat. Whenever she felt this way, everything seemed to flatten out until her surroundings felt fictional.

"Hmmm." Dr. Dave gave her a pitying look. A feeling of complete unreality descended over her. Could this entire place, everything that was happening, just be some kind of hard-core intervention? That any second, her friends were going to jump in to read tear-streaked letters, followed by her mom and Nate? Lily would be revealed at the end, alive, but as a cautionary tale on how drinking and partying leads to dead girls. Which would also mean she hadn't really killed her last fan.

Please let it be that, please let it be just that. But of course not—the one time she wanted an intervention and it couldn't be an intervention.

"Anyway, please have a seat." Dr. Dave gestured to an overly tufted brown leather couch as he moved behind his ornate desk. "So, we missed you this morning at drumming." He rested his chin on his fist and made a sad face. Katie hated when people did this—made general statements to avoid asking an outright question and yet still expected an answer.

"Oh, well, we were just really into our solitude and walking and lost track of time."

"Yeah? I figured that, when I saw you girls drive up, that you must still be out on your meditative walk." Dr. Dave chuckled in a way that annoyed Katie. "But hey, no judgments. You're not prisoners here or anything. We just want you to get the most out of the retreat, that's all."

Katie didn't say anything; she just wanted to get to the point. Get this whole thing over with. Dr. Dave continued to make small talk about drumming and how it worked out his shoulder muscles better than pretty much anything else. He rotated each shoulder as proof.

"I want to be hypnotized. Like, in the traditional sense."

"All right. Okay. I can do that. But I would also like to teach you how to do self-hypnosis, because you know what? You can pretty much hypnotize yourself to do anything, be anyone, if you master the skill. Sky's the limit on achievement and personal modification. The possibilities are endless."

Katie's eyes slid over to the diplomas on Dr. Dave's mantel, and she realized she didn't recognize a single college or university.

"Sure, that sounds good. Are you going to put a shirt on?" Katie asked. Dr. Dave was still shirtless from drumming and made no attempt to cover himself up.

"Ha! You're right. Man, oh, man. I didn't even notice." Dr. Dave stood and did a quick stretch, the ample hair in his armpit springing out like a forest scene in a pop-up book. His back muscles rippled.

He pulled open a closet door with a crystal knob, revealing a mix of glaring white shirts, each hanging equidistantly apart. Katie looked away as he slid on a cotton white V neck that made his tan a rich copper. When he sat back down, chair squeaking, he distinctly smelled like Tide and not some scentless organic detergent as Katie would have expected. A quip started to build on her tongue about how he kept his phosphate use in the closet, but it fizzled out. Brief as an electric shock.

"What exactly are you hoping hypnosis will do for you?" Dr. Dave rubbed his hands together like he was warming them up. Katie noticed that the veins around his bottom eyelids were puckered.

"Just, um . . ." How to start? How much should she say? Did the doctor-patient thing *really* hold up at a *wellness retreat*? "Well, it's a sleep thing; I have trouble sleeping. Most nights. Probably every night. And I want to sleep better."

"Even here?" He made a hurt expression.

"Yes. Even here."

"Huh. Well, what kind of sleep issues are you having, Katie? You haven't really been specific. Are you having difficulty falling asleep, or can you fall asleep but are unable to stay asleep?"

"I sleepwalk."

"Oh. Sleepwalking. Huh." He nodded, taking some time to think about it. "Well, sleepwalking is basically being able to perform a series of complex tasks while still in a REM state. There are a few causes of sleepwalking. Often, if someone is sleep-deprived in some way, he or she will have difficulty fully waking if they are suddenly triggered awake by a noise or a touch, even if they have to go to the bathroom."

Katie blinked, and held back from saying, *Yeah, I know, dickwad; I'm the one who sleepwalks.* Instead, she nodded politely.

"Right. But I want to know something I might have done while I was sleepwalking." Then, because she thought that sounded too suspicious on its own, she added, "And what's causing it and hopefully a cure."

"Well, y'know, Western doctors will give you some bullshit about sleep apnea or overactive bladder or restless leg syndrome. They'll give you a condition and hand out some pills, but what does that tell you?" He wiggled his eyebrows at her. "Absolutely nothing. Maybe a pill will mask the problem, but it won't cure it."

Katie wasn't really sure what the difference was if it stopped her from sleepwalking, but so far, she hadn't found one; antidepressants hadn't helped, and muscle relaxants didn't, either. Ambien made it worse.

The only thing she could consistently rely on was the tranquilizing properties of alcohol—and no, she wasn't just giving herself an excuse to get tipsy every night.

"But sleepwalking is caused by stress, man. You need to meditate, to get your head straight." Dr. Dave tapped a finger to his temple. Apparently, even in this setting, Dr. Dave was still going to sound like he was doing slam poetry at some campus bar.

"Right. I know meditation is the cure-all, but I was hoping to remember—" Katie was about to say, *What exactly I fucking did last night while sleepwalking. Did I kill my last fan?* But Dr. Dave cut her off.

"I understand. You want to know why it started in the first place. You want an answer because that stress was probably caused by some buried trauma, and the sleepwalking is a symptom of that, or what we psychiatrists refer to as a protective dissociative mechanism."

"Exactly." Katie looked around the room, trying to come up with a vague but sensible reason. She felt a burst of self-loathing that she was even there, needing to ask to be hypnotized. Only she could fuck up a wellness retreat this badly. For a second, she worried she was going to cry.

"When did you last sleepwalk?"

Katie wasn't going to admit it had happened last night. "Not long ago, like last week. Yes, that's my freshest sleepwalking incident, and working my way backward makes sense to me." She immediately regretted lying. If Katie had done something horrible, her entire defense would be that she was asleep for it and so not responsible. And now Dr. Dave could refute all of that; tell some stern-looking jury that Katie said she didn't sleepwalk at the Sanctuary at all.

Ellie better be right, that this session with Dr. Dave was confidential.

"That's really insightful, Katie. To work backward. You're lost and you're trying to find your way back by *retracing your somnolent steps*." More overly enthusiastic nodding. She felt like Dr. Dave might actually reach over and pat her on the head. "Luckily, you're in the right place. Okay, well, let's get started. Lie back. I just want to say, if you find this helpful—especially in conjunction with the tea— please give us a shout-out on any of your social media platforms."

"I will. In fact, I've already mentioned the Sanctuary on my Instagram account." She was getting that tingle of a hidden agenda, and any second she was going to bolt.

Dr. Dave's eyes lit up. "That's great. Yeah, how many followers do you have, anyway? It must be quite a lot."

"I'm not sure," Katie answered without a wisp of sincerity. She had exactly 115.5 thousand followers left when she signed in yesterday. A third of what she had had before the tweet.

"Well, I do appreciate it. Also at the end of the month, we're hosting a self-hypnosis seminar. You can learn to master this yourself. That's what we're all about—empowering people. Handing them the reins to get back to their own lives. We're also having a special for a weeklong retreat we're doing in late October, where we offer the ayahuasca ceremony three nights in a row because consecutive ceremonies can allow you to go deeper into your psyche. Is that something you would be interested in signing up for?"

She didn't have any intention of ever coming back to this place, but Katie mumbled, "Sure," anyway and reclined, just to shut down Dr. Dave's verbal spam and because she thought he might try even harder to wow her with his hypnosis if he thought she was going to be a returning customer.

As she tried to relax, Katie was met with an unwelcome memory. In season, 6, episode 8, "You're Getting Sleepy," Shelby Spade's nemesis acquired the ability to hypnotize by stealing a pocket watch from a traveling carny, and turned the entire student body at Bay View Middle School into his minions. Spade managed to get the pocket watch he'd used, but not before getting him to cluck like a chicken in front of the entire school. It was the first time Katie had argued over a script. "It's what the audience will expect, that he'll cluck like a chicken. Couldn't Shelby get him to do something else? Something they wouldn't see coming?" She remembered how the head writer had offered a placating nod, praised her for her "thinking outside the box," and said that a writing career might be on her horizon. He'd ended the conversation with a condescending *awww* she was far too old for, and Katie had known she wasn't being taken seriously.

Dr. Dave wheeled his office chair closer to Katie's head. "All right, Katie, I want you to focus on loosening up your body. Feel your spine relax. Picture your bones so supple they can bend. Your muscles are feeling airy and limp. All feelings of heaviness are gone. It's like you're filled with helium and floating. Try to keep your eyes closed. You can feel at ease now. Block out all else but my voice. I want you to imagine a staircase, Katie. It can be as ornate or as plain as you wish. My voice, Katie, listen to it. You are descending. Everything else has fallen away, and all you want to do is to get to that plateau where everything is revealed." Dr. Dave's voice crackled like a warm fire, but Katie wasn't feeling at all lulled. Instead, she felt nervous and tight.

"You're going down the steps, Katie. Imagine feeling increasingly weightless with each step." Dr. Dave started counting the steps on her staircase. "One, two. Your body is getting lighter and looser with each step. It's almost like you could step out of your body completely. Yet your mind is sharpening. Three, four. Feel the bannister."

But Katie wasn't picturing going down steps; instead, she was climbing up them. She was racing up the spiral staircase in their West Hollywood home, the one she'd bought with her Spade money, up to her gigantic bedroom. Those stairs. The ones she would sit on to watch Lucy's dinner parties unravel into boozy bashes that ended up in the pool, with white stripes being sucked up through cocktail straws.

The landing where Nate would step over her, his eyes buggy from too many hours playing video games, and snarl, "Go to bed, all-star," in that blameful way like she was responsible for the booze-fest and their mother arranging herself in stumbling poses she thought were sexy.

AJ would meet her on those steps, sit down next to her, his lanky legs bunched up against his chest, pressing his shoulder into hers and ask, "What's up, buttercup?" or "Why so glum, chum?" AJ was always there, always sober. Staying on late, he told her, until he knew she was safe in bed, away from all "the yahoos." He would make sure her teeth were brushed and face washed. AJ hated when she wore makeup off-set; he would say he didn't understand why girls always wanted to look older when they were already perfect little flowers. He'd fix her a warm glass of milk, and they'd both pretend she hadn't been draining the bottoms of the guests' wine and cocktail glasses.

He was the father she never had. The one she needed.

"You're going down, Katie, down, down, down. Deeper. The bannister makes you feel safe; the steps feel secure beneath your feet. You're getting more comfortable and relaxed. You see the last step now. How many more steps do you have, Katie?"

"Twelve." She rattled off that number because that was what usually went with *steps* in her mind.

Dr. Dave started counting backward from twelve, but in Katie's mind, she was still on the landing. Looking. Watching the parties. The stain on the wall from when her father hurled a gin and juice at Lucy's head, then noticed Katie on the stairs. "Katie, honey, I need a loan. Your mother is kicking me out."

The feeling of AJ's warm hand on her back later that day when he took her out for ice cream and told her she had every right to be upset, that divorce can be processed like a death in a child's mind. "Let yourself mourn, darling." Her father hated AJ. He thought he was always taking his cut. "If only AJ, in his faggy suits and smart-ass eyewear, would get the fuck out of the way so I can take care of things."

Katie remembered this so well because she didn't want AJ to be gay. She knew nothing about him, in that self-centered way kids think someone stops existing when they're not around. But AJ seemed like he existed only for her. That was why she loved him so much. She wanted to marry him one day, but in that confusing way girls wanted to marry their fathers.

"You're at your last step, Katie, and now you've entered a room full of beautiful art, or maybe it's not a room but a place. Maybe there are trees, soft cushy grass, maybe you can hear a stream in the distance. What does your room look like? You don't need to describe it out loud, but visualize it."

Katie continued to picture her childhood bedroom. It looked like a toy store, so jammed full with stuff. She loved having other cast members over to admire all her things, the things only the star could afford to have.

"Now that you're in your special place, calmness washes over you," Dr. Dave intoned, and the words *special place* made her feel queasy.

Her bedroom, with the bed AJ always ushered her off to, always warning her how early she was going to have to get up the following morning to shoot. "You don't want those baggy eyes, do you, Miss Spade? Because I know your audience doesn't. You need to look sharp."

She wasn't sleepwalking then. She never sleepwalked in that house. They put it up for sale right after AJ went berserk and sliced her cheek. They rented after that, until Katie finally fled LA for New York with loose goals about becoming a serious *acteur.*

She could never put it together, the AJ she knew and the disgruntled employee.

As an adult, she viewed her mixed-up feelings for AJ as clear evidence of how damaged she was, that her childhood was so full of longing she thought her manager, *someone she was paying,* genuinely cared for her.

"Now think about sleep, Katie. Falling asleep, how it makes you feel. Think about your last moments just before drifting off . . ." Dr. Dave's voice slowed, went hazy. She tried to put herself back upstairs in the Blue Bliss Room. She was looking at the door as she always did right before she fell asleep. At home, after triple-checking the outside doors on their shared brownstone—even while knowing Nate would do the same to make sure it was locked—she'd still fixate on her bedroom door handle before drifting off. She'd thought it was just an extension of her compulsive safety checking, brought on by her sleepwalking.

A flip-book of all the doorknobs and latches she'd obsessively stared at in her life suddenly tumbled through her head—in hotels, in her trailer when Shelby Spade went on mall tours, all those doorknobs from one-night stands just before passing out. Even there, in Dr. Dave's office, she glanced quickly at the brass doorknob on the wood-paneled door in case she really did get hypnotized—which was like sleep.

Then for some reason, her mind again settled on the long lever door handle of her overstuffed childhood bedroom. The pre-sleepwalking handle. She remembered exactly how the lever's faceplate caught the reflection of the twinkly fairy lights Katie had strung across her ceiling because it was too babyish to have an actual night-light. She would watch that handle, fixate on it; almost wait for it to open, soft and slow. For a hand to dart inside and flick off the lights, then a voice to say, "Go to sleep," and watch the door close again. Softly.

But there was always someone turning off her bedroom lights. Nate. Lucy. AJ. Even her dad, when he came around.

She'd want to get up and turn them back on, because she wasn't quite asleep yet and the dark had gone swirly black, and she'd feel like she was drowning in it and couldn't get up. Couldn't move at all. Anxiety pooled in her chest, and she'd try to force herself to fall asleep to make it all go away. To speed time up so it would be morning and sunlight would stream again into her room. The urge to get up and turn on the lights would make her twitch but not completely wake up. She'd feel trapped, skimming just above the surface of sleep. She needed to turn the lights back on before . . . Before what? Before something. It felt urgent. She needed to stay awake, but she never could.

Sleep—it would come at her soon after the lights went off, as aggressive as a hand gripping her ankle and pulling her underwater. She couldn't get up. There was a voice in her ear. *Get up, open your eyes. Get up, open your eyes. Open your eyes.* But she couldn't move; she felt paralyzed.

Then her door opened again. A quick burst of music and light from the hallway that should have startled her back awake but only her eyelids would lift; she could see a figure standing at the door. Not just a hand but the entire body now. A faceless silhouette, obscured by the light beaming in from behind it. It scared her to death, the sight of it. It was stretched out to funhouse proportions. The door closed, and there was always a moment when she thought she'd imagined it, or maybe it was Lucy checking in on her, but she knew that was too hopeful. Lucy wasn't the sort of mother who stood in doorways to admire her children sleeping. She could never stay still that long, and there was nothing to admire when her children weren't trying to tap dance their way into America's heart.

But then she would hear it breathing. It was in the room with her, this shadow-creature.

Who was it now? This looming, elongated thing. She couldn't sit up. She couldn't keep her eyes open. She felt trapped in herself, like a living corpse.

Its mouth was open; she knew this because she could hear its tongue run over its lips, moist smacking, and the drag of breath over the back of its tongue. It was on the move now. A night terror loping its way toward her. Its long, skinny fingers reaching for her, pulling back her Hello Kitty comforter. *Hello, sleeping beauty.*

Get up, open your eyes.

A crushing weight in her chest.

Open.

She could hardly breathe.

Your.

Something wet. On her face. A finger hooked into the waistline of her pajama bottoms, tugging them down. She went cold and raw.

Eyes.

If she could just get up, if she could go toward the music, she'd be safe. Get to the party downstairs and everything would be fine, but she couldn't. She was pinned down. Her body bending like she wasn't in it.

Go, go, get up. Go.

Katie jolted up from the couch with her hands out in front of her like she was defending herself from being hit. A panicked scream jangled her ears.

What the fuck, what the fuck.

"Oh shit, I'm sorry; I was trying to guide you out slowly. You looked really distressed." Dr. Dave had his hand on her shoulder.

She just looked at him like she was surprised to see him there. She hadn't been hypnotized; instead, she had been remembering something. As thin and shapeless as it was, she had been remembering something.

It was just the wrong thing.

ELLIE

Nate.

He was here. Just moseying around the side of the house.

He only ever used public transportation, which meant he actually rented a car, got in it, left their cozy and safe home, and drove three and a half hours to do what? To see her? Why?

And now he was giving her a happy wave like it was perfectly normal to crash her weekend away. He must have seen her reaction, because his hand quickly went limp.

What is he doing here?

Thank goodness she asked Anthony for a moment of privacy to keep working out her "shit," as he put it.

Before they'd left, he'd jokingly given her an escape plan if his sister became *too much*. Something she'd only half listened to. She was supposed to text a code word, and then he could call and demand that she come home right way because of something. She didn't pay attention because she knew she wasn't going to need him to rescue *her*.

This was a mistake on her part. She should've known Nate had texted, probably several times by now, to check in with her. He likely took her silence as some kind of SOS and thought he'd better come galloping in, high on a white-knight fantasy, to save her from a disastrous weekend.

Ellie had dropped her drumsticks in the grass and clomped toward him. She had to get rid of him. If Katie saw her brother, all hell would break loose. Katie couldn't keep a single thing from

Nate. She had to detail even something as banal as buying milk or using the ATM for Nate. Share some grievance that had happened to her along the way. "What is with people disregarding personal space? Like if you cough while I am reaching to grab a carton of milk, and your cough rustles my hair like a light breeze, you're standing too fucking close, asshole."

She also had no trouble barraging him with crude jokes and provocative sex stories. Like that time when Katie was dating a guy she dubbed "Cliffhanger Dick" because he drank too much and could never finish.

Nate and Katie had an entire roster of chirpy one-liners for Cliff.

"Do you think Cliff's go-to sex song is Sarah McLachlan's 'Building a Mystery'?"

"Do you think Cliff is planning to turn it into a series?"

"'*Until next time*' is Cliff's best pickup line."

It would go on and on, *endlessly*, such that Ellie would have to flee the room. Even if they made it a joke, it was still about his sister having sex, something Ellie couldn't imagine wanting to ever picture about her own sibling, if she had lived. But then maybe that was because her sister was twelve when she'd died.

Nate teased her by calling her a prude. "Sheesh, I know my sister has sex; so what if she tells me funny stories about it? I'm not her *father*."

Theirs was a strange brother-sister relationship. They told each other far too much, and Katie would certainly tell him about the knife and Lily, and Nate would do the right thing and call the cops.

"What are you doing here?" Her voice was all sharp edges, but she couldn't help it. She was seething.

Nate winced. "You didn't answer your phone or any of the texts I sent." Like this was explanation enough to just show up. If he was anyone else, under any other circumstance, she would have called him possessive. Smothering. Controlling.

"I had to surrender my phone, Nate. Everyone did! It's a rule here," she snapped.

He dropped his head to the side, and his hands shot up. "Sorry! I was just worried about you." He looked genuinely hurt that she wasn't happy to see him, and immediately Ellie regretted her tone. Nate was a fixer. If she told him she was angry that he was there, that it felt like he was checking up on her, Nate would just stick around longer to try to appease her. He'd pace and linger and wouldn't leave until she could convince him she wasn't mad at him—not an easy feat, since Nate would keep asking if she was sure she wasn't mad until she started to get angry again and then they'd start all over.

Ellie forced her voice to go light and puddly. "Oh, well, that's sweet of you to check up on me, really. It's just that you surprised me, that's all! I thought I was seeing things."

"Well, I would have come right up to get you, but you were going to town on that drum. I didn't know I was engaged to Keith Moon." He laughed. Ellie was suddenly aware of what she must look like—sweaty, red-faced, and with frizzy hair. She wasn't even sure of when she'd last shaved her armpits.

"Ha, funny. But good on you for referencing an English drummer. Let's go for a walk." Ellie grabbed his hand and tried to draw him toward one of the trails, but Nate drew her back into him. He wrapped his arms around her, bent down, and kissed her. He pulled back and said "hi" with a thick glaze of sugary romance. It took so much for Ellie not to bat him away and drag him out of view from the Sanctuary. It was sheer luck that Katie and her squad were all somewhere else right now, but that could change any second.

"So where's my sister? Don't tell me she's already riding the tea trolley." Nate flicked his eyebrows twice.

"I want you to myself first. Come on." She went ahead of him, hooking her pinkie in his, forcing him to follow her down a trail. Knowing too that she probably looked better from behind; her blond hair would catch all those rays of sunlight breaking through the canopy of trees. "It's beautiful here, isn't it?" she said in a breathy voice, really trying to sell *breathlessly beautiful.*

"Yep. I guess. If you're into trees." Nate looked around and nodded.

He was dressed in a pressed denim button-down that had been faded in all the right places in a factory. His sleeves were meticulously rolled to the elbows. His beige chinos tapered at the ankles and ended with shiny, pointed boots. When he slid his aviator glasses back on, he couldn't have looked more city slicker if he'd tried. Even his woodsy aftershave was overpowering the real deal of the actual woods. In a few seconds, he would probably start worrying about sunscreen and wood ticks.

Ellie wondered if she could really marry such an un-rugged man. "So how was yesterday?" They'd been apart for a single day. Did Nate realize that?

He immediately started talking about the restaurant, about some bland drama between two waitresses, which inevitably led to his obsession with finding out who was skimming the cash register. He felt like he was closing in on the culprit—a single mom who worked the lunch crowd. Ellie pretended to be interested so he wouldn't notice how far she was taking him from the house. Finally, she turned around again and fiddled with his shirt collar.

"If you think it's the single mom, just fire her."

Nate lips parted like he was about to say something, probably about needing to gather more evidence, but Ellie knew the truth was, he didn't want to fire a single mom. He'd feel too bad about it.

"Nice is no way to run a business, Nate."

He cleared his throat and nodded. "Yeah, I know. You don't have to remind me. I'll talk to her on Monday."

"Look, babe, I am so, so happy you came. I really am, but I wish you hadn't driven all the way out here. I don't need any saving. Katie is doing really well here, so much so, I don't even want her to see you in case it breaks her momentum." Ellie turned to face him now that they were far enough into the woods to be obscured by trees. No one could see them there.

"Seriously?" He made an overly pronounced surprised face and hooked his thumb into his pocket.

"Yes, she really is."

"Huh. Well, that's good. It really is. I never thought my sister would take to a place like this. Wait, did she drink the magical tea yet? Is that it?"

"No, the ayahuasca ceremony isn't until tomorrow."

"Ceremony?" A little smile played on Nate's lips, the one he got when he thought she was being pretentious. When she'd try to call him out on it, he'd deny it by saying he just thought she was cute, but it still annoyed her.

"That's what it's called." Ellie shrugged. She knew he knew it was Sunday. It was like he just wanted her to say *ceremony* out loud so he could give her that look.

"Well, I also have some news for you. Another surprise. I was going to wait, but since I'm here, I might as well tell you." Nate waited a beat or two to draw out whatever he was going to say next.

"What is it?"

"We're moving out." He moved his arms out from his sides as if he were getting ready to catch her gleeful leap into his arms, but she couldn't muster it, so she grabbed his hands instead and swung them in the space between them.

"What? Are you serious?"

"Yes, very serious, Ellie. I know you hate living so close to my sister."

"We don't just live close, we *share* a building. One she owns." It was a sore spot for Nate, and it slipped out of her mouth before she could stop herself. She was messing everything up; having Nate there was clouding her thinking.

The natural thing would be to tell him about how his sister woke up with a bloodied knife, and there was a missing woman named Lily. She should be panicking, clutching at Nate, thanking him for saving her from Katie's insanity, telling him how afraid she was, that she was even worried if she didn't comply with Katie today that she might be her next victim. But without a body, without knowing for certain that Lily was actually dead, she didn't know what to say to Nate. She felt trapped in some kind of limbo.

But then Nate wouldn't leave. He would need to talk to Katie. The police would be called and questions would be asked, and Ellie couldn't trust suspicion wouldn't shift to her. She was Katie's roommate; her fingerprints and DNA were on the knife too.

And whom would Nate choose at this point? His sister or his fiancée? He was in love with her, she knew that, but there were so many pressure points the police could squeeze until Nate wouldn't know what to believe. He'd been Katie's "fixer" far longer than Ellie's fiancé.

Plus, she should have already told him. It wouldn't come across as honest now that she'd waited this long. If Lily's body did turn up and Katie was arrested for her murder, then this exchange between them right now, she'd hoped, would get lost in the chaos. It would give Ellie a chance to obscure the timeline or come up with a good reason why she wasn't telling Nate about the knife this very second.

"Yeah, and that's why I put a deposit on another place."

Ellie was genuinely surprised that'd he'd taken this step. The hopeful look on his face did something to her and she suddenly wanted to tell him everything. About the knife. She suddenly believed he just might choose her over Katie if he had to. "I just didn't think . . . I mean, that wasn't the plan."

"It was always part of the plan. You know that."

"I know, but just not yet." She touched his face. "Where is this new place?"

"You're going to love it. It's in Morningside Heights, West 110th. It's huge. The subway is a minute away, and you could get to class in under five minutes."

"That sounds really expensive, Nate."

"Don't worry about that. I've got it covered." He winked, and she almost expected him to flip up his collar in some cool-dude gesture.

"You've got it covered? But how? I'm just curious as to how you have it covered." Ellie was serious. What was he thinking? What kind of math was he doing in his head? The truth was, Ellie contributed very little to their household income—Katie did have *that* right—so how did he suddenly have the money to move out when the restaurant hadn't even been open a year? Ellie did push to move out—as any sane person would in her situation—but Nate always gave the excuse that he didn't want to leave his sister to live on her own. *For her own well-being,* while they both knew the cheap rent and constant financial aid his sister provided was also a pretty good reason to stay behind and care for her *well-being.*

She thought she'd convinced him that the retreat was their best option. That Katie's *conversion* from a tipsy, bust-in-the-door day-drinker and bust-in-the-door sleepwalker to a sober, yoga-loving, mindful human being who would become so self-absorbed in her own betterment, she would leave them alone and they'd all live together in peace.

Ellie genuinely did not want Nate to mess up his own life over this weekend.

"Well, I met with a guy who thinks we could open a second location in St. Louis." He grabbed a skinny twig, snapped it off, and started plucking the leaves off one by one. Nate had a whole name-less network of guys and buddies who could all do something for one another. It was like he moved around in this highly skilled man-horde. You need some electric work? Nate knew a guy. Need someone to move you? There's a guy. Need someone to sharpen kitchen knives? Nate's buddy just happened to do that.

Nate's phone trilled. He looked at his display, then his face darkened. "I thought you said guests weren't allowed their phones?" He looked up at Ellie again with an accusing glare. "It's my sister."

Heat rolled up the back of Ellie's neck. "Well, isn't that typical? Katie has obviously broken the rules. Don't answer it." Ellie put her hand on his phone, forcibly blocking him from answering. "She's really making progress, and she's probably looking to self-sabotage by asking you to come get her or something. Just don't."

He eyed her suspiciously but put his phone away. That was the thing about Nate—his grand gestures and white-knight aspirations also came off a tad clingy and possessive. She knew that going into their engagement, but to drive all the way there—first with an excuse that he was worried about her, then with big news to cover up his lame excuse for showing up—was all too desperate, even for Nate. Still, she didn't want to fight. She just needed to give him what he really came for and send him on his way.

"You don't need to worry about Katie. I thought you came here for me." Ellie slipped both her hands into Nate's pockets and kissed his neck, slowly leaning her entire body into him. She wanted to send him off as a happy camper. She could feel him respond, and she took hold of him through the thin cottony material of his pockets.

"Ellie, no," he whispered. "We're outside."

"So?" She took her hands out and started to unbutton his pants. "I want you."

"What, right here?" Nate looked around.

"Yes, here. Now."

"But what if someone sees us?"

"No one can see us. I really need you." Her voice dipped into baby talk. His sister worked it over him all the time. There was something off-putting that he responded so much to it. Eventually, she would have to break him of it, but for now, a fiancée put up with such things. His cheeks flushed, and she knew she had him, that he would forgive the discrepancy with the phone.

She pulled down her Lycra pants—not all the way, but enough—turned around and grabbed onto a skinny birch tree, and looked back at him with her best sleepy-eyed gaze, full of pleading that he do her a huge favor and fuck her right there. It was how Nate liked her best—full of need, of want, dependent. She even moaned, "Please."

Nate's face went slack. Ever the trooper, he pulled his own pants lower. He wound her hair into his fist as he pushed himself into her—roughly, the way he thought she wanted it. He liked her like this, the bad girl in the sheets, the English rose in the streets. It would be hotter this way, the genuine quickie Nate liked in his office with the kitchen staff a stone's throw away, clanging their pots and pans, muttering curse words. The dishwasher describing some fantasy woman he most certainly didn't bang the night before. Hotter even if there was a knock on the door, and Nate had to shout, "Just a minute!" And then it really would be that—just a minute.

When it was over, she kissed him longingly. "Now go home, and let me and your sister have some girl time before the wedding." Ellie squeezed his hand. "I'll see you Monday night."

"Fine, fine." Nate kissed her again. "I'll drive the entire three hours back, because that's what I was hoping to do with my day— drive six hours in a rented car without my fiancée."

"Are you telling me you're disappointed? Maybe I should get Katie's friend Ariel for you?" She gave him a pouty look, hoping the mention of Ariel's name would compel him to leave quicker.

Nate's ears burned red. "No. I just . . . I thought I'd be sticking around a little while, that's all. Maybe get in on the trippy ceremony." His voice put ceremony in air quotes.

"Nate."

"No, it's fine, I'll go." He did a mock mope up the path and back to his car, with Ellie urging him to hurry up so Katie wouldn't see him. She watched him pull out of the lot and disappear completely before doubling over, her hands on her thighs, as she sucked down gulps of air. It was like she was physically trying to swallow back down the anger roiling inside of her. How could this weekend go so wrong? It was her chance for wellness too—a weekend to let her grief out like a dog left in a kennel too long. People expect you to get over something that happened so long ago, but how was that possible when her sister died so young? When each time Ellie reached a milestone, she had to acknowledge her sister would never experience it.

She wiped at the sweat on her forehead and took off into the woods again, this time to look for a body.

ARIEL

Fiiiiinally.

Dr. Dave and Katie's session came to an end.

Ariel was sitting next to Paula in the living room, coloring a chakra wheel. Both their heads snapped up when Katie scrambled down the hall, thumped up the stairs, and shut the door to her room.

Ariel dropped her colored pencil and followed her.

"Katie? Can I come in?" She knocked softly.

"I just want to be alone right now." Katie sounded congested, like she'd been crying. How did Dr. Dave make her cry?

"You sure? If you want to talk—"

"I am sure."

"So what happened with Dr. Dave? With your session?" Ariel pressed her forehead against the door.

She tried the door handle. Her mind flickering to standing outside Rob's very lovely ranch-style house. The ease with which their front door had opened. A cute turquoise-colored door. How quiet the house had been when she stepped inside.

"Please go away, Ariel. I need to be alone right now." A sharp, sputtering command.

Ariel flinched back. What was she going to do? Storm into Katie's room and do what she did to Rob's wife?

But that was an accident.

It was.

She wandered back downstairs. Paula was gone and she didn't

want to color anymore. So she moped outside and made her way over to a hammock. It took two tries to get into it and get comfortable.

There was a light wind. She closed her eyes and listened to the lake gently lapping in the distance. Immediately a thousand images of Katie and Dr. Dave buoyed up like dead fish. In order to chase the images away she imagined a version of herself that lived by the ocean. Another too in which Ariel married Nate and was still living in New York, in the brownstone with Katie—in this kind of sitcom merriment. Never getting on each other's nerves. If only Nate had liked her that way.

It was a game she played in her head, one in which she'd made better decisions and as a result had a more fabulous life. If only she'd been more willing to go without nice things and work nights and weekends, she could have stayed in New York without her parents' financial help. Some internship would have led to a corporate career with lots of travel. She'd have money for a personal trainer and dietician, and be her ideal weight. She would never have worked at the Holiday Inn, never have met Rob, never have hurt Rob's wife.

Something warm started to trickle down her scalp and she thought a bird had to have shit on her, but when she touched her head and looked at her hand, she saw a smear of blood. She was pulling her hair and not noticing. Now her scalp was lightly bleeding.

For a second, Ariel thought she might be sick.

Alone and thinking.

This was never a good mix for Ariel. It made her fretful.

Now she would be alone for the next two meditative hours. Carmen had taken off on a hike. Katie was locked in her room for some reason. It seemed like she was only confiding in Ellie about whatever was bothering her.

Even if she saw Ellie, she wouldn't try to hang out with her. And then she felt a pulse of jealous anger toward Ellie for trying to take her place as Katie's pillar of support. It should be Ariel who Katie needed to talk to, just like in college.

She was craving something. Something she couldn't describe. Like those moments when she caught herself thinking, *I just want to go home*, when she was already home and not knowing where it came from. Or what it meant.

Dr. Dave was right about having too much static in her head.

Why couldn't she just could drift off and go to sleep? It's what people did in hammocks.

But she was having trouble staying still and now her scalp was throbbing. What was happening in Shakopee right now? Her parents were waiting for her to call back. Maybe her mom had googled defense lawyers, or had already called one she spotted on a bus bench. Or maybe not. Maybe they weren't going to help her at all. Her parents thought abortion was murder!

What were her ex-coworkers saying about her? What was Rob thinking? He must hate her now. He was probably calling her an obsessive psycho, like he was the other victim in all of this.

She couldn't sit still, so she hauled herself out of the hammock with an ungraceful flop and went over to the spa.

She'd love a massage. She'd been staying away from the spa, after Naomi's healing session that morning, in case it was more of the same, but now she felt less skeptical of every aspect of the Sanctuary.

A massage would make her feel better, but Paula had beat her to it. The masseuse told her to come back in half an hour and handed her a sprig of lavender to tide her over. "Breathe it in. It will give you calming, patient thoughts as you wait for your massage."

She took the sprig, pressed it to her nose, and inhaled its craft-store scent. She really did feel a belch of hopefulness. Maybe Rob's wife didn't get hurt that badly. Maybe she didn't lose the baby. There had to be some chance that everything would turn out to be fine.

Suddenly, she felt an overwhelming need to tell someone.

Not *someone*, but Dr. Dave. She knew he could make her feel better about it. Maybe he would tell her something like, *There's no such thing as bad acts, only opportunities to learn to do better.*

She strolled around the grounds, casually at first, then slightly more frantically, and walked into the house looking for Dr. Dave. It was a strange moth-to-a-flame feeling. She just wanted to be around him.

She heard him talking in the kitchen. She moved toward the sound of him. His deep voice was hushed and cajoling, "I told you, we have nothing to worry about," he said.

"Are you sure?" Naomi asked pleadingly. "They almost shut us down."

"Baby. Come here." Dr. Dave was embracing his wife from behind, kissing her neck. They were standing by the sink, facing the other way. Toward the window. Ariel hovered in the doorway. They didn't notice her.

"We have nothing to worry about. This isn't anything like last time." Dr. Dave slid his hands over Naomi's skinny hips. Pulled her tight against him. "There's nothing to worry about," he repeated with more bite in his voice. He pulled her face around by her chin, and then they were really kissing.

Before Ariel could back out of the kitchen, Naomi's eyes sprang open, looking directly at Ariel like she'd sensed her there the entire time.

She kissed her husband harder.

CARMEN

Carmen jogged down the trails, a trowel shoved down the back of her shorts. Its sharp tip was grazing her left butt cheek.

After lunch she couldn't bring herself to jab the needle into the pinch of fat on her belly. She'd set the syringe down on the edge of the bathroom sink and stepped away from it like it might follow her. Then, before she could change her mind, she grabbed it, squirted its contents down the bathroom sink, and tossed the empty syringe in the garbage.

The fertility drugs were starting to give her headaches this time around, and she couldn't remember the last time she didn't feel a persistent low-level cramping in her uterus like she was physically suffering from reproductive whiplash from plumping her ovaries up. And Megan just seemed too anxious to be a great mother. Probably by the time the kid was three, she would have it diagnosed with defiant personality disorder or chronic pessimism, something clinical sounding to explain why the child wasn't always giving her mommy-dearest smiles.

And so now she was jogging, thinking, *if, if, if, how.*

If she were going to steal the cocaine, she wouldn't just snag it and take off. One, she didn't have a car. Two, she'd prefer to be much stealthier than that.

So stealthy that Simon and Marie wouldn't even know their cocaine was missing until they were all the way back in Canada. Even better if they were completely clueless as to who'd stolen it from them.

Carmen's fingertips were buzzing.

Her mom's life advice skidded through her head. *Carmen, you gotta steal it like you already own it, like it's already yours.* This particular gem was given to Carmen when her mom took her back-to-school shopping to get new shoes. She convinced twelve-year-old Carmen to put her old shoes in the box and wear her stolen sneakers out of the store. Carmen was caught, of course, and her mom accused her of walking like a willy-nilly pussy, looking around as if she were wanting to be caught. "You know Ted Bundy picked his victims by how they walked," a connection that still made little sense to Carmen other than once she went for it, to not falter. Not even a little.

And then she had to think of Lily again. Her sponsor said she wouldn't just take off in the middle of nowhere, and even if the girl came off as unstable, it was an odd thing to do—leave in the night, next to a forest preserve. She had to have been picked up by someone else.

Or.

She couldn't ignore the fact that Lily was missing at a retreat where drug dealers were also guests. Had Lily seen something she shouldn't have? Did Simon and Marie try to initiate a threesome with her as well? Then Lily saw the bag with the foam blocks and pried one open just like Carmen had, and they what? Killed her in the cottage?

Were Simon and Marie much more dangerous than they looked? Of course they were. Someone had to be dangerous to get into the drug trade, had to be willing to take a certain amount of risk, commit a certain level of violence.

But then she had just been in Simon and Marie's cottage. There hadn't been any evidence of a struggle. There wasn't blood splatter on the ceiling or walls. And the foam blocks were still sealed. And wouldn't they leave, if they'd just committed murder?

Whatever had happened to Lily, Carmen would avoid because she was smart. She would think it through. She was definitely smarter than Lily.

She was looking for a good spot to dig a hole because *if* she were going to steal the drugs, the hiding spot would have to be far enough away from the house, in a secluded area, where no one would see her with them. But also a spot that she could access quickly.

Theoretically, if she were to steal the cocaine, she'd want to bury it as fast as possible because the less time she had it on her, or in her room, the less chance she was going to be caught with it. The less chance she'd end up buried in the woods.

Then, right before they left the Sanctuary, Carmen would take one last meditative walk, dig it up, put it in her backpack, and carry it out. Easy-peasy.

It would only work, of course, if she replaced the product in Simon and Marie's duffel bag with an authentic look-alike.

When Carmen thought she was far enough away from the house, she took a left into thick brush and then climbed up an incline.

She found a tree, indistinguishable from all the other trees except for the X she'd chipped into it with the tip of her trowel, then she started to dig at the base of the tree. It was muggy and hot. Her skin was sticky with sweat, and mosquitoes swarmed. She managed to pull out a chunk or two of earth.

She hadn't anticipated how hard it was going to be to dig a large enough hole for ten bricks of cocaine with a trowel. It wasn't like she'd gone to summer camp. Especially between giant, snaking tree roots where the earth was packed so tightly. What she needed was a jackhammer.

She rubbed her forehead, leaving behind a streak of dirt. She looked around. She would have to split it up and dig three smaller holes. She kicked at the ground here and there, looking for some buttery soft spot. Nothing. She could cover up the drug bundle with leaves and branches and any soil she managed to get loose. Of course, that would leave a mound rather than the seamless flat ground she had envisioned. A mound made things obvious, and there was a chance the wind or an animal or rain could expose it. No, she'd have to dig a hole.

Twenty more minutes until paddleboarding. For all the feel-good jargon of this place, Dr. Dave and Naomi ran a stiff schedule. When the drumming session had started without Katie and Ellie, they'd worn the faces of disappointed parents.

Carmen suddenly heard something, the kind of scuttling an animal would make. She stumbled back and moved down a path that took her closer to the lake where the trees were more spread apart. It was farther from the highway, but she could figure that part out later.

She carved another couple of Xs into trees. One marked tree was probably not enough—it would be too easily missed. She'd double mark where she put the drugs.

She started chipping away at the earth, and again it was just too hard. She was running out of time. Fuck it. The cocaine would be wrapped in cellophane, so couldn't she just put it in another garbage bag and then put it in the lake?

She knew how to tie a good knot, and this was a lake, not a river with fast-moving currents. She added rope to her mental list of supplies.

Carmen scouted the exact spot she would put the bag—the lopsided tree close to the shoreline. She could tie the bag to it. She took the trowel and carved XX. Probably not necessary, because there'd be rope. No, something less noticeable than rope, more like fishing line or a thin cord. Putting it in the lake would also cut the time it would take to dig it up. Then she noticed all the dirt she had under her nails and over her hands. Streaks of it were on the front of her shirt, probably on her face too. The lake would prevent needing to explain why it looked like Carmen had rolled in dirt.

She rinsed her hands and splashed lake water on her cheeks to clean up.

Yes, the lake would be best. It should all work out fine.

If she were going to steal it.

If.

She had a vision of herself still living at home in five years, by then caring for her siblings' offspring because at least two of them were going to inevitably get knocked up early.

Debt would be unrelenting. Her teeth would be jaundiced because she wouldn't be able to afford to see a dentist. Maybe she would start taking more nips from a bottle to ease the bitterness spreading through her like a cancer.

Her dad would be completely held against his will in his tremulous body, and he'd cast her pleading looks to kill him.

And what would Carmen think about as she sat in a rocker on their pockmarked front porch? *You willy-nilly pussy idiot, why the fuck didn't you steal it? A golden ticket was right in front of you, and you walked away. Like there would ever be a second shot at that kind of money in your lifetime.* What was more terrifying right now? Getting caught and killed by Simon and Marie or not even trying to steal it and then living with that? *I would hate myself. I would look in the mirror, and through gritted decaying teeth, baggy eyes, and wrinkles two decades too early, start each morning by telling myself, "I fucking hate you."*

She hadn't felt this—a flicker of hope—in her chest in so long, and that made her dangerous too. Maybe more so than both Simon and Marie, who . . . what? Would lose out on a lake house? A second home? Fuck them.

She tucked the trowel back into her shorts and then was suddenly hit with a palpable feeling of being watched. She stopped moving. Looked around.

She saw something off in the distance; it was red. Like a small flag sticking out of the ground.

She took a few steps toward whatever it was, then heard something snap behind her.

"Whatcha doing?" a chipper, male voice asked. Carmen whipped around. No one was there. Her heart hammered in her chest. She whirled around again. "Up here. No, *here*." A deep chuckle.

She looked up. There was Anthony clinging to a tree like a black bear.

"What're you doing up there?" Carmen shouted.

"I've climbed a tree!"

"Yeah, I see that."

"Dr. Dave said to do this to get in touch with my inner child to move past my creative block."

"How long have you been up there?"

"I don't know. Dr. Dave said not to come down until I had a creative breakthrough."

"Can you get down?"

"Uh, I dunno. I haven't tried yet."

"All right, then. Have fun." Carmen waved bye.

"Wait! I don't think I can get down."

Carmen stood at the bottom of the tree and spotted Anthony's very awkward descent. He was a large man, tall and wide. When he finally landed, his skin was coated in sweat, his arms scratched up.

"So did climbing a tree help you?"

Anthony retied his white-and-navy bandanna that had been knocked off on the way down. He stopped and closed his eyes for an uncomfortable moment. "I don't know yet. Maybe? I guess I sort of cheated by coming down before a breakthrough."

"Well, I'm sure it'll come to you. Anyway, we should get back. Paddleboarding is starting soon." Carmen began walking toward the lodge.

"It's a nice day, isn't it?" Anthony galloped up behind her.

"Sure is." Carmen nodded.

"What do you usually do on a day like this?" It took her a second to get that Anthony was trying to chat her up.

"Ah, probably not this." Carmen gestured to the trees.

"And what do you do for work and do you enjoy it?" A two-part question. Carmen sucked down a groan. Anthony was trying too hard to be conversational. She could picture him on a date, asking rote questions he'd downloaded from some site that helped male gamers through the painful task of pretending that women's brains were interesting to them.

"I am a home-care aide and it's fine." Anthony's shoulders slumped when Carmen didn't ask him any questions about himself.

"Hey, you never said what you were doing." He gave her a side-eyed glance behind his glasses that was trying to be friendly but somehow wasn't.

"Looking for, uh, truffles." It was the best Carmen could think up on the spot.

"Pssht. Truffles don't grow in New York." Anthony guffawed at her ignorance—fully shattering his attempt at making artificial first-date conversation with her.

She should have said mushrooms. "Yeah, I guess. No harm in looking, right?" she quipped and started walking faster.

KATIE

"Everything you need to know about life, you can learn on a paddleboard." The group was ankle-deep in the lake, holding their boards and paddles and listening to another one of Dr. Dave's motivational talks. "Because once you get on this board and in the water, it's all about finding focus and balance. When you shift from your knees into a standing position, it's important to look up and in front of you. If you look down at the board or the water, you go down. Your body goes where the mind takes it. Take a second to really absorb that—the body goes wherever the mind takes it." Dr. Dave waited until he felt his profound tidbit had been sufficiently absorbed before getting up on his board with feline ease. He continued to draw parallels between paddling techniques and job promotions.

Naomi was floating farther out behind him in a stark white wetsuit that hurt Katie's eyes. She was treating everyone to a showcase of her paddleboard yoga moves that defied gravity and made her shimmery muscles pulse.

Katie tried to listen, tried to shake the panicked feeling whenever it came back. Tried to stop feeling that *tick, tick, tick* of her pulse in her neck by pressing a finger against it, as if doing so would slow down her jittery heart. *The heart is a time bomb; that's why it ticks.* She'd been feeling off since the hypnosis. Strangely blank. Her head was eerily quiet. Maybe that's why the thumping of her heart was so loud.

Ariel whispered at her that someone had shown up looking for

Lily. "She was lying about her name, by the way. It's Rachel! Why lie about your name at a wellness retreat? Maybe she's a fugitive. Told you she was a nut!" She delivered this news with a disproportionate amount of self-righteousness.

Katie's gut fizzed. What did it mean that Lily was lying about her name? Did it mean anything at all? Katie looked at Ellie, who mirrored her baffled, panicked look. Then she shrugged, like Lily's name was inconsequential: a bloody knife was a bloody knife.

"How was your session with Dr. Dave? What did you do?" Ariel asked her for the second time.

"It was okay." Katie wasn't going to talk about it.

Paula pulled her board out of the water and started to do a dry-land attempt at kneeling on the paddleboard, but it looked like her knees were locking and she was wincing in pain.

Naomi power-paddled back to shore. "Paula, what did we discuss? Arthritis is just a symptom of negative thinking."

"I know, I know, but it sure doesn't feel that way." Paula rubbed her knees. "I guess I overdid it yesterday." Naomi silently placed her hands on both of Paula's shoulders and pressed her down. Paula let out a yelp as her knees buckled and yet, she managed to kneel.

"See? Just as Dr. Dave said, the body goes where the mind takes it, and your psychic pain is manifesting as arthritis in your knees. You need to outthink it, Paula, outthink it!"

Paula's face was white. Her eyes were wide and shiny with tears. For a moment it looked as if she might pass out; instead she looked up at Naomi and said, "Thank you."

"Good grief," Carmen muttered.

"C'mon, everyone, let's get going," Naomi shouted like a spin-class leader.

The group waded farther out so the fins of their boards wouldn't hit the bottom of the lake. Katie stood there, knee-deep, eyeing her board. The water. It looked smooth and calm.

This had been the part of the weekend she'd always envisioned herself doing. Or, well, getting a pic of herself doing it, holding her paddle over her head, because it seemed like everyone else she knew had one.

"Who wants to take bets on who's taking a dive into the water first?" Carmen grinned.

"Well, I have no plans to stand up on this thing," Ariel said back, her voice a nervous wobble. "Why do people want to do this? I don't get it. Why can't we just boat around the lake and sightsee? Yoga is a land activity. And why don't they provide life jackets?"

"Come on, Ariel, I thought you were trying new things." Carmen's voice had a teasing edge to it.

"It's easy. It really is." Ellie got on the board, belly down, and then eased up onto her knees. The board gave a tiny shake, and then in one quick, easy movement, she was standing up and digging her paddle into the rocky lake floor so she didn't float off.

"I guess it's not your first time," Ariel mumbled.

Carmen went next. From her knees, she took on a gymnast's landing standing stance, the board shaking beneath her until she stood straight up. "Not bad, eh?" She stuck the paddle in the water and gave herself a push off, somehow managing to turn around and come back.

It was Katie's turn, but she stayed on her knees. The board felt too uncertain, and she couldn't be bothered to try to stand. The fetid fishy smell of the lake was tickling the back of her throat.

And then Ariel. They all tried not to watch too hard as Ariel struggled onto the board in her unathletic way. She grabbed onto it, belly down like it was a piece of wreckage on the open sea, before slowly getting up onto her knees. And then, in that slow-mo way that makes something exceptionally funny, she tipped over. Her eyes bulged, and her arms did a series of circles to try to keep her on the board, and when it was clear she was going down, she held out her arms like the water was going to break her fall.

When she face-planted into the water, they burst out laughing.

It was one of those things they couldn't help laughing at. Katie tipped her head back and let out a raw giggle. It felt like pent-up steam rushing through her throat, her own board trembling under her. When Ariel came up sputtering, shouting, "See what I mean?" Katie laughed even harder.

This would've been an inside joke that Carmen and Katie could endlessly use to tease Ariel—*See what I mean?*—were Katie not so aware of how soon the moment would be over, how soon she'd snap back to her misery of the bloodied knife.

Carmen wobbled, jumped off her own board. Made a point to float on her back and kick her legs so she splashed everyone around her. Katie took her paddle and splashed her back. Carmen dived, disappearing under the water, then coming up behind Katie and shaking her off her board.

They stood in a tight circle, laughing hysterically as they splashed one another. Katie jumped on Carmen's back; Carmen flopped backward so they both went in the water. Ariel splashed at them as they stood up. Katie sent her a tidal wave back, and Ariel cried out that she'd gotten water in her mouth, *ewwwwww*. Katie could feel Ellie watching, and she avoided eye contact with her. She was worried she'd see that questioning look. *How could you be so callous to laugh and play around at a time like this?* Katie would need to again face that she was a dog killer and a possible murderess. But for now, she was neither, because what she didn't know, she didn't know. She was glad that Nate hadn't answered. If nothing else, Katie was an all-star at tucking away unpleasant things until she forgot about them completely. Her ability to repress was the closest thing she had to a superpower.

"All right, girls, come on, let's go!" Naomi took it upon herself to paddle over, like they were the bad kids in gym class smoking behind the bleachers. Ariel stayed kneeling after her fall and bobbed along next to Katie. They were trailing Carmen and Ellie, who were ahead, but still within talking distance.

"It's like cross-country skiing on water, and who wants to cross-country ski?" Ariel was still complaining.

"I miss you, Ariel." Katie felt a sudden burst of needing to get her affairs in order in case she really went to jail, to do the list of things she would do if she were dying, like tell her friends she loved them.

"Well, I miss you too, Katie. How was your session with Dr. Dave?"

Why is she asking that again? "You've asked me that twice already! Like I said, it was fine. Good."

Ariel wilted slightly and looked away.

"It's so beautiful here." Carmen dipped her paddle and glided forward. It was.

Now that they were moving, the smell of the lake cleared, and Katie took in a deep breath of clean country air, feeling the sun on her face. There was a warm, silky-soft breeze brushing over her skin. The shoreline looked impossibly green and wild, and that fidgety mania always simmering in her chest just went *swoosh*. She could almost feel it leaving her body like an exorcism. For the first time, she felt like she was at a wellness retreat. *Peaceful.*

They paddled along the lake, soaking up the sun and scenery, until Katie gave up on paddling, lay back on her board, and tanned. "Oh, good idea," Ariel gushed and did the same. Carmen and Ellie paddled farther ahead.

"Do you think I'm going to get a tan line from this leash thing?" Not that Katie tanned so much as burned with her white, freckly skin without a thick layer of SPF 50, but the cuff was the size of an ankle monitoring bracelet, and Katie didn't exactly need to look at an outline of that for the rest of the day, so she ripped open the Velco and slid it off.

"I don't think you should take that leash thingy off, Katie."

"We're so close to land, we could probably still stand up in this water."

Katie stared up at the sky, so clear and blue it almost looked like a solid thing hovering over her. Her body ached with exhaustion. Her eyes fluttered closed, and then just like that, she was asleep. A deep drifting into nothingness. She floated along that way until the distant sharp buzz of a speedboat half roused her.

Off in the distance she heard Naomi shouting that they should all get ready for some waves. "Shift your weight. Find your center of balance."

Still, sleepy, Katie tried to sit up, but she wasn't prepared for the wild swaying of her board. She saw she was much farther behind everyone else. Even Ariel.

Instead, Katie slowly rolled over onto her stomach and hugged her board as it rocked back and forth until the water started to calm back down.

She stared into the hazy green lake at the little flecks of beetles resurfacing. Then she caught sight of something deeper in the water. Something white and engorged looking. Seaweed fluttered around it like hair. "Lily?" Its bulging eyes flicked opened and a face rushed up at her. Katie jerked back, and suddenly she was plummeting fast and hard into the water and then she was really awake.

Her eyes opened. Her own hair swirled around her. All she could see was weedy green. The water was freezing cold and bit into her after the baking sun. The shock of it turned her all around. She couldn't tell up from down. The lake floor wasn't there. She felt like she was doing somersaults in outer space. She hadn't even gotten a chance take in a breath when she fell in. Her chest instantly tightened.

Her mouth opened, and she took an involuntary breath; her throat and mouth filled with water. She choked and let out a short gust of air bubbles. Her vision sparked. She could hear distant shouting overhead. Her body twisted and contorted. Everything was being squeezed out of her.

And then she saw a door. *The* door. Her little girl door with the

Hello Kitty stickers and the hook with the pink feather boa that fluttered when the door opened.

The handle was turning. A fuzzy silhouette, backlit from the hallway light. His head tilted, and then he was gone again in the dark when her door closed.

Now she could see it was a man, but then she knew that already. It was his smell. So familiar.

She shut her eyes. Could hear him padding toward her on her thick beige carpet. She counted, *one, two, three,* but she couldn't sit up. And then he set himself down on the edge of her bed, *one, two, three.* A pull of the covers. A hand.

He shifted, bounced up and down harder. Touched her hand, picked it up, then let it go like he was testing how asleep she was, but she wasn't all the way gone yet. Her mind was still conscious and she tried to gather all of her mental energy to tell him to go away, to not touch her, but she couldn't get the words out.

Then he shoved something into her mouth; it jabbed the back of her throat, and she couldn't breathe, just like now.

She would be safe if she could only get up. Get to the party. To her mother. AJ. Nate. If she could just open her eyes all the way.

Then he put all his weight on her, squishing out the shriek building inside of her. His wet mouth was in her ear, repeating, *I'll be gentle, I promise. I'll be gentle. You won't remember anyway.* A sudden sharp burning seared through her vagina.

No one would understand it. I'd get into trouble. Shhhh.

He was so heavy. His voice sounded like gurgling water. *My little superstar. My doll. Oh, such an angel when you're so quiet.*

She was trapped like this. Drowning under the weight of him. She marked time by listening to the sounds of the party. She focused on the music, looping choruses, the end of one song and the start of another. A trill of laughter. A man's blobby voice.

And then it was over because she disappeared into sleep and was gone.

Katie took in another gulp of water, felt her eyes bulge, blood vessels spidering the whites of her eyes. Veins popped in her forehead. Her lips parted, secreted more bubbles. Slow and barely there now. Something inky was closing in on her. Then her foot touched the bottom of the lake.

She looked up. A beam of sunlight. Ellie was peering down at her from her paddleboard. And then Carmen was there, thrusting her paddle into the water, and Katie pushed off and was reaching, reaching, feeling around half-blind, finally gripping the paddle in her hand.

When she broke through the surface, Max the paramedic was there, and he hauled her up onto Carmen's paddleboard so she was lying across it. "Are you okay?" someone asked but her ears were too full of water to tell who it was.

Katie coughed up a throat full of water, and then her stomach crumpled and she retched the water back into the lake. Carmen speed-paddled them both back to the Sanctuary, dropping into the water as they neared the shore, pulling Katie the rest of the way like a floating stretcher. Max started checking her over. Katie wanted to scream at everyone to stop touching her, but she had no air left to scream.

Ariel and Carmen huddled around her. Someone wrapped her in a towel. Her teeth wouldn't stop chattering. Her lips were numb. Her face was numb, but eventually she managed to tell everyone that she was okay.

But she wasn't okay.

She'd been molested. Raped.

The memory of it was like a clot in her brain, wrapped in its own membrane. It had just been stretched and pricked and was trickling out. She could feel it fluttering at the base of her skull. Breathing down her neck like its own entity. Threatening to burst open all the way.

Someone had done this to her, and she knew from the feel of the weight on her chest and from his smell that it was someone familiar. That it hadn't just happened once. It had been more than once. She had been raped over and over in the shadows of a childhood she thought she remembered.

Those parties Lucy threw, so many men wandering drunkenly through the house, swinging her door open when she was half-dressed, looking for the bathroom.

She couldn't see his face, only a featureless blob of black. The mental equivalent of a blurred ski mask. Then a disconnected twist of a thought.

Shelby Spade was sexually abused. Not me. Shelby Spade.

Anything to distance herself from whatever was buoying up in the black whirlpool that was her memory. But it didn't work. She could feel it too much, pressing on her windpipe. The rage.

I was sexually abused.

ELLIE

Katie went straight to bed with one of her bottles of vodka, cradling it like it was a hot water bottle for a stomachache. Ellie didn't even try to stop her. Katie knew the rules about the tea, and if she decided to break them, well, Ellie just hoped that everyone else saw it too. So she had no trouble letting the girl squad into their room to fawn all over her.

"So that's where you two went this morning. Couldn't last a full twenty-four hours without a little tipple, eh?" Ariel remarked in a cheery, singsongy voice when she saw the vodka.

"Listen, why don't I go into town and get you some mix for that vodka? Some soda? Orange juice? Red Bull? Whatever. But you're going to need your stomach pumped if you keep downing it like that. Did you even eat lunch?" Carmen was antsy and tensed up like she was about to take off out the door. Ellie thought it must be caffeine withdrawal.

Katie shook her head in a far-off way. Carmen placed her hand on Katie's forehead as if she were a feverish child.

Ariel crawled into bed next to Katie and stroked her hair and cooed that the fall into the lake wasn't that bad.

Ellie couldn't believe the enabling that was taking place. She fought an urge to fling open the drawer with the knife, pull it out, and say, *Take a look at this. See what I found in the bathroom sink this morning? You want to cheer her up?*

"I'm just going to sleep for a while," Katie said quietly, her lips hardly moving, as if her mouth were numb.

"I'll go and get you some diet soda, Katie. Where's the key to the Escalade?" Carmen was up and off the bed. A little too eager to get out of the room. Definitely sugar or caffeine withdrawal.

"Yeah, and some snacks since you haven't eaten. I can go with you, Carmen. I tried one of Naomi's granola bars, and it was like sucking on a rock," Ariel chimed in. Ellie was sure she'd probably return with a box of hundred-calorie packets of Cheetos or some other junk food passing itself off as sensible because it contained two pieces per foil bag. So much waste.

"I can go pick up diet soda and snacks. I don't mind," Ellie volunteered. Better that she went. Who knows, maybe she'd see a beat-up Lily hitchhiking along the road. She had planned that she and Katie would take another long, meditative walk to scour the woods for Lily's body. It would be so much better if Katie found her, not Ellie, because the person to find a body was usually a good first suspect.

Just like Katie to give up so easily and leave it all to Ellie.

"No, I got it," Carmen said flatly, already searching for the keys.

Ellie reluctantly pulled them out of her pocket and handed them over. Carmen started for the door.

"Wait for me," Ariel called after her.

"It's all right, Ariel. I can go by myself. Stay with Katie; she'll need you here."

Ariel's face shifted into an overly pleased expression, and she flopped back down next to Katie.

Carmen couldn't leave fast enough.

The whole scene of Ariel petting Katie was making Ellie uncomfortable. What if Katie, in this vulnerable state, just spewed everything to Ariel?

How much would that vacant-brained girl love to be the center of that drama? She'd immediately sound the alarm, then stick to

Katie's side like a barnacle to make sure she was in every single media shot. Playing up her role as loyal friend in interviews until she was Katie's full-blown publicist.

And fine. Why did Ellie care? She didn't really. She just didn't want it to happen yet. Not until after the weekend, not until Ellie thoroughly extricated herself from Lily's probable murder, and then Ariel could leech away after that.

Worse, though, was if Ariel suggested a new theory.

It surprised Ellie that it hadn't yet occurred to Katie that she might have stumbled upon Lily's murderer while he or she was in the act.

And that the killer, realizing her somnolent state, had pressed the knife into Katie's hand and watched as she weaved her way back to her room. Now the killer was waiting, maybe even watching Katie more closely to see if she would remember—and if she did, she'd have to die too.

The only reason Ellie hadn't voiced this scenario out loud to Katie was that she knew it would send her flying back to the city. It would give her a way out of the retreat and the tea.

And how did it make sense, when there was no body? At least not yet.

The sponsor showing up there had certainly ratcheted things up, hadn't it? Ellie couldn't have predicted that, and so soon after Lily's "departure."

Time was ticking now.

"I think we should let Katie sleep for a little while." Ellie parked herself at the door. She wasn't going to leave Ariel in the room. It was too dangerous.

"And I think Katie can decide for herself if she is tired," Ariel yipped back at her.

"She already said she wanted to go to sleep." Ellie made her voice firm, same as when you're training a dog.

"S'okay, Ariel. I just want to sleep." Katie's eyes slid over both of them, and it looked like she was about to say something, but then she rolled toward the wall. The bed squeaked. The floral wall-paper seemed to move in around her.

"Well, then, we will leave you to it." Ellie opened the door and waited for Ariel to follow her out, which she did with a slow, droopy shuffle.

"I'll check on you again soon," Ariel said over her shoulder, shooting Ellie a defiant flick of her eyebrows before darting down the stairs.

ARIEL

Ariel clomped down the stairs and out of the house, her jealousy pinballing again from Dr. Dave giving Katie a "session" right back to Ellie.

How dare Ellie practically kick her out of Katie's room? What was her problem? There was something unhealthy about the way Ellie seemed to be keeping Katie away from her friends. She was controlling, and Katie didn't even seem to realize it.

Ariel couldn't believe how Ellie had stood at the door with those icy-cold blue eyes of hers. There was an edge to Ellie she hadn't picked up on until now. This entire weekend, she'd thought Ellie had this one-dimensional personality of blandly pleasant—the way beautiful women do because they don't need to develop a real personality—but now she saw something different. Unpleasant. Dark, even.

Maybe it had to do with money? Did Ellie think Katie was too generous with her friends and by isolating her was hoping to be the sole recipient of all that generosity?

She wouldn't put it past her.

And Ariel *needed* to be with her friends. She certainly wouldn't have any left by now in Shakopee. Her Holiday Inn coworkers had probably already banned her from their after-work cocktails and fried desserts at Applebee's because sleeping with a pregnant woman's husband was akin to drowning kittens. Never mind what she had done to Rob's wife.

Once again, she was alone.

Thinking. Fretting. Worrying.

Twining her hair around her finger, feeling a satisfying rip of her roots as they separated from her scalp.

Simon and Marie were doing slow tai chi movements on the lawn. She couldn't see Dr. Dave anywhere. Paula and Anthony were sitting on a blanket together. Anthony was blowing bubbles, and Paula was laughing like a toddler as she popped them.

Ariel noticed the woodpile. The ax sticking out of the tree stump. She went over and pulled the ax out.

It was heavier than it looked. The handle was warm from the late-afternoon sun. Ariel had earned a wood badge during her time in Girl Scouts. She picked up a log, stood it upright, and swung the ax down into it.

The blade caught, and she had to raise the ax with the log stuck to the end of it and bring it down once, twice, before splitting the wood into two.

Now *this* was cathartic. The smooth swing of an ax, the perfect splitting of one thing into two, then three. Rivulets of sweat were already running down her back and gathering on her forehead.

With each log she placed on the stump, she thought of someone before swinging the ax like she were practicing to become an ax murderer.

Rob.

Rob's wife, who was never real to Ariel because Rob turned her into a caricature of the sort of wife men cheated on—withholding, histrionic, nagging, and threatening. Whenever Ariel tried to push Rob on when he would finally ask for a divorce, he'd snap at her because he took so much bullshit at home he couldn't deal with any more of it. He'd stop talking to her for a few days, then he'd text a room number followed by an emoji with its tongue out that she'd liked to think was his way of flirting.

And in return, she felt sorry for him. She'd rub his shoulders, tell him how his wife didn't appreciate him enough, then eventually jump on his dick and do some porny performance full of unrequited yearning until she was practically singing that old Cardigans' song and waving jazz hands as she rode him. *Love me, love me, say that you love me.*

Ellie. For being a haughty British snob who was trying to take her best friend away from her.

Carmen. For not wanting her to come shopping with her.

Lily. Who had nearly burned her face off.

Naomi. For kissing Dr. Dave like that.

Her parents. For not having enough money to keep her afloat in New York long enough to establish herself, forcing her back to Shakopee and the Holiday Inn. And Rob.

Herself, for going up to Rob's house. For trying the door after no one answered. For going inside and everything that happened afterward.

"Yo, Ariel. I like what I see here." It was Dr. Dave, and suddenly everything was all right.

How long had he been watching? Ariel had lost all sense of time, and when she saw the scattering of hacked-up wood pieces sprinkled around her, she was surprised. *I did all this?*

"Oh, thanks." She set the ax down with delicate care, like a cocked gun she was suddenly frightened of, and rubbed the sweat off her forehead with her arm.

"You know what?" Dr. Dave tapped his chin, like he was deciding something. "Come with me. I have something for you. Another challenge."

And then everything went brighter, like a dimmer switch had been cranked all the way up. *He's so beautiful,* she thought. Looking at Dr. Dave was like looking directly into the sun. It almost hurt. Now Ariel was practically skipping behind him as he led her away from the Sanctuary and down a narrow, bushy path. "What is it? What's the challenge?"

"I can't tell you; that'll spoil the surprise. Y'know, every retreat my wife and I put on, there is always someone who stands out as being vibrationally higher than all the other guests, and this weekend, well, that person is you."

"Really?" Ariel's heart soared. Should she ask him if her good vibrations called for another treatment? And then she wondered what he thought of Katie's vibrations.

Dr. Dave stopped so suddenly Ariel almost bumped into him. He turned around and took hold of her wrist, his grip pinching her skin. "Yes, really. Why would I say something that wasn't true?" He looked hurt. "Don't you trust me?"

"I do trust you. I trust you a great deal." Ariel reached out and ran her nails down his forearm. She wanted to kiss him. Wanted him to give her another "treatment." She wanted him.

Dr. Dave slid away from her and started walking again. "Then don't ask me, 'Really?'" He mimicked her voice in a way that made her feel stupid. She started to think that maybe what had happened at the rope course wasn't going to happen again. Ariel mumbled an apology and followed along. She listened to their feet crunching leaves and dirt. They walked in silence for a few minutes and it felt like a wasted opportunity to Ariel. She wanted to know more about him.

"So how did you meet Naomi? Was it love at first sight?" Her voice sounded thinner than air.

"We met a few years ago."

How, not when. Not what I asked. "Was she a patient of yours? Kind of like how Katie was today?" She sputtered out a cringeworthy giggle.

"I met my wife at exactly the right time—it was like all the right elements coming together to create the planet Earth. Naomi was unhappy and I led her out of her darkness." Ariel thought about the family picture in the basement. Had Naomi been one of those unhappy mothers who walked out on her children? "We shared a vision. I had the know-how and she had the finances and together we're able to help people." Ariel knew it. He'd married Naomi for her money! Now she could be his younger, prettier (once she dropped this extra weight) wife. "If you're asking me questions because you're feeling jealous or possessive, you need to know that I don't engage with petty emotions like that, Ariel, and neither should you. It's below people like us."

Her heart skipped. *People like us.* "Yeah, sure. Of course."

They kept hiking in silence, Dr. Dave pausing here and there to wait for Ariel to catch up. She watched him from behind, his broad shoulders, the sway of his back giving way to a shelf made of muscular butt, his calves pulsing with the strength of a man who was always moving. She pictured calling up her parents and sister to announce that she was in a serious relationship with a *doctor*.

"We're in the nature reserve now," Dr. Dave announced, once again as congenial as an airline pilot. "Ariel, do you know how many choices people make in a single day?"

Was she expected to answer, or was this a rhetorical question? Five, ten? How many choices were real choices and not just reactions? What was the difference?

Rhetorical, because Dr. Dave answered himself. "Thousands and thousands of mundane choices piled on other, equally dull decisions. And you know what happens then? You're so inundated with monotony that you forget all those decisions have brought you to this very moment and that you did this—you haphazardly created your life, the life you have to live with until you die."

Ariel wasn't sure about that. It seemed a lot was already decided for a person depending on the place and parents they were born to, or at least that's what Carmen kept saying. Dr. Dave seemed to know what she was thinking.

"Now imagine if you became highly aware of all those decisions and treated each one as a life-or-death decision. It's how I live, Ariel. I don't tumbleweed about; I'm not a translucent jellyfish coasting on waves in the oceans—I am a man. I create my existence."

There was an excited edge to Dr. Dave's voice.

Just then, Ariel noticed how the air had shifted.

And then she became aware of a kind of ragged wheeze.

Ariel noticed the flattened grass—like something had been dragged—a streak of blood. Her throat went dry and tight.

"Can you make a life-or-death decision, Ariel?"

"Yeah, yes, I can." Ariel just wanted to get to the next part of whatever this was about.

"Then you're going to need this." When Dr. Dave turned around, he was holding a long curved knife.

CARMEN

Carmen found a cluster of big-box stores. She went to a hardware store first, then drove diagonally across a nearly empty parking lot the size of two football fields to a Walmart.

She speed-walked the aisles, filling her cart with some diet 7UP and Red Bull for Katie, some random snacks. She tossed in four rolls of Saran Wrap.

Once, when she had gone to Tommy's house, she had spotted several tins of baby formula on his coffee table.

"What? You got a new baby, Tommy?" Tommy was an overly chatty guy for a drug dealer, so Carmen avoided starting any conversation with him. Her head was usually filled with thoughts of disbelief, *I am not here, this isn't my life, this isn't me, it's not my life*, but the sight of it filled her with dread for whatever baby was living there.

"Nah. I just got some higher-end clientele."

Carmen gave him a puzzled look. "Like cokehead mothers who are still breastfeeding?" Her joke fell flat and Tommy rolled his eyes at her.

"I usually cut everything with baking soda. Never flour, man, because it gets clumpy if it gets wet, and screw icing sugar because it gets everything sticky. Plus, I ain't no baker." Tommy grinned. "But baking soda burns nostrils and people can tell if you mixed in too much. So because I want to keep these new customers, I am gonna use this shit." He nodded at the formula.

Obviously Carmen wasn't cutting cocaine. She was completely

replacing it, but still, if Tommy said baby formula then that's what she should get. Might as well go with a professional's advice.

Carmen loaded her cart with canisters, first with ten cans for ten bricks, then worried it wouldn't be enough, so she went for a full dozen. A frazzled-looking woman with a bawling baby wheeled up and scowled like Carmen was trying to hoard all the baby formula in town.

Carmen gave her an empathetic look and handed her a canister. "They say breast is best, but my little one guzzles this stuff down like he's at a keg party," she quipped without meaning to. What the fuck was she saying? She sounded like Katie. The woman took the canister, placed it in her cart, and swiftly wheeled away. Carmen could suddenly feel the store cameras watching her as she moved to the front of the store to pay. Sweat was gathering in her armpits.

The twinkly music from a speaker above played "Daydream Believer" as she placed canister after canister on the conveyor belt to be scanned. The cashier eyed her but didn't say a word, even after Carmen finally blurted, "Nanny problems. It never ends!" with a shrug and a giggle that didn't sound like her at all. How was she going to pull this off if she couldn't even keep her story straight with Walmart employees? *Take it like it's already yours.* She let out a puff of air, rolled her shoulders like she was about to get into a boxing ring, then added a pack of gum.

Carmen tossed the plastic bags dangling from her wrists into the back of the Escalade. *Time to make some cocaine.*

She pulled into a rest stop off the highway that seemed to be from another time. The men's and women's bathrooms were divided by a portico, dark as a back alley. There were two vending machines, lights out and empty except for a lone pack of chips. Someone had spray-painted NO FUTURE against the brown cinder block.

Maybe all rest stops felt this anachronistic, like the broken remnants of a long-ago utopian dream of a place where families could get out of wood-paneled station wagons, stretch their legs, and maybe enjoy a picnic lunch in an isolated, overgrown place and not a welcoming spot for any murderous psychopath to lurk.

Carmen got out and crawled into the back of the Escalade.

She took out her purchases and arranged them around her in the order she would go in like a little cocaine-packing buffet. Cocaine was just powdery white stuff—easy enough to replicate, but the packaging had to be precise. So precise that Simon could check on his stash and not feel compelled to cut into one of the packets because something seemed off.

It had taken an entire roll of cellophane and a canister of baby formula before Carmen had finally figured out how to wrap the cellophane into a tight enough brick that it would fit nicely into a foam block. She'd gone to Walmart's sports section, found half an aisle of dusty yoga equipment and everything one might possibly need for a zombie apocalypse: tents, knives, guns, ammo. She lingered over the knives and gazed at the guns locked in the glass case, but retreated before she made a bad decision.

Instead she took down the measurements of a foam yoga block and bought a spool of nylon rope. On her first brick, she'd tried to adjust the duct tape, ripping the cellophane open, and *poof,* it was like a powder bomb had gone off in the back of the SUV. The back window was coated with a fine dusting of Similac, and Carmen's lips tasted like sour milk.

She was going to have to find a car wash and vacuum this damn thing out. She had to keep the car running, because it was too hot not to have the AC on.

Now, several attempts later, she had ten very fine, convincing bricks of cocaine.

Ten.

She really just couldn't stop herself from making ten. She knew her odds of getting away with it would be better if she just took one or two, and that's what she should do—take just a little bit and hope it went unnoticed. But she couldn't stop herself from fantasizing about taking all ten, and then it was like her greedy fingers couldn't stop toiling until she had enough.

Greed slithered through her head, coiling around her brain and squeezing.

She had started to reason that the risk was high either way, so why not make off with the entire pot of gold? And not just pocket change. *The risk is justified.* She kept repeating it. *The money justifies the risk.*

She heard the rumbling of another vehicle pulling in.

It parked right beside her. *What the fuck?* It was like being on a bus with plenty of empty seats and then some dude gets on and sits down right beside you and you know you're in trouble.

Carmen's head twitched. A door opened.

Her heart started racing. *Fuck, fuck.* She was in an Escalade (wasn't the Cadillac every drug dealer's vehicle of choice?) with a shitload of stage prop cocaine. She was probably about to get carjacked.

She heard the crunch of gravel as whoever it was stepped around the Escalade.

A sudden knock on the driver's-side window—

She shoved the fake cocaine into the Walmart bags, lunged over the back seat, and squeezed through to the front. Rolled down the driver's-side window. "Oh. Hey, hi. Everything okay, Officer?"

KATIE

"Hey, funny girl, I've been looking for you. How're you feeling?" It was Max bounding up the porch steps.

"Waterlogged." Katie gave him a shrug of a smile. She couldn't sleep, so she'd poured some vodka into her yellow Nalgene bottle with the intention of sitting by the water and drinking. Maybe even hiking around a little to clear her mind. But she got to the porch and felt too overwhelmed to go any farther and flopped down on a porch swing.

Max grinned. "Yeah, that was a bad spill."

"Uh-huh. It was," Katie said noncommittally.

Max lingered.

"Y'know, I used to watch your show. I mean, I wouldn't have admitted it to any of my friends or anything, but yeah, I liked it. The show and, well, you. I think you were one of my first crushes."

Katie took a slug from her Nalgene bottle. "Oh, that's nice. I'm glad I caused you a great deal of shame."

"Oh, I didn't mean it that way—"

"Relax, Max! I'm kidding. Just messing with ya."

"Yeah, I knew that." He sat down on the sectional covered in cheery aqua-blue pillows. The porch was overly stuffed with leafy ferns, rustic lanterns, and starburst mirrors. There was one of those hunks of rock that plugged in that was supposed to purify the air, which made no sense to Katie. "You look sad."

She shrugged. "I just . . . I guess I *am* sad. It's all too much."

"What's too much?"

She looked at Max, and her eyes started to water. An angry scream sounded through her head, a plea to go back in time and fix this weekend. Her entire life. That's what a true wellness retreat needed: a fucking time machine.

"Everything." She sighed the word, annoyed at herself for saying anything at all.

"You want to talk?"

"No. I don't want to talk; I want to drink." She lifted her Nalgene bottle and took a sip, the vodka burning her throat. He scanned her face.

"What's in there?"

"Vodka. Want some?"

"No. I'm good. I can't drink; it's, uh, not good for my psyche." Max's eyes lingered a beat too long on the bottle. Clearly, there was more to the story.

"Well, it's good for mine." Katie took another stinging mouthful.

"How about we do something?"

"Like what?"

"Something to get your mind off *everything*. We could go to the spa. Get a massage? Sit in the hot tub?"

"I think I've had enough water for today, thanks."

"A massage?"

Katie shook her head. She didn't think she could bear to be touched right then. "I think only a lobotomy would do the job." She wanted to be unconscious. A blank space.

"Ha! Right. Well, unfortunately, I didn't seem to pack my lobotomy kit." Max did a fake pat down of his body. He was wearing a red T-shirt that hung just right, tight dark-washed jeans, and white sneakers that seemed to reflect the sun. "So how about a board game? I spotted some in the living room."

Before Katie could say no, Max darted back into the house and came out holding up a deck of cards and Life. "Which one?"

"I can't tell if you're trying to be ironic." Katie's little Life car would be devoid of other family pinhead pegs. It would just be her on the run from the law. Then, just to feel extra bad, she remembered how she hadn't even bothered to renew her license.

"How about I show you the one card trick I know?"

"Oh, yes, magic tricks. Is that how you woo all the girls at parties, Max?"

"Damn right. Works every time too." He fanned out the cards in his hand and held them out to Katie. "Take one. Look at it, remember the card, and put it back in."

Katie pulled out a ten of clubs, put it back in the deck. Max had her do this two more times until she caught on. "You don't know any card tricks, do you?"

Max started laughing. A good, hearty laugh right from his belly. "What? How could you say that? Because clearly this is your card or one of three of your cards." He whipped out the queen of hearts. Katie shook her head.

"Nope. Not even close."

"Okay, fine, you got me. I don't know any card tricks, but hey, you're smiling a little now. You know any card games?"

"Just one. War." Katie slowed down on the vodka as she sat opposite Max and slapped down cards, one after the other. The swing, gently swaying back and forth, made her feel weightless.

ELLIE

For once, the wood-chopping had stopped. That noise had been in the background most of the day. What a strange noise to get used to.

Ellie had returned from another unsuccessful hike in the woods. She spotted Naomi padlocking the storage shed next to the garden. She was wearing an oversize straw hat, gloves, and a billowy, beige jumper with dirty knees. Not good gardening attire, that jumper.

Ellie marched over to her. "May I speak with you for a moment?" She didn't try to hide how worried she felt. She would have preferred to talk to Dr. Dave but couldn't find him, so Naomi would have to do.

"Hello, Ellie. Of course, you sure can talk to me. I was just picking some spinach. It's hard to get the right bunch of spinach. It can be too earthy or wilted." She touched the spinach in the basket hanging from her arm with warm affection.

"So, I was hoping to find out how Katie's hypnosis went earlier. Did Dr. Dave happen to say anything to you?"

"How is Katie doing now?" Naomi echoed Ellie's question.

"She's shaken up, but no worse for the wear."

"Wonderful." Naomi then shook her head, clicked her tongue. "Not sure why she would have removed the safety leash like that. I told all of you to keep the leash on." Naomi wagged her finger like Ellie had done something wrong too.

"Yes, well, Katie is impulsive and does not always behave in ways that make any bloody sense to those around her. It's actually why we're here. Katie has had mental health issues most her life, and she wanted to try some alternative treatments."

"I can personally attest that Dr. Dave's program will free Katie of any mental anguish."

"I hope that's true for her sleepwalking issues as well. Katie *thinks* it's her most pressing issue, and I can understand why since I've witnessed her doing all sorts of bizarre, even disturbing things while sleepwalking." Ellie hoped Naomi would press her for details.

"Oh dear!" A mosquito landing on the back of her hand suddenly distracted Naomi. She brought her hand up and examined the insect with wonder before gently blowing on it until it released its syringe-like mouth and flew away. "Fortunately any sleep issues can be resolved through my husband's program."

For a wellness counselor, Naomi was very difficult to talk to. "So how was Katie's session with Dr. Dave? Because I feel her sleepwalking is a symptom of something more deeply rooted. She can be very erratic at times."

"Well, I can't tell you specifics. That's confidential."

"I understand, but I'm practically her family. I'm her sister-in-law."

"Sorry, I can't," Naomi said, singsongy. And that was why Ellie would have preferred to talk to Dr. Dave. She hoped she could have batted her eyes at him, hinted at something more, and he would've spilled everything that Katie might have said. "I am sure, however, that my husband's hypnosis session had an impact on her. He is incredibly talented."

Ellie thought she would continue and say Dr. Dave was talented at hypnosis or even talk therapy or something specific, but Naomi left it as a generalized talent.

"I suppose the reason I'm asking is that I want to know if there's some way to help her. She just seems especially stressed since we've arrived."

That got Naomi's attention. No one came to the Sanctuary and got worse.

"It's like something has happened and she's really stressed out by it."

Naomi's eyes narrowed into sharklike slits. She was offended. "Oh? Are you saying Katie has gotten worse since she's arrived at my retreat? That's not how it's supposed to work."

"I don't think the retreat itself has anything to do with it; it's just that Katie seems to be especially, well, haunted since we've arrived." *Haunted.* It was vague enough. People can be haunted with anxiety that they'd left their iron on back at home. She wasn't giving too much away.

"Well, you both sure missed a lot of the activities this morning, and we've designed the in a certain way that if you work it, it will work for you." Naomi was veering from where Ellie was trying to take her.

"Oh, no, it's not that. I think she's getting quite a lot out of being here. I almost feel like it might have to do with Lily. The girl who left."

"How so?"

"I think she was a reminder of Katie's glory days, of when she was famous, and this has somehow had a negative impact on her. At first, she seemed bothered by the girl's presence. And then with that woman showing up, Lily's sponsor, I don't know."

Naomi's eyes scuttled away, toward the house. She looked like she was in a hurry or maybe worried. Ellie continued, "Is it true that Lily was going by a different name? That her name was really Rachel?"

"Her sponsor called her Rachel, yes."

"Did she say why?"

"No." Naomi shrugged. "But sometimes people like to pretend to be someone else when they go on trips."

"Right. Hmmm. I just . . . well, Katie has had some trouble with a stalker, and I wondered . . . with Lily using a different name . . ." Ellie let her voice drift. Naomi just looked at her. "But then, it seems Katie is equally as stressed by her absence. I find it all very baffling."

"Tell her to come to me for a treatment. I can help."

"I will." Ellie had been hoping for more information about the sponsor. Whether she was coming back or if this sponsor had other people looking for Lily now. But at least she'd started to lay the groundwork; in case Lily's body was discovered, she had to start protecting herself now. There was no way she was going to go down as an accomplice to Katie Manning.

"Now I think you better come with me." Naomi dropped her basket of precious spinach.

"Oh, um, why?"

"Because you're the one in need of immediate help. You're emitting a very anxious aura and I think your preoccupation with your friend is a way to self-sabotage your own wellness journey. Come, come." Naomi was already walking away and expecting Ellie to follow, which she did, because Naomi was right. She *was* feeling anxious. She needed to slow down her thoughts and take some time for deep breathing, or else she was bound to make more mistakes.

ARIEL

A deer looked up at her with one lashy, mournful eye, its nostrils flaring. It struggled to get up, legs doing a feeble Bambi-on-ice twitch and then gave up.

"It's been hit by a car," Dr. Dave said solemnly, pressing the knife into Ariel's hand. "It made its way this far, and now it's slowly dying. Probably bleeding out."

Ariel held the knife. Her eyes skittering between the deer and the knife. "And you want me to . . ." Her voice edged up toward a shriek.

"I don't want you to do anything. I'm just showing you a life-or-death situation and giving you a tool to handle it. It's up to you to decide what to do."

Probably bleeding out? What if it wasn't? What if it was just hurt, like something was sprained and tomorrow it would be doing just fine and back to doing whatever deer did in the woods? It's not like its vitals had been taken or an X-ray was done. A doctor didn't just look at someone and say, "Slit 'er neck, because it looks like she's on 'er way out."

"I can't. I'm sorry, I just can't."

"You can. I know you can."

"I'm too scared."

"Ride that wave of fear, Ariel. I want you to know how powerful you are, how you can take a new path rooted in infinite possibility. There are no mistakes, Ariel, only choices that lead you to the place where you are right now—this situation with me—and if you open yourself up, everything serves your deepest awakening. You can't escape yourself, so why not be your best self?"

The doe was making heavy, ragged bleating noises that made Ariel squeamish. "I can't. I really can't."

Dr. Dave looked annoyed, and then he just shrugged. "All right. Okay, then. If you can't, you can't." He took the knife back and emitted a disappointed sigh. "Let's go, then." He started to walk away. His sudden movement made the deer try to get up again—a sad, pathetic sight.

"You're just going to leave it here? Shouldn't we help it?"

"You decided not to help it, Ariel."

"And what about you? Can't you do something?" She was getting angry now. She did not do well under pressure, especially not when she was feeling criticized.

"I chose to help you and not the deer." Dr. Dave whipped around and grabbed her shoulders. Ariel braced herself, expecting that he was going to shake her, but he didn't. He let her go with a kind of resignation that made Ariel feel desperate.

"Give it to me. The knife." She held her hand out for it.

Dr. Dave stood there a second, then made a big production of taking it back out of its sheath hanging from his belt. "You need to be quick, Ariel. Straight across the neck. You'll torture it if you don't go hard and all the way."

Ariel stomped back toward the deer. Again, this was not how she had envisioned this weekend. Among all the cashmere throws and steaming cups of hot chocolate that had danced in her head, there were no mercy kills.

And yet she knew she was capable of violence, maybe even of killing something. Someone.

But that was different. Rob's wife had attacked her first.

It was only five days ago when she'd driven over to Rob's house. At first, it was just one of her masochistic drive-bys, where she would park across the street and watch his house. Knowing Rob had his tidy little life inside. A wife and a child on the way.

Then Ariel had felt the biting urge for equilibrium. Why should Rob get to have it all and leave her single? She had believed in that moment that if she hadn't met Rob, if he hadn't promised a future with him, she wouldn't have stayed so long in Shakopee. She *would have* gone back to New York City, *would have* had a different, much more fabulous life.

He was to blame.

She wanted to tell Rob's wife about their affair. The timing was right, because Rob worked late on Tuesdays. And maybe too because she knew she was going away that weekend or because again, she was already feeling a tad high from watching all Dr. Dave's self-empowerment YouTube videos. She went up and knocked on the door.

No answer.

She tried the handle, and the door opened.

It was dusky and quiet inside.

A large wedding picture hung over their fireplace, Rob in his tux, clinging to his wife from behind. Bridget smiling so hard that it looked painful. Another large multi-photo frame with shots from a trip to somewhere tropical, with wall decals looped over it that spelled FAMILY.

Ariel suddenly had a burning urge to see the second floor. Where Rob slept with his pretty wife. She made her way upstairs and was immediately drawn to the freshly painted pink nursery. Little onesies were tightly folded and lined up in a basket under the changing table patterned with ladybugs, DADDY'S GIRL, and baked goods that this baby girl would one day beat herself up for eating. And then there was the requisite framed picture of the sonogram. This black-and-white blotch of a thing.

The ceiling light, a pink chandelier, flicked on.

"Why don't you make yourself at home?" It was Rob's wife standing at the door of the nursery, her skin glowing, cheeks red. She was perfectly pregnant, in the way that her pregnancy hadn't touched any other part of her body. Her face wasn't puffy, no extra weight had been gained. Bridget rested her hands protectively across her adorable beach ball–size belly. "I know why you're here." Bridget smirked at Ariel. "And you need to leave my husband alone."

"Leave him alone?" Ariel practically guffawed. "We've been sleeping together." Her voice sounded tinny in the pink room.

"You think I didn't know that? I've been with my husband since eighth grade." Rob had never told Ariel that. "You think you could show up here, tell me that my husband stuck his dick in you, and what? I would meekly move out so you could move in like the interloper you are?"

This wasn't how Ariel had planned it. She'd pictured tears, then wine being poured, the two of them forming an alliance. Rob's wife wasn't taking her seriously. Pretty, thin women like her never did. It was as if her fatness was an advertisement for own lack of willpower. They thought she was weak.

"I'm pregnant," Ariel lied. She couldn't stand to be dismissed like this. Couldn't stand that Rob's wife had hijacked this whole confrontation.

"No, you're not. You're a frumpy, unassertive, emotionally stunted idiot. I've already called the police. You're going to be charged for stalking and trespassing. Now get the fuck out of here." Anger, hot as bile, crept up Ariel's throat.

"Fine, but I am really pregnant, and Rob will have to pay child support for the next eighteen years, at least," Ariel said as she tried to pass Rob's wife, still standing in the doorway. Bridget lunged and grabbed Ariel's hair and used it like handlebars to shake her head back and forth.

They tumbled out into the hallway.

Ariel tried to get loose from the woman's grip. Her eyes were watering. She couldn't see anything. She wanted to get away. She wanted to go home.

Ariel still wasn't sure how it happened, but she tried to buck Rob's wife off her, and the next thing she knew, his wife was at the bottom of the stairs, screaming, "My baby! My baby!" her legs pointlessly writhing like the deer's were now.

The deer snorted as Ariel moved in close.

She knelt next to it, murmuring, "It's okay, s'okay, s'okay," to the deer. It was panting now, so fast its tongue lolled out of its mouth. She took the knife and pressed its sharp tip into the animal's neck. Hesitated. Ariel's arms were rubbery from the ax chopping.

The doe's eye was fixed on her. Was it pleading for her to stop or to hurry up?

She lifted the knife and brought it down hard, stabbing the deer in its neck. She shifted and straddled the deer. Lifted its head and started to drag the knife across its neck.

Viscous blood spilled out.

Her heart beat wildly in her chest, and every nerve ending in her body was perked and alive.

Ariel's hands were still dripping blood when Dr. Dave came up behind her. He wrapped his arm around her waist. He was so rangy and tall, she felt petite in his embrace. "I knew you could do it, Ariel." He pulled her back into him and pressed his hard-on into her.

How did he know she wasn't going to say no? How did he know how much she wanted him?

She turned around and kissed him, leaving a bloodied handprint on his cheek. He pushed her down to the ground. Ariel peeled off her shorts as he unbuckled his pants and then parted her legs that looked so ridiculously office-white next to his sun-bronzed skin.

He thrust into her, squeezing her breasts through her shirt.

Ariel was surprised and oh so pleased when she came, quickly and hard, and they were finished before the deer had bled out.

CARMEN

Carmen arrived back at the retreat just before dinner.

She'd managed to get rid of the officer easily enough. She'd told him she was staying at the Sanctuary and that she just needed a little break from the healthy eating and that she was so, so ashamed, but she'd finished an entire box of powdered doughnuts.

He rolled his eyes but nodded like he understood. "You ask me? That place is full of wing nuts. I would just keep driving if I were you."

Carmen flung herself out of the SUV, set on going straight to her room to hide her backpack, which was now full to the brim with "cocaine."

Dr. Dave cut her off in the driveway.

"Welcome back, Carmen." He gave her a stiff smile. "We've all been waiting for you." He motioned toward the front lawn, where all the retreaters were gathered in a circle with what looked like sleeping bags.

"Oh, sure. I just need to put my backpack up in my room."

"I will take if for you, the group has waited long enough." Dr. Dave tried to take the backpack off her shoulder but she swung, too wildly, away from his reach.

"Nope, I'm good. I'll just keep it. What's the exercise this time, *Dr. Dave?*" Carmen's voice dipped into sarcasm but she couldn't help how irritated she felt. She wanted to immediately stow her backpack someplace safe.

"I'm about to explain. Take a seat, please." He motioned for her to take the only vacant spot in the circle. She sat down between Ariel and Anthony. Simon was across from her. She'd cleaned herself up as much as possible in the bathroom at the car wash, but there were still some powdery streaks on her tank top and shorts. Did Simon notice?

"What took you so long?" Ariel leaned in and whispered.

"I got lost."

"He made us wait for you, you know," Anthony piped in, sounding very irritated at the delay.

"Where's the snacks?" Ariel asked.

"Uh, still in the car," Carmen answered. She still had her backpack on.

"Keep them away from me, okay? I don't want to break my diet."

Dr. Dave cleared his throat in their direction. Ariel sat up straight, her hands on her knees like a good little student.

"We are the alchemists of our own bodies and minds. We are now going to symbolically renew ourselves. Think of the bags before you as a place of transition. You might even envision them as cocoons or your mother's womb. The point is, you're going to get inside of them. Naomi will pull the drawstring tight, but don't worry, these bags are burlap, so you can't suffocate. Focus only on your breathing. Ask yourself this one question over and over, 'Who do I want to be? Who do I want to be?' When you have an answer, I want you to burst out and complete the transformation."

Everyone immediately stood up and started stepping into their giant bags.

Carmen didn't want to lose sight of her backpack. "I'm not really interested in getting into what is basically a body bag."

Katie snickered. Simon was looking at Carmen again. Studying her body with a look on his face she couldn't read.

"Then it is essential you do get into the bag; you should be interested in your own transformation, Carmen. Naomi can help you." There was a testiness to Dr. Dave's voice. Carmen knew that she was drawing attention to herself, and that she should just get into the bag.

Would it look odd if she kept her backpack on? She was going to keep it on. Naomi hustled over.

"You're not Dora the Explorer, are you? Let's take this off." Before she could stop her, Naomi pried Carmen's backpack off her. She flung it to the ground and Carmen's body clenched. For a split second she expected one of the powder bricks to bust open and explode a puffy white cloud, and then the gig would be up. "Lean over, please," Naomi demanded so she could tie the drawstring.

I can't believe I am inside a fucking bag. What is the point of this? All of Dr. Dave's exercises seemed like random salad bar offerings; too picked over, ultimately insubstantial, and left you hungry for something more.

And now she was standing in a burlap sack waiting to be reborn. Wasn't Dr. Dave also promising that everyone was going to be reborn, transformed, or whatever tomorrow at the tea? How many times could one person be reborn over a single Memorial Day weekend? Dr. Dave was just an entrepreneur masked as a wellness evangelist, and not a very good one at that.

He was stretching out an ayahuasca tea ceremony, which should take a single evening, into several days, calling it his *program* and charging an exorbitant amount of money.

To what? Sweat inside a bag! Wasn't this rebirthing technique used by quacky psychiatrists in the seventies? Didn't people suffocate and die?

And what was his program exactly? It was like a variety show and if nothing stuck, then Dr. Delusional had the Hail Mary of the ayahuasca tea that he served at the *end* of the weekend, so that a hallucinogenic experience would bleed over or obscure everything else preceding it and people would go on to recommend the retreat as life-altering.

Carmen's breathing went shallow. Panic was bubbling up her chest. She had forgotten she was a little claustrophobic. Maybe more than a little.

Breathe, breathe. Calm down. I can easily get out of this thing. Just focus on the backpack.

Carmen stood there, breathing, trying to keep an eye on her

backpack through the burlap fabric. It had been right there, she was sure of it, but now she couldn't see it. Where was her backpack? She jumped in a little circle looking for it, like she was in some blind potato sack race.

Someone was crying—was that Paula or Ariel? She couldn't tell.

Where was the backpack?

Anthony was humming something familiar—was that the Super Mario Bros. soundtrack?

"I feel like I'm a giant bottle of Crown Royal!" That was definitely Katie.

Carmen still couldn't spot the backpack. Naomi had to have taken it and put it somewhere. It had to be Naomi. Everyone else was inside a bag. *That's it. Calm down.* Naomi had no reason to go through her bag. *Calm. The. Fuck. Down. Breathe.*

After what seemed an appropriate amount of time, she pushed her hands through the top of the sack, untied the knot, and tried to look like a totally new person than she had been fifteen minutes ago.

"How do you feel, Carmen?"

"Different. I actually feel amazing." Inexplicably, Ariel *whoop-whooped* and hugged her.

"I told you we like a challenge." Dr. Dave gave her a self-satisfied smile.

"Where's my backpack?"

Suddenly Anthony burst out of his bag, sputtering and gasping, "I know what to write! I know what to do next in the game." Dr. Dave took Anthony in an embrace and oddly, kissed the top of his head. Then Dr. Dave moved away from him, arched his back, and flung his arms out.

And there it is, Dr. Dave's messiah complex on full display.

Carmen spotted her backpack; it was under a hammock. She grabbed it and darted back inside the Sanctuary.

* * *

The meal passed much like that of the night before.

Once the dishes were cleared, Naomi clapped her hands together and with over-the-top giddiness declared, "And now, let's dance!"

Naomi and Dr. Dave led everyone outside, toward the lake.

Carmen guessed this beach party was supposed to come across as impulsive, but the fire was already lit on the beach, a variety of musical instruments were laid out, and there was a speaker hopefully cued to play good music, when the enthusiasm waned for the disharmony of untrained musicians.

It was as spontaneous as a set change. Even the beach was man-made. The dock was lit up with solar and rope lighting and had the look of an airport runway against the darkening sky.

Carmen and Katie, Ariel and Ellie all sat together on an itchy blanket.

Naomi immediately started drumming on some bongos, to get things going. Paula had maracas. Ariel hit some claves together. Katie had claves too and laughed her way through it. She was definitely drunk. Carmen knew by how her left eyelid was starting to droop. Katie's Nalgene bottle was half-full of vodka, she could tell by the attention Katie was giving it. Once in college, Carmen went shopping with Katie, and by the end of the afternoon, she was inexplicably wasted. "I thought everyone drank on the down-low out of these." Katie held up the Contigo thermos that Carmen had assumed was full of coffee.

Naomi finally hit Play on some half-decent music and stood up to dance. Soon other guests sprang up, one after the other.

Katie jumped in, bumping and giggling with Ariel. Ellie danced with only the top half of her body, her feet planted firmly in the sand.

Marie grabbed hold of Carmen's hands, her hips rotating. She was wearing a long, flowy skirt and a white tank top that showed she wasn't wearing a bra. Her nipples were hard. Carmen let Marie pull her up. Marie looped under Carmen's arm, did a little twirl, then rolled back into Carmen's arms. She shimmied down and let go. Her toned arms shimmered up over her head, her hands twisting at the wrists.

Simon came up and laid claim to his wife. Marie danced with him, and Carmen was surprised at how much she wanted her. She wondered why Simon and Marie had chosen the Sanctuary. Were they not worried about security there in the deep, deep woods of the Catskills, or did they think stashing cocaine inside foam blocks was disguise enough and made them safe? If Marie hadn't hurt her ankle, Carmen would never have known. They hadn't accounted for letting anyone inside their suite.

Or maybe it was Dr. Dave. They were truly his loyal followers who just also happened to transport cocaine. Or else Dr. Dave was their middleman, the guy they picked up the cocaine from.

Everyone was dancing now.

Katie thrust her Nalgene bottle at Max; he laughed and shook his head. Katie whispered in his ear, and Max uncapped it and took a long draw. He winced and shook his head after. Then went for another. Then another.

Katie turned around and aimed her ass at Max's crotch. Ariel grabbed Carmen's hand, and they spun around. The earth tilted.

Carmen looked over at the rolling hills across the lake; in the dark, they looked like a sleeping animal.

Marie moved up behind her, put her hands on Carmen's hips, and pressed her breasts into her back. Carmen grabbed her hands this time, to keep her there. Marie's hips rotated against Carmen.

Simon sat back down, elbows on his knees, and watched them. Normally, this would piss her off—being part of a show put on for a husband's or boyfriend's pleasure. But she was enjoying Marie's hands on her, her body next to hers. Carmen felt suddenly flush with twisted desire. She wanted to fuck this woman but also knew she was going to fuck her over.

A life-or-death feeling hung in the air, and it made Carmen feel an electric buzzing in her skin. *Enlivened*. That was the word. *It's this place*. Carmen felt like she was someone else.

Maybe because he wasn't getting enough attention, Dr. Dave suddenly walked away from the fire and stood at the end of the dock.

"The lake's right here, and you're all just ignoring it." He laughed, stripped off his clothes, placed one hand loosely on his hip, and turned toward them again like he was trying to make sure everyone knew how well-endowed he was before he jumped into the cold lake.

Paula wasn't far behind. She flung her clothes off as she ran toward the dock and plunged off, dog-paddling straight for Dr. Dave. More followed—Naomi, Simon, and Marie, who needed some help undressing from her husband. "Come on! All of you. The water is beautiful." Naomi, treading water, waved them in.

"Don't be such prudes!" Paula splashed, her purple streak looking especially inky dark now that it was wet.

Ellie also started to undress, carefully folding her cowl-necked poncho, frayed jean shorts, underwear, and bra into a little pile next to the fire, like she was at a Laundromat.

Katie nudged Carmen and said in her ear, at what she probably considered a whisper, "See? She even looks prudish *whilst* skinny-dipping."

Ellie had the sculpted body of a supermodel, and when she walked toward the lake and down the dock, she did so slowly. Runway style. For everyone to admire her.

Anthony immediately jumped up and followed Ellie into the water, tearing off his clothes as he went, leaving them wherever they landed.

Max went next. Katie's eyes widened as she watched him undress. The dock was just a big pile of clothes. Then, surprisingly, Ariel stood and undressed. Quickly, as if she wanted to do so before she changed her mind. This was the girl who'd once managed to change into a different outfit without removing the one she was already wearing. She plugged her nose and dropped off the dock. When she came back up, all the other guests cheered.

The lake was shimmery and moonlit.

From there, it almost looked like a mass baptism. When Marie beckoned her in, Carmen also stripped and went into the lake as if she were under some kind of spell.

KATIE

The wheedling for Katie to get naked and join the group in the lake quickly ended when she said, "No way; I've already met my near-drowning quota today."

The only time she was reminded of her near drowning was when she laughed and felt a sharp pull in her chest. After her fourth drink, she'd stopped worrying about where the knife had come from. It had to come from somewhere—the blood belonged to someone—but a knife without a body was just a knife as Ellie had so wisely put it. This was her thinking. Alcohol gave her the warmest, most loving hugs sometimes. Under the influence was the only time she could genuinely think positive. She knew she hadn't really seen a body in the lake—that it was just anxiety. And the other things she'd felt, she couldn't feel anymore. Right now, she could take a pin, pierce her skin, and feel nothing.

Maybe that's what people would remember, how she'd danced while Lily was missing or murdered or whatever the hell happened—she wasn't going to think about it right now. She had reached the peak of why she loved to drink: her head was quiet, and she was living in the immediate present as if she were floating inside a pink bubble.

Max got out of the lake fast enough when he realized Katie wasn't going in. This pleased her, that he was still more interested in her after seeing Ellie naked.

He dressed and huddled near the fire to warm up.

"You want my sweater?" Katie started to unzip her hoodie.

He gave her an exasperated look. "No. I'm good. I don't need your sweater."

Katie handed him the Nalgene bottle of vodka instead—"This'll warm ya' up"—which Max was happy to take and nearly drained. "Well, well, looks like I am getting you drunk tonight." Katie flicked her eyebrows at Max. He smiled. She liked how he smiled at her. It turned out the paramedic did like to drink. See, that's how the real world dealt with shit—not flouncing around and breathing in solariums.

Max fumbled slightly when he handed her back the bottle. He was a lightweight, but Katie wasn't and she wasn't done drinking. She wouldn't be done until she passed out. Finishing off the last sip, she held the empty bottle up and shook it. "Oh, no, we're empty. Good thing I have more back in my room." Katie stood up.

"It's so dark, I think you'll need an escort."

"You're hired! I would love to have you as my escort." Max made a face and Katie giggled. The next thing Katie knew, she was loosely holding hands with Max and stagger-running across the lawn toward the Sanctuary. The lanterns that dotted the pathway blurred and streaked.

They didn't make it.

Up at the barn, Katie pressed Max against the barn door and kissed him.

When they broke apart, Max slid open the barn door and disappeared into the darkness. Katie waited a beat for him to turn on a light, and when he didn't, she called out, "Max?" She took a step into the barn and heard a labored grunting. "Seriously, not funny. Max?"

He jumped out and hugged her from behind. Katie screamed, then laughed. They couldn't find a light switch, but with the glow from the Sanctuary coming in, and the moonlight, their eyes adjusted. And then they were kissing again, and in a tangle of an embrace they made their way over to one of the massage tables.

Katie hopped on it and leaned back. "Is a massage included in your fees, my escort?"

He grinned as he kissed her. He grabbed some massage oil and squirted it into his palm.

Katie unbuttoned her jeans and pulled down her underwear, which she flung onto the floor. Max's oil-slick hands started running all over her. His lips followed, up and down her neck, his tongue in her ear, across her belly. Katie shifted and kneaded his shoulders and pressed into his hard-on. She moaned in his ear. Max gripped her ass.

She grabbed at the button on his jeans. Max was adorably sheepish as he undressed. "You know I've already seen you naked, right? Like less than fifteen minutes ago."

Katie lay back on the table and locked her legs around his hips.

Max kissed her again and pushed himself inside of her. Now that it was happening, Katie realized she was too drunk to enjoy it, to get the pleasure she so desperately wanted right now. She stared up at the rafters; were those pendant lights swaying? She started to catch whiffs of menthol and she didn't like the smell. Like Vicks VapoRub.

Suddenly the rocking motion was starting to make her feel woozy. The edges of her vision had significantly dimmed, and she wondered if she was going to remember any of this.

The roof twirled, and Katie needed a visual anchor, something to look at so the spinning would cease and she could stop herself from throwing up. Her eyes focused on the moon outside the window. A knot in the wooden rafters. A single pendant light. Nothing was helping.

She heard a gentle scraping sound; someone was coming into the spa-barn. She turned her head to look at the door, but it was closed. Back to the moon and rafters.

Normally, she would never do this. If she'd initiated, then she'd let the dude finish, but right now, she wanted to stop.

Then she saw it. Hovering up in the rafters.

It was so odd and out of place, it took her a second to understand what it was—a star-shaped foil balloon with a long twirly string. It suddently dropped down and floated across the barn about five feet off the ground, its long string dragging against the floor.

Was it the same balloon from the woods? But that balloon was deflated and tangled in a tree. This one looked new. The helium bulged the corners of the star.

Who put it here? Is this some kind of prank? Did Lily do it? Is she here?

A burst of dread flooded her. *Balloons don't move like that on their own. What the hell is going on?* Katie tried to tell Max. Tried to tell him to stop. She wanted to sit up, push him off her, and grab the string, but she couldn't. Her body was suddenly paralyzed.

She couldn't move a toe, a finger, even blink.

She tried to call out again to Max, but nothing came out. She tried to scream, but there was no sound.

The balloon hovered in one spot, a blank mirror, before it slowly turned. Foil crinkled. And then she was looking at a graphic of Shelby Spade smiling down at her. She was sitting sideways, same position as a silhouette on a mud flap. A balloon meant for girls' birthday parties and sick kids in the hospital. She had on impossibly clunky-heeled shoes that no one should have to endure, never mind a fourteen-year-old. Pink jeans, tight tank top. Her trench coat was hooked on her finger and flung over her shoulder, and her red hair puffed up so big that her photoshopped body looked even skinnier. YOU'RE A STAR was spelled out in glitter over her dead eyes.

The balloon bobbed like that a second or two before it started a slow descent toward her until it loomed just an inch away from her mouth and nose. Her neck stiff, eyes streaming, she couldn't turn away. It moved in closer and closer until it pressed against her mouth. But it didn't stop. It continued to press itself inside of her. Into her mouth. Through her pores. Trying to possess her.

Tears rolled out of the corners of her eyes. She couldn't breathe. She was suffocating, drowning all over again. A voice. Not hers. Not Max's. It was as if it were coming from the balloon. *There, there, my sleeping beauty. My doll. It wasn't so bad. Shh, shh, you won't remember a thing.* A wet kiss on her forehead, a moist wipe between her legs.

And then like that, her body became unpinned from the table. She bolted upright and released a terrified high-pitched scream. Max stumbled back. "What's wrong? Are you okay?"

"Did you see it?"

"See what?"

"That balloon. It was right here." Katie was on her knees on the table now, looking wildly around.

"Katie? I didn't see a balloon. Are you all right? Did I hurt you?" Max was standing there, full hard-on bobbing.

The balloon was gone. Or was never there to begin with. She was losing her fucking mind, and she knew she was about to cry. "Go. Please just go."

"I just . . . why?" He pulled his pants up and tucked himself in.

"Please," Katie said, and when Max opened his mouth to say something, thinking he could possibly have the right words for her, she shouted, *"Go!"* Her voice reverberated around the barn like a bullet.

Max stood there for a second, looking wilted and confused. "Yeah, sure." He shook his head, swung open the barn door, the night air hitting her like another shot of vodka, then gently closed it behind him.

Katie quickly turned around and threw up onto the floor. She felt sick. Sick and dirty. Her skin was crawling.

Upstairs in her room, she stood at the sink and drank a handful of water, tried to fix her makeup and smooth out her tangled hair, and wondered if she could drink herself pretty again and go back outside. Apologize to Max. She knew she couldn't because puking had hardly sobered her up at all.

My doll. My doll. My doll. These words tickled the back of her throat like a finger, and she was kneeling at the toilet again. Bringing up more until her stomach crumpled in on itself.

ELLIE

What a pathetic sight!

Ellie found Katie passed out by the toilet. The ends of her hair dangled in its water. She leaned her back, then hauled her up under her armpits, dragged her backward, and dumped her on the floor next to her bed. So relieved to be free of her sour vomit smell. She pulled off Katie's Converse sneakers, which were probably made by small Indonesian children in a horrid factory, and they hit the floor, *ka-kunk, ka-kunk*. Ellie went into the bathroom and ran the water cold and brought out a glass of it for Katie, but she was still passed out. So Ellie set the water down next to her on the floor, tossed the quilt from the bed over her and drew it up to her chin. "You're like taking care of an invalid," she said out loud, and it felt good.

She dug around inside Katie's purse for her phone. It was in a ridiculous bejeweled case. She tapped in Katie's unlock code—Katie was never discreet with her phone. She had two text messages that Ellie was interested in. One was from her ex-boyfriend, Walker. It started with, *I didn't want to tell you this over text, but since you aren't taking my calls . . .*

Ellie texted him back: *Don't contact me again, or I will call the police and say you're stalking me.*

Another text from Nate. Ellie tapped it opened.

Katie: DID I KILL RICHARD?

Nate: ?

Katie: REMEMBER MY DOG? IN LA? DON'T LIE!

Nate: ??? | IF ABOUT WHAT?

Nate was not an astounding texter, but Ellie didn't mind. She'd prefer a slew of bland, lazy question marks over bland, lazy emojis and LOLs any day, which were downright emasculating, in her opinion.

Katie: DID I KILL MY DOG RICHARD WITH A KNIFE?

Nate: WTF???? NO, YOU DIDN'T. WHY WOULD YOU EVEN ASK ME THAT?

Nate's last text had been unread. Katie was probably too drunk by then, all her focus shifted to Max. Ellie wondered where Nate was, if he were still at the restaurant or back at home now, breaking his vegetarianism by eating a cheeseburger with a side of bacon behind her back. No, she really didn't think so. Nate was committed to her, to her version of them as a couple.

Did she need him right now? Ellie's thumb hovered over the Dial icon.

She didn't expect to have an urge to call him, but she did. She allowed herself a moment of yearning to be back home with Nate. In what she had come to call "their bed," "their kitchen," "their place," like she really had planted a flag and staked ownership on that brownstone, or at least the garden and main level. When she was in her little studio, making jewelry, she could almost pretend Katie's presence wasn't looming over her.

Homesick. Was that what she was feeling? She couldn't tell. It was like opening the fridge because you had a yen for something but couldn't figure out what it was.

She hadn't felt a sense of home since Violet died. Since she had gone to wake her mom up one morning, five months after Vee was gone, and saw that she was dead. She'd been taking a handful of pills a day to cope with the loss of Vee. Her heart was already broken, and so it just gave out in her sleep. It couldn't have been suicide. Her mother wouldn't have done that to her. How long had Ellie pretended she was still alive? Whispering at her through the closed door so she didn't have to see her body again? Didn't have to admit she was completely alone? "Do you want some soup, Mom? I made extra. No? You sure? You really should eat something."

Ellie sat there and thought about her own sister. Poor Nate, even if everything were different Katie could never be a satisfying sisterly substitute for Ellie's brilliant, talented sister who was reading poetry when other kids were still riveted by picture books. Violet was also a musical prodigy. They never would have known that if the last tenant in the run-down bungalow they'd rented hadn't left behind a piano. It was too expensive to have it moved; her mother had planned to take it apart in pieces and toss it in the trash, but then Violet was eighteen months and started to plink away at the keys. *Anything that entertains a baby for any amount of time is worth its weight in gold.* This was her mother's line. She always started the story this way. Tossing in words like *fate* and *destiny*. Ellie was three years older than Vee, and so she only had her mother's version of how Vee started on the piano. How her plinking turned into melodies, and those melodies turned into these haunting things that startled their mother so much she wondered if Vee was possessed by something else. If she were even real. More fate and destiny.

But these were Ellie's memories. When Vee played the piano, their small, boxy living room would soar. There were moments Ellie was sure if she opened her eyes, even she would be levitating off the ground, her body lifted up by the sheer force of her sister's hands running across those keys. Violet could read music by age four and was writing her own by seven. At eight, she was accepted into Julliard Pre-College to attend courses. They were all going to move to New York, and Violet was going to light the world on fire, and when she did, all their lives would change forever.

But then she got sick. It started with a sore throat. She was prescribed all kinds of antibiotics, but nothing seemed to work.

Vee collapsed one morning, halfway through a lesson from a

fancy piano teacher their mother worked double shifts to afford. Her forehead hit the piano keys with a doomful *plink, plink*.

It was acute leukemia, and Violet was going to have to stay at the hospital for a long time.

But it wasn't the cancer that killed her.

Now Violet was just one of the many vibrant lights snuffed out by darkness.

Ellie put Katie's phone away before her willpower cracked and she found herself doing something stupid and calling Nate. She buried it deep in Katie's purse, which was really a portable trash can with straps, going by the sticky, gooey things that were inside it.

As she set the purse back down where Katie had tossed it— clearly she'd been aiming for the desk but missed it by a foot— Ellie noticed she had a spot of blood on her shirt just over her hip. She must have aggravated her wound by moving Katie. She lifted her shirt to examine it better. Not her wound but the mark on her shirt. She couldn't believe it; the bloodstain was almost heart-shaped.

Ironic, considering who'd caused it.

SUNDAY

ARIEL

Ariel spent half the night afflicted with sweaty dreams full of bloodied knives and the sound of hooves coming for her as Dr. Dave
pumped inside of her.

Her crotch was throbbing when she woke up.

She lingered under the covers, thinking about yesterday. How
she'd slit the deer's throat and felt an exhilarating mix of horror
and power. Tried to recapture the feel of Dr. Dave's sinewy body
moving next to hers. The grit of dirt against her bare skin.

She got out of bed, stretched, and felt the sharp spikes of a hangover in her temples even though she hadn't had anything to drink
the night before. Carmen was already awake and brushing her
teeth in the bathroom.

"You must be happy we're leaving tomorrow," Carmen said, tossing her toiletry bag into one of her canvas grocery bags. Ariel noticed that Carmen hadn't unpacked at all. She just took things out
of her canvas bags and put them right back in, like she wanted to
be ready to leave at any given moment.

"Why do you say that?" Ariel was actually horrified the weekend was nearly over. She couldn't go back home and be plopped
back into her old life.

Carmen gave her a look, like she was about to say something
but then changed her mind. "Oh, no reason. I just know I'll be
happy to go home."

Ariel couldn't think of a single reason Carmen should want to leave the Sanctuary either. All she did was complain about her life, her job, and having to take care of all of her siblings.

Ariel went into the bathroom and started to get ready for the day while trying not to sob. She put her hair up, but it wasn't falling right, and she knew the bald spot was exposed. She let it down again and mussed it up, but then her hair looked too windblown. She tried a ponytail but again couldn't get it to stay in the right spot. She'd pulled too much of her hair out. Her entire head was ruined. She could just cut it all off!

She thought about last night. How it had been one of her most freeing moments. To strip down, to expose her imperfect body and not care what it looked like to anyone else. Dr. Dave had swum up to her in the water and said, "I'm proud of you, Ariel." She'd thanked him, and Dr. Dave had kept treading water close to her. So close she'd thought he was going to kiss her.

"You should come back again and try our Premium Warrior package. You are more than ready; hell, you could probably run it." Dr. Dave had reached over and brushed away a wet strand of hair stuck to her cheek. "You're so close to overcoming your crutches." His eyes had flickered up to her hair. He'd rested his palm on her cheek, and Ariel had pressed her face into his hand like a cat.

"I would like that." She'd known then that she would return to the retreat. As much as possible. Over and over. Something was vibrating inside of her now, higher and louder than ever before. Dr. Dave was right; she was vibrationally superior.

Over two short days, her life had advanced further than it had since she'd graduated. She felt genuinely different since she'd arrived there, like the husk of her old self was at the bottom of the lake and she was blossoming into something new.

Ariel tried to slide a hairband on, and pulled out hair spray. She aimed the nozzle at the back of her head with plans to shellac her hair into place, but decided it wasn't worth the sting of alcohol on her scabby scalp. Her comb-overs weren't going to work out today.

She had fallen asleep with damp hair, so now she would need to go through her entire hair regimen to get it to do what she wanted— wash, dry, styling paste, roller brush, curling iron, hair spray. Her hair was her nicest feature; that's what people say to women who are chunky: "You have such nice hair."

Forty minutes later, she exited the bathroom, expecting Carmen to look pissy because she'd taken so long, but surprisingly, Carmen didn't. She was just sitting in the chair and staring out the window. "It's not even 8:00 a.m., and they're already starting another ritual outside." She rolled her eyes, got up to leave, and held the door open for Ariel to follow.

Back on the beach, the group—minus Katie, who would probably languish in bed until noon, given the shape she had been in last night—were standing around the same firepit from the night before. Their heads were down, and from afar, it looked like they were writing into their palms, but as Ariel and Carmen got closer, it was clear they were writing on small squares of paper. Ellie was there, and when she saw them, she offered up a blunted smile. She looked like she hadn't slept much. Dark circles under her eyes and a wariness that hadn't been there on Friday muddled her usual gloss. Ellie looked like she wanted to go home too.

It struck Ariel again how much she didn't want to go home.

"Good morning, ladies." Dr. Dave gestured to a small table with a basket of paper and pens. "I invite you to write out your burdens then toss them into the fire to be released from their power over you. Nothing quite like watching your troubles go up in a blaze."

Ariel took some paper. She looked out at the lake. A mist was hanging over the water, and it bled into the gunmetal-gray sky. There was so much Ariel wanted to write. She didn't know where to start.

Carmen immediately started writing. Ariel glimpsed over her shoulder and saw that she was writing *Dr. Dave is a douche.* Carmen folded it and tossed it into the fire, then doodled on the next piece of paper. Ariel felt defensive of Dr. Dave, but instead of saying anything she took a cleansing breath.

Yes, Ariel was definitely vibrationally superior to Carmen—she doubted they would continue to be friends after this weekend.

Paula started sobbing, her pen wagging back and forth. She was tossing paper into the fire as if she were personally responsible for keeping it alight.

Max went over and asked Ellie how Katie was feeling, and they had a whispery conversation.

Anthony wrote something and made a big production of squishing his paper into a tiny white ball and then lobbed it into the fire like a basketball.

Ariel pressed the pen to the page, and like that, everything came spewing out in an inky frenzy.

I hope the baby is okay. I hope I'm not arrested, that no one presses charges. That Rob doesn't hate me. That my parents don't think I am a psychopath. I want to stop feeling bad. I want to succeed. I think I am in love again with a married man. I want to stop pulling my hair out.

If wishes were fishes, we'd all swim in riches. It was something her dad would say to her. *That's all I'm doing—writing out wishes.*

Ariel wanted to make a bigger gesture. She wanted to externalize her internal change. If she had to return to Shakopee, she wanted to look so different, her transformation would be undeniable.

"I want to shave my head." Ariel said it out loud, her eyes directed at Dr. Dave as if asking for his permission.

"What? No, you don't," Carmen cut in.

"Yes, I do. I pull my hair out. I know you know that," she said to Carmen. "I pull my hair out to cope with my anxieties. I have since middle school, and I want to shave my head. I want to be free of my crutch so I can learn to deal with negative feelings in a healthier way."

"You go, girl!" Paula cheered.

"Cool," Anthony said blandly.

Dr. Dave left and returned quickly with scissors and a cordless razor. He handed both to Ariel.

"I can't let you do this. You'll regret it," Carmen said.

"It's just hair, Carmen." To prove her point, Ariel grabbed a big chunk of her hair, pulled it taut, felt the usual surge of tension that could only be relieved by tearing it out by the root, and started cutting. She dropped the chunk of hair into the fire.

"Oh my god, I can't fucking watch this." Carmen threw her hands up.

Rather than feeling a surge of panic, Ariel felt immediately lighter. Like her neck had a kink in it that was being kneaded out. She continued to fist big swaths of hair and cut them off until all that was left was a stubby, uneven carpeting of her hair.

"Anyone want to help me with the back?" Ariel asked, half laughing because she was feeling almost high right now. She handed the razor to Dr. Dave, but Naomi stepped forward and took it. She motioned for Ariel to sit down in one of the Adirondack chairs, and she buzzed it up the back of her head.

Ariel could feel the sting of it on the scabby patch of scalp where she'd torn her hair out. "How brave of you," Naomi cooed before handing the razor to Anthony, who took a turn, and then Paula, Simon, and Marie. Ellie pressed it to her skin. "Don't be shy," Ariel chirped, but Ellie just held the razor to the same spot before passing it back to Ariel.

Carmen refused, of course.

By the time it was Dr. Dave's turn, Ariel had no more hair to shave, which made her feel so disappointed she almost started to cry, but then she decided maybe it was a sign. Of what, she had no idea, but feeling like it was a sign was so much better than feeling disappointed.

Ariel ran her hands over her scalp, surprised at how soft and new it felt, like baby's hair except for her bald patch, which was mottled with scabs. But it was her bald patch, and she was going to let it out of its burial plot. Own it to disown it. That's what Dr. Dave had said in one of his YouTube talks, and there she was, doing both at the same time. She had no more hair to pull. No more hair to cover up her compulsion with. Here she was, out in the open. Cured. She looked at Dr. Dave and knew she'd done the right thing when she saw his look of approval.

With both hands, she picked the hair from her lap and tossed it into the fire and watched her crutch burn up.

When she was done, she was met with long, tight hugs from everyone and another round of compliments for her fearlessness, courage, and pluck. Things Ariel had never been described as having before in her life. Dr. Dave encircled her, lifted her up, and gave her a twirl.

She felt like a debutante making her debut. Naomi hugged her last, her embrace quickly shifting so that she was holding onto Ariel with a full-body vise grip.

And then Naomi's lips moved to her ear, her breath wet as she whispered, "Follow your own bliss, girl. Don't come near mine or you'll be sorry. I always make them sorry."

CARMEN

Oh my god, what did Ariel do? She'd drunk Dr. Dave's Kool-Aid, that's what she'd done. She'd lost contact with reality. *There's blankness in her eyes. She's speaking with a crazy joyous inflection— like Naomi. I have no idea who she is. Ariel has no idea who she is. She is one of those people who send out their DNA to ancestry firms, and whatever they churn back out to you, that's who you are.*

The thought made Carmen's skin go cold.

Now as they walked back to the house for breakfast, Carmen couldn't take her eyes off her, and it wasn't the shaved head that was most disturbing but Ariel's self-satisfied look. It was the zeal of the newly converted, and it looked cemented to her face.

And when a corn-colored sun poked through the overcast sky, Ariel tilted her chin upward as if the sun were shining down just on her.

When Ariel saw that Carmen had noticed, she didn't get embarrassed.

It suddenly clicked too that Ariel had . . . what? A crush on Dr. Dave? But *crush* wasn't the right word. More like *adulation*. It was the way she'd looked at him as she cut her hair off. Like a rosy-cheeked bride-to-be. Naomi had to have seen it too; there was an obvious bite in that hug she'd given Ariel.

It was like Dr. Dave flipped houses, and Naomi was the finished product. He was ready to sell her off and start on another one: Ariel.

If things were different, Carmen would wake up Katie, maybe

even start some kind of deprogramming that included immediately whisking Ariel away from this place, but Carmen had her own agenda. She knew that today's itinerary was loose and less structured than that of the last two days. Something about preserving one's energy for tonight's psychedelic tea ceremony.

Breakfast, given how chilly it was outside, was served inside at the dining table, and Carmen sat through it, all smiles and pleasant small talk. She ate quickly and went upstairs to pack her backpack. She changed out of her jeans and into comfortable, breathable clothing. Lycra—good for yoga and committing most crimes. She grabbed the chair and propped it under the door to their room in case Ariel tried to burst in.

She gathered the bricks of formula from under the bed, along with her carpenter's knife and glue, which she triple-checked was odorless. All she needed was for Simon and Marie to return to their cottage with the burning reek of superglue. She touched each brick of fake cocaine. All ten. *Cha-ching, cha-ching.*

Just pack two or three. Steal just four or five of Simon and Marie's cocaine. But it was like she couldn't control herself.

She packed all ten, almost rotely. As if she were possessed with greed, cloying as sulfur, like all ten already belonged to her, and to change her mind now was the equivalent of flushing *her* money down the toilet. She couldn't have stopped herself even if she'd tried.

She went downstairs and parked herself on a hammock, watching for Simon and Marie to leave their cottage. Carmen would have preferred to make the switch later in the day, even during the tea ceremony, but there were just too many unknowns. It was still risky to do it so early in the day because it gave Simon and Marie more time to figure out their cocaine was gone, but Carmen calmed herself. *The yoga blocks are already sealed. They're taking them up to Canada. They have no reason to open them up again.*

Plus, Carmen wanted to plan for error. If something went wrong in the morning, she'd have a second shot that night.

When Simon and Marie finally made their way toward the spa, dressed in thick, white robes, she jumped up, went inside, and grabbed her backpack. She had to pass Ariel, who was sitting cross-legged in the middle of the lawn with that same beatific look on her face.

She circled through the woods to the back of the cottage. The rear sash window was still propped open about five inches. Carmen had been keeping an eye on that window.

It was too high for her to reach without a boost, but she'd planned for that too. Last night, after the skinny-dipping, when Naomi pulled out enough glow-in-the-dark Hula-Hoops for everyone—making it easy to keep tabs in the dark that Simon and Marie were still lakeside—Carmen said she was going to get warmer clothing.

On the way to the Sanctuary, she had assessed the height of the cottage's bathroom window, and then taken a wooden crate she'd spotted next to the wood-chopping pile and stored it nearby, patting herself on the back for her foresight.

Now, she picked up the crate, turned it upside down, stood on it, and immediately wished for a taller crate.

Goddammit.

Barely reaching the windowsill, she kicked out her legs and gained a grip against the clapboard. Carmen pushed the screen in, accidentally bending the aluminum frame. It clattered inside onto the tiled bathroom floor. She shimmied her way in and dropped down next to the toilet, grabbed the screen, and loosely leaned it back into place.

Carmen pulled opened the cupboard doors on the bathroom vanity and felt such palpable relief to see the bag was still there that she almost swooned. The bathroom was a mess. There were wet lumpy towels that looked like they were just used and dropped to the floor. Carmen needed more space to work, so she grabbed the duffel bag and moved into the main room, between the foot of the bed and the fireplace.

She had taken the alarm clock from her room and was carrying it in her backpack (who, under the age of thirty, owned a regular watch anymore?) to keep time. It made a little *ding* noise as she set it down on the dresser.

Quarter past ten. The spa treatments lasted about an hour, so she had half an hour to get this done.

Sitting on the floor, Carmen dug through the foam blocks, pulling out the light ones and putting them to one side, the ten heavy ones to the other side, lining them up.

Pushing out the fresh blade on the carpenter's knife, she picked up a foam block, cut through the line of clear glue, and pried it apart.

She pulled out the first cocaine package and compared it to her fake cocaine. It wasn't a perfect replica. The baby formula was a bit too white. Too fine. It'd pass a quick glance but not a close inspection.

If Simon and Marie opened these up before they left, they'd know. For sure, they'd know.

They won't. She had to believe they wouldn't. This was what believing in oneself was, right? Taking a risk and knowing it would work out.

Carmen got to work slicing open all the blocks, then pulling the real-deal cocaine from each and sliding them first into ziplock bags and then into her grocery bag.

She stuffed the baby formula into the yoga block, but it was too big. She tried tucking it in and pressing the powder in tightly, but nothing worked. *It's not fitting.* She couldn't get the edges of the foam to even meet. *Fucking Christ.* She'd overfilled them.

She had to dump some of the formula out.

Twenty-seven minutes after ten.

She rushed into the bathroom and turned on the water, jabbed the knife into a corner of the first brick, and poured some of the powder down the sink. Her hands were shaking; she was rushing. Powder was spilling out on the counter. She wet some toilet paper, wiped up the powder, and tossed it in the already overflowing garbage can.

She ran back into the main room and stuffed a slimmer brick into the first foam block, careful to tuck the opened corner in first, then cut open the tip of glue. She squeezed, and the glue came out in a fast shot, down the side of the block. *Fucking fuck.* She used her finger to spatula off the excess glue, but she couldn't get it all, and the glue started drying into a crusty yellow drizzle. She'd bury this one at the bottom.

Slower now, she dabbed the glue over the dried glue and pressed the halves of the yoga block together. It was still not sealing as tightly as Simon and Marie had them. But what could she do? It wasn't like she could put back the real cocaine at this point.

Carmen stuffed the blocks with varying degrees of authenticity. She noticed that there was a white dusting from the bathroom to where she was kneeling and stuffing blocks. She was botching this like the bungling amateur she was, but Carmen kept gluing and vise-gripping the blocks, wishing she could use a hair dryer to speed up the drying time. Two more blocks to go. This was taking so much longer than she'd wanted it to.

And then she heard their voices.

Her heart screeched in her chest.

It wasn't even 11:00 a.m. yet. Why were they back?

They were speaking in French. Carmen had no idea what they were saying, but the tone suggested that they were arguing.

Carmen tossed the unglued foam blocks into the bottom of the bag, burying them under the others. She grabbed her backpack and rushed toward the bathroom, trying to wipe up the Similac soot with her feet as she went. She threw the duffel bag back under the sink.

Please, please, don't let them have noticed the crate. Their argument was growing more heated. Standing on the toilet, about to hurl herself back out the window, Carmen glimpsed Marie taking off down the side of the cottage, toward the woods. Simon followed her

Carmen let out a breath. She turned around and walked into the main room again. The air was a haze of dust.

She should just leave.

Two bricks weren't finished. If Simon and Marie checked the cocaine they would know immediately that it had been tampered with. She had to finish. Leaving two empty split bricks was too much of a risk. Plus there was still baby formula in the bathroom sink and a dusting of formula on the floor next to their bed. All she needed was another ten minutes.

She snagged the duffel bag and slid back into the main room like a baseball player coming into third. She dug for the first block, jammed in the formula, blotted on some glue, and put the halves of foam together. She squeezed the glued foam block under one arm while stuffing the last block with her other hand. Sweat rolled down her back, and she was starting to feel dizzy.

Carmen quickly packed the blocks back into the duffel bag, zipped it up, and again stuffed it back under the sink. She wiped up the sink, then rushed back to desperately kick at any remaining powder with her foot. She jammed the grocery bag of the real deal into her backpack.

There was a brushing noise against the cottage door, and then the jangle of a key to the lock.

They were back.

Fuck, fuck, fuck.

She was caught. It was over.

The dead bolt was turning open.

Then, desperate and shaky, Carmen tossed her backpack toward the door, ripped off her shirt, and flung herself into the middle of Simon and Marie's bed.

KATIE

Katie hated to be alone when she was hungover, and there wasn't even a television to keep her company. She was stuck in bed, feeling queasy, and there was nothing to do but think, think, think.

Thinking was the last thing she wanted. Her thoughts were spinning, and she felt feverish and sweaty. A lone buzzing horsefly was bumping against the window. She needed a hair-of-the-dog solution—a couple of sangrias or Bloody Marys to quell the wooziness churning through her. She'd already looked for the remaining vodka but couldn't find it. Ellie had probably taken it. She rolled over and lay on her side, staring at the door. Then at the door handle, until she swore she saw it jitter back and forth. She grabbed her pillow, buried her face in it, and screamed.

I was molested.

Raped.

Now that the memory had buoyed from whatever dark crevice it had been hibernating in, she knew it was as true and real as anything else that had happened to her. She knew it last night. And what did she do with this information? She went out and drank herself cross-eyed, and had sex with someone she barely knew.

Wasn't that what sexually abused girls turned into? Promiscuous, self-destructive scarecrows who roamed around at night? Addicts and cutters? Didn't abused girls twist a predator's perversion into festering self-loathing? Isn't that what was meant by *damaged goods*? Her development as a human being had been fucking derailed in lieu of someone else's orgasm.

Didn't they lash out and sometimes commit murder?

I was sexually abused. At night. In my childhood bed, in my childhood room, where I should have been safe. Someone came into my room while I was sleeping and molested me. And now I sleepwalk, like my psyche shattered into two. One half comes alive at night, taking control of my body, always trying to get away from a predator. While the other, the daytime half, is just a haunted shell of my full potential.

Katie's stomach went oily; she felt like her skin was curdling. Why didn't she remember more of it? Why hadn't she screamed? Why hadn't she been able to move? Why had she just let it happen? She knew him. When she closed her eyes, the silhouette in the doorway was familiar.

So, so familiar.

Katie stumbled out of bed and threw up before reaching the toilet. A scream caught in her throat, pushed on her windpipe like a thumb from the inside. She was splayed out on the bathroom floor unable to move, the pulse so strong in her temples she was sure her skull was cracking open.

When she could stand up, she ran the water cold and splashed it over her face. Blood gathered behind her eyes. Her left eyelid was twitching. She made her facecloth extra cold and held it to her forehead. It was something AJ would do for her whenever she felt sick, and in that last year he was working as her manager, she was sick a lot.

She grabbed her phone out of her bag that she'd drunkenly dropped in the middle of the room last night and called Lucy. She hadn't talked to her mother in four months.

The last time they'd talked was when they'd met at Nate's restaurant and Lucy had brought along a man she'd tried to pass off as a new boyfriend until he ambushed Katie with a contract at his D-list agency, where she'd be guaranteed sporadic offers of soft porn and guest spots on humiliating reality television series. Katie thought it was a way for Lucy to humiliate her after losing what was supposed to be her big comeback role. When Katie had said she wasn't interested, Lucy made a comment that Katie only had a good year or two left to get back into the business. "What else are you going to do? You need to do something. It's not healthy to rest on your laurels." This coming from the woman who'd sold her daughter's childhood off to the highest bidder.

"Katie?" No one's mother should sound that surprised when her child called. She could tell Lucy had been sleeping. She could picture her pulling up her silky eye mask in her king-size bed, thick curtains drawn tight so no light could get in, her face greasy from heavy night creams. Lucy was a firm believer in beauty sleep.

"What happened to me?"

"What?"

"What the hell happened to me?" She was sweating again; her entire body was on fire. She slumped down on the edge of the bed.

"Oh, Katie, I'm just not sure what you're talking about." Her mother's voice was alert now. She was probably sitting up, holding her phone with both hands.

"I was sexually abused." A long silence. Katie heard Lucy swallow. "I was sexually abused when I was doing *Shelby*." Katie's throat was raw.

Lucy made a sticky *oh* noise on the other end. Absent from her voice was any shred of genuine surprise. Not a confused *oh*, as in *What the hell is Katie talking about?* but something else. Her mother had known this was coming.

"Oh, sweetheart, I am so, so sorry. It's all my fault." Lucy let out a long, agonized sob. Katie felt the usual bubble of rage when Lucy cried. When Katie was growing up, Lucy would always make her emotions so big that they squeezed Katie out of the room.

If Katie ever complained about being tired or not wanting to make some appearance, Lucy would cry and say she must be a bad mother and twist it all up so that Katie was the one comforting her. All of her successes and failures seemed to belong more to her mother than to her.

But her mother sounded different right now.

"What are you keeping from me?" Katie roared into the phone. Blood rushed in her ears.

"I was hoping you would never, ever, ever remember. The psychiatrist said you had a dissociative disorder, and I thought that it was a good thing that you didn't remember. I didn't want to make you remember. Why would I ever want you to remember?" Something flickered in Katie's mind, and she had a memory of Nate standing in the hallway, looking at her. "Nate."

"Nate's the one who found you. With him. With AJ." She sputtered out his name, AJ, as if her lips were refusing to say his name.

AJ.

It all rushed back to her with such force that her spine snapped up straight and her neck whipped her head back. Memories were clawing their way out from wherever they were buried. A horde of memories saturated her brain all at once. For a moment, she heard only white noise. Then AJ. His hot, whispery breath—she could feel it pooling on her skin.

You're my special girl. My star.

My doll.

AJ.

Details were zigzagging back to her. How he was always there when Lucy had a party, *he said* to make sure she was all right. "I will stay until you're snug as a bug in your bed." The warm milk he made her drink to help her relax. The taste of it filled her mouth. There had to have been something in it. Something that made her dozy and unable to move.

The milk. The way her muscles turned wobbly and how AJ would shoo her off into her bedroom. Then the soft click of her door, the creak as he sat down on the bed, and the way her girl body sank toward him from his weight. The roll of her head on the pillow toward the doorknob as she felt her body bouncing up and down. The music from the party. *Get to the door, get to the door, will the door to open.*

And then blackness.

When Katie thought she'd lost her virginity at fourteen to a sleazy DJ, she was genuinely confused why there wasn't any blood.

"Nate found you. He told me AJ was in bed with you and I sat him down and had him tell me exactly what he saw. I had no idea. No idea. Honey, I know I wasn't the best mother. I wasn't paying enough attention, and I trusted him. I stopped drinking immediately after that."

Like it mattered that she'd stopped drinking *after* Katie was abused. But it was true. Lucy did change; she went from being out all the time to staying home so much it annoyed Katie.

But Katie had always associated that with her cut-up face. That Lucy's golden goose had been marred and so the high times had ended.

Right then, the memory of the balloon came rushing back to her like an explosive mushroom cloud surging up from the back of her brain from last night's blackout: the balloon inching toward her and the panic of being pinned down and unable to move.

"My face." Katie stepped back into the bathroom and stared at her scar in the mirror. It was flecked with dried mascara that had crumbled off her eyelashes. Her throat had tightened to a pinprick. An explosion went off inside her head; her vision sparked white. The bathroom tilted and morphed into the one in Lucy's house.

"Yes. It all happened so quickly. Nate told me the night before about what he saw, and I was in such shock. I didn't sleep at all that night. I wanted to kill AJ. I knew that much. I didn't even want to send him to prison. I wanted him dead for what he'd done to you. The next morning, I completely forgot you were scheduled to appear at the—"

"Hospital." Katie finished Lucy's sentence. That morning, AJ was supposed to take her to the hospital to visit sick kids, but he didn't show up. It was always AJ who took her. He kept everything organized. Her publicist and security detail always met her at the hospital so she and AJ could go for dinner afterward, usually someplace fancy, and he'd order wine and look the other way when Katie took sips from his glass. He would tell her how much he admired her and what a good thing she was doing.

That day Lucy took her, using the drive to explain that AJ would never set foot in their house or their lives again.

"Why are you saying that? Of course he will. He's my manager and he loves me."

"Oh, honey, no, no. AJ doesn't love you—he's a sick man. He used you, what he did . . . listen, Nate told me something last night, and we need to talk." Lucy reached over and took her hand. "I know how important Wish Come True is to you, but, Katie, I think maybe it would be best if you skipped your appearance today."

Katie's head started to swim. It was like there was a lag between Lucy's lips moving and what she was saying. All Katie heard was that AJ didn't love her. AJ used her. She would never see AJ again.

"Yes, he does! AJ loves me. You're just jealous because I love him more than you." Katie was screaming in Lucy's face. She wanted to grab the wheel and send them both into incoming traffic.

Inexplicably, her mother started sobbing, and Katie wanted to get away from her even more. When Lucy pulled into the hospital parking lot, Katie jumped out before she'd even made a full stop. "Don't follow me. If you do, I will do something terrible."

She remembered walking inside, dressed as Shelby Spade. Her publicist handed her a fistful of balloons to hand out to patients. The puff of stale air, and the smell of heated food and sickness, hit her harder than ever. It was as cloying as a rag held over her nose and mouth.

She wanted to walk right out the back and take off, but the photographer her publicist had hired was already there, already telling her to smile because no good deed was worth it unless it was documented. She felt her face click over. "Turn that frown upside down," and her lips congealed into a smile, as trained as Pavlov's dog. A blast of white light from the camera's flash stung her eyes.

Her memory dropped off right then. It was like she'd fallen

through a trapdoor into blankness, or entered some kind of fugue state. It was as inaccessible as trying to remember a dream. The next thing she remembered, she was staring at her fifteen-year-old self in the mirror surrounded by Hollywood vanity lights, still dressed up in her full Shelby Spade costume for the big event.

She remembered having these feelings: she wanted to die. She wanted to carve herself up and let everyone who claimed to love her take their pound of flesh.

She was used up and unlovable. She felt a tidal wave of revulsion toward herself. Toward Shelby Spade. No one loved her, but everyone loved Shelby.

She blamed Lucy. A selfish, self-absorbed stage mother who'd been using her for money the minute the umbilical cord was cut. How could she fire the only adult Katie could count on? And then she realized it was all an act. Not even AJ really loved her. Everything was an act. Was she even real?

She didn't remember bringing a knife with her to the bathroom. It was just in her hand. *Smile, smile, smile.* Like she was a fucking decoration that had to always be pleasant to look at. *I don't own my face. It's not mine.* And so she took the knife and tried to carve a permanent smile up her own cheek.

"Katie, are you still there?"

"I cut my own face." It sputtered out of her. Her bones went loose and saggy. She bent over at the hips. The tiny tiles on the floor bubbled. Wooziness roiled through her.

"You didn't know what you were doing, Katie. You didn't understand what had happened to you. You were just so mixed up; you thought AJ was the only one who loved you. That man, he manipulated you. Something snapped when I said you wouldn't see AJ again."

"And what? You just fired him! Why didn't you have him arrested? That's a pretty understated response to sexual abuse, don't you think?"

"I would have, but, Katie honey, he had you so turned around,

I don't think you would have testified against him. You were so much under his control at the time. How . . . how did I let that happen?" She let out a guttural sob that Katie couldn't listen to. Did she expect Katie to answer that for her? How? Deep-seated rage pulsed through Katie. She eyed the window, imagined herself leaping through it. Glass flying. Skin flaying. She held the phone away from her.

"Katie? Katie? You there?" Lucy's voiced buzzed.

"Yeah, I'm here."

"Listen, Katie, you're right. AJ should have been arrested for what he did to you. I just didn't think . . . You were so mentally fragile, I just couldn't, I couldn't put you through it. Could you imagine the circus? The cameras on the courtroom steps? How AJ would twist it and claim it was all a lie? And you didn't remember any of it, or didn't seem to. Oh, how that man could *talk*! He was so charming; that was his profession. He could spin anything, and I could just picture him making appearances with women in pantsuits who wanted to believe him on talk shows. Who would *debate* your honesty for entertainment."

"So that's where you drew the line in terms of publicity? Public slut-shaming?"

"Oh, Katie. You would have been victimized over and over. You would never have gotten away from it. I talked to our lawyer, and he said without evidence, your lack of memory, and your current mental state, it would have been next to impossible to charge AJ. And say if he were charged. How much time would he serve? We live in a sick world when a man goes to jail for less time for raping a child than he does for tax evasion. I was scared for you. So scared. And that's when I realized how to get him. I'd worked out a way to save you from all that ugliness of court dates and testifying and your character being questioned. No. No way. I couldn't do it. But I was going to put AJ in jail. I had moved money around and was going to nail that bastard for embezzlement, but then you had your breakdown."

"So he didn't steal from me?" It was a pathetic thought, like it mattered, but Katie was still catching up to this new reality of not just being blamed for acting like a privileged victim but being an actual fucking victim.

"He stole something much worse than money, Katie. *Much worse.*" Lucy's voice went gummy again. "When you cut your face, you were so distraught. You didn't even feel it. You were laughing. By the time we got you to the hospital, you didn't remember it at all. The psychiatrist later called it an acute amnesiac episode. It was part of your dissociative condition, and so I made a quick decision. It was easy to blame AJ for it. To have him arrested for that too. A gash like that on your face is indisputable."

"He died in jail. He died for cutting me, but he didn't do it. I said he did it, but he didn't." Katie remembered Lucy coming into her room at Willow Place, where she'd stayed for "exhaustion," and in a clipped voice delivering the news that AJ was dead, followed by a single sentence about putting the past in the past before a cheery segue into having made an appointment with the same plastic surgeon of some other celebrity. He put her face back together after her DUI accident. Katie thought Lucy had no feelings, that she was the monster.

"No, baby girl, I made you believe it. I put the words in your mouth. I whispered it into your ear for three days, *AJ did it, AJ cut you, AJ did it.* Nate was the perfect eyewitness too. The hero of the story, even. He said what needed to be said, because he's only ever wanted to protect you. It could have been worse if Nate hadn't interrupted you; you were going to cut both sides, Katie. Or, I should say, AJ was. He was going to disfigure you. See? Even as I tell this story, I still almost believe it. That's how easy it is to blame AJ, because regardless, he might not have been the one holding the knife, but he was still the one responsible anyway. You have nothing to feel to guilty about. That man had just started working with another little girl, trying to shape her into a star, and who knows what horrors that girl would have endured? You saved her from him." Katie suddenly remembered that deep pang of jealousy when AJ began mentioning another, younger, presumably cuter client he'd started working with. He was paying less attention to her, coming around less. That gnawing panic of being ignored by another adult, one who had only recently showered her with attention, swirled like a cyclone of razors in her stomach. "Sometimes there is justice, Katie. It doesn't happen very often, but that scum got exactly what he deserved in county jail."

"Did you arrange that too? To have him killed?"

"Oh, Katie, I'm not some mob boss. He went to jail as a man who hurt a beloved little girl; we all know how those men are received by other inmates. It was just pure luck that he was sharing a cell with someone who followed through."

The milk. The taste of it was filling up her mouth again, and her legs were going wobbly. She felt physically whiplashed.

"I'm sorry, Katie. I should have protected you. I should have been a better mother."

"I want to get off the phone now." Her voice was flat and distant. Her lips felt numb. The bathroom was closing in on her. The white walls rolled around her liquidly.

"I am going to have Nate check on you, and then I'll be there soon. I want to help you work through this."

"I'm not at home." Katie spoke with an airy lilt she'd never heard in her own voice before. "I am at a retreat. I'll call you later. " She pressed End.

Everything she'd thought was true was a lie. AJ was not a father figure but a predator. No one is who they say they are. With jagged, robotic movements, Katie stripped off last night's clothes and got into the shower. She turned the water to searing hot, letting it hit her skin until it felt as if it were blistering and running off her bones like hot wax. She sank into the tub and pulled her legs up.

When the hot water ran out, she stepped out of the shower. Written in the steam on the mirror was I'LL SOOOOOLVE IT. She wiped it away because she wasn't sure if it was really there or not. Reality was always going to be a tenuous thing for her.

She looked again at her face, her scar. She'd never hated it and knew it was the wrong way to feel. She didn't even really hate it now. Right now, she felt crazy. Fucked up. Her skin was crawling. She was so fucked up. What happened to her was like lead in water; it had been slowly poisoning her all this time.

Katie crawled back into her bed and curled into a ball.

She wanted to do the tea. She had to do the tea.

It helped heal childhood trauma, and that's what she wanted. To just spew and purge AJ, his sick semen that had pooled up somewhere in her girl body, bulging and swishing like a cyst that had been blocking her memories like a dam. Memories that were trapped but still alive and skittering around, banging on the inside of her skull to be let out, to wake up.

She had never been more certain of anything—that the tea just might free her of feeling so trapped, so stuck, like a windup doll endlessly marching into a wall. She would do the tea tonight, and then on Monday, she would turn herself in. She would bring the knife in a ziplock and say, "Here, I think I might have used this to murder someone while I was sleepwalking. Do with me what you will."

She wouldn't think beyond that. Only that she was doing the right thing.

ELLIE

Ellie's meditative walks were really one-man search parties for Lily. She still couldn't find a body. All day, she'd been walking the woods, poking at things with a long stick to see if some body part would come loose. Lily had to be dead. Had to be. Ellie kept coming back to it, the possibility that this girl was still alive and out there, that maybe she'd made it off the retreat—but then, why hadn't she gone to the police? Because she was still in the woods and had other plans?

Ellie's skin prickled.

No, there had been too much blood. She had to be dead.

So she searched while Katie lay in bed, nursing a hangover.

Of course, Lily's body could be in the lake, and if it was, then Ellie had little chance of finding her. Instead, Lily would wash up two towns over or get tangled up in some fisherman's line. When would that happen? A day from now? A week? Three weeks? The waiting would be torture.

And by then, Katie could be in a totally different frame of mind. Right now, it seemed like the feelings of guilt needed just a tiny little jab to come spewing out at the nearest police station, but give her a few days and that would change.

Katie could talk herself out of anything.

Ellie felt defeated and listless. When she came to a rock ledge that overlooked the lake, she sat down on it. Dark clouds were brewing.

That morning, while Katie had still been asleep, her mouth gaping, Ellie used her phone to google a few things. First, she searched if there were any reports of a dead girl in the area, and second, how long it took for DNA to degrade in nature.

It was an electronic trail, and maybe Ellie was being paranoid, but she had to protect herself. Especially considering that Katie was capable of continuing on her merry way by downing vodka and pairing off with a man she barely knew, despite thinking she'd killed another human being. When Max had asked about Katie, she had almost felt sorry for him. He had been so apologetic, so genuine, so sincere—someone like Katie would suck him dry. "She's very hungover," she'd told him, almost adding that this was Katie's usual state. "Max, did Katie happen to say anything to you last night? She was babbling a lot. Mostly it was incomprehensible but some of what she was saying was quite disturbing."

Max ran his hand over the rough stubble on his chin. "Just something about a balloon. She kept asking if I could see a balloon, but there wasn't one. It was like she was hallucinating or something."

Ellie's mood immediately lifted, so much so, she had to physically refrain from smiling by chewing on her bottom lip. It was like a shot of relief, no, much more than relief, it was more like complete self-validation jolted through her.

Katie was fraying, she was coming undone.

Ellie gave Max a grave look. "Thanks for letting me know. I am very worried about her."

Again, she had to keep laying tracks that would lead back to Katie.

She wanted it over, the weekend to end, to be a memory. She wanted to be home. Wanted the feel of Nate's soft lips on her mouth, his large hands sliding up and down her body, and that furrowed look of concern that he should be doing something more. Touching her better. Offering her more pleasure.

Ellie couldn't picture herself in jail. She'd gotten too used to the finer things in life; she wouldn't be able stand how loud it would be, or the competing personalities and their accompanying body odors, all invading her space.

She couldn't let that happen.

Not for Katie.

If Lily was out there and her body was discovered in a week, or two, or even a month from now, and say, all the forensic evidence had been degraded (as per her earlier Google search, forensic evidence was destroyed at a much faster rate outdoors, especially if it came in contact with water), how would Ellie be implicated? What evidence would be on the knife now that Ellie had handled it so much?

Suspicion runs fast and hot, while the truth lags so far behind.

Katie had the money to hire the best lawyers, who would probably twist things up so much that Katie would eventually believe what they were telling her. Right now, she believed she'd killed someone without so much as a trace of a memory of doing so.

There was just the knife and the blood.

Ellie and Katie were sharing a room.

That could be the focus.

And then it would get twisted into Ellie's word against Katie's, and who would a jury believe? Adorable Shelby Spade or Ellie with her jerry-rigged past that functioned to make other people think she was more refined than she really was? Less damaged?

Ellie pulled the knife out of her backpack, unwrapped it from its towel, and flipped it back and forth, and looked at the dried blood. She could almost pick it off with a fingernail. It occurred to her to do that too. Clean it and put it back in the kitchen. But that wouldn't be something Katie would do. Ellie made a decision. She stood and moved toward the edge of the stony cliff and tossed the knife into the water. She watched the lake suck in the knife, then immediately return to glassy and smooth.

Ellie continued on her search for a body, desiccated leaves crunching under her feet, and when a misty sun-shower started to fall, she smiled.

ARIEL

Oh my god, I killed the baby. I killed Rob's unborn child. They're here to arrest me. They're going to take me away.

This was Ariel's first thought when the police drove up.

She was still sitting on the lawn on a purple mat. Legs crossed. Eyes closed. The heat of the buttery sun on her shorn head felt strange and beautiful. She was trying to meditate but couldn't make her mind empty.

She bet Naomi could stop thinking on will. Her threat was still ringing in Ariel's ears, but she had it all wrong. Ariel wasn't trying to infringe on her bliss, because what Ariel had with Dr. Dave transcended marriage and affairs and all things seedy. She'd killed something for him, and that level of intimacy meant something deeper than any of the mundane weddings she'd seen go through the Holiday Inn. Dr. Dave was too big of a force to be married to only one woman.

And what did marriage really mean anyway? It seemed like a silly, dated institution to Ariel. Just something people did because they thought they were supposed to, and the next thing they knew they were miserable and cheating on their spouses.

"I always make them sorry." That's what Naomi had said. What did she mean by *they?*

Part of her was wishing that Dr. Dave would see her and unroll a yoga mat right next to hers and that they could meditate together. They could try to listen in to one another's thoughts and test out Ariel's budding theory that they were linked on a supernatural level.

It was why she'd chosen to meditate so close to the house and not down at the dock, so she was visible from most windows of the Sanctuary and could imagine Dr. Dave watching her, until he *was* watching her. She was trying to manifest her yearning into reality. Then there was the sound of a car door slamming shut. She turned around and saw a police car parked aggressively close to the house. Two state troopers had stepped out.

All she had managed to manifest were the cops.

Ariel jumped up, pulled the hood of her sweatshirt over her head, and tried to beeline away from the house, with loose plans to hide out somewhere until they left.

"Hey! You!" Too late. The woman officer was calling after her. The beige uniform hugged the woman's hips; there were starbursts creased around her crotch. The troopers' cheery purple ties fluttered in the wind, looking so at odds with the guns on their belts as they walked toward Ariel. She stayed turned the other way a beat too long, her eyes watering, almost expecting the feel of handcuffs being slapped on her wrist. "Helloooo?"

Ariel turned around and pulled down her hood, and the woman's eyes popped at her shaved head. "Can you tell us where Dr. Dave or Naomi are? They inside or outside?" She gave a sweeping glance at the vast property. The woman wasn't wearing the broad-rimmed hat like her male partner, and her hair was pulled back into a stern ponytail that still showed the rake of comb marks.

"I'm right here." Dr. Dave came out of the house. "What can I do for you, Myrna?"

Never good business to be on a first-name basis with the police. The thought whipped through Ariel's head like a warning.

The troopers met him at the porch, and Myrna introduced the other officer. "You remember Lieutenant Gonzalez?" The troopers climbed the porch steps. "I am sure you do."

Lieutenant Gonzalez offered his hand, which Dr. Dave shook with overt confidence. "We just need to ask you a few questions," Gonzalez said. Though Dr. Dave didn't offer them a seat, the officers sat down on a pair of wicker chairs, sinking into their giant pillowy seats.

Ariel rolled up her yoga mat and took her time sliding it into the tubed basket on the porch so she could eavesdrop.

"Yeah, so we received a report that one of your guests," Myrna continued to speak, "a Miss Rachel Mueller, had been staying here and according to her sponsor, she is currently missing."

"She told us her name is Lily, and I don't quite understand why this woman thinks she is missing. She was already here yesterday morning and my wife explained to her that Lily, or Rachel, simply decided to check out early. All of her things were packed up—her room is empty." Dr. Dave perched on the edge of a porch railing across from the troopers, looking gangly and oversize compared to the sitting troopers. "I'm sorry you both wasted your time taking a trip up here." He stood up again, like the matter had been cleared up and therefore the officers would leave.

Neither officer made a move to leave.

"Dr. Dave, Dr. Dave, Dr. Dave." Myrna was shaking her head. "Once is a coincidence; twice is a pattern."

"Nope. No patterns here, Myrna. The other time was an entirely different scenario; you know that. You also know that our guests each sign a liability waiver before imbibing ayahuasca and all participants acknowledge and accept the risks, which are minimal." Dr. Dave sat down again, this time on a wooden bench. Ariel made the decision to sit down next to him. The troopers traded a look.

"Tell me this, then—did Rachel Mueller drink your witch brew before she went missing?"

Dr. Dave chuckled. "It just kills you, doesn't it? That I am religiously exempt from the law to serve my *witch brew* as you so offensively put it? You should try it sometime, Myrna; I think you would find out a lot about yourself. The ceremony is tonight, and you're more than welcome to join in."

"I'll pass."

"What are you afraid of?" Dr. Dave was aiming for congenial, but there was too much hostility in his voice and it fell flat.

"I don't know. Maybe fleeing your tea ceremony at night while under the influence and getting lost in a forest reserve for three days, having search and rescue airlift me out and take me to the hospital, where I would be treated for severe dehydration and a broken collarbone. Not sure that's my idea of a fun weekend."

Dr. Dave nodded. "Yes, well, once again, that was an unfortunate event, but one we've learned from, and we've since taken the necessary precautions."

"What time did Rachel leave?" The male trooper broke up the stare down between Dr. Dave and Myrna.

"We don't have an exact time; *Lily* didn't officially check out. It's probably safe to assume she left sometime late Friday night or early Saturday morning. I don't really know. From what I've heard, she did arrange for her sponsor to pick her up, but I guess something changed for Lily and she had someone else pick her up."

"Huh." Myrna looked incredulous. "That's weird."

"What's weird?"

"That someone would come all the way out here, pay for the weekend, then just take off halfway through before the big event—which you said is tonight. Especially since the cost to stay here for the weekend is . . . gosh, it's a lot of money. It just doesn't really make sense to me."

"I agree. We haven't had anyone leave prematurely like this before, but I respect Lily's, er, Rachel's decision. What we do here, like you said, it's not for everyone." Dr. Dave's jaw tightened.

"Is this really a good place for someone with a drug problem? I mean, it was Rachel's sponsor who was coming to get her," Gonzalez said.

"Ayahuasca tea is renowned for helping addiction issues."

"So more drugs help a drug problem? I just can't wrap my head around that one." Gonzalez shook his head.

"The sponsor also said that Rachel didn't have a fixed address either and that she could never afford attending your retreat without someone else paying for it or even comping her stay." Myrna's eyebrows flicked up like *comped* equated something salacious.

Naomi flung the door open and came out onto the porch. "Hello, hello." She was holding a tray of lemon-infused water. Her eyes were sparkling until they landed on Ariel. "'Scuse me, Ariel." Naomi stood over her, waiting for Ariel to move in a standoff that lasted a beat too long. The ice in the pitcher jingled, and the officers watched them with matching bemused expressions.

Ariel couldn't stand the awkwardness, and so she gave her seat up to Naomi.

Refusing to be edged out completely, Ariel faced the troopers. "On Friday, Lily practically burned my face off during the fire-starting challenge. FYI: she's completely unstable." Gonzalez wrote that down. Dr. Dave visibly winced.

"Fire challenge, now that doesn't sound safe," Myrna tutted.

"Yeah, playing with fire is just never a good idea. I mean, I learned that in preschool." Gonzalez turned to Myrna. "You know what that reminds me of? Who was that guy who convinced his followers to boil themselves to death in the desert?" Gonzales tapped his pencil on his pad of paper.

Myrna didn't even pretend to think. "That was James Ray. Those people paid thousands to be cooked to death."

The ice in Naomi's pitcher jingled before she set it down too hard. "Well, *unstable* isn't a word we use here. Anyway," she practically sang the word *anyway*, "I am glad you're here, since I was about to call you. I just received a call from the credit card company and it seems that Rachel Mueller was using a stolen card." Naomi cast Dr. Dave a victorious flick of her eyebrows. Dr. Dave put his hand on the back of her neck, and Ariel's gut churned like she'd swallowed a windstorm.

"Is that so?" Myrna looked skeptical. "You just got that call now?"

"Well, we don't run credit cards until a guest has checked out, just like your average hotel. I think the fact that Lily, or, I am sorry,

Rachel, did everything she could to stay here and access my husband's program is very telling to how powerful and transformative our retreat is for people. I think it also explains why she left without officially checking out."

"It certainly wraps things up with a shiny silk ribbon, doesn't it?" said Gonzalez.

"Look, we don't want to pursue this any further." Dr. Dave gave a resigned shrug. "We can eat the cost of Rachel's outstanding bill. I certainly don't wish to add further stress to someone who is clearly struggling. I can forward you the credit card information she used to book with us, Myrna, but I'm going to have to ask that you both leave now so we can continue to prepare for this evening's ceremony." Dr. Dave stood up.

"All right. We'll be waiting for that information," Myrna said before aiming herself toward Ariel. "You be careful now. We don't want to have to come back tonight."

"You won't." Ariel jutted her chin out. As the troopers were getting back into their car, she caught Myrna saying to Gonzales at the tail end of a whistle, "What a piece of work the bald girl is."

CARMEN

Breasts exposed, her back arched, Carmen presented herself like a sexual gift. Remembering her silver dollar—size bruises that dappled her abdomen from her IVF shots, she yanked the sheets up to try to cover them.

Simon burst into the cabin, his face red and sweaty. "What are you doing here?" he snapped. A quick glance at her breasts. Marie came in behind him, a worried look on her face. Her eyes ran over Carmen's body once before bumping into Simon. They looked panicked and frozen to the spot. Like they had no idea what to do with her.

"Oh," Marie said breathlessly.

"I thought . . . oh my god, I am so sorry. I've completely misread your signals. I should go." Carmen pulled the sheets up to cover her breasts. Her face was already burning red with fear, so it was easy to fake tearful embarrassment. She wanted to reach for her shirt on the floor next to the bed but knew the move to leave would look too eager.

"How did you get in here?" Simon's eyes darted toward the bathroom.

"*C'est bien*, Simon, calm down." Marie placed a hand on her husband's chest. "When have you ever been made upset by a beautiful young woman in your bed?"

"I tried the door, but it was locked, so I slipped through the window. I thought if I waited, I'd lose my nerve. I realize now that I should have . . . This is so intrusive, I should go."

"We are leaving," Simon said, his voice gruff. He was already heading toward the bathroom. She heard the cupboard door open, and Simon was back in the room holding the duffel bag.

"Yes, we have a family emergency and, regrettably"—Marie gave Carmen a hungry look—"we must go right away."

Immediately, Carmen stood and dressed. *Please, please, don't look in the bag.* But Simon placed the bag on the dresser, and with his back to the room, started to unzip it.

Marie touched her shoulder, drew her around as Simon parted the opening of the duffel bag. All the air went out of Carmen's body, and she clamped her eyes shut. She expected Simon to grab her by the throat, slam her into the wall, and blow her brains out. Her legs turned to rubber. She was going to give herself away if she didn't calm down.

"Au revoir, Carmen." Marie kissed her on the lips.

"*Dépêche-vous*, Marie! Snap, snap." Simon dropped the duffel bag by the door—right beside Carmen's backpack—then grabbed their suitcases, one after the other, and flung them onto the bed.

Carmen was stunned as she stepped out of the cottage. *Could it really have been that easy?* And then she saw the police car. *That's why they're leaving.* The police were either there to arrest Simon and Marie, or else it was Lily. Her sponsor had called the cops just like she had said she would.

Carmen made a sharp left as soon as she was out of view of the cottage. When she reached the woods, she started to run. Hot tears started to fall down her cheeks. She felt immune to the branches whipping against her skin and the soft and spongy ground sucking at her feet. Nothing slowed her down.

A smile broke out over her face, and she tilted her head back.

She did it.

She followed her own Xs. Found her isolated spot at the lake.

She moved fast to hide the cocaine, triple-checking everything was sealed up before twirling the two plastic grocery bags tight, then placing those bags into a large, black garbage bag. She then secured it with the fishing rope and dunked it into the lake. To make extra sure it didn't go anywhere, she dropped several rocks onto it.

As she made her way back up into the woods, she again spotted that red thing. The flag she'd seen when she'd first come down there.

It was a red paisley headband. Much like the one Lily wore.

Carmen didn't take a closer look. She didn't stop walking. Instead, she broke out again into a jog, convincing herself that the dark spot on the bandanna wasn't really blood.

KATIE

When Katie could finally muster the will to leave her room, it was late afternoon.

She knew the police had been there. From her bedroom window, she'd watched as they'd arrived and then left. Her feet glued to the floorboards, the rest of her body straining to go downstairs and turn herself in, she was a twisted centaur of indecision.

She decided that if the police were there because they'd found Lily's dead body, then she would be called down. Every guest would at least be interviewed. It was what Shelby Spade would do—take down names, get a statement from every single guest staying there, search the grounds to figure out a possible murder site. Well, not a murder site, more like the teacher-staff room to see if Coach Griffin really was stealing Mr. Palmer's math quizzes and giving the answers to his best football players. (He was.)

But then the police left.

She could still do the tea.

Her last night of freedom had not been cut short. And maybe— and here she allowed herself this short-lived burst of optimism— maybe something would buoy up from the blackness that was Friday night while she was under the tea's influence that could save her from turning herself in. But what would that be?

She could not think of any other scenario with a bloodied knife that didn't include cutting herself or someone else, and Katie didn't have a new mark on her body. Clearly, she could bury the things

she didn't like about herself down deep until they were mere pinpricks in her brain.

Unless.

And here, a bubble of hope fizzed in her chest.

Unless she had stumbled upon Lily's dead body and plucked the
knife out of her and then, what? In her sleepy stupor, she took
the knife back to bed with her? It would explain the blood. But
where was the killer during this? Lurking in the shadows? Did
he know she was sleepwalking? From what Nate told her, she
sleepwalked with her eyes open.

Did he wait for her to leave before hiding the body, and was now
carefully watching Katie to see if she'd remember anything? And
if she did? What? He'd kill her too?

The bubble of hope popped. It sounded ridiculous. Like something the *Shelby Spade* writers would come up with for a reunion
episode in an attempt to be edgy and set up a twist ending so far-
fetched it left viewers dizzy and indifferent.

It was probably better not to present outlandish theories to the
police tomorrow—just present the facts, as she knew them. She
had the knife, the blood, and the history of stabbing living things
in her sleep. Yes, she was going to turn herself in. The decision was
made. She was going to a police station as soon as she left the retreat, handing over the knife, and holding her hands out to be
cuffed. She imagined a Nickelodeon version of a police station in
her head.

Katie's life as she knew it would end tomorrow.

The rest of the day was spent whittling down the hours to the tea
ceremony by moving around the grounds of the Sanctuary with
Ellie, Carmen, and Ariel. Stiff and mostly silent, they went from
the spa to swimming in the lake to sunbathing on the dock right
up until the baking sun cooled off.

Ariel's hair, or lack thereof, should have been more disturbing to Katie, but it just wasn't. Hair seemed like such an inconsequential thing, like a doily. *Who cares?*

Everything seemed so suddenly trivial: birthdays, the days of the week, five-year plans, self-betterment, the endless cycle of wanting, then getting or not getting, then getting depressed either way because none of it really mattered. Then moving on to another brand of self-betterment to figure out why you're so fucking unhappy. It didn't work, because the pursuit of wellness was just a big distraction from the truth that life was a mix of tedium and chaos with fleeting bursts of grief and happiness. It gave a false sense of progress—to count calories, drink only smoothies; to post pictures of acrobatic yoga poses, screenshots of one's daily steps, and reposts of inspirational quotes. Now it seemed like a soul-sucking way to mark time; counting your steps? Keeping a journal of your negative thoughts? Would a diet journal be read at one's funeral? Should it be, if it took up so much of someone's life?

Not that Katie did any of these things, but she was convinced of others' wellness journeys and she'd always wanted in. *If only I could be like these people, then I could better ignore the constant gnawing in my chest because I am in a perpetual state of fight-or-flight but can't do either. There is always some beast at the door, trying to break it down and turn your world upside down. And if you live through it, it will come back, again and again.*

It all seemed like so much effort to pretend.

To what end?

You're here, and then you're not.

You're a child, and then someone cuts your childhood out of you. You're not a killer, then you are one.

Just like that.

"How is everyone feeling about tonight?" Ellie asked in a chipper voice. She seemed uncomfortable in the silence and tried to start a conversation every once in a while.

"Great!" said Ariel, her eyes shining.

"Better than I was." Carmen was twisting a piece of string that was hanging from the hem of her T-shirt and rolling it around her finger tightly.

Katie shrugged and stared at nothing.

"How is everyone feeling about the weekend overall?" Ellie tried again.

"Amazing!" Ariel's eyes went from shiny to misty.

"Very enlightening," Carmen said, snapping the string from her shirt. Her finger was blue.

Katie shot her a look that said, *How could you even ask that?*

Ariel told them that Naomi had an effigy of her old self hanging in the basement, and didn't that seem crazy? Did they think Naomi might be crazy? "She was Dr. Dave's patient once, y'know."

Carmen laughed. "Not surprised. I think anyone who spends this amount of time thinking about themselves would go mental."

Another cavern of silence.

"I really need to go home." Carmen suddenly sounded uneasy and urgent. "Hey, Katie, do you mind if we leave tomorrow before the sunrise salutations or whatever?"

"But that's like 5:30 a.m." *The earlier I leave, the sooner I go to jail.*

So her friends thought the weekend was a bust and wanted to go home. Katie couldn't blame them. She hadn't exactly had a good time—and in Ariel's case, maybe she was now responsible for her friend going too deep into Dr. Dave's brand of new age spirituality—but she was hopeful the tea would change all that.

That the tea would be a positive experience for each of them; that they'd have at least one fond memory before learning that they'd been hanging out with a murderer the entire weekend.

"Sure," Katie finally answered with a shrug.

"I don't want to go home," Ariel said in a quiet voice. Katie's thoughts were too much of a tumbling mess for her to say anything back.

* * *

Max made a point to find her. He asked if she was all right "with everything," and Katie's chest almost split in two, right there on the porch. She managed to nod and say yes.

"I don't know if I believe you."

"I am okay with you. Believe that."

"All right, then. Is it okay if I look you up sometime? Make sure you're still okay down the road?"

She wanted to say he wouldn't need to, because she'd probably be on TMZ. Instead, she nodded. "That'd be nice." Of course she met a genuinely nice guy just when she was headed off to prison. Her mind tipped toward making a conjugal visit joke. Would she ever stop being like this? Always trying to be a ra-ta-ta piece of entertainment in exchange for being liked?

In the evening, they moved to the living room, where Dr. Dave gave his final pep talk, something about how they were all official warriors now, ready to rage against the ordinary. Warriors who could manifest their own realities and create the lives they'd always wanted. That in the end, nothing mattered but their own happiness. Their own bliss. "Stop at nothing to cultivate infinite bliss," were his parting words.

Then they had to go back upstairs and get ready for the ceremony.

Katie dressed in the required loose-fitting clothing for the ceremony. White linen pants and a tank top. She debated on bringing her phone but decided to leave it. To go all in with the ceremony.

She grabbed a sweater for when it cooled off. Right now, she was still so warm, but she couldn't tell if it was the air that was warm or her own churning anxieties that were keeping her feverishly hot. There was a big, gaping question mark of what was going to happen to her tomorrow. She had an end-of-life feeling, like she was heading into an unfamiliar realm so different from anything she'd ever known.

Things had been closing in on her all afternoon. The egg yolk sun was hanging too low. The wood smoke was getting stuck in her throat, curling into her hair and pores. The lake and trees had crept in closer. Her scar was aching on the inside of her cheek as if she were hanging from a fishhook.

Ellie was in the bathroom, running the tap. When she came out, Katie was waiting for her and asked her for the knife.

"Why?" Ellie's eyes shifted around the room. The look Katie associated with people who pretended they forgot their wallets when the bill came after an expensive dinner. (It happened to Katie a lot.)

"I just want it. To put it with my own things." Katie was sitting on her bed, her hands folded loosely between her knees. "I am going to turn myself in."

"You are?" Ellie dropped onto the opposite bed. "Are you sure? I thought we would dump the knife tonight. When we come back from the tea. It would be good time, considering everyone will be feeling its effects. If someone did spot us, well, they won't exactly be a reliable witness, right?" There was a twinkle in Ellie's eye, and Katie wondered if a part of her future sister-in-law was enjoying this a little bit too much—being lured over to the dark side. The excitement of covering up a crime.

"I have to turn the knife over. It's the right and responsible thing to do. I can't hide from what I might have done." Katie's voice was flat and distant. Like she was fading away.

"And what will you tell the police?" Ellie eyed her. Katie realized how nervous Ellie was, as if Katie would try to blame something on her.

"I won't say anything about you. If you want, I'll say you didn't even know about the knife at all."

Ellie looked at her. "Do you feel guilty?"

The question jarred Katie. A new rush of panic surged through her. She wasn't sure how to answer it. "It's hard to feel guilty about something I don't remember."

"You still don't remember anything?"

"Not about Friday night." Katie was almost tempted to tell Ellie more. What she did really remember. After everything they'd been through this weekend, Katie felt that Ellie was someone she could trust, but she wasn't ready to talk about AJ. And she was fairly certain she would never tell anyone that she'd cut her own face. "Friday night is a blank."

"Well, do you mind if I keep the knife overnight, then? All things considered, I would just feel safer that way." Ellie averted her eyes.

Katie let out a burst of breath. "Right. Good idea."

ELLIE

At 7:00 p.m., Dr. Dave gathered everyone on the lawn. "Unfortunately, we are down two more members this evening—Simon and Marie were called home to Montreal due to a family emergency. They will be missed, but all that means is that there's more tea for you and me." Dr. Dave waggled his eyebrows. "Now, are you all ready to unfetter your minds?"

Ellie wondered at Simon and Marie's sudden departure. If maybe a missing girl was too disturbing for them to stay and enjoy the tea. And if so, what did that say about everyone still there?

The sun was setting, and the light hit the windows of the lodge in a way that turned them into interrogation mirrors. Dr. Dave was dressed in a poncho, cargo shorts, and an outback hat. He was holding an old-fashioned torch, complete with a doused rag. Carmen made some jabbing Indiana Jones reference. Ellie could picture the conversation between Naomi and Dr. Dave; they would have decided against a regular flashlight for the purpose of "authenticity."

Dr. Dave led them down a path away from the house and far from the other manicured pathways. It had been hidden by a loose bushy branch that he removed and tossed to the side. The path was narrow and leafy, and the group had to do a single-file march, swatting away at branches as they went. The entire time, Ellie thought Dr. Dave's torch was going to graze one of the trees and ignite a forest fire.

"And into the dark we go, to find enlightenment," Dr. Dave said over his shoulder.

Enlightenment. The last two days had been very enlightening indeed.

The path eventually widened into a clearing, which was lit up with tiki torches that encircled a brick firepit.

Dr. Dave and Naomi had gone to a lot of trouble to create the feel of the Amazon in the middle of their wooded acreage, but the site was too clean to be convincing. Too nice. The bamboo mats too new looking.

It was the kind of place that reality TV stars would gather on an elimination episode.

A fire was already lit and sparking up into the dark sky. Beside each mat were cheery pastel-colored puke buckets and rattles.

"What're the rattles for?" Anthony picked one up and shook it in Dr. Dave's direction.

"Right. I'll get to that, Anthony." Dr. Dave didn't try to hide his contempt for being asked preemptive questions as he dropped his torch in a large orange Home Depot pail full of water. It sizzled out.

Dr. Dave waited for everyone to be seated before taking two large glass bottles with screw tops out of his canvas bag and setting them down on a small wooden table. "As you all know, since it's stated in the itinerary, the tea can cause a physical purge, and so the buckets next to you are there in case this happens." Dr. Dave also pointed toward an outhouse with a little half-moon-shaped cutout nestled between trees. "But of course, vomiting and diarrhea are a small price to commune with your personal version of God. As Anthony pointed out, you're each outfitted with a rattle. Please know that sometimes your first visions are the darkest; please use the rattles to dispel negative thoughts and make the visions flee. Remember to mentally state your intentions before drinking."

Ellie's chest started to tighten.

Naomi took the bottle and served up the first cup in a shot glass. It poured thick. She handed it to Dr. Dave, who closed his eyes for a second. His lips moved slightly before he downed it in two throaty gulps, then closed his eyes for a long, uncomfortable moment. His eyes flicked open again, and he released a long "Ahhh!" like the tea was thirst-quenching.

Naomi filled another cup, and drank it down.

"Whoa, shouldn't there be, like, a designated driver here?" Carmen said, but no one paid her any attention.

"Everyone relax, get comfy, and buckle in, because your soul is about to go on a ride." Dr. Dave lit a bundle of sage to "purify the area," as Naomi poured more tea into cups and handed each one out.

"Cheers." Ariel tipped her glass toward Katie and Carmen.

"To the end of a girls' weekend like no other," Katie added and clinked her glass into Ariel's, then Carmen's. Ellie had made sure not to get stuck in the middle, and so was on Katie's left. When Katie turned around, she gave Ellie a knowing look of resignation before taking her first sip of the tea and immediately started gagging. The tea sputtered out of her mouth. "Oh my gawd, this tastes like a mix of ashes, rotted fruit, gasoline, and aspirin."

Ariel took her cup, sniffed, and grimaced. "I don't think I can."

"Just down it, Ariel." Dr. Dave was walking the circle. He'd taken off his poncho and was now in a fresh tank top so white it glowed in the dark. His eyes were already red-rimmed, maybe dry from the fire or maybe something else. Ariel nodded obediently before swigging it back and then looking up at Dr. Dave for some kind of pat on the head. Dr. Dave gave her a narcotized grin and said, "Good girl."

"Drink up." Ellie nudged Katie. Watched as Katie took another tiny sip. She grimaced as if a live fish were going down her throat. "You're going to have to down it, like Ariel." Katie nodded, plugged her nose, and swallowed.

Good, thought Ellie. Finally something was going right.

Ellie took a sip of her own tea and let it sit in her mouth, its granular earthiness stinging her tongue. She held it in her mouth, savoring its crude oil taste because she had enjoyed this part of the tea ritual—suffering through the physical purge. It was a bit like self-flagellation, and it really did feel cleansing.

So, Katie was going to confess. It was far more difficult to convict someone without a body—she knew this from the many hours of *Dateline* she'd watched. Still, she felt more relaxed about the situation. Katie really thought she was guilty. The police would comb the woods and divers would search the lake. Eventually Lily's body would be found and Katie would go to jail.

Ellie was so tempted to swallow the tea and ride out this final night convening with her dead sister and mother. She'd seen them the one time she drank the tea, and knew in her heart that the tea would always bring them back to her.

Instead, the first chance she could, she brought the cup back up to her lips and carefully spit it out. When no one was looking, she dumped it into the dirt.

Another thing ruined by Katie.

Dr. Dave started to sing what was called the icaros, meant to provoke heightened and profound states of awareness, if he were a proper shaman. But unlike the gentle, lulling warble one would expect in an ayahuasca ceremony, Dr. Dave's singing veered into a Broadway rendition. He was too distracting. The way he was dancing around, his arms over his head, one hand shaking a large bundle of leaves at a consistent tempo like he was the star of the show and not the tea. And then they waited.

Ellie looked around the circle at the people she'd spent the weekend with, not just Carmen, Ariel, and Katie but everyone. Weepy Paula, Anthony with permanently dry-looking eyes, a bandanna tight around his forehead, his glasses fogging. Wood-hacking Max.

She watched as they each folded under the influence of the tea.

ARIEL

Naomi hated her. Ariel could feel it rolling off her like heat waves full of radiation. When Naomi handed her a cup of tea Ariel said, "Thank you," accompanied with her warmest smile. It was a peace offering, one that Ariel hoped would say, *Hey, I'm not here to infringe on your bliss, only add to it.*

But Naomi ignored her. Completely dismissed her.

Earlier, Ariel had made a point to find Dr. Dave one last time and asked if she could stay on at the retreat. Work for him. Be part of the kitchen staff or do landscaping. Heck, she'd even clean the toilets. Anything to stay there and continue her spiritual journey— and of course not return to Shakopee.

Dr. Dave had given her a long assessing look before saying yes.

Ariel had sprung up into his arms, like she'd just accepted his marriage proposal.

He had gently pried her off him with one of his late-night-talk-show-host chuckles, then added, "You'll have to work on winning over Naomi. She can be hard on the staff."

Ariel wondered at that now. The women who made up the staff. The way Naomi sniped at them. Was that what she meant by making "them all sorry"?

Had Dr. Dave slept with all of them too? Was he still sleeping with them? Did he run closer to Warren Jeffs than Eckhart Tolle?

But then Ariel couldn't concentrate anymore. Her thoughts fluttered away. Her hands were starting to tingle, her fingers were feeling as if they were growing and stretching. She thought, *I could do anything with these hands.*

The tea had officially arrived in her brain.

Ariel flopped back on the bamboo mat and watched the sky tilt, the stars swirling and then shifting into geometric shapes until they arranged themselves into the sonogram image of Rob's baby. Somehow she just knew the baby was fine. She felt her insides go warm and gooey.

She could see herself at an incredible distance, her life up until now playing out like a movie reel against the dark sky.

There was her grandma holding her at two years old; she missed her grandma so much. The last dance class she attended—she had been eight, maybe nine years old. She had caught herself in the mirror and had known it was a joke to wear a bodysuit with her body type. When she had said this to her mom, she had agreed, taken her out of dance, and started her on a barrage of diets. She would never look the way she wanted to. A single frame started to flicker and replay over and over. It was Ariel at the Christian camp she'd attended, which she had later found out was a Christian camp for fat kids. Her zealot of a camp counselor had liked to put them to sleep with campfire stories about how Satan was coming for them to turn them into whores because they already couldn't control their sensual desires for sweet treats. "Just think about it. Was Jesus fat?" She had withheld food and sunscreen, and Ariel's body had felt fried up and weak. She had put herself to sleep each night by plucking at her hair. That's where it had started. She'd had no idea.

It all seemed so clear to her now. She was always seeking validation from others, and the more it was withheld, the more she zeroed in on the person withholding it, as if they were a safe and she just needed the right code.

It was as if she were addicted to rejection. And that rejection affirmed the negative voice inside of her head: *you're not lovable.*

She had to stop doing that to herself. Life was too short.

Other images popped up. Lovely memories of going to the beach with her family, of arriving in New York for the first time and walking down to Times Square, openly jubilant, before learning that it was considered the antithesis of New York to the locals. Her sister, her husband, and the birth of her nieces and nephews no longer inspired jealousy, but joy. She had so much love to give and knew she was going to be an incredible asset here, at the Sanctuary. She was going to help so, so many people.

Ariel was suddenly crying so hard that her sternum was clattering in her chest. And then Carmen started to frantically shake her rattle and Ariel's movie abruptly ended. All she could see was a black abyss.

CARMEN

When Carmen first saw an orb of light approaching through the brambles, she thought she was hallucinating a tiny sun by the way the spokes of light pinwheeled around it. The sun was there, just for her, because brighter days were on the way. These were tipsy, zany thoughts—a cocktail of her giddy outlook and the trippy tea. She felt an urge to whistle, but couldn't feel her lips.

She hadn't intended to drink the tea, but then she couldn't think of a reason not to try it.

She wasn't going to donate her eggs anymore. Of course not. Simon and Marie were gone. Her treasure was buried. She was in the clear, so why not? Over the weekend, she had become increasingly curious about the tea. It wasn't like she would have another chance to do it. Would the tea really expand her consciousness? Help her live a better life? Why not purge her old self and get ready for her new fabulous one? Fuck it. She'd won.

Now that Carmen had stopped gagging, the DMT in the tea had settled into the grooves of her brain and was working its black magic. She'd been sucked into a euphoric bubble. She couldn't feel her face but could feel every single one of her organs working inside her. Churning, churning. The little engine that could. What a perfect machine the body was, when it worked.

She felt a burst of sadness for her dad and his degenerating body, that the light switch on each of his nerve endings was being flicked off, one by one.

Then she saw that sunny light again, bouncing toward her. No, she thought suddenly as she looked harder. No, not a sun but an egg.

She could see cells splitting inside its yolky orb. It was one of her eggs, fertilized and ready to go, dancing toward her.

Could everyone else see it? The floating, glowing egg? Through lid-heavy eyes she looked at everyone, but the fire distorted their faces, and suddenly they all morphed into her siblings. They were all there, tossing her a thumbs-up for being such an incredible role model and for taking care of them. When she blinked, they mutated into sickly looking creatures with jagged teeth. She knew if she let them, they'd feed off her. She blinked them away.

Anthony made a groaning noise, then was rolling on the ground, throwing up so violently he looked like a dog with its head stuck in a bucket. Carmen was transfixed until the bucket-head snapped toward her. Time stretched out, it seemed like hours had passed.

Then the egg-light split and a second egg came bouncing behind along the pathway of the first. Twins.

Carmen again wondered if anyone else was seeing it. But then Naomi stood up. "Oh, you're back," she said and then emitted a sudden, creaky noise. A strange scuffling followed. The table holding the bottles of tea was knocked over.

There was a definite lag in the connection between Carmen's eyes and her brain. Her "eggs" were flashlight beams. Those heavy, night-security-guard kind of flashlights. And because her stoned mind was having trouble making connections, she was more interested in the flashlights than who was holding them.

It was Simon and Marie, and they had guns. Marie was waving hers at their entire hookah lounge circle, but Simon was coming straight for her. "You little cunt bitch, where is it?"

Dr. Dave stumbled up, and once he was standing, his legs looked suction-cupped to the ground. "What's this about, Simon?"

Simon turned around, and even though he kept the gun on Carmen, Naomi still flitted over and blocked her husband's body with her own. "There are no problems here, Dr. Dave, if I get back what's mine. I don't want you involved. You know following our bliss does not include hurting you."

"This is a sacred ceremony, Simon. I can't have you here waving a gun," Dr. Dave slurred, pushing Naomi aside. "Whatever this is about, we can tackle it together. Just give me the gun." He put his hand out like a schoolteacher asking for a homework assignment, but the motion seemed to knock him off-balance and Dr. Dave suddenly wobbled and swayed like an AirDancer in a used car lot. Suddenly everyone around the fire turned into AirDancers, and Carmen almost laughed out loud.

Simon stared at Dr. Dave's hand like he was considering handing over his gun. Dr. Dave was his guru, after all. *Please, please, please give him the gun.* "Give it to me," he repeated, reaching for it.

Simon pivoted and thwacked the butt of the gun into the back of Dr. Dave's head. Ariel cried out like she was the one who'd been clobbered. "I didn't want to do that," Simon said calmly, "I really didn't."

Max made a move to stand up, and Marie swung her gun, one-handed, and aimed it at him.

Dr. Dave stood there a second like he was still registering the blow. His ear was bleeding. Simon hit him again. "Get on the ground. Stay there! Or I will have to really hurt you."

Dr. Dave sank back down onto his mat. Naomi clung to him, crying, cupping his wounded ear like she was already trying to heal it.

Simon was coming for Carmen now. She tried to stand up and make a run for it, but her body had liquefied. The air was rippling.

Simon knelt in front of her and pressed the gun under her chin. It was a cold kiss. "Where the fuck is it?" He was suddenly on top of her. His French accent so thick in his rage that she hardly understood him. "You're the only one who was in our room. What did you think? You thought spreading your legs was worth that much?"

Paula made a gasping noise. Anthony continued to retch into his bucket.

"What are you talking about? Where is what?" It was too surreal, this scene, of having a gun pointed at her while under the influence of an ancient medicine meant to fill her with feelings of spiritual buoyancy. Carmen still thought she could walk away from it, that she could manifest a different outcome.

Simon walloped her in the side of the head with his fist, sending her sideways to the ground. She could immediately feel her skin split and the warm rush of blood. Her ears roared. Simon kicked her in the abdomen, her money-making ovaries heaving. This sobered her up enough to grasp that she'd lost. She wasn't getting the drugs or the money.

Katie and Ariel were screaming, "Stop! No, stop!"

"Get up." Simon pulled Carmen upright by her hair. She felt like a limp marionette hanging from strings. Her scalp was on fire. Her eyes were sparking white. "All of you. Up. Get up now." Simon swung his gun at Ariel, Katie, and Ellie.

Katie was staring at her with big, questioning eyes. "What did you do, Carmen?"

Did Katie ask that just with her eyes? Or was she actually talking? Carmen put her hands up in front of her. "No, they had nothing to do with it. It was just me, Simon. I needed money. I saw it when I helped Marie after she twisted her ankle. I took it. Just me. Please, please, leave them out of it."

Ariel was keening now, adding an even worse layer of panic to what was happening.

"I told you all to get the fuck up. Tell me where my shit is or I start shooting your friends one by one until you do," Simon growled at her.

"No, no, please. It's in the woods." Carmen choked out the words. "I hid it."

Simon got them into a single line, pulling Carmen's arm roughly, while Marie kept her gun on everyone around the fire. "Let's go get it."

"They don't need to come with us, they don't know anything—" Simon shook her back and forth by her hair.

"I don't fucking believe you," Simon shouted down the back of her head, then pulled her upright again, twisted her around, and aimed the gun at Ellie's head.

"I can kill this one now. Is that what you want?"

Ellie was remarkably calm.

"No, no, please don't."

"Then shut the fuck up and do what I say." He dragged her forward. "Any of you try to run and I will kill Carmen. And then I will kill each of you slowly and painfully."

They were all moving now. They walked away from the safety of the ceremony, across the lawn, past the house, toward the paths. No one stopped Simon. He kept her at the end of the line (how poignant), in what felt like a death march into the woods. Away from the light of the fire, Carmen felt as if she were being swallowed whole by darkness. Her eyes felt crossed. Simon's grip was a vise on her bicep. She felt small, child-size, compared to his rage, his gun.

Katie was in front of her, mindlessly whispering into the night air, "What did you do, Carmen? What did you do? Who do you think you are? Who do you think you are?" But then Carmen realized it wasn't Katie but a snakelike hiss cycling through her own head.

Ariel kept up her pitchy weeping. Simon told her to shut up, his fingers flexing tighter around Carmen's arm. "Which way now?" he asked her, thrusting the gun harder into her ribs. She'd hardly noticed, but the manicured, wood-chipped path had split into two.

Which way? Carmen didn't know. She felt so turned around. She thought she could hear the lake but couldn't figure out where exactly it was. Everything looked so different at night, and she was feeling so woozy. The piney smell of the woods was like a stinging resin flicking into her eyes. Sweat was gathering on her nose; waves of heat were rolling up her back. She was trying hard to swallow down the bile crawling up her throat.

"This way," she managed to reply with a surprising level of confidence. Simon grunted, jabbed her forward with the gun. A few minutes and they hit another divide in the narrowing trail. "Here," she said, and led them down the left trail. When the path split again, Carmen almost admitted she was lying, that she didn't know where she was, but then she spotted the lake through the trees, moonlit and gleaming. But it was still too far away; it was all the way at the bottom of a thickly treed slope.

She wasn't anywhere near the spot where she'd sunk the drugs.

What was she going to do? Keep everyone hiking through the woods until it was obvious she didn't know where she'd put the cocaine? Try to buy time and keep Simon's spirits up by mumbling that it must be there somewhere, like she'd just misplaced a set of keys?

The earth was shifting; the forest kept rearranging itself. Everything looked the same. Every little dip and opening toward the lake looked identical. When the trail they were on wound back to the previous trail, Simon pushed the others out of his way and got right in Carmen's face.

"Stop playing games! Where the fuck is it?"

Think. She'd never felt so stoned in her life. She lifted her finger and pointed in the vague direction of the lake.

"In the lake? Are you fucking kidding me?" Simon's arms were out, and he pressed a fist hard into his forehead. "You're telling me you put $350,000 of cocaine in fucking water to just . . . what? Float away? *Putain!* You've got to be fucking kidding me!"

"It's wrapped in plastic. I made sure it wouldn't get, like, wet." Carmen's tongue had gone woolly. She was using filler words, and no one trusted anyone who used filler words. "They're, like, tied to a tree with rope."

Simon's veiny forehead was slick with sweat. He winced and scratched his ear with the gun. "Where in the lake? Where?"

Carmen gazed around, but nothing looked familiar. "I can't see properly. Could I have the flashlight?"

Simon moved ahead of them, handed it to her, then aimed the gun at her head. "Any of you bitches move and I'll shoot her, okay? Understand?"

Carmen waved the flashlight around, feeling the barrel of Simon's gun pressed into the back of her skull. She couldn't see Xs on the trees. The trees themselves looked like stretched, funhouse versions of trees. Her friends were giving her pleading looks. "There. That's the tree. It's down there."

"You lead, and if it's not there, you die."

She was lying, of course. She really had no idea where she was.

And then Katie started puking.

KATIE

Bewildered, her legs hardly working, Katie kept telling herself none of this was really happening. Her vision was pixelated as if everything she was seeing were a mere suggestion. Tree branches were floating over her head, bright and vibrant as peacock feathers. She would blink, and the trees shifted into black antennae reaching up into the night sky. She'd blink again and she could see the trees expanding and contracting like giant lungs. Her own breath swirled in front of her, like a zigzaggy light show. She knew what she was seeing wasn't real, so maybe Simon wasn't either. It was just a bad trip that would be over soon. It was too discordant with the spiritual purge she wanted so badly. Now she was being taken hostage for something she could hardly grasp.

How could Carmen steal drugs? Fucking Carmen and money. She would have lent her more than a paltry three grand. She would have lent her ten grand or twenty or thirty or whatever it took to talk her out of something so dangerous. How could she have put all of them in such danger? Ariel was blubbering in fragmented, teeth-chattering sentences that sounded like the start of a prayer, "Dr. Dave . . . Dr. Dave . . . save us . . . please, please save us. I know you can hear me."

Why was Ariel praying to Dr. Dave?

Dr. Dave wasn't going to save them.

Katie's thoughts spun frantically. *We should be able to take him. There are four of us and only one of him. And a gun. But don't think about the gun. A distraction.* She had to distract Simon and then maybe her friends could get away. She had this odd, puffy-chested urge to be the hero again. Just like when she'd played Shelby Spade, she'd be the one to spin things around in a few compact minutes and make everything right again.

Plus, she was planning to turn herself in tomorrow anyway. Who cared if she died? And if she didn't, wouldn't it work in her favor to be the one who'd saved her friends from a homicidal drug dealer?

Katie doubled over and started to throw up. She didn't even have to really fake it; her gut was churning. Simon grabbed the flashlight back from Carmen, and as he moved toward Katie, she stood back up and screamed, "Run! Ruuuuun!"

Simon whipped around and waved his gun, scanning the flashlight over everyone's faces. They all just stood there. Carmen swayed back and forth, Ariel continued her pitchy wail, and Ellie stepped backward but then stopped. Katie had misjudged how close they all were. How hemmed in they were by the steep incline of trees on their left and the drop toward the lake on their right. Simon could easily pick them off one by one as they slowly scrambled either up or down. The tea had completely distorted her sense of space.

"Are you fucking stupid? *Tabarnak!* Any of you run and I'll kill you." Simon grabbed Katie in a headlock and shouted down the back of her head as he dragged her forward. She kept her eyes clamped shut, expecting a bullet to hurtle into the back of her skull, Simon making an example out of her. She could hardly breathe. "Next time, I am just going to start shooting. It's the last time I say it. You understand me? I will kill all of you. Now just get me my fucking blow. I've had enough of this bullshit."

"Simon, Simon, it's okay. It's down there." Carmen had her hands out, as if she were standing on a balance beam. She pointed vaguely down a narrow bushwhacked trail that sloped toward the lake. Simon grunted, kept his arm around Katie's neck in a stiff choke hold, pressed the gun even tighter against her head, and dragged her along in awkward tandem. "Come on, all of you. Go down there. If it's here, you can all go, but if you try to run, I will kill her, and as I already promised, I will find each of you and kill you too." He gestured for them to go.

Simon was walking backward, using his gun to point at each of them. Suddenly, Simon grunted, and the flashlight whirled. He was dragging Katie down with him. He let go of her as they fell. A gun blast rang out. A flock of birds shot out of the trees. Ariel screamed. A rancid odor burst into the air.

Something hard jabbed Katie in the back. She rolled onto her side.

The flashlight had dropped and spun fully around, illuminating what they'd tripped over. It was Lily.

Katie was within kissing distance of her corpse.

Her face was cement gray, and her flat, dead eyes were aimed skyward. Her lips were puffy, and it looked like an animal had been gnawing at her nose and her ears. Her torso was bloodstained; her dried-up shirt had several slits down the front. Her ropy, braided hair was fanned around her head like a rake stuffed with leaves.

Seeing the body was too horrible. Something inside Katie snapped. She was a murderer. She had to get away from it. Without thinking, she ran.

No, no, no.

ELLIE

Ellie moved quickly. She slid forward, grabbed the flashlight, and hammered it into Simon's head while he was down, once, twice. She heard a splotchy cracking noise like his skull was giving way. His grip on the gun loosened. She grabbed it and shot him in the head.

She flopped down, heaving, trying to catch her breath.

Of all the potential ways Ellie thought this weekend could end, this was not one of them. Never did she think she'd be giving a police statement about being held at gunpoint by some Quebec Mafia couple and led into the woods because Katie's idiot friend stole cocaine from them. This was never on her list of possible ways the weekend could go wrong. The entire time she was being led into the woods, she knew they had to do something. If Carmen gave him the drugs, he would kill them all because that's the way these things went. She wondered if the other three would do something. Anything at all? Or would it all be left to her? And then Katie had tried and failed, of course.

And Lily. Her body had finally been found. Poor thing. She had to have died a slow, slow death, her organs shutting down one by one as her legs came to a stuttering stop, until she dropped and went to black all alone. She saved them in the end. Sweet irony.

If Simon hadn't tripped over her body, they would probably all be dead. Now what?

The police would come. They would take statements for something she'd never planned for. *And where is Katie?*

Surprisingly, the flashlight still worked. Ellie picked it up again and passed the light over Carmen. Still clutching the gun with her right hand, her finger twitched over the gun's trigger. "I think I've been shot." Carmen held her hand out, and it was slick with blood.

"Oh, thank you, thank you, Ellie. *Oh my god,*" Ariel's voice squawked out of the dark, jangling Ellie's nerves again. She resumed her blubbering—or maybe she'd never stopped—and Ellie had only managed to tune her out while bashing in Simon's head. Her unrelenting, watery panic was like cutlery squealing against a dinner plate.

She couldn't see Katie anywhere. "Where's Katie? Which way did she go?"

Carmen looked around from where she was splayed out. "I don't know."

"Katie? Where is she? Did you see her, Ariel? Kaaaatie? Kaaaatie?" Ellie called out into the darkness. She weaved her flashlight back and forth into the trees. Nothing. Katie was gone. She had taken off like a coward. She had left all of them behind and run away.

"Ellie, what happened to your accent?" Carmen was trying to stand up. Everything went suddenly quiet. Even Ariel paused in her whiny weeping.

"My accent? Whatever do you mean?" Ellie said with Emma Watson precision, but she knew it was too late.

Fuck, fuck, fuck. I keep slipping up at the last moment. Now everything is fucking ruined. Again. I can't do this anymore. I can't try again. Not after putting in all of this effort. All of this time. No. No. Not unless.

"Yeah Ellie, it was like you didn't even have an accent," Ariel said. The sound of her flat, nasal Minnesotan accent announcing Ellie's moment of failure did something to Ellie. Two full days of looking at Ariel's insipid face, of listening to her distort Dr. Dave's mantras into something she would probably turn into a bumper sticker and slap on whatever candy-colored hatchback she owned back home, was too much.

Unless.

Again Ellie adapted to this new situation. Took control.

Carmen was up now in a kneeling position, one hand pressed over her hip.

Ellie felt the gun in her hand. Carmen was already, at the very least, grazed by a bullet. It would all be stitched up so perfectly. She tilted her head back, allowed herself a second to look up at the universe smiling down at her.

She turned and aimed the flashlight at Ariel. In one swift movement, Ellie brought the gun up and shot Ariel in the face. Her stupid bald head—what had she thought she was proving?—snapped back. Her face didn't even get a chance to register surprise. Her body slammed to the ground.

"Gawd, I've wanted to do that all weekend."

CARMEN

"What the fuck! What the fuck? Why did you do that?" Carmen screeched. Ellie emitted a harsh cackle, and Carmen scuttled backward.

What the fuck was happening?

Ellie pivoted toward her. Under the silver glow of the moon, she looked gruesome. Her features had turned steely. Spritzes of Simon's blood stippled her face. She cocked her head slowly like she was getting something out of watching her reaction, and then she slowly lifted and aimed the gun at Carmen. *The tea, the tea made Ellie deranged. She's hallucinating some other scenario right now that's making her homicidal.*

Carmen ducked low and took off into the bushes. Ellie got off two missed shots that brought up the ground around Carmen, then another that chipped a tree just ahead of her. The glow of the flashlight switched off.

Carmen weaved through trees, going deeper and deeper into the woods. The bullet hole in her side was pumping blood as she ran. Branches slapped at her face and arms. She couldn't really see where she was going. It was so dark. She focused on dodging low-hanging branches and the trees themselves so she didn't run headlong into one and knock herself out for Ellie to come up and shoot her execution-style. She was so focused, she nearly went off the side of a rocky ledge, her legs braking, her body practically rearing into reverse.

The crunch of feet. The flashlight beam turned back on. Ellie was on the move. Hunting her down.

Carmen crouched down behind a frail bush growing out of a rock and watched the flashlight move in the opposite direction, stop, and slowly pass over tree trunks behind a large stump. *Keep going, keep going.* Carmen couldn't breathe.

The flashlight swiveled around and started to move toward her. Carmen had nowhere to go. She was trapped on a ledge.

She inched forward and looked down at the lake. It was inky black except for the reflection of the moon scything the surface down the middle.

Another *pop, pop* of the gun. Bullets whizzed by her.

She had no choice. She had to jump.

Fuck.

She hurled her body off the ledge into the lake. The bullet hole in her hip searing white hot pain as she hit the cold water.

Ellie got off a few more missed shots, water splashing up like sparks.

Carmen tried to keep herself submerged underwater so Ellie couldn't see her. She tried to guess at how many bullets might be in that gun. Ellie kept turning the flashlight on and off, to confuse Carmen where she might be, forcing her to swim around in circles, frantically paddling away from the strobe of lights.

Ellie didn't have such good aim when her target was moving instead of just standing there, thanking her. She heard Ellie shout, "Oh, for fuck's sake!"

Her prim English accent was completely gone now. In its place was a West Coast grinded drawl.

Who is this woman? Who is Ellie? This wasn't the tea. Someone doesn't lose their accent just because they took a hallucinogen.

She'd had no reaction when she saw Lily's body, or when she'd hammered Simon's head in with the efficiency of a carpenter banging a nail into a board.

The flashlight continued to flick on and off.

On then off.

The only thing that even made sense was that Ellie wanted the cocaine. Simon had said how much it was worth, and in a split second, she'd decided she wanted it for herself. Or maybe she'd been in Simon and Marie's cottage too? She'd take $350,000 over a marriage with Nate and a sister-in-law she clearly had to put up with, and she was willing to kill them all for it. So she really was a gold digger; Katie—if Ellie didn't kill her first—would feel so vindicated.

Carmen tried to swim farther across the lake.

Immediately, a cramp shot up her side. Her teeth chattered fiercely. She could float back to the shore, but for now, she had to stay there, treading water in the middle of the lake, where only a trained sniper with a scope could reach her, and Ellie wasn't that good of a shot.

The flashlight was still off.

From this far out, Carmen could see the lodge. It was lit up and inviting, a massive house that announced that the people living there did everything right in their lives. The sight of it and her own vulnerability got twisted into that feeling she'd had when she was younger as the failure treading water in the public pool.

Obviously, she couldn't go back there. What would Marie do when she saw it was Carmen and not Simon returning? She scanned the shoreline; thought she glimpsed a dock farther down the lake but she could never make it that far. And it could be a fallen tree or her eyes playing hopeful tricks.

She had to get to the road and try to flag someone down. From this vantage point, Carmen knew where she was now. In her panic, the tea peaking in her body, she hadn't taken Simon far enough, and then had taken him left when she should have gone right.

She knew where to go now to get to the road.

She was starting to go from cold to freezing. She was almost sober now. All the rushing adrenaline, the searing pain of being shot, and the cold dip in the lake were like strong black coffee.

Her entire body shuddered, and the cramp in her side gnawed into her. Suddenly all she wanted was to be at home. To smell the soap in her youngest sister's hair after a bath. She wanted to give her dad more of those reassuring looks he had started to seek from her like a child, as if she could actually make things all right. Her muscles were becoming too fatigued to keep her head up; her eyelids were getting heavy. She could fall asleep right there. She had to get out of the lake. Now.

Carmen managed to half float, half swim to the shore and immediately took cover in the brush, sand and grit sticking to her wet skin, her bullet wound. She sat there, not breathing, not moving, just listening and raking her hands through dead leaves on the ground for something she could use to protect herself, finding only a piece of driftwood that would likely shatter on impact.

Where was Ellie? Was she waiting for her somewhere in the dark?

Minutes passed, and Carmen heard nothing. She moved as soundlessly as possible a few steps, then stopped and listened. A few more steps. Now she was crouching low and heading away from the lake.

Carmen wove through the trees, nearing a walking pace toward the road, branches sighing above her as a wind came up.

And then she saw it, moonlit and glowing. An X.

If Ellie hadn't bashed in Simon's skull, Carmen would have given Simon his cocaine, and they would probably all be returning to the retreat in one piece.

Don't do it. Don't. But still, she swiveled back around. Another X. Yes, she knew exactly where she was now. Exactly where she'd submerged the bag of cocaine.

Her sister's hair would smell better if they had a working hot water tank.

Ellie wasn't taking her money. She knew that much. Not after all she'd had to do to get cocaine.

Ariel was dead.

There was no way she was giving it up now.

KATIE

This place made a killer out of me. I killed Lily.

I am a killer.

She was running in no clear direction, with no clear reason other than to get away from the sight of Lily's body and the hard truth of what she'd done while she was sleeping. Yes, she'd planned to turn herself in, and she liked the sound of it in her head, but what came next?

She realized she'd been hoping that the police would tap a few keys and tell her that Lily or really, Rachel So-and-So had just used her ATM card an hour ago, and so no, she clearly wasn't dead or missing. The officer would have kind eyes and chuckle at her over-reaction, and then there'd be a sheepish request to get a picture of Shelby Spade for their twentysomething niece who'd get a kick out of it.

What must lurk inside of her to kill in her sleep? She had to be a latent psychopath.

This place made a killer out of me.

This thought kept shuttling around in her head as she slowed to a half stumble. Her heart felt as if it were being squeezed in a clawed fist. She had a strange urge to go back and cover up Lily's body because she must be so cold; that didn't make sense because Lily was dead, but it seemed like an act of kindness she deserved.

Her skin felt as if it were burning.

She wanted to scream, to pull her hair out.

She was in a small clearing now, lurching around like a dog tied to a post. What did she do?

I killed Lily.

She dropped to her knees. The wind was hissing. Her brain was on fire. Suddenly, her head was flooded with the memory of slicing her face. It kept repeating like a GIF. Over and over, she could see herself standing in front of the mirror, the light bulbs over the vanity mirror buzzing as she brought the paring knife up to her face and sliced herself open, starting at the corner of her mouth and working her way up.

Turning her mouth into a joker's grin.

Warm blood dripping onto the floor.

Her face switched to Lily's face, but this time, Katie was stabbing her in the chest over and over. *Leave me alone! Leave me alone!* she screamed as she killed off her last fan.

Lily's bloody hand came out and caressed Katie's scarred cheek.

Yes, that's what happened.

Katie tried to make out the when and where, but it was like she'd killed Lily on a closed set. Everything was black.

A gunshot suddenly popped in the air, and it jolted her back.

Katie scrambled up. The gun had gone off earlier. This bit of information was finally reaching her overwhelmed psyche.

Her spine went ramrod stiff. She listened to the air.

A short gurgle of eerie quiet and then a flurry of more gunshots. *No. No. No.* Katie started running again, wild and frantic through the woods, blind in the dark, toward the sounds. Toward her friends.

ELLIE

Carmen's stupid little Xs were like a bread crumb trail—so easy to follow.

Ellie knew the greedy bitch would come back for the cocaine. No one went to this much trouble, took this kind of risk without at least trying to come out of it with their windfall intact.

All she had to do now was sit and wait. She thought Carmen would draw Katie out, that at least she'd try to save her friend first before going for her jackpot in the lake, but it turned out Carmen wasn't that good of a friend, after all. Here she was, dripping wet and slinking along the shoreline. It was almost too easy.

Ellie felt a moment of pure wonder at the turn of events. She'd been so angry at Katie for inviting her friends, at how she'd believed they'd ruin everything, make everything messy and uncontainable, and now, she felt grateful to Carmen for her haphazard actions.

Already, Ellie was inventing a new story: Simon killed everyone. Unbeknownst to Ellie, the other three had stolen his drugs.

Katie was the likely ringleader even if she didn't need the money—she would have wanted the adrenaline rush or just a cut of the drugs, and then Ellie would again point out how odd she'd been acting the entire weekend.

I made a point to express my concern to others at the retreat.

Ellie was the only one who'd managed to get away from Simon (and then she might even mumble the word *karma* when being interviewed).

He'd brought them directly to Lily's body to show them he wasn't messing around. That he would kill them. That he was already a killer. She wouldn't know why he killed Lily, but Lily did happen to be an addict, so maybe that had something to do with it?

Carmen had brought him to where she'd hidden the drugs. She then, in a baffling move (*she was high as a kite, Officer*), had tried to fight Simon for the gun, and while this struggle had been happening, the rest of them had fled into the woods.

Ellie wouldn't be able to explain it—the why or how, since she was running in the other direction—but Simon shot Ariel.

The rest of them were quickly separated. She was halfway back to the retreat with plans to take the SUV to get somewhere safe to call for help when she saw Ariel's lifeless body. She'd stopped to check her vitals, because she was just that kind of person, but it was clear by the gaping hole in her face that she was dead.

That was when Simon came upon her. She would describe her panic, the way she'd squeezed her eyes closed when she'd felt the muzzle of the gun pressed into the back of her head. She'd say she'd thought she was dead, but then Simon suddenly had other plans. He'd made her lie down and had started to pull down her pants, but then she'd noticed the flashlight and somehow managed to grab it, and she'd hit him until the gun came loose. Best to keep that part as close to the truth as she could.

It was Simon's gun, after all. And the drugs made for a neat little irrefutable bow on the story.

She really couldn't have imagined a better outcome. And for all her meticulous planning, the months of effort, her failures, there she was having it all just fall into place.

Even if it looked like chaos, it really wasn't, because the universe just had a way of taking care of good people.

Of course, the police would probably find out who she really was, so she shouldn't use an accent. She would have to tell Nate the truth, blubber into his lap that she'd come to New York to reinvent herself—the police would understand, because she certainly wasn't the first twentysomething to pretend to be someone else in the Big Apple. She hadn't expected to fall in love! And then she'd *confess* that she'd thought her emotional baggage would be too much for him, considering how much baggage his sister already heaped on him. She hadn't wanted to treat him like a bellboy.

Hopefully, he would forgive her. If not, well, she would have to adapt, and she was sure that wouldn't turn out well for Nate.

Carmen waded back into the lake, her one hand trailing along some invisible line, and for a moment, Ellie wondered if she were still hallucinating until she realized it was a rope.

She could tell Carmen was really hurt from the way she was hobbling around in the water, struggling to reel in her big ole bag of coke.

Ellie moved in; she had to get closer. Her aim really was terrible. She plodded forward through the dark, carefully. Almost soundlessly.

It was too bad. She actually didn't mind Carmen. Under other circumstances, they may have been friends. Maybe even good friends, because like Ellie, she clearly felt a sense of duty to her siblings.

But Ellie had to finish what she'd started. The first rule of success was to just damn well complete whatever you'd set your mind to.

The lake softened the sound of Ellie's slow creep up behind Carmen. She wanted to get close enough so she wouldn't miss. Truth was, even if things were turning around now, it was much harder to kill people than she'd thought. Maybe because of the ease with which her sister's life was snuffed out.

Katie was like Rasputin. Ellie had tried three times to kill her. Each attempt had been made to look like an accident, because there was no way she was going to do any time for that bitch, but if straight-up murder was hard, staging an accident was way harder than she'd thought.

The first time she went to Nate's place and saw a series of locks on the outside door, she thought she was in trouble. "My sister is a sleepwalker," he'd explained, and then added how Katie liked to *roam* at night. Ellie had thought it was going to be so easy; all she had to do was unlock the door and let her get mowed down by a car or freeze to death. Of course, Katie, floating on a cloud of horseshoes, somehow evaded that fate, and Nate became even more vigilant about checking the locks at night.

Her second attempt had been lame, and Ellie was almost embarrassed by it now; she'd made dinner one night and served Katie some very undercooked chicken Parmesan slathered in marinara sauce. Ellie was a vegetarian and had convinced Nate to become one too, so they were both safe from eating it, but a slow, painful death by salmonella just didn't happen. Nate had noticed how undercooked it was and batted it out of Katie's hand. "I'm sorry; I just don't know how to cook meat," had been Ellie's excuse, her eyes welling with tears.

Nate had comforted her in the kitchen as Katie ordered pizza.

She'd waited a month before she tried again.

One night, when Nate was working late, she had brought Katie a bottle of wine, which she'd laced with several tablets of Ambien. Katie drank wine like it was wrapped in a paper bag and she was riding the rails. Once Katie was good and dozy drunk, Ellie had suggested she take a nice, long, relaxing bath. Ellie had filled the tub, led her to the full, frothy bubble bath, helped her get in, and then left.

It was exactly the way someone like Katie should die—young and alone with nothing but years of floundering behind her. Shelby Spade would be mentioned as the last thing she was known for—a silly, sugary caricature that she'd never risen above.

Ellie had gone back downstairs to her own place and waited for her to drown. She had even tried a few distraught-looking expressions in the mirror, her eyes welling as she practiced her lines. "No, no, not Katie." She had would make a good actress herself.

But then, what does a sleepwalker do when plastered on Ambien and wine? She gets out of the tub and walks around for a bit before finally passing out on her dry living room floor. She had greeted Ellie in the late afternoon, proclaiming to have a "killer" hangover. God, what kind of tolerance did she have?

And so Ellie had decided that the universe was telling her something. It was telling her that dying was too easy and that Ellie should fuck with Katie first. Because you know what? It wasn't fair that someone could upend your life and then go on with their own like nothing had happened, so completely unaffected by the misery they had caused. She had to make her suffer. Feel loss. Feel guilt. Misery for misery.

Ellie had taken Katie's phone and sent out that tweet and then watched with glee at how Katie unraveled. Each angry tweet had hit her as sharp and brutal as a spiked whip.

Ellie had screwed Katie's boyfriend, Walker—a disgusting grunter in the bed who shouted congratulations when she faked an orgasm. She'd waited until she knew he and Katie were out for dinner to pepper him with texts and send him a headless naked picture of herself. She knew Katie's neediness and petty insecurities would cause her to look at his phone as much as it made her ignore Walker's signals that he wasn't taking her seriously; he'd certainly cheated on her easily enough.

She was the one who'd listed Katie's address on a Reddit thread. Soon enough, Katie's stalker had started sending his deranged artwork. Ellie had hoped that the stalker would take care of Katie for her. How easy would that have been? It would have been like getting a hit man for free. But nope. Unfortunately, Katie's stalker was as lazy as she was, and he preferred to do his stalking through the mail and email.

And so Ellie did what she always did.

She adapted.

Still in knee-high water, Carmen had reeled in a black garbage bag and was awkwardly hugging it. Ellie was right behind her; she could almost press the muzzle of the gun to her head.

She pulled the trigger, and *click. Click. Click. Click.*

Out of bullets.

Carmen whirled around, her eyes wild, and slammed Ellie in the face with the garbage bag. Ellie staggered back, gasping in pain. Carmen swung it again, harder this time. Ellie felt the wet crack of it against the side of her head. Her jaw flung loose. She stumbled backward into the water. Maybe she would have passed out right then, but the cold lake shocked her out of the agony that was her face. Underwater she clawed blindly for Carmen's legs, trying to take her down too, but her hands fluttered around, feeling nothing. Then, realizing she'd dropped the gun, she felt around for it and picked it up.

Ellie shifted up onto her knees.

The shoreline tilted, but she could see Carmen. She was limping her way out of the water. The heavy garage bag was slowing her down. She still couldn't let it go.

Ellie got up and staggered after her, water splashing.

She grabbed Carmen's hair.

Carmen turned and smashed her forehead into Ellie's nose. Ellie's vision flashed crimson, and her teeth started to ring. A pummel of fists followed, all over her face and body. She felt her mouth fill with blood. A tooth came loose and dangled on pulpy threads.

Ellie was still holding the gun; she managed to knock it against Carmen's head, forcing her to stagger backward. Ellie hit her again, this time accidentally dropping the gun into the water with a plop. Carmen's knees buckled. *The rope.* Ellie grabbed it and wrapped it around Carmen's neck and started to choke her, the thin nylon burning into her own hands.

Carmen's neck had been cut. Her jugular was spewing like a faucet. Her hands were trying to stop it, but they couldn't. Her body sagged, her legs giving out, and Ellie helped her along by pushing her under the water.

Carmen fought, but she was so weak now, and all Ellie had to do to keep her there was press her knee into her chest until the surface of the lake turned smooth. . . .

And now she was off to get Katie. The main attraction.

KATIE

The gunshots had stopped. She couldn't hear a thing.

The woods were dead quiet. Just the twittering of nocturnal insects.

The dark sky loomed large.

Simon shot them. He shot them.

He could be anywhere.

She tried to figure out where she was, but the woods had swallowed her whole. She was running in circles. Katie was directionally challenged on her best days. She could get lost in a parking garage, never mind a forest at night.

Everything looked wrapped in cellophane. The air was thick and wobbly with inky rivulets running through it that she could almost touch. Blood pounded in her ears. Her skin was ice, and yet she was coated in a layer of sweat, soaked in dread. Shadows moved all around her.

The air seemed to bulge, and Katie questioned if any of it were real. Would her eyes flicker open again and she'd be safe and snug around the fire? That the tea, after its initial gush of well-being, had just been replaced by a very, very bad trip? Did she trust her own cracked psyche anymore? How could she when she could murder someone in her sleep?

The angry blasts, those had to be real because Katie had felt the ground shudder. She scrambled between trees, trying to find her way toward the road. To get help. She had to get help.

She wished she had her phone. That she hadn't chosen tonight, the tea ceremony, as the moment to give herself over to this place. If she had known what Carmen was doing, she would have talked her out of it.

Katie staggered down another rocky dip that suddenly turned steep, and then she skidded down it until she dropped on her ass into a shallow pool of moldy-smelling water. A mostly barren creek. The water was only a few inches deep.

Her insides started to heave, and when she stood up, she had to steady herself against a tree. Her peripheral vision flooded with streaky lines, and then she felt the tree pulsing, the deep ridges in the bark fluttering like fish gills beneath her palm.

She snatched her hand back and moved forward, careful not to slip on the mud-slick rocks that made up the creek bed.

Her head was churning.

Lily's body, the excruciating details of it, played out as clear as a hologram. She was seeing dead Lily everywhere she looked.

It wouldn't leave her alone, wouldn't let her think. Lily's blue-white face bloated and fissured with blood vessels was seared into her eyes.

But there was something else. She'd seen something. It was pulsing right there in the middle of her brain, but the tea was like a fog machine, obscuring whatever it was she wanted to know. She couldn't get to it. Something so obvious. It fluttered around her mind like a moth.

"Katie? Katie?" A disembodied voice plunged through the dark. Ellie was calling her name.

"I'm here. Here! Where are you?" Katie whirled around. It was too dark to see her. Ellie called out again. Katie answered.

They did this a few more times, a game of Marco Polo in the dark woods, using sound to close the distance between them until finally, Ellie found her.

"Oh my God, Katie, thank God." The voice was closer. "I'm up here." Ellie flicked on the flashlight. It seared into Katie's night-adjusted eyes. She staggered toward it.

"I heard gunshots," Katie hissed up at her. The flashlight landed on Katie like a spotlight that she couldn't see beyond.

"There you are. I see you," Ellie said with a slight peekaboo lilt in her voice.

"Where are Ariel and Carmen? Are they okay?" The flashlight that Ellie was aiming directly at her eyes was still blinding her.

"I don't know. Simon started shooting after he saw *you* run off, and we all just scattered. I don't know where Carmen or Ariel are, and Simon's still out there. We have to get back to the car. I have the fob. We just have to get to the car, then drive to a phone and call the police."

Why does Ellie have the fob? Katie was sure she'd put it back in her suitcase along with her phone. There was something else in Ellie's voice nudging at her. Not just its sharpness but also its volume. Katie was whispering because there was a drug dealer after them, but Ellie—there was a lack of urgency in her voice.

Katie couldn't think straight.

"Are you hurt? I'll come down and help you."

"No, I'm fine. I'm coming." But the flashlight started to wobble toward her anyway.

Behind her was the rocky ledge she would have to climb up, and in front of her was, well, Ellie, which inexplicably flooded Katie with a sudden wave of dread. She heard the splotchy noise of Ellie hitting the ankle-deep water. Her flashlight—or really Simon's flashlight—zigzagged and landed on her again. How did she get his flashlight if he'd just started shooting? Her dazed head churned.

And then it connected.

What she'd seen on Lily's body.

There was a chain necklace that had bunched up around her neck. If Lily had been wearing it earlier, it was long enough to have remained hidden under her clothes. But there it was, a tiny glass bauble gathered in the hollow of her neck.

A dandelion seed necklace. The ones Ellie made and called her make-a-wish jewelry. "You can hold it up and blow whenever you need to make a wish," she'd said. Nate had smiled, and Katie had thought, *Wow, this manic pixie dream girl is doing a real number on my brother.*

But how?

"Come on, Katie, we have to go. Simon is a total psychopath." Ellie spun the light around. "Come this way. The road is this way; I just heard a car."

An alarm bell went off inside her. She was feeling lured. Drawn out.

With the light pointed away and with a shifting of clouds, the moonlight burst through and cascaded down. Katie saw that Ellie was coated in blood. "What happened to you?"

"What do you mean? I think I look good." Ellie swung the flashlight under her chin, fully illuminating her face, and gave a gruesome grin. A front tooth was missing. Her face was a beaten, pulpy mess and yet her eyes were alert and gleaming, like she didn't feel any of it. Ellie let out a witch's cackle. "Maybe I don't. Your brother is going to be so mad—he loves my face."

She's crazy. She's fucking crazy.

I knew it.

Katie started backing up until she bumped against the hard crest behind her. Her hands searched for something, anything to use against Ellie. A rock, a branch.

Ellie turned back around and swept her flashlight over Katie cowering tightly against the ridge. Let out a growly, fed-up sigh. "You're such a cunt bitch. You can't make anything easy, can you?"

Katie was startled by Ellie's harsh, accentless voice, even thinking for a moment that a third person had shown up.

Ellie made a fast, sweeping gesture like her arm had been released from a spring.

And then Katie noticed the large rock in Ellie's hand. All she managed to do before the rock came smashing into her skull was ask, "But why?"

Katie's vision turned bloodred, her ears flooded with whooshing air, but she could still hear Ellie's voice as it bubbled like it was coming from underwater. "Why? Because you ruined my fucking life. You killed my sister."

ELLIE

Her sister had been dying for as long as Ellie could remember. Her tiny, emaciated bird-bone body was always emitting an odor of doom. It was like her slow, slow death replaced any memories of when Violet was healthy. It was just the sounds of the piano, followed by a cutaway to chemotherapy treatments, then dialysis, the long, long wait for a new kidney, and the constant drone of *Shelby Spade* on her portable DVD player that she took from waiting room to treatment room to hospital bed.

Katie was writhing on the ground, sputtering in the filthy water. She was trying to say something, but it was all gurgles. Ellie set the flashlight down on the rock shelf so she could watch. She was enjoying the sight of Katie like this. "What was that? Huh? Can't hear you. Did you finally shut up?"

"Lily was your sister?" Katie managed to finally spew out. Her gashed scalp was running blood, and her hair had gone from its toned-down auburn color right back to the hyper red that it had been when she'd played Shelby Spade.

"No. Lily's name is really Rachel, and she was a junkie. She was playing a role. I hired her because I wanted you to feel what you should have felt all those years ago. Guilt. Guilt for killing my sister."

Nate told her one late night that Katie had cut her own face. That she'd suffered a psychotic break, and they'd decided to let the police think it was AJ, Katie's old manager. "Why? Just for stealing money? Don't you think that's a tad excessive?"

Nate's face had darkened. "He got what he deserved."

Certainly there was more to the story, but Ellie didn't care. All she knew right then was how susceptible Katie would be to suggestion. So why not frame her for murder? She was almost angry with herself for not thinking of it sooner. It was so much better than just killing her, which would give Katie an easy way out. Better she felt punished. Tarred and feathered. Any remaining fame would forever be eclipsed by "her" crime.

Never once did Ellie buy Katie's *poor me, I'm getting recognized by strangers* act.

Ellie immediately started looking for a victim. Someone who would go along with anything for a little bit of money—who'd be willing to even play dead.

An addict who knew her way around a needle would be best, because Ellie would need a fair amount of blood.

A homeless shelter was an obvious place to start, so Ellie volunteered using a different name. It was a badly run, smelly room in a church basement.

And that's where she'd met Rachel, aka Lily. Ellie did plan on calling her Violet, but she couldn't. Rachel was too grubby. And saying Violet's name out loud did something to her. Her eyes would well, and her sister's name would get stuck in her throat. So another flower it was. A proxy. And Katie would "kill" her all over again, but this time she would be punished for it.

Ellie had planned to send Lily away right after the tea ceremony and plant the knife. No one was going to find her because she technically didn't exist.She was staying at the Sanctuary on a stolen credit card. The money Ellie had used to pay her was all taken from Nate's restaurant and completely untraceable to Ellie's own bank account. Ellie was going to give a statement to the police, vague enough to make her sound reluctant to accuse her sister-in-law-to-be but with the right amount of hinting and worry to lead them to Katie.

Lily would be long gone, jacked up on meth in some rest stop bathroom. Ellie hoped she'd overdose in the next few months so she wouldn't have to worry about her.

It might be more difficult but people were still convicted without bodies all the time.

And it wasn't like she was going to just kill someone for no reason. She wasn't a psychopath. But then she realized *Rachel* probably had a police record. Her DNA could be obtained from the blood that Ellie had been storing up (she kept it hidden in one of Nate's freezers at the restaurant, tucked behind the baby back ribs) and so unfortunately Lily was really going to have to die. Plus, when she thought more about it, it was just all-around better if there was a body. Rachel was a terrible person anyway. A meth addict who, at the tender age of twenty-four, already had two—maybe it was three—children in foster care. No one would really miss her—this was before Ellie knew about the sponsor.

The minute they'd pulled up to the retreat, Ellie knew Lily was as high as a kite by the way she aimed that shaky-handed heart at them.

Friday was cringeworthy. Her panting and fawning over Katie was too over the top, too manic. She was going to scare Katie back to the city. Ellie was not going to be foiled again.

On Friday night, after Katie had fled the partnered breathing exercise, Ellie had whispered to Lily to meet her at the dock, later that night.

"You need to tone it down; you're coming on too strong. If you keep that up, she'll leave."

"I thought that's what you wanted. That it would help with her intervention." This was the story Ellie had told Lily—that she was going to play a small role in some elaborate intervention to help Katie stop drinking. But give an addict some money and the addict wants more. "Look, I gotta run back to the city, like, quick. I can be back in a couple of hours." Lily was jittering on her feet. She had already snorted or shot through whatever she'd brought with her and wanted to go back to the city for more. Ellie registered that

Lily was wearing her bulging backpack. She must have already called her sponsor to courier her back to the city. The girl was so fucking desperate for another hit of meth.

"No. We had an agreement, Rachel, you need to stay until Sunday." Ellie wasn't going to get reckless now. She had planned to kill Lily on Sunday night, while everyone was under the influence of the hallucinogen. If something went wrong, well, there would be no credible witnesses. Who would believe that someone who'd just spent a night communing with dead relatives or turning into a dragon saw something that implicated Ellie?

Even Ellie would have been deemed unreliable, so if she fucked up her story at any point or it didn't match up exactly to other statements, she would still be in the clear.

It was supposed to happen after the ceremony ended, when everyone was still hazy and bleary-eyed after traveling into their mired psyches. Ellie had promised Lily that she would pay her the rest of her money on Sunday, after the tea.

She would go to her room, and while Lily was teetering toward sleep, her body weak and wrung out, Ellie would stab her. It was always going to be a knife from the kitchen. It had to be in order for it to be plausible that Katie went on some crazed killing frenzy while sleepwalking.

Katie didn't remember killing her sister, so now she wouldn't remember killing someone else, but this time she would rot away in jail for it. It would drive her mental, trying to unlock a memory that simply didn't exist. Maybe then she would finally remember Violet and even appreciate the poignancy that Ellie chose Memorial Day weekend for her downfall.

"What's the big deal? I can be back before morning. I'm not tired. Could I get the keys to that Escalade? I'm not tired," she repeated, her buggy eyes getting buggier. "I can drive right through. Like there and back."

"We had a deal, Lily. I need you to stay."

"No one'll know I'm gone. I just need the keys." Lily took a step toward her. Her sweaty sheen of desperation was picked up by the rope light snaking the dock. When Ellie didn't immediately hand the keys over, Lily snapped, "Fine, fuck you! If you don't give me the keys, you can do your own intervention. I don't care; I'm out." Lily turned to leave.

"Okay, fine, wait here. I'll go get the keys." Ellie marched back to the house. Crept into the kitchen and pulled a knife from the butcher's block.

She hemmed and hawed about going back upstairs for the latex gloves and hairnet she'd brought along, but she didn't want to risk waking Katie up prematurely or Lily, in her erratic state, suddenly taking off. Plus the lake was right there, surely that'd get rid of most of Ellie's DNA, and whatever was remaining could easily be written off as transfer DNA. Ellie had spent a lot of time researching the beautiful ambiguity of transfer DNA.

When Ellie returned, Lily was waiting for her in the driveway, her hand out. Ellie made like she was handing her the keys but instead plunged the knife into her stomach, then pulled it out. Aimed the knife to stab her again, but Lily had just stood there blinking. She was too high to feel pain, and rather than crumple to the ground as Ellie had expected, she'd clamped her own hand over Ellie's and twisted it around so the knife nicked Ellie's hip.

For a second, Ellie thought she was going to be killed. Lily, all skin and bone and jacked on meth, was stronger than she looked. Ellie managed to elbow her in the nose and regain control of the knife. Lily had pivoted, bent slightly at the hips, and Ellie thrust the knife into her back, once, twice, and was about to stab her a third time when she took off toward the woods.

Fuck. Lily wasn't dead.

Not yet.

Ellie started to go after her when the screen door creaked open, and she heard the shuffle of someone out on the porch. She crouched down behind the Escalade. It was Anthony, standing there in shorts and a T-shirt, stargazing for what seemed like hours but was probably twenty minutes. Enough to give Lily a good head start. After Anthony went back inside, Ellie scoured the woods, but it was too dark and she didn't have a flashlight. She was tired too. Stabbing someone was physically taxing. It was something you just didn't think about.

By the time she got back to the Sanctuary, the sky was lightening.

Ellie decided that if Lily hadn't returned to the Sanctuary for help, she had to be bleeding out in the woods. There was no way someone could sustain that many stab wounds, in the woods, in the middle of nowhere. There was too much blood. And bravo to herself—she was right about that! Oh, poor Lily—she could picture her running around the woods, not realizing it would have been better to stop moving and let her wounds clot up because her meth-infused heart was spewing out all her blood.

Someone would find Lily's body in the morning. They had to. And so Ellie adapted once again. Moved her plan up to Friday night. At least she wouldn't have to spend the next two days with Katie and her dim-witted friends and all their screechy laughing.

So she'd stood over Katie, still asleep. Gently squeezed a small amount of Lily's blood out of the plasma bag she bought online into her own hand and pressed a bloody handprint to Katie's face. She then pinched the valve, made a flicking motion, and spritzed more blood down her tank top. Then she tucked the gory-looking knife right next to her. Drained the rest of the blood into the sink, cut up the plasma bag into tiny pieces and flushed it.

In the morning, she would have pushed Katie to go to the police right away, but she couldn't. Not until she knew for sure that Lily was dead, because if she weren't, she'd reveal everything. If, miraculously, Lily hadn't bled out and really was huddled up in the woods someplace only half-dead, well, Ellie had to finish the job and pull that necklace off her with her Ellie-Rose brand logo, an oversight she wasn't proud of. She'd given it to Lily when she was trying to befriend her. *Every time you feel like using again, just take this out and make a wish for something better.* Something like that. It was why she'd had to spend the last two damn days looking for a dead or dying meth-head.

This weekend had been incredibly stressful for her.

Until Simon turned it all around for her.

Just another way the universe was telling her how right she was.

KATIE

"Your sister? Who's your sister?" Katie wanted to keep her talking. She didn't understand what Ellie was talking about. Ellie was clearly having some kind of psychotic break brought on by the tea.

Katie tried to stand up, but the world tilted and she sank back down to her knees.

"You still don't know?" Ellie cracked an angry smile.

"I don't, Ellie."

"No, of course you don't, and you know why? Because you're a self-absorbed twat who is so totally incapable of, well, everything." Rage was building in her, her voice was vicious. "My sister's name was Anne-Violet Gardner, but she preferred Violet, and so that's what we called her. Me? I stayed Ellie-Rose. What can I say? Our mother wasn't particularly creative when it came to names. Violet was only twelve years old when you killed her."

"Killed her?" Katie sputtered. She was feeling woozy. She still couldn't grasp what Ellie was saying. Katie killed a kid? A dog, another woman at the retreat, and now a kid? Wasn't three victims the threshold number of a serial killer? How was that possible? "I don't understand. How? I don't know a Violet."

"You're expecting a murderer's soliloquy here, aren't you? That's what happened on your ridiculous show, wasn't it? That whoever was caught would then spend the next sixty seconds spewing what drove them to do it, exactly how they did it, and why? God, I fucking hated you then too. Just your voice was enough to curl the skin off my body. But Violet, well, she loved Shelby Spade. Your character was everything to her."

Katie was trying to piece things together. The show had been over for more than a decade. Whatever Ellie was talking about happened at least twelve years ago. But that was before Katie had started sleepwalking, and what did it mean that Lily was a junkie? That Ellie had hired her? Her head was throbbing; her scalp was weeping blood over her face, and her eyes were stinging with it. Her vision was red-streaked. Holding herself up, she dug around in the water to look for her own rock, but they were all so heavy and suctioned into the wet ground. All she could do was grab a fistful of mud instead.

"And your scar, that was the worst part. My brilliant, achingly good sister didn't even make a ripple, she didn't even register yet in this world, when she died. No one mourned her aside from me and my mother and her piano teacher. She had no friend, she'd been out of school for so long. And yet you were the one in the newspaper and on TV. Those ridiculous talking mannequins on entertainment shows would go on and on and on about poor little Katie Manning. They called it a breaking story that you had a little cut on your face and flashed to an *outpouring* of sympathy. I remember all those balloons and flowers and candles that swelled against the closed gate of your driveway. But you were still alive. Still healthy. You went on to live another twelve meandering, useless years."

Twelve years ago, Katie was fifteen.

She was fifteen when she'd had her breakdown.

The day of her breakdown, she went to the hospital to fulfill her obligation to the Wish Come True foundation.

The hospital visit. She had seen so many kids that day. But then there was that one, the "big fan." That sweet girl she'd hung out with. What was her name? Was it Violet? She'd given her a balloon. It was all Katie could remember.

"And so no. You are not allowed a comeback. You deserve to die in a ditch, because you and your friends were trying to rip off cocaine. And me? I plan to convert your apartment into a studio where I can make jewelry full-time. Oh, and we'll have to put that thing you call a cat down."

"Ellie, please, whatever happened to your sister, I'm sorry. If I did something, I don't know what I did. I really don't." It was a plea.

"That's just it; you don't know. You killed someone, and you don't know. Just like Friday night, but of course that was me—do you know how much focus and organization this all took? I just want you to take a second to appreciate that. Really appreciate the work I've put into wrecking your life. I think I deserve my own moment of recognition."

"Whatever happened, we can fix it, Ellie. We can do it together."

"Pssht. Stop. You can't undo killing my sister."

"But how? How did I kill her? I don't understand!" Katie sobbed.

"I *coooould* tell you"—Katie watched as Ellie tilted her head back and forth as if weighing her options—"but it's especially tortuous if I don't, right? This is one you'll never *sooooolve*."

"Please, Ellie, whatever I did, I'm sorry."

"You know what? If you had stayed under your rock, we wouldn't be here. I almost forgot about you, actually. Almost. But then I read that article in *Variety* about you getting a part in that movie and that Katie Manning just might have herself a comeback. Well, that couldn't happen. I was okay sharing the Earth with you when I knew you were a washed-up loser with an ugly scar who'd drifted into obscurity. But no, you weren't allowed a comeback. My sister is dead." Ellie was circling her, tossing the rock back and forth in her hands like it was an apple she was about to eat. "And now you're going to die in a ditch, and no one will even care. Maybe Nate, but I'll make sure to comfort him really well. We'll wait a year to get married, and at the reception I will dab my eyes and say things about how sorry I am that you're not with us any longer, and people will drop your name in their speeches, but everyone will forget about you by dessert."

Katie was slow to catch up. "Nate? You just used him get to me?"

"*Ding, ding, ding.*" It was a hard, ugly sound in the dark woods. "I never planned on really marrying Nate. He was just a means to an end, but now, I don't know." Her voice took on a girlish wistfulness. "We do really get along. He does what he's told. It's sort of hard to resist."

Katie hurled a fistful of mud at Ellie. She was aiming for her eyes, something to momentarily blind her so she could make a run for it, but the mud landed on Ellie's upper chest and rolled off. She didn't even flinch.

"God, I hate you." Ellie lunged toward her. Katie sprang back and managed to land a kick to Ellie's face. This sent Ellie staggering for a moment, and Katie scrambled upright and tried to run, reaching the jagged incline, but Ellie was on her. She pounded her twice in the back with the rock she'd been holding. Katie felt something in her back give way; a rib snapped.

Katie flipped over and used her feet to kick Ellie off her, connecting with her chest. A gasp of breath. Katie lunged forward into a half crawl, spotting a loose dead branch on the ground. She grabbed it and held it up like a baseball bat and cracked it against Ellie's face, freshening up the dried blood there.

"Fuuuuuck!" Ellie snarled. Katie swung again but missed and lost her footing. Ellie pounced on her and delivered a frenzy of punches and slaps all over Katie's body, finally grabbing Katie by the hair and ramming her forehead against the rocks. Once, twice.

Ellie then picked up the branch that had fallen from Katie's hand. She placed it across Katie's neck and pressed all her weight against it. Katie could feel Ellie's breath against her face; Ellie wanted to watch her die close up.

Act like you're dying.

Act.

It's what you do; it's who you are.

The voice came from somewhere outside of her.

Act more hurt than you are. Pretend you're dying.

And then a black curtain rolled over Katie's eyes. Her breathing slowed, her heart was conducting shallow, weak flutters. The last thing she heard was, "Just die already," before everything turned to static, and Katie was sure she didn't need to pretend anymore.

ELLIE

Ellie was singing as she climbed over the tumble of rocks and out of the creek. A shallow valley. She did it. Right now, she wouldn't mind a victory pose shot, her arms V'ing over her blood-drenched body.

She did it. She finally killed Katie Manning. And it felt so good.

The world was a better place without her. Nate especially.

She was glad she'd gone ahead and filled out that life insurance policy. In every single way, they were going to be better off without Katie Manning.

Ellie had walked the woods enough looking for "Lily" that she knew her way back to the retreat. First she swung by Carmen's floating body and grabbed the garbage bag of cocaine she'd left on the lakeshore. She thought about keeping it. How much was it worth again? It would be enough to make a fast exit, but then she hadn't been lying when she'd told Katie she wanted to stay with Nate.

She hiked farther, the bag of cocaine heavy as she retraced her steps back up the path to the little pile of bodies.

When she saw Ariel's dead plank of a body, she stepped over her to where Simon had tripped over Lily. And again, seriously, how much better could this have worked out? "Oh, Lily, you really did come in handy, after all." She leaned down and snatched the dandelion necklace off her neck.

She dropped the bag of cocaine at Simon's body. It didn't fit the narrative that he didn't have the drugs with him when Ellie killed him. Lily's body, too, might be a head-scratcher for the police, given that she'd died two days earlier, but she was sure an autopsy would reveal Lily's chronic meth use, and they'd assume she was some how in with the drug dealers.

Ellie toyed with the idea of playing catatonic. Too shocked to speak, her memory cloudy from trauma and the tea she'd pretended to drink.

It would save her from possibly giving conflicting stories to a sharp-eared detective. But then, the amount of cocaine was a sure thing when it came to detracting suspicion off her.

Ellie wanted full control of the story. She needed to push the police in the right direction.

The few times she'd been out with Katie when someone had recognized her, when a restaurant waved her to the front of the line, Ellie saw the allure of fame. She knew she was going to leave this place with a certain level of fame, a hero of sorts, even if just because she was the sole survivor. Everyone loved a Final Girl.

Her jewelry business would take off; who wouldn't want to wear something with such a savage story attached to it? Nate would totally understand too when she "withdrew" from Columbia and she wouldn't have to waste another day skulking around the city pretending to be in class.

She was practically floating.

When Ellie neared the house, she circled around to where the tea ceremony had been. She stood from afar, watching the others still cowering away from Maric's gun.

The fire had whittled down to glowing embers.

Ellie rearranged her face to one of terror.

It took a bit of rustling of bushes for Marie to swing herself around. "Simon?" she called out before Max and Dr. Dave and Naomi brought her to the ground just as Ellie had expected them to do. Apparently, Anthony's proclivity for violent video games didn't transfer to real life.

Paula cried out when Ellie stumbled back into the ceremonial circle and, for a moment, Ellie had an urge to hurl something at her, but then Paula swept toward her and covered her in a blanket.

This was exactly what she needed; someone like Paula to mother her like this. It would set the tone for when the police arrived. Ellie was a victim.

"Where is Simon? What happened to my Simon?"

"Shut up." Max had the gun now and held it on her as he pushed her back toward the house. "An ambulance will be here right away, okay? Keep breathing," he said to Ellie with reassuring masculine authority. Then to Paula, "Paula, make sure she doesn't fall asleep. Keep her warm."

Max was actually pretty cute.

Then he yanked hard on Marie's twisted arm to get her moving again. Ellie allowed herself a small smirk that only Marie could see.

Now all Ellie had to do was wait. Her teeth were chattering. Paula added more wood to the fire. Ellie liked watching the sparks dancing up into the sky. These were her fireworks, for now.

Sitting by the fire, it took so much willpower not to smile, not to openly grin like an idiot that she had to tighten her puffy, split lips against it.

The fire warmed her up. The police would be there soon. She had her story ready.

Oh, Violet, I hope you can see me right now. I hope you know what I've done.

The morning of Katie's visit, the doctor had announced that Violet was stable. The kidney transplant had taken, and the chemo she'd had to endure months earlier had worked. Now all Violet had to do to keep healthy was continue on immunosuppression medication and limit her exposure to germs. Her immune system was a frail thing, but Violet could go home as early as the end of the week.

Her mother gripped Ellie and her sister's hands and cried. They all cried. In that moment, Ellie realized how scared she'd been, how much she'd been holding her breath.

Violet asked the doctor in her small, worried voice, "Does that mean I have to return my Wish Come True? Shelby Spade is coming today."

The doctor chuckled and said no, of course not. Vee smiled and gripped their hands harder, equally happy to be alive, to live, as she was to meet Shelby Spade.

Katie Manning was late, because why not make dying children wait for you?

Ellie brushed her sister's hair as they waited. Tried to make her laugh with her funny accents. Ellie had gathered and mastered a whole variety of drawls, twangs, and brogues—all to make her sister laugh during those times in the hospital when the batteries in Violet's portable DVD player were drained. But Ellie couldn't make her laugh this time.

Vee picked at the bedsheets as she grew increasingly anxious. "What if she doesn't come?"

Ellie decided then that she hated Shelby Spade for making her sister wait, sitting alert in her bed, jumping with hope at every sound in the hallway that it was Spade making her appearance.

Their mom finally had to leave for work.

Katie eventually showed up, sunglasses still on. Reeking of perfume to cover up what Ellie was sure was the odor of stale alcohol. At fifteen years old!

Violet smiled so grandly that for the first time, she just looked like a kid. Not a sad, sick kid who'd spent the last few years propped up in a starchy hospital bed—just a kid. There was new color in her cheeks. There was hope. A life. Until that cunt Shelby Spade came strolling in.

She had a foil balloon in tow—of herself, of course.

And here Ellie needed to take a moment to pat herself on the back for strategically placing that foil balloon in the woods on

Friday, before Katie hurled a potato at her, and then herded the girl squad toward it. She loved how much it had disturbed Katie. She had snuck the balloon from Lucy's house, where the woman kept a basement full of *Shelby Spade* paraphernalia. No wonder Katie couldn't grow up.

They knew Katie had finally arrived by the way the nurses squawked and cooed. Ellie peeked out the window of Vee's door to where Katie stood and posed with one leg in front of the other with the nurses, trying to look sexy in a fucking pediatric oncology unit.

The moment Katie stepped inside that room, Violet lit up. The sharp angles of her cheekbones softened.

Along with a balloon, Katie had also brought with her a pink fedora. "Just like the one I wear on the show," she said. Violet already owned the pink fedora and a *Shelby Spade* notepad and pen and comforter and pillowcase and doll. There was no end to the merchandising that her sister fell victim to.

Ellie managed to intercept it. "My sister is on an immunosuppressant. It would be better if I took it."

"Oh, gawd, Ellie. My meds are just to help me accept an organ, which has already happened. If I had to live in a bubble, the doctors would have me in one. You're such a germaphobe." Then she said to Katie, "I am getting out in a few days."

"You might be getting out in a few days," Ellie corrected her.

Katie offered them both a glazed look. She shrugged and let Ellie take the fedora. Ellie wondered if she was on something.

Vee tossed daggers at her. She mouthed at Ellie to leave. Ellie wasn't supposed to. Her mom told her to stay for the visit and watch over her sister to make sure nothing happened, but she couldn't possibly imagine what bad could happen. She gave her sister an exaggerated eye roll. When she stepped outside, some twat nurse smiled at her and said, "Nice to give your sister some space to enjoy meeting her idol; I'm sure she needs it."

She went down to the cafeteria, where a cute orderly chatted her up and paid for her lunch. In her mind, Ellie pretended she was in her high school cafeteria, sitting with the captain of the football team. She'd all but dropped out by this point.

Before long, an hour had passed, and Ellie went back to her sister's room. She'd expected that the big-time teen celebrity would have stayed for less than ten minutes, and that Violet was probably disappointed and going to need some consoling.

But when she got back to Violet's hospital room, she was gone.

Ellie asked another twat nurse on duty—this one was extra bubbly and stroked her ponytail like it was a pet ferret resting on her shoulder—where her sister went, and she said that Violet was still enjoying her visit with Katie Manning.

"They're still together?"

"Oh, yes, Katie Manning took her out for a walk in her wheelchair. Isn't that the sweetest?"

Ellie was reeling. "I didn't say Violet was allowed to leave her room."

The nurse made a frowny face. "Of course Violet is allowed to leave." There was an accusation in the nurse's voice and Ellie knew the nurses thought their mom was far too overprotective of her sister. Once, one of the nurses gave Violet a chocolate bar and their mom tried to get her fired, accusing her of sabotaging Violet's cancer treatment.

"I think it's nice that Violet is getting some time out of her room."

"How long ago did they leave?"

"Oh, well, hmm, I am going to say about thirty or forty minutes ago. Now don't you worry, hon, they'll be back anytime, I am sure. Your sister is not made of glass." The nurse clucked, all chipper, and continued to jerk off her ponytail.

Ellie scoured the hospital, floor by floor, getting increasingly panicked when she couldn't find her sister. Where was she? Why would that idiot nurse let Katie Manning take off with her sister?

It was because she was rich and famous. That stupid nurse probably still watched *Shelby Spade*.

Suddenly, Ellie's lime-green flip phone buzzed in her pocket. "Ellie?" It was Violet. Her voice was shaky, and Ellie could tell she was crying.

"Violet, where are you?"

"She left me. She just left me here!" A wet, sputtering sob filled the line.

"Tell me where are you and I will come and get you."

"I'm just a couple blocks away, at that mall. I'm outside on a pay phone, next to Macy's."

Ellie wanted to stay on the line while she walked over there but Violet said she was tired of holding the phone and hung up.

Ellie ran the entire way there. She circled around to Macy's but Violet wasn't there. That's when she noticed a commotion in the far end of the parking lot and she saw her sister's wheelchair toppled onto its side. One wheel was still spinning.

A lump of clothing on the pavement.

There was a moment of relief that Ellie could still remember for its bitter cruelty because at first she knew that the small lump of clothing she was seeing, a purple hoodie and stiff-looking jeans, couldn't possibly be her sister.

Violet would be in her hospital gown. And there were so many plastic shopping bags scattered around the pathetically small lump. They didn't have any money after all of Vee's hospital bills to go shopping.

But it was her sister.

Violet had been hit by a car.

Ellie sank down next to her and pulled her body onto her lap. The blood coming from Violet's mouth spilled onto Ellie's leg.

Her sister lived another eighteen hours before she died. Before her breathing tube was pulled out because even that couldn't keep her alive anymore, and they wanted to see her face one last time.

Katie Manning took her sickly, wheelchair-bound little sister to a germ-infested mall and ditched her as soon as her brimming admiration grew stale and tedious. Like Violet was a thing she discarded as soon as she grew bored with it.

Her mother sued the hospital for negligence; what kind of hospital lets a twelve-year-old leave the premises without an adult? She sued the Mannings for damages (what a paltry term for killing her sister). Both the hospital and Lucy Manning swiftly settled out of court with a hefty sum that allowed her mother to quit her job and start drinking. She spent her days ranting and raving. She blamed Violet's disease on aspartame, on shitty processed foods, microfiber materials, and cell phone radiation.

She blamed the doctors, the nurses, and their faulty Western medicine. She took on the look of other parents whose children finally succumbed to a brain tumor or cancer or other cruel ailments that Ellie had witnessed so many times before—hollowed out, like clothes hanging from hangers. Their faces weren't even there anymore.

But mostly she blamed Ellie, her less loved, untalented child. It was a stinging, venomous blame. "You should have known better than to have left Violet alone with that girl. How could you have let this happen? You had a hand in killing her too. Never forget that. You killed her too. I hope you make up somehow for your sister's death." It was always some variation of this day after day until her mother decided she'd rather join Violet than stay living with her other daughter. The line of opened, half-spilled prescription bottles was another reason she'd kept the door to her mother's bedroom closed after she died. Ellie didn't like to think that her mother had committed suicide, but who was she kidding?

Her mother's last words to her were the most comforting words she'd said to Ellie since Vee died. "You're beautiful enough to find someone to take care of you. You'll be fine."

If only Shelby Spade hadn't come waltzing in that day.

If only they had refused the Wish Come True.

And Ellie knew on some level that it was bat-shit crazy to want to kill Katie so badly. At least she *knew* that. She knew it would not bring back her sister or mother. In her single session with a therapist, she had revealed her deep-rooted anger toward Katie Manning and the idiot therapist looked almost confused and said, "But what happened was just one of those tragic things, there's no one to blame. It's not as though Katie pushed your sister into traffic."

Ellie walked out right then.

She didn't believe it. She knew it was Katie's fault.

There was a single, inciting factor that took her sister away— and that was Katie Manning. She abandoned Violet, and Violet died. It really didn't matter anymore.

Following her bliss meant exacting revenge.

And she deserved to be happy, didn't she?

Now all there was left to do was sit through a D-list celebrity funeral, where everyone would suddenly adore Katie Manning again, and endure another display of stuffed animals and half-dead flowers piling up outside their brownstone that Ellie knew would flood her with rage.

But all she would have to do was remind herself that it was her brownstone now and Shelby Spade would fade into meaningless nostalgia.

Heaving for breath, she could feel her heart conducting shallow, weak flutters.

The branch Ellie had used to crush her throat was still delicately balanced across her neck, and she felt too weak to push it off. A grotesque cracking-whistle growl flared from somewhere deep when she breathed. Ellie hadn't choked her long enough.

So now she was going to die slowly, painfully.

She had to get up.

But couldn't get up.

Her body felt pinned to the ground.

She lay there, the moon peeking through branches hovering over her. And just like that, in her dying moments, she remembered Violet. The day of slashing her own face came back to her in its entirety.

Violet was the last kid she had met that day. Violet was twelve, and yet she still looked like a little girl in her hospital bed.

Violet asked all about the show, and Katie rotely delivered the answers she always gave.

Being on the show is an amazing experience.

No, the actor who plays Lacey Evans is actually very nice in real life.

It was so embarrassing that my first kiss was on-screen.

A nurse came in and asked Katie to sign something for her niece. Violet asked if Katie could take her for a walk around the hospital, before Katie could think of an excuse to leave. Usually AJ kept track of her time during these visits, and he'd cut in after about fifteen or twenty minutes. Now without him, she had no idea how how to segue to saying goodbye.

"Sure." The nurse brought in a wheelchair.

Next thing, Katie was wheeling Violet around the hospital. The girl loved to talk; it was like she'd been stranded on an island and words streamed out of her like engine exhaust.

Then Violet abruptly asked what it was like outside. "What does the air feel like on your skin? What does it smell like?"

"Smoggy," Katie answered because it was LA.

Violet said she wouldn't mind the smog. She couldn't even remember what it was like to breathe in anything but the stale, reheated food smells of the hospital.

Katie felt sorry for her, but more than that, she liked her. "How long since you've been outdoors?"

"I don't even know. The nurses say fresh air is good for me, but my mom doesn't believe them. She thinks everything, the air, tap water, cell-phone towers, milk, sugar, especially sugar is going to kill me. She wants to keep me under quarantine and it's so stupid because the thing is, we're always dying."

"That's a really cool way of putting it. So true."

"Sylvia Plath said it."

"Who's that?"

"The poet?"

"Oh, right, I forgot." Katie was embarrassed that she didn't get a literary reference being made by someone three years younger than her.

They went outside into the hospital courtyard. Violet tilted her head up at the sun, then looked again at Katie, one eye squinted against the brightness. "Will you please take me somewhere? Anywhere other than this hospital?"

"You want me to break you out of here? I don't think that's allowed."

"But I'm all better now. My mom said I can't have sugar or fats. That that's what cancer feeds off of, but I don't have cancer anymore and I've got a new kidney. Pleeeease? Pretty, pretty pleeease?"

Katie was already feeling rebellious. Here she was, out without AJ, without her mom. She asked her security guard to get her and Violet something to drink from the vending machine, and they took off out of the courtyard.

"To be honest, I don't remember the last time I went anywhere without some adult following me. My mom or my manager." Katie's voice faded off.

"Ugh, me too. I don't even think being healthy is going to change anything for my mom or sister. I think they will try to keep me in bubble wrap for the rest of my life."

Katie knew that feeling. Violet had been living with the fear of never growing up, and Katie had been afraid to grow up and be abandoned. And now it had happened. She'd been abandoned again, by her AJ.

The mall wasn't very far, and Violet was so light to push. The walk seemed even shorter because Violet just chattered away, and soon they were there. Violet wanted to immediately go to the food court and so they did. She had Katie wheel her around to sample something from each restaurant.

Katie bought her french fries, a milkshake, an oversize slice of pizza, a taco, a greasy stir-fry, and then a bag of candy from The Sweet Factory. Violet tasted each like she'd never eaten food before.

"Aren't you going to eat?" Violet asked her.

"No, I already did." Not true, but there was no way AJ would ever let her eat this much junk food. But AJ wasn't in her life anymore, she reminded herself, and so Katie joined in, shoveling salty fries into her mouth and washing it down with liquid sugar from Orange Julius.

They went to the Gap afterward, where Violet admired a purple hoodie, so Katie bought it for her and then the same hoodie in four more colors. Violet ripped the tags off and put the purple one on. Then Violet mentioned needing some jeans, so Katie bought her some of those too and helped her to put them on in the dressing room. She still wouldn't take off the fedora, which Katie thought was adorable.

They kept shopping and whatever Violet showed any interest in, Katie swiped her credit card and got for her. But it seemed the more she did this, the more Violet wanted. Soon Violet's wheelchair was loaded like a shopping cart and the benevolence Katie had been feeling about making this girl's Wish Come True was draining away. Wariness was descending over Katie. She was starting to feel like the butt of some kind of joke. That Violet was taking advantage of her. *Even a recently dying girl doesn't like me for me.* And then Katie realized she had never expected her to.

The fried foods were going sour in her stomach.

Next Violet wanted to go to HMV, and she greedily filled a plastic basket with CDs and DVDs that were much more grown-up than what one would expect for a fan of *Shelby Spade.* "Do you really need all of these?"

Violet scoffed, "I nearly died! And it's not like you can't afford it."

Katie reluctantly paid what turned out to be an exorbitant amount. "We should get back now."

"I really need some sneakers." Violet's voice skidded upward into a whine. "I'll be going back to school soon and I need something stylish, because my mom won't be able to afford—"

"Shelby! Shelby Spade!"

Katie turned and saw that a crowd had gathered outside HMV. Mostly tween-aged girls with their moms and dads. Katie waved and smiled, and the girls giddily started to jump up and down with pens and various things to sign. Their parents had that pleading look that said, *Please don't disappointment my child.*

"This is so cool," Violet squealed.

"I have to go and say hi, and probably sign some stuff. Then we have to go back, okay, Violet?"

"Fine," Violet pouted.

Katie wheeled Violet out of HMV, and left her just by the entrance as the crowd encircled her. It was the usual posing for pictures and signing autographs and answering the same questions she always answered.

The actor who plays Lacey Evans is actually very nice in real life.

Suddenly, it was as if the crowd tripled. Where did all the people come from? People were thrusting pens at her to sign whatever they had on them, and the next thing Katie knew she was signing receipts, plastic shopping bags, and bare skin.

The crowd had circled around her, and she was starting to feel like trapped prey. There was a man, too old to be interested in Shelby Spade. He had the same kind of black-rimmed glasses as AJ.

The crowd started pressing in on her. Someone was touching her hair. The back of a hand grazed her breast, and she felt a stark wave of revulsion run through her. *Don't touch me, don't touch me, get away.*

"Whoa, whoa, please, can everyone back up a little?" But no one was listening. She was just an object to be touched, grabbed at, used. Someone tugged on her trench coat. She was so stupid to come here still dressed as Shelby Spade, and now someone was pulling the belt loose from her trench coat. What had she been thinking? AJ would never have let her get into this situation.

"Please give me some room. I have to go. I gotta get back to my friend over there." When Katie looked for Violet she realized the crowd had somehow shuffled her away from HMV and she couldn't see her anywhere.

"Stop it!" she screeched at all the clutching hands. "Stop! Please stop." But the hum of the crowd drowned her out. Her voice broke down into a whimper. "Stop. Go away."

The man with the black-rimmed glasses was coming closer and the memory of AJ coming into her room at night pulsed through her, quick as a heartbeat, there then gone. Panic set in. She felt dizzy and sick. She couldn't breathe. Her vision was narrowing into pinpricks—when mall security showed up and created a tiny opening, Katie fled.

She'd left Violet behind because she'd been forced to, but she didn't kill her. What was Ellie talking about?

Suddenly a freckled, apple-cheeked face peered over her. "Well, well, look at what the cat dragged in!" A burst of canned laughter, shrill and menacing, echoed through the trees.

It was Shelby Spade, real as anything. "Guess it's gonna be hard to make new friends now that all your old ones are dead." Katie's eyes popped and watered. She tried to sit up, but her head rattled. Her spine felt like shattered glass.

The air fizzled.

"Go away," Katie mumbled. If she really were dying, she didn't want the last thing she saw to be Shelby Spade.

"Nuh-uh. Never. Ever. You are me, and I am you, and let's just say I'm not ready to make my final exit just yet." A big, toothy smile. "You should really be asking what Shelby Spade would do in a situation like this." Another jarring burst of laughter. "First thing I'd do is get up, because when the going gets tough, the tough get going." An audience *awwww* whipped through the air. Shelby thumbed at the dark woods over her shoulders. "If you die here, no one'll know the truth, y'know. She'll get away with it. So are you just gonna lie there stargazing, or are you gonna get up and soooooolve this case?" Shelby's can-do attitude was as grating as ever.

She took off her pink fedora, spun it on her finger, then whipped it up in that old move Katie had to repeat over and over at the end of every episode. "Case closed," she'd announce as she coolly caught the fedora and placed it on her head, then tilted her head with a hard smile. But when the fedora landed, her Shelby Spade apparition was gone.

Katie too felt like she was about to disappear.

But she couldn't. She couldn't die in a ditch like this. She wasn't going to let her brother marry a murderer. What would Ellie do to Nate if he did something to piss her off? If he stayed out late one night or burned her morning crêpes? If he ever stopped being exactly what she wanted him to be? Her friends were all dead, but there was one person left she could save.

She pushed herself up and gingerly scrambled up the creek

rocks on all fours like a wounded animal. When she reached even ground, she started at a limping trot back toward the retreat, toward the stream of smoke swirling into the air.

They were all dead. It was Katie's fault for bringing them there.

A feral rage overtook Katie.

Her rational mind shut down; she knew exactly where she was going and what she needed to do. The effects of the tea were gone, and now there was a siren wailing inside of her.

By the time she reached the retreat, her pulse was beating faster. Her hands had curled into fists. In the distance, she could hear an actual ambulance bleating, but it could not overpower her own internal alarm.

She spotted the woodpile. Loosened the ax from the tree stump.

Camouflaged with mud and her own dark blood, no one even noticed her.

The scene on the porch was pitched with worry and chaos. Max was holding a gun on Marie, who was flanked by Dr. Dave and Naomi. Anthony was huddled on one of the porch benches, hugging himself.

Ellie wasn't there.

She noticed the thick plume of smoke billowing up into the fading darkness.

Katie crossed the lawn and made her way back to where they'd had the tea, toward the ceremonial fire that was still burning. Somehow, she knew Ellie would be there. Probably savoring a last moment of peace before she had to snap back into character. Another character.

When Katie burst through the bushes, Ellie looked up, her face full of shock and maybe even awe. Paula gasped and said something about Katie being all right, but then she saw the ax and froze. Ellie's lips moved to say something—maybe "Wait!"—but Katie wasn't listening. She swung the ax.

"Case closed, bitch."

KATIE

Katie was arrested and held without bail for the murder of Ellie-Rose Gardner for exactly two weeks.

For those two weeks, Ellie got exactly what she'd wanted. Katie suffered a burst of infamy as an ax murderer. She was kept in isolation, but this didn't stop the other inmates from shouting out what was supposedly her new moniker, Shelby Blade.

Nate hated her.

But she felt nothing. Even her lips felt numb.

Something inside of her had died in those woods with her friends.

She spent her time in her cell watching a narrow beam of sun travel across the room. Jail is a retreat of its own in a way. Nothing to do but think, think, think.

When she slept, she'd wake up with her body pressed against the corner of her cell or crammed under the piss-stained cot. Her bad dreams had shifted from a dark, shadowy monster penetrating her room and her body, to running lost and frantic through the woods, to the feel of the ax as it had entered Ellie's skull.

It didn't stop when she woke up.

She was continuously plagued by the sight of her friends' bodies being zipped up in bags.

Two bright lives gone to black.

Once the police finished sifting through the evidence, Katie's charges were reduced to manslaughter. The private investigator she'd hired had come through. Ellie-Rose Gardener was her real name, but she wasn't a student at Columbia University, nor had she attended Cambridge University. That was what he'd called Katie about that Saturday.

If only she'd answered.

Clive had managed to trace Ellie-Rose back to Northern California, and in turn to her mother, who was still receiving settlement checks and paying the rent despite no one having seen or heard from her in years. When police searched the house, they found that Ellie had been living there right until she moved to New York; the body of her mother had been placed in a suitcase and stuffed in the crawl space.

Ellie had told everyone that her mother no longer left the house, that she was too depressed. But in order to mollify her mother's distant relatives, she had pretended to be her on the phone. It was a talent of hers, voices and accents.

This was the first chip in Nate's denial that his fiancée was a vengeful psychopath: she was never home when her mother called. He'd thought they sounded alike, but what was odd about a mother sounding like her daughter? Nothing. Then he went over the times he'd overheard Ellie casually chatting with her mother, sprawled out on the couch—knowing that no one was on the other end of the line. It made him sick. His own guilt set in. He should have noticed more, he should have admitted to himself that Ellie's stories had too many discrepancies to be true, that he made the fatal error of believing that she was perfect.

Later, they would both study a picture of Ellie and her sister that Nate found among her things. Violet was a sickly looking girl with hollowed-out eyes. In the picture, they were sitting on a bench outside the hospital. Ellie's arm was slung around her sister, and they wore matching smiles. It was a posed picture, but their eyes were shining and it looked like they'd finished laughing at something.

Two dead sisters.

Both involved Katie.

There was other evidence too. Ellie's search history on her laptop was telling, full of macabre Google searches on how to poison, strangle, dissolve a body. Katie's body, to be specific.

Clearly, Ellie had been arrogant enough to see no need to sanitize her search history.

Considering the extenuating circumstances that pushed Katie to drive an ax into Ellie's skull, her lawyer was able to strike a plea deal that included not spending any more time in jail.

When Katie returned home, survivor's guilt overwhelmed her. All her friends were dead. Her mind was a war zone of what she could have done differently. Images of inputting her credit card to book the rooms at the Sanctuary, choosing the Escalade, picking Ariel and Carmen up and leading them off toward their deaths. It was like being slowly choked to death with barbed wire, something she felt she deserved.

She could only find a handful of archived articles online and she had to specifically search her name and the children's hospital to access them. One included a photo of herself with Violet at the mall. Katie was smiling down at Violet, as Violet gazed into some glowing store.

Her face unscarred. Violet's life, recently restored, was in that single frozen moment still ahead of her.

She printed the photo and stared at it for great lengths of time throughout the day, as if by doing so she could crawl into its frame and go back in time and change everything about that day.

CHILDREN'S HOSPITAL PATIENT WITH KATIE MANNING PRIOR TO GETTING HIT BY CAR.

Ellie was right. The sympathy Katie garnered for her cut face had overwhelmed the interest that she was with an ailing girl at the mall in the hours before that girl was killed by a car. Or maybe it had been Lucy's doing. No matter how bitter or resentful Katie had felt toward her mother, she had to respect her talent for controlling Katie's image and sheltering her from reading anything negative about herself in the media.

She wasn't even angry anymore with Ellie for wanting to kill her. If only she had succeeded sooner, Carmen and Ariel would still be alive. Maybe she deserved to die.

She stopped leaving her apartment, stopped eating and showering. She was a toxin that killed everyone she came in contact with. The first falling domino in a chain reaction of doom.

She even drove Nate away. When he brought up her mail or let her know that the guy who delivered her booze was there "yet again," she kept the door chained and only spoke to him through the narrow opening.

Eventually she stopped opening her door at all.

One day, Nate broke into her suite and found her on the floor of her apartment, having nearly drunk herself to death. He scooped her up and took her to their mother's house on Long Island. Lucy jumped at another chance to mother her, and Katie let her.

Lucy cooked for her, making elaborate dishes just to break up the quiet with clanging pots and pans and flavor the air with roasted garlic, sautéing rosemary, baking cookies. Whenever Katie managed to stay out bed for any length of time, Lucy delivered lengthy, detailed monologues about whatever she was making as if she were hosting her own Food Network show because she thought cooking was a "safe" topic. Katie appreciated it; she liked listening to Lucy's chatter, through her thick fog of misery and Xanax.

Each night, she served Katie hot chocolate and tucked her into bed—"Hold on, baby girl, hold on"—and pressed her hand to her forehead like she was trying to heal her, before kissing her goodnight.

Books appeared on her nightstand that had titles like *Adult Survivors of Child Abuse* and *Grieving Is a Journey Not a Destination*.

Time trickled by. Lucy made sure she took her medication. Eventually they started to go for walks.

Nate had stayed in the brownstone but visited frequently. They ate dinner together. Some nights they played board games and watched hockey. She listened to Lucy and Nate talk around her. One night, Katie laughed. It was such a jarring and horrendous sound, she immediately threw up. She wasn't allowed to laugh anymore.

On the one-year anniversary of the retreat, Katie sleepwalked and woke up in the basement. She'd had another dream that she was back at the retreat. This time she was running frantic through the woods, trying to find her way out, but she kept passing Carmen and Ariel's bodies over and over because she was trapped there and going in circles. Each time, she'd check to see if she could rouse them back to life but couldn't, and the grief that they were both gone would hit her again and again like a splintered projectile.

When her eyes snapped opened, Shelby Spade dolls still in their original packaging surrounded her. Her mother had to have kept fifty of them. Each doll's fixed beady eyes were staring down on her.

Immediately Katie felt her throat start to close over. She wanted to hurt herself, and be numb at once. She wanted a drink, a random hook-up, to go out and get lost in a stupor. She wanted to flee, crawl out of her own body, escape herself, but there was nowhere to run. She stood, reached for one of the boxes, and clawed it open.

Holding a doll by its legs, she studied the details of this cheerful approximation of her childhood face. The freckles were perfectly spaced out, the pink fedora was elasticized to her oversize head, and the matching trench coat hugged a body that didn't exist in nature. The eye shape was wrong, too cat-like, the color also. The doll's were a perfect indigo, while Katie's eyes were a dull hazel.

The only thing that was right was the flat, empty little-girl smile: a white dab of paint between red ribbon lips.

That smile.

She grabbed a hammer sticking out of a nearby tool bag and hammered the doll's head in.

One by one, with methodical, white-hot rage, she smashed doll after doll until there was nothing left but plastic parts. And when she laid a sheet over the wreckage of her former self, something jolted inside of her. She released a scream from the darkest, deepest pit of her body. It was so guttural, so fierce, it left her breathless and heaving. Her body went slack.

She climbed the stairs, and stared out the front bay window. The sky was a cloudless, pink membrane—the shade of new skin.

Her friends were dead.

Shelby Spade was dead.

Katie Manning was not.

ACKNOWLEDGMENTS

First and foremost, I need to thank my babysitters who allowed me to carve out the necessary time to write. Scott and Terry Nicholson—you are incredible grandparents. Krista Nicholson and Jenna Harrison—you are both such fab aunties.

I am also so grateful to my parents, Alan and Carole Smith, for all of their help and support over the years.

Deep appreciation goes to my brilliant editors, Kristin Sevick and Amy Stapp, who elevated this book with their insightful notes and advice.

I want to thank everyone at Forge who worked to get this book ready and onto the shelves, from the extremely talented copy editors to the designers, and marketing teams.

Much gratitude to my earliest readers: Stacey Hauser and Sherry Graham who have put up with the earliest, crappiest versions and have always found a way to encourage me to keep going.

To Marcie and Kent Wood who have shared their expertise in law enforcement with me.

I also need to thank Caroline Ingrid for trusting me with all of her psychology notes.

To Cindy Horvath and Dayna Hatland at Horizon's—thank you for being so amazing at your jobs. I never have to worry when my son spends the day in your care.

Immeasurable love and gratitude to my beautiful, talented, brilliant wife, Tara, for always believing in this novel and in me—I couldn't do a thing without you!